"*The Metropolitan Affair* is a second-chance love story set amid the glamor of New York City during the Roaring Twenties. The novel weaves historical mysteries with a fascinating behind-the-scenes look at museum work and the problems of art fraud. I loved the fast-paced jaunt through elite museums, Jazz Age parties, and antique-filled mansions on Long Island's famed Gold Coast. With smart leading characters, a compelling storyline, and a deep dive into Egyptian antiquities, this novel is a richly layered delight."

—Elizabeth Camden, RITA and Christy Award–winning author

"A splendid and fascinating world is captured both in the golden age of the Met and through Green's marvelously painted New York. With a dash of Elizabeth Peters's Amelia Peabody that is sure to delight fans of *Miss Fisher's Murder Mysteries*, *The Metropolitan Affair* finds Jocelyn Green at the top of her game as one of the reigning queens of inspirational fiction."

—Rachel McMillan, author of *The London Restoration*
and *The Mozart Code*

"As always, Jocelyn Green pens a novel rich in history, character, and meaning. A complex exploration of family and loyalty lends depth to a thrilling mystery and a swoony romance. Steeped in fascination for ancient Egypt and 1920s New York, *The Metropolitan Affair* delivers on all fronts! Savor every word."

—Sarah Sundin, bestselling and award-winning author
of *The Sound of Light* and *Until Leaves Fall in Paris*

The
METROPOLITAN
AFFAIR

On
CENTRAL
PARK
1

The METROPOLITAN AFFAIR

JOCELYN GREEN

BETHANYHOUSE

a division of Baker Publishing Group
Minneapolis, Minnesota

© 2023 by Jocelyn Green

Published by Bethany House Publishers
Minneapolis, Minnesota
www.bethanyhouse.com

Bethany House Publishers is a division of
Baker Publishing Group, Grand Rapids, Michigan

Printed in the United States of America

Library of Congress Cataloging-in-Publication Data
Names: Green, Jocelyn, author.
Title: The metropolitan affair / Jocelyn Green.
Description: Minneapolis, Minnesota : Bethany House Publishers, a division of Baker
    Publishing Group, [2023] | Series: On Central Park ; 1
Identifiers: LCCN 2022047543 | ISBN 9780764239632 (trade paper) | ISBN
    9780764241321 (casebound) | ISBN 9781493440634 (ebook)
Classification: LCC PS3607.R4329255 M47 2023 | DDC 813/.6—dc23
LC record available at https://lccn.loc.gov/2022047543

Scripture quotations are from THE HOLY BIBLE, NEW INTERNATIONAL VERSION®, NIV® Copyright © 1973, 1978, 1984, 2011 by Biblica, Inc.® Used by permission. All rights reserved worldwide.

This is a work of historical reconstruction; the appearances of certain historical figures are therefore inevitable. All other characters, however, are products of the author's imagination, and any resemblance to actual persons, living or dead, is coincidental.

Cover design by Laura Klynstra
Cover model photography by Ildiko Neer / Trevillion Images
Cover image of the Metropolitan Museum of Art interior staircase by MB_Photo /
Alamy Stock Photo

Author is represented by Credo Communications, LLC.

Baker Publishing Group publications use paper produced from sustainable forestry practices and post-consumer waste whenever possible.

23 24 25 26 27 28 29   7 6 5 4 3 2 1

To Mindelynn
Of course

Do not fear, for I have redeemed you;
I have summoned you by name;
you are mine.

ISAIAH 43:1

CHAPTER 1

Dead people were easy to talk to. It was the living ones that often gave Lauren trouble. Even her father.

No. Especially him.

Rolling her shoulders back, she headed toward the Central Park bench where he waited. At seventy years old, he'd diminished from the giant he'd been to her in childhood. And like the giants in her storybooks, her father had been just as fabled. Outsized in her heart and mind and not quite real.

Bridles jangled on a pair of horses pulling a carriage full of tourists. Lauren watched it pass, then crossed to the lawn spreading from the Egyptian obelisk erected by her employer, the Metropolitan Museum of Art.

Lawrence Westlake stood to greet her. "I wasn't sure you'd come."

She wouldn't stay long. "You said there was something specific you wanted to ask me?" She sat on the opposite end of the bench from him, near a barrel sprouting orange chrysanthemums. Behind the obelisk, trees flamed with autumn's glory beneath an azure sky.

He lowered himself to the bench. "There is. But first, how are you? How is your work?"

"Busy as ever. We're expecting another shipment of crates from the team in the field any day now." As assistant curator of Egyptian art, with the curator on an expedition, Lauren was doing the work of at least two people until the team's return next spring.

"Anything exciting?" Lawrence's eyes glinted. From a nearby pushcart, the smell of roasted pumpkin seeds and apple cider carried on the breeze.

After a quick glance at her watch, Lauren told him about the most recent mummy and coffin to arrive and felt herself relax. Lawrence Westlake might not have been the best father, but he'd been the one to instill in her a love for Egyptology. Aside from the curator, Albert Lythgoe, and the expedition director, Herbert Winlock, she couldn't think of anyone else who might share her enthusiasm for the nuances of ancient Egyptian artifacts.

"I'm proud of you." His smile brought a gentle tapping on the wall she'd built around her heart. Then he pulled a photograph from inside his jacket pocket. "Look what I found."

Lauren took it and stared at the little girl in the photo, standing as close to the man beside her as he would allow. It had been taken twenty-seven years ago. She'd been five years old.

"How small you were," Lawrence murmured. "Do you remember that day?"

"Of course." She recalled every detail. Someone from a geographical society had come to their home to photograph Lawrence before one of his many trips. Lauren had pestered to be in one of the photos, and they'd finally appeased her. She'd wanted to sit on her father's lap but hadn't been brave enough to do more than hold his hand.

She fingered the torn corner of the image. "Do you remember *this* day?"

He frowned. "When you tore off the corner? It was an accident. Out of character for you since you were always so careful with your things. You treated everything as though it were in a museum even then."

His expression held no hint that he remembered the circumstances. Lauren had been upset that he was leaving her behind again.

Lawrence had tucked the photograph into the front pocket of her dress, saying that she was to keep the picture close, and in that way, they'd always be together.

Lauren had ripped the photo when she yanked it out of her pocket and thrust it back at him. She didn't want a piece of paper. She wanted him.

"I'm going on another trip," Lawrence announced above chittering sparrows. "To the field. Come with me."

Snapping the photo into her handbag, she thought of the times he'd said this to her before. There was always a reason she couldn't or shouldn't come after all. But all she said was, "I thought you'd given up traveling."

"I tried. Staying in one place won't stick." A sigh gusted from him as he leaned back against the bench. "How long do I need to do penance for missing your mother's death?"

But it was the *life* he missed that bothered her most, both before and after her mother died. He didn't understand that or didn't want to.

"You had your aunt and uncle and your cousin," he said. "You and your mother left Chicago to spend every Christmas vacation with them. Staying there after your mother died was best for everyone."

She hadn't said a thing about Mother, and still he argued, bringing up feelings and memories she'd rather leave buried. Was it any wonder she hadn't sought his company during the last four months he'd been living in Manhattan?

Wind teased a strand of hair from Lauren's chignon, and she tucked it behind her ear. "I don't want to do this today."

"It's time to make good on a promise I made to bring you with me."

A promise made and broken more than once. She was unwilling to argue with him anymore, and yet unable to agree.

"The only problem is, the board isn't convinced you ought to have a spot on the expedition team."

"Since I never asked for a spot, we're in perfect agreement." She plucked a petal from the chrysanthemums beside her.

"You're qualified to come. I know that, and you know that. But you need to prove it to the board. You know, with publications, that sort of thing."

Lauren stifled a dark laugh. She had proven herself to many people and institutions along the way to earning her doctorate in Egyptology and attaining this position at the Met. She most certainly did not need to prove anything for a role she hadn't looked for.

"I have no time to impress some nameless board," she began.

"Not nameless." He cut her off, handing her a business card: *Lawrence A. Westlake, executive board, Napoleon Society.* A phone number and Manhattan PO Box followed.

She'd heard of the society but hadn't known that her father was involved with it, let alone on the board. Still in a fledgling state, the organization was devoted to celebrating Egyptian history and culture, and was named for the man whose explorations in Egypt inspired so many others.

"Imagine what this could do for your career," Lawrence said.

Lauren had gotten further in a career in Egyptology than most women could ever dream of. Still, she couldn't deny the pull of the field.

"We've secured the perfect spot for our new office building and museum in Newport," he went on.

"Newport? That's a little out of the way, isn't it?"

"It's perfect!" he repeated. "New York already has the Met, and Boston has the Museum of Fine Arts. But Newport is where all those patrons spend the summers, and the Providence Athenaeum, a short drive from there, holds all twenty-three volumes of Napoleon's *Description de l'Egypte.* It's only fitting for the Napoleon Society to host a world-class collection nearby. I've been curating it for a few years now, and I expect it will be ready to open to the public in another two. Eighteen months if we're lucky."

"So this expedition is for that purpose?" she asked. "To discover and bring back artifacts for your new museum?"

"Precisely. We'll have to do some maneuvering around the new regulations over there, but that won't stop us. I'm inviting you to be part of that."

She broke from his dancing gaze and watched the wind move through the trees. Beyond those, Manhattan's skyscrapers needled the sky. *Far* beyond that lay an ancient land she'd been to as a tourist and then later as a student, but never as a professional.

As much as she'd like to believe this opportunity would work out, that she could uncover history herself, she knew better than to hope.

"No, thank you." Rising, she looked down at the white-haired man who had so often broken her heart. "But best wishes as you go about your business."

She tried to ignore the hurt etched on his face. She refused to feel guilty for rejecting the offer before he had a chance to take it away.

As he walked her back to the Met, she tried to talk to him of something else—anything else. But the conversation fell flat.

Little wonder. Egyptology was all they had in common.

"One more thing." Lawrence extended an engraved invitation. "The Napoleon Society's fundraising gala will be November 21. Please come and hear more of what we're all about."

She took it, and he tipped his hat to her. "Thank you for meeting with me today. I am sorry, you know. And I am proud of you. I would recruit you to this expedition even if you weren't my daughter. You're good enough to be on the team, Dr. Westlake."

Lauren hated that she didn't believe him. She hated that she wished she could.

———○———

THURSDAY, OCTOBER 15, 1925

Humming a melody from Verdi's *La Traviata*, Joe Caravello emerged from the subway station into the mottled dark of predawn Lower Manhattan. The sky was a bruise, the sidewalk a series of cracks and broken pieces. He trod the final few blocks to work, eager to reach the place where his thoughts had been for more than an hour. Longer, if he counted thinking in his sleep.

At 240 Centre Street, the five-story granite and limestone police headquarters filled a wedge of land bordered by Grand, Centre, and Broome Streets. Streetlamps illuminated the columns and porticoes over the three arched doorways but failed to penetrate the shadows gathered in his mind.

The clock on the dome began chiming the five o'clock hour as he climbed the steps and entered. After passing through the marble reception room and into the detective bureau, he poured himself a cup of tar-black coffee and took it to his desk.

"Detective Caravello?" A lanky figure approached. His sleeves were a half inch too short. Must be fresh out of the Police Academy on the fourth floor. "Oscar McCormick." He shook Joe's hand with a firm grip. "We're neighbors now, so I thought I'd introduce myself." He jerked a thumb toward the desk across from Joe's. Up until two weeks ago, it had been Connor's.

"I heard about what happened with Connor Boyle," McCormick added.

"Yeah." Joe took another gulp of coffee, not minding the scald on the way down. "Not surprised."

"Right. Well, I'm real sorry things went down that way, and I wanted to tell you that straight off, but we don't have to talk about it again."

"Smart." Joe wasn't cutting the kid any slack, and he felt a twinge of guilt. If the new hire had come a month ago, Joe would have taken him for an espresso at Ferrara's. Ever curious, Joe would have asked for his story, what made him want to join the NYPD, and what his goals were on the force. He would have shared his own insights about the job and been the unofficial one-man welcoming committee. At thirty-five years old, Joe was a veteran, and if he could set an example for young officers, it might help them withstand corrupting influences.

What a joke. Joe couldn't even keep his own friend on the straight and narrow.

The young man shifted. "And I have no reason to believe what they're saying about you, either. I never judge a man based on rumor."

Joe studied McCormick's face, which had turned a ruddy shade to match his hair. "And those rumors are?" He figured he knew them all, but it wouldn't hurt to be sure.

"Oh, uh, just that you could have sprung Boyle from jail with your testimony but decided not to."

"I told the truth in my statement. That's it." Connor's story was that he thought the man Joe had been handcuffing during a speak-easy raid had a gun. Connor claimed he needed to neutralize the threat. The truth was that Wade Martin had been unarmed and already neutralized.

"Well, they say bullets were flying that night, and the one that killed Martin could have easily come from some other miscreant. If you'd kept quiet, maybe Boyle would still be free. They say you ought to have been more loyal to your friend."

"I'm loyal to the oath I took when I swore to serve and protect this city. My friend shot an unarmed man I had already subdued. Is anyone saying that Boyle simply shouldn't have taken the shot?"

McCormick kicked at the foot of Joe's desk, sending his coffee sloshing. "Well, me, for one. I say that."

With a nod of acknowledgment, Joe wiped up the coffee spill with a napkin, then tossed the sodden wad into a nearby waste bin. If the kid had scruples, Joe could only pray he held on to them longer than Connor had. The man he'd shot left behind a young widow about to give birth to a fatherless child.

That senseless killing never should have happened.

Aware McCormick still stood there, Joe felt his mouth twitch at one corner in his best attempt to stop scowling. "Welcome to the force."

McCormick excused himself, and just in time. Joe had an appointment to keep.

At the doorway to his boss's office, he cleared his throat. "Inspector Murphy? I'm ready if you are."

After shoving a stack of files aside, the inspector in charge of investigations motioned Joe inside and gestured to the chair across from his desk.

Joe sat. "This isn't working," he began. He'd called this meeting and saw no sense in not getting straight to the point.

Murphy's blond eyebrows knit together. "After you tell me exactly what you're referring to, you'd better have a solution to propose."

Of course he did. Joe hadn't come here to whine. "Sir, every time we raid a speakeasy and padlock the door, violence breaks out, people get hurt, and five more speakeasies pop up within the week anyhow. I'm sure you read the commissioner's annual reports." In one year alone, the NYPD made ten thousand arrests on Prohibition-related charges. Only two hundred thirty-nine of those accused were convicted. Three thousand cases were dismissed, and the seven thousand remaining cases languished in the enormous backlog overwhelming state courts.

"Is this about Boyle?" Murphy's grey eyes narrowed.

Joe had expected that question. "It's not about what happened that night. But that does serve as one more example of the risks we take and the little reward we gain—if any—with these raids. We aren't succeeding in shutting down the illegal sale of alcohol. We're only moving it around."

In truth, he'd been disillusioned about Prohibition enforcement almost since the Volstead Act went into effect more than five years ago. "This entire bootlegging underworld is a Hydra. Cut down one outfit and another one takes its place almost immediately. We're chasing our tails. Spinning our wheels. Pick your own metaphor, but you know what I mean."

Murphy folded his arms over his barrel chest. "Are you getting to the part where you tell me how to solve the problem of Prohibition in Manhattan?"

"You and I both know that's a problem that can't be solved completely. All I'm asking is that we try a different angle." Joe drew in a breath. "Egyptian art and forgeries."

"You're kidding." Murphy's expression suspended between amusement and the very opposite.

"Ever since King Tut's tomb was opened a few years ago, there's been a demand for all things Egypt. And since the Egyptian government closed off the exportation of antiquities, the demand for forgeries has gone up. Forgery is another form of money laundering, just like bootlegging."

"And you have proof this is happening?" The inspector lit a Chesterfield and sent a plume of smoke into the air.

"I have no proof that someone is going to get robbed tonight, but you and I both know it'll happen. Crime happens all the time, including forgeries, whether we're savvy to it or not."

"You didn't answer my question."

"Okay, how's this: two days ago, the antique dealer Reuben Feinstein made a call about his property getting egged. I went over there to check things out, and when I chatted with him, he mentioned that the restoration side of his dealership is slowing down because the specific supplies he needs are out of stock all over the tri-state area. I spent most of yesterday visiting his suppliers. Feinstein was right. Gold, turquoise, a certain kind of black paint—all consistent with Egyptian art—are in high demand." He paused to let Murphy absorb that.

"I couldn't get a list of his customers without a warrant," Joe continued, "but it doesn't take much math to put two and two together here. My gut tells me that if we find those involved in making or dealing forgeries, we'll find criminals who are guilty of other crimes. Racketeering, trafficking, and Prohibition violations. One crime leads to another."

The inspector tapped ash into a tray. "Even if what you say is true, you're forgetting one problem. Where are the victims, Caravello? When is the last time someone came to us to report that their artifact was forged?"

"I'm well aware of that dilemma. If it's a good enough forgery, they won't even know it's not genuine. If it's obviously fake, they wouldn't have acquired it in the first place. Or if they figure out it's fake after the purchase, they may be too embarrassed to report that they've been duped. That's why we go looking. You've told me yourself that purely reactive policing is bad policing. Here's a chance to be proactive."

Murphy took a deep breath, but Joe wasn't done speaking yet.

"Remember the oyster shell?" he asked. When Murphy didn't respond, Joe went on. "You read my report. When I was handcuffing Martin, I noticed he held a gilded oyster shell dripping with gin. There was an Egyptian carving on the inside of it. When I asked him about it, he claimed that Boyle had dropped it into his drink before the raid. Why? What does that shell have to do with anything?"

"It's not your job to find out. That's up to the investigators assigned to that case."

"But there's a connection there. And that's not all. I've been looking around at some art dealerships and antique stores. There's an undercurrent of Egyptian art flowing through Manhattan, and it's cloaked in secrecy. I'm telling you, it's worth looking into. Something is going on."

Murphy pinched the bridge of his nose. "I can't possibly sell this to the public, you know. Nor can I get funding from the Board of Aldermen or the Board of Estimates for this. More resources for murder investigations? Sure. Armed robberies? You bet. But to look into crimes that haven't even been reported . . ." He took a long drag and exhaled. "We've known each other a long time."

Joe nodded.

"So I know you have an appreciation for art that most cops on the force do not. I also know you have a thing about fakes. It's personal for you. Can you deny it?"

"Sir?"

"Scams. No one likes them, but you have more reason than most to crusade against them. I get that."

"This has nothing to do with my father, Inspector. It's a proactive avenue of investigation we haven't tried yet. What we've tried so far isn't working."

"You said that already."

"It bears repeating."

Murphy's mouth slanted in what Joe hoped was resignation.

"I wouldn't come to you with this proposal if I wasn't willing to do the work myself," Joe pressed.

A beat passed, and then another. The inspector blinked. "You're qualified to tell a fake from the real thing?"

"I know who is."

CHAPTER 2

Textbooks and translations sprawled over Lauren's desk, topped by a reproduction paperweight she'd picked up from the sales desk: a twelve-inch-tall statue of Hatshepsut, female pharaoh from the eighteenth dynasty. She tipped her mug, only to find a shallow swirl peppered with leftover grounds.

"Knock, knock." Only Anita Young, Lauren's assistant, entered that way. It had begun because her hands were often full, but even when she was perfectly capable of rapping her knuckles on the door or its frame, she preferred to speak her arrival.

"Come on in."

Anita's black bob grazed her jawline as she nodded toward the small plant wilting on the corner of the desk. "I'm curious why you even bother, Dr. Westlake. You're clearly not trying to keep it alive. It's only gathering dust."

"Oh, I barely even notice that thing anymore. It was a gift from my cousin. Elsa works in the American Museum of Natural History and insists I ought to have something living in my office. Other than me." She wiped one fleshy leaf with her fingertip, then dumped the last swill from her mug into the pot. "Drink up, little one."

Anita snorted. "The living is not your specialty. But the long dead is all the rage anyway. Speaking of which, the new shipment is here, and Mr. Klein is done unpacking. Want to go see?"

Lauren left her chair before Anita finished asking.

Together, they headed to the receiving room designated for their department, and Lauren thrilled at the sight of crates and lids and sawdust. After Egypt's declaration of independence from Britain, which came eight months before Tut's tomb was discovered, archaeologists hadn't been sending as much back to their home countries as they used to. A revised agreement with the Egyptian government meant most of it stayed there. Nationalist pride surged among the Egyptians, and they were taking much more interest in preserving and celebrating their rich and noble history. Whatever Albert Lythgoe and Herbert Winlock sent back to the Met was granted by special agreement.

Pulling on a pair of white cotton gloves, Lauren lifted an alabaster lotus flower from a nest of wrappings. As she finished unwinding linen from the object's base, sand sifted between her fingers. She rolled the grains between her forefinger and thumb and imagined brushing the sand away from the object for the first time, after discovering it herself.

Anita turned toward approaching footsteps. "Good afternoon, Mr. Robinson," she called out as the Met's director strolled through the door.

"Ladies." He nodded, his hair and mustache the color of moonlight on the desert. "All is intact from this shipment so far, I hope? As intact as the pieces were before they shipped, at least."

Lauren brushed the sand from her hands. "We've only just begun here, but Mr. Klein didn't say otherwise."

"Who?"

"The registrar," she reminded him. Fred Klein was the most unassuming man she'd ever met, always shying away from attention and meticulous about details. He was well-suited to his job of carefully unpacking every single object that arrived.

"Ah yes, yes, of course. Well, that's something, I suppose." The crescents beneath his eyes held more than their usual share of cares.

"Did you need to speak to me, sir, or were you just checking up on the delivery?" Lauren asked.

"I've had a meeting with the Morettis. You remember Ray and his wife, Christina?"

"Of course." They were longtime patrons of the Met, and more generous in their financial support than most. "Their donation to the Egyptian department helped fund the current expedition."

Mr. Robinson winced. "Right. I'm afraid they think we aren't sufficiently grateful. Mr. Moretti came today with an offer to give the Met a portion of his collection, but with the caveat that all of his items be grouped together, and the room in which they are housed be named for him."

Anita released a low whistle. "That's nervy."

A smile cracked the placid planes of Mr. Robinson's face. "Previous directors have gone along with such strings-attached proposals, but I won't. I explained the museum can't meet those stipulations since the exhibits change routinely, and we need flexibility with how we use the space. Mr. Moretti rescinded his offer to donate his items altogether. He may choose to withdraw his financial support, as well."

He looked pointedly at Lauren, though she had no idea what she had to do with the situation. "We can't afford to lose any more support. We certainly can't afford bad press, or even the appearance that the Met is exclusive or discriminatory. Given the Morettis' interest in Egyptology, it would go a long way if you could make some kind of overture to them."

A ridge formed between Lauren's brows. "I'm no donor relations expert, Mr. Robinson."

"You don't need to be. Just be yourself."

Anita gestured to the sawdust-packed crates. "Dr. Westlake is most herself when surrounded by inanimate objects. The older the better."

Mr. Robinson's mustache twitched. "If you want your department to be as robust as possible, you'll find a way to steer the Met back into Ray Moretti's good graces. Don't underestimate yourself."

"Why would she do that when you're doing it so well for her?" Anita muttered so quietly that only Lauren could hear.

"I know you don't like conflict," Mr. Robinson said, "which is why you're so good at making it go away. You should have listed soothing egos as a skill on your résumé."

The tease drew a smile, but he was right. Her dislike of conflict made it hard for Lauren to push back against him now. "Anita and I are already swamped. We've got to sort all Mr. Lythgoe is sending back from the field and get ready for the spring exhibition, too. Next year, I'll ask him to switch places." She kept her tone light, but she wasn't joking. She'd worked here six years and hadn't once been included on an expedition.

Mr. Robinson's mouth firmed into a tight line. "Oh no, you are right where you belong, Miss Westlake. We need you right here."

The words cinched like a fetter around her chest.

Barely covering a huff, Anita broke in. "*Dr.* Westlake, shall we get on with cataloging these priceless artifacts that only you can understand?"

Mr. Robinson took his leave, and Anita indulged in a gigantic roll of her eyes.

Resigned to the task he'd left with her, Lauren turned her attention to an inscribed coffin and the mummy inside. "Hello, Hetsumina," she breathed, in awe of how well preserved everything was. "We've been waiting for you. What do you want to tell me?" Several moments passed while she inspected the hieroglyphs.

"Not that it bothers me, but you're doing that thing again," Anita said.

Lauren lifted a shoulder. "Habit."

"Sure, I get it. I chew the end of my pencil. You talk to mummies." Her blue eyes danced with good humor.

"Oh, come on. It's not like I'm conducting a séance. I know they can't hear me. It's my way of thinking out loud as I look for clues among the inscriptions, the amulets buried with them, their jewelry and textiles. If you knew how to listen, they'd talk to you, too."

Anita gave an exaggerated shudder worthy of Charlie Chaplin. "Pass."

Lauren laughed, unperturbed, and went back to inspecting Hetsumina. "Well, she's easier to work with than most people around here."

"Aha, you mean mummies don't need their egos soothed, and they don't make unreasonable demands of your time or disturb your inner peace."

"Now you're on the trolley." Lauren smiled. "They don't fight. They don't make promises, and they certainly don't break them. Mummies don't lie."

There was no way around it. Joe needed an expert in Egyptology, and the Metropolitan Museum of Art employed the best.

"You may be able to catch her if you hurry." The woman at the information desk hung up the phone and pointed through the Great Hall toward the rear exit of the building. "Her assistant says she just left."

Thanking her, Joe hustled through a labyrinth of classical sculptures, then through a hall of decorative arts. Upon pushing out of the double doors, he paused at the top of the stone steps and scanned until he spotted her. She crossed the lane and took a left turn on one of Central Park's countless paths.

He ran down the stairs and darted after her.

"Dr. Westlake!" he called.

Halting, she pivoted. Shadows draped the brim of her hat and fell over the contours of her face. He wasn't surprised to see that she hadn't followed the trend of bobbing hair and wore hers in a thick knot at the nape of her neck. "Joe Caravello, is that you?"

Out of habit, he showed her his wallet ID and badge.

She trotted toward him, radiant, and grasped his hand in both of hers. "Please tell me I didn't hear you call me Dr. Westlake. We go back much further than that."

Joe wasn't sure how he'd expected her to respond to this surprise meeting, but he hadn't expected this. "Yes, we do," he admitted, disoriented by her warmth. "But that was a long time ago."

"It's so good to see you again." Her voice had softened to velvet. The gloaming called out every detail of her face, from the dark lashes framing sparkling blue eyes to the subtle cleft of her chin. "I see you've followed in your hero's footsteps. Well done, Joe. I knew you could do it."

He took a step back, hoping to clear his head if he wasn't so near her. Inspector Murphy was right that Joe had an interest in art most cops didn't share. What Murphy didn't know was that Lauren Westlake had been the one to introduce him to it. That was a lifetime ago, before they'd pursued their separate careers and lost touch.

Joe hadn't come here with any hope of resurrecting what they'd had before. He was here on a mission. "Actually, my work is why I'm here."

"Oh. Yes, of course. How can I help?" A flush entered her cheeks, and he hoped it was from the cold, not from the embarrassment of learning this wasn't a social call. She resumed walking.

He kept pace with her. "I need your expertise, if you don't mind. I need you to tell me if a particular piece is fake or genuine."

"Egyptian, I assume?"

"Allegedly."

She led him deeper into the park. Good grief, would she have taken this route without him? Didn't she realize this wasn't a safe place for women alone after dark?

"Do you have the object with you?"

"It's locked away as evidence, but I have photographs."

"There's better light by the castle, especially since the Weather Bureau took it over as a weather station," she said. "It's on my way home, up ahead. Let's take a look there."

The Belvedere was a miniature castle atop a huge rock outcrop, complete with pavilions, terraces, and the best view of the park. The path curved, and they followed it up the stone stairs. Joe stayed several paces behind her, yet close enough to catch her if she were to stumble in those heels. Her hips twisted as she climbed.

He dropped his gaze to her ankles instead, until they reached a gazebo type of structure. Lauren stood in silhouette against a sunset over Central Park, and for a heartbeat, Joe forgot what year it was.

They'd been here before, the two of them. She'd been eighteen, and he twenty years old. Something squeezed in Joe's chest for the lovestruck, naïve young man he'd been. This was where he'd thought he would finally kiss her.

This was where she'd told him she was leaving for college, and that she might never come back.

Joe wondered if she remembered.

"Here we are again." Lauren's smile was wistful, and he had his answer. "Shall we sit?" She approached the nearest bench, which was dotted with evidence that pigeons had made themselves at home here recently.

Joe shrugged out of his jacket and spread it over the seat for her. "Please."

With thanks, she lowered herself. Sitting beside her, he withdrew a few photographs, taken from different angles, of the gilded oyster shell Wade Martin had been holding the night Connor had shot him.

With astonishing speed and confidence, she pronounced it a fake.

"You're sure?" he asked.

"Positive. This is a pendant for a necklace. You see this hole at the top? A genuine piece would have two holes, not one. That's how they strung pendants so they would lay flat."

Joe didn't know what this meant for Connor's case, but as Murphy had pointed out, it wasn't his to begin with. All he could do was pass the information along and let others decide what to do with it.

It did, however, confirm his hunch that Lauren's expertise would be invaluable. He slipped the photographs back into his pocket. "I wish I could do that. It would make my job a whole lot easier."

"You can." Her lips tilted in the same lopsided smile she'd given him thousands of times before. He beat back the memories and focused on the task at hand. "All you need to do," she was saying, "is study Egyptology since childhood, earn a degree from the University of Chicago, and study abroad, not only in Egypt but also in Germany since they have the best translations and dictionaries of hieroglyphs—which means, by the way, you'll have to learn to read the German language, too."

He sat back against the bench. "Trying to impress me?" She'd practically recited her résumé, almost as if proving herself. He supposed she'd had to do a lot of that, working among men who may not believe that behind that beautiful face, a brilliant mind could spar with them—and win.

She colored.

"I was impressed even before all that, you know," he reminded her. "Listen, I'm looking into Egyptian forgeries. I have a hunch they've been flowing through Manhattan along with King Tut fever. But to find the forgers, I first have to find the forgeries and work backward. Would you contact private collectors you know to see if they have acquired anything new—so to speak—recently? And if they have, would you be willing to sleuth out real from fake?"

"You want me to be a consultant for the NYPD?"

"I do."

"Aren't your consultants usually men?"

"You're the one I want," Joe said. "That is, you're the best, and I need the best. I wish I could pay you, but this will have to be pro bono. We have zero appropriated funds for this."

She waved a hand. "Don't worry about that. I'll do it. Thank you for believing that I can. It will be a service to our patrons and to the Met itself in the cases where the patrons have promised to bequest their acquisitions to the museum. Better to root out the forgeries before they ever enter our building."

"Exactly." He was glad she saw it that way. He figured that being a police consultant would be a boon to her résumé, too. "If you need me to talk to your boss to get the time off work for official police business, I can do that."

"I'm already overwhelmed at work. I'll have to help with your investigation after museum hours."

That changed things. He'd imagined her conducting these meetings in broad daylight. "Walk me through what you're thinking."

"I'll go in the evenings." She said this as if it were a perfectly reasonable solution.

But the evenings were dark. It was barely past six right now, and night had already fallen. "Alone?" Disapproval made his voice rough.

She cocked her head, the whites of her eyes gleaming. "Who is it that you don't trust? Is it me, the collectors, or the people I may meet along the way?"

From the second highest point in Central Park, Joe looked out over the oasis. City lights twinkled in the deepening darkness. More than two million souls lived in Manhattan alone, and nearly six million when counting all five boroughs of New York City. "I don't trust anybody," he said at last. It was a lesson he'd learned too often, and too late.

CHAPTER

3

An insistent purring vibrated in Lauren's palm. Cleopatra, the black cat she'd adopted shortly after moving to the Beresford, insisted on attention while Lauren drank her morning coffee from the comfort of the sofa. The dining room in the Beresford hotel-apartment complex offered excellent breakfasts, but she could not live without her own coffeemaker in the small space she called home.

Sunlight poured through square windowpanes, beckoning Lauren to appreciate the tenth-floor vantage point. If she couldn't be gazing at the pyramids of Giza, the view of Central Park, especially in autumn, was a lovely consolation. Between treetops and skyscrapers, she could make out the top of the massive Metropolitan Museum of Art.

"I still think we could have a bird in here without any trouble." Elsa shuffled out of the bedroom with a limp from a childhood bout of polio, tying the belt around her robe. Her chin-length blond-and-copper hair had already been finger-waved into place.

Lauren turned to her, amused. "The poor bird would disagree as soon as Cleo decided to break into the cage and go hunting one day when we're all at work."

"You're not really a killer, are you, sweetie?" Elsa rubbed under

Cleo's chin. At twenty-five years old, she was an ornithologist at the American Museum of Natural History, which was right next door to the Beresford.

"And you're not really willing to put up with all the birdseed hulls and feathers a live bird would fling out of its cage, are you?" Lauren teased.

Elsa sighed. "I suppose not. I can barely stand the cat hair as it is." After washing her hands, she poured herself a cup of coffee. She leaned one hip against the counter and took a sip before asking, "Are you seeing Joe today?"

"No plans to."

"Shame. By the way, you never told me if you recognized him right away when he came looking for you in the park. Does he look the same as you remembered?"

Lauren smiled and made her way back to the couch. "The last time I saw him, he was twenty years old and lean as a beanpole. He has matured and filled out since then, as one would expect." Honest to goodness, thirty-five looked better on Joe than twenty. The fine lines fanning from his grass-green eyes did nothing to lessen how striking they were, framed by kohl-black lashes.

There had been something else there, too, both spark and shadow, when he confessed he didn't trust anyone. Years ago, she would have asked if he was referring to more than what happened to his father, and he would have told her. But too much time had passed for her to be his confidant now. Besides, he was a detective for the NYPD. The loss of trust in humanity probably came with the job.

"I'll bet he has." Elsa grinned. "I know my parents didn't approve of your friendship with him when you were living with us, but I think it's the bee's knees you're working with him. It might almost feel like a social life. At least, the only kind you'd allow time for, anyway."

Before Lauren could form a reply, Elsa raised her mug in a one-sided toast and took it to her bedroom to finish getting dressed.

In the next moment, Lauren's other roommate burst into the

apartment and closed the door behind her. "Oh good, you're here, I was afraid I might miss you!" Ivy said all in one breath. She swiped a berry-pink cloche from her straight black bob and swept her bangs to one side. "I hope you don't mind." She extended a small brown bag to Lauren.

Lauren reached inside and withdrew a silver filigree picture frame. Inside was the photograph her father had given her earlier this week. The photo had been trimmed and matted with black, so one would never know the corner had been torn. What she had intended to discard, Ivy had restored and given a place of honor.

If only restoring the relationship could be as easy.

Lauren smiled, struggling to form a response.

"You're not angry, are you?" Ivy blurted. "I know you said you didn't want it. But look how cute you are, and how proud your daddy looks. He's the only parent you have left, and if I were you, I wouldn't throw that away."

Ivy Malone had lost both her parents and her brother to illness. She'd taken a job as a widow's companion and live-in personal secretary while completing her education, and now worked at the New-York Historical Society, down the street from the Beresford.

"You're right," Lauren told the young woman, who was one year Elsa's senior.

"To my thinking," Ivy went on, "having a distant, complicated relationship with your father is better than not having one at all. Don't focus on what you lost when he went away on all those trips, but see what you still have."

Lauren pulled her into an embrace and whispered her thanks.

The ringing telephone broke the two apart. While Ivy hung her coat and purse on the coat-tree, Lauren answered the call.

"Lauren?" It was her father.

She glanced at the framed photograph in her hand. "Hi, Dad."

Ivy whirled to face her, and Lauren nodded in silent agreement that this time she would not be dismissive.

"I called to see if you've given my proposal any more thought.

To make a good showing before the Napoleon Society board and join me on our expedition."

She had less time now to jump through hoops than she had before, and she told him so. "I've been tasked by the police with checking for fakes among our top patrons, as a service to them, the Met, and the NYPD." Her father had never met Joe, so saying his name would mean nothing to him.

A beat of silence. "Isn't Newell St. John one of the Met's biggest supporters?"

Lauren hesitated before conceding that he was. St. John had the largest private collection in the state.

"Then that's the perfect place for you to start. Come with me today. He and I were in the same fraternity in college. He's hired me to catalog his collection. You can check for fakes at the same time. I'll ring him and let him know you're coming. That is, unless you've already made other arrangements?"

"I—no, I haven't," she stammered. "I rang him a few times this week, but no one answered."

"He was traveling last week and let the staff take time off. There's your trouble. Come with me today," he said again. "What do you say?"

Even without her roommate's influence, Lauren could find no reason good enough to keep her from this opportunity. "Pick me up in thirty minutes. I'll be ready."

She would have to be.

The St. John estate on Staten Island sprawled over the land with spires and turrets fit for a medieval fortress. The Westlakes had always had enough money to be comfortable, but they'd been paupers compared to the millions represented by this mansion alone, not to mention all of the original masterpieces within. Separate galleries held different types of art: oil paintings, sculptures, and antiquities, which was where Lauren and her father would spend the day.

"Have you come across anything suspicious so far?" she asked him as soon as the butler left them alone. "Anything that could lead you to believe it was forged?"

He smiled at her. "That's why you're here, my dear. You are the expert. If it was my opinion the police wanted, they would have asked for it."

She turned away from the warmth in his eyes before she could mistake it for fatherly pride. She was far too old to care about that.

And yet, how could her spirit not respond when the one thing she'd wanted for years seemed to dangle so near her grasp?

Lauren was being ridiculous. She was here not as someone's daughter, but as Dr. Westlake, assistant curator of Egyptian art and special counsel to the NYPD. It was in that capacity that she carried on her work. Joe had asked her to do a job, and she would do it well.

That afternoon, Lauren mused aloud, "None of this was intended to see the light of day ever again. Yet here we are, handling these treasures half a world from where they came."

Lawrence looked up from his notebook. "Are you saying it's wrong? That we should forgo discovery altogether?"

She shook her head. "It's not that simple. Ancient Egyptians didn't want to be forgotten, and these discoveries help us learn and remember who they were, what they gave to us. So many firsts can be traced back to them."

"I agree. We are not tomb raiders, wishing only to steal and sell for personal gain. We are learning and preserving the culture. At least, that's how I see it. That's the mission of the Napoleon Society."

"But that's what the Met and Boston's Museum of Fine Arts are already doing," she said. "Why go to the trouble of starting a brand-new institution when you could be partnering with one that's already established?"

"What a question!" Lawrence chuffed a laugh. "There will never be too many museums in the world. Besides, mine will be accessible to people who may not want to navigate a cacophonous metropolis. Boston and New York are intimidating, loud-mouthed bullies to most folks. But Newport is a hospitable cousin near the shore.

Dedicated solely to Egyptian artifacts and culture, the Napoleon House will appeal to the true enthusiast. Come look at this."

She crossed the hardwood floor, polished to the shine of citron. From outside, she could hear Mr. St. John's beagles barking. "What did you find?"

He held up a gold necklace, turning it slowly so all angles caught the light. "Such fine workmanship. Feel how heavy it is." He laid the collar across her open palms.

"I can't imagine wearing it for any length of time," she murmured.

"But you can imagine the woman who did, can't you?" Lawrence smiled, and then he was off, spinning a story about a noblewoman in Luxor, based on the piece and its provenance, and filling in the blanks with his own vibrant mind. His stature had diminished over the years, but clearly his mental acuity remained needle sharp.

His breath smelled of black licorice, as it had since she was a child. If she closed her eyes, she could imagine the years peeling away until she was a little girl, spellbound by her father's stories. When he drew her inside the wonder of ancient Egypt, she felt his warmth pour over her. There was no other place she'd wanted to be in those moments. She belonged.

But was it love for her she'd felt, or simply his love for ancient cultures?

Lauren's eyes popped open. Even if Egypt was their only connection, she ought not cut that single thread. Ivy was right. As painful as the realization was, it was better than nothing.

MONDAY, OCTOBER 26, 1925

Joe rolled his sleeves to his elbows and punched a mound of bread dough on the floured table.

"You don't have something better to do at four in the morning?" Greta Caravello propped one fist on her aproned hip while flipping bacon in the cast-iron pan.

"Better than helping the best cook in the best boardinghouse in Manhattan? Forget about it." He winked at his mother. Besides, kneading dough proved better than a punching bag for working out stress—and it smelled a whole lot better, too. He jerked his chin toward the sizzling bacon. "Who could sleep with such a tease, anyway?"

"The rest of the house, apparently. Except for Doreen, who's in the dining room."

Joe nodded, but his thoughts had already veered elsewhere. He pounded the dough again. More than a week had passed since he'd asked Lauren to help track down forgeries, and so far he'd had no progress to report to his boss, other than being able to identify that the oyster shell in play the night of Wade Martin's murder had been a fake. That was something, but not enough. Still, how could he push Lauren to cover more ground, and faster, when she wasn't being compensated and had little time to work with? He couldn't. Neither could he get far without her. So while he waited for movement on the forgery front, he continued to work on various other cases, from robberies to missing persons.

"Your father will be down any minute." Mama pulled the bacon strips out of the pan and onto a sheet of brown paper. "Mornings aren't easy. He's not getting younger, if you haven't noticed."

Neither was Mama. Age lined her face, bowed her shoulders, and frosted her brown hair. Finished with the dough, Joe set it back in a greased bowl for a final rise.

Sal Caravello shuffled down the stairs and into the kitchen, buttoning his collar. "On schedule for breakfast?" The question implied authority, but his demeanor did not.

"It's all right, Pop." Joe squeezed his shoulder, nearly wincing at how thin he'd grown. "Everything will be ready in time."

Only then did Pop lift his chin. Almost as though he'd been a child expecting punishment and was relieved to escape a scolding.

Joe regretted his part in that. For years, Joe had blamed his father for the mismanagement of money that had led to losing the family restaurant. Desperate for funds, Pop had made a risky investment that turned out to be a scam. It wasn't Pop's fault. It was the confidence man who'd taken his money and run. Inspector Murphy had been right that Joe had a thing about fakes. But that didn't mean his new assignment tracking forgeries wasn't a completely legitimate mission on its own.

Joe checked his watch. "I'll see to Doreen." The only one of their nine boarders who wasn't a college student, fifty-year-old Doreen Boyle was a flower vendor at the Union Square market. She needed to be in place there well before sunrise to receive deliveries from Long Island and New Jersey nurseries.

After passing through the short hallway connecting the kitchen and dining room, he pushed through the swinging door and greeted her. "About ready to go?"

"I'm perfectly capable of walking myself." Doreen dabbed her napkin to her mouth, then folded it beside her plate. Silver threaded the black braid coiled at the back of her head.

"You certainly are." Joe made it his business to escort her anyhow. Union Square was only a few blocks away, but it was dark. "I just like the company on my way to work."

Chuckling, she stood and pulled on her coat. "I doubt your day starts this early, Joe. Connor's never did."

"In a city that never sleeps, New York's finest rarely do, either." He kept a smile in place for her, even as the mention of her nephew soured the coffee in his stomach. Connor had provided for his aunt right up until he'd been arrested. She would have been completely alone had Joe's family not taken her in. But it didn't take a detective to see that room and board did nothing to mend her broken heart.

The walk to Union Square Park held the chill of a season on winter's doorstep. "Speaking of Connor, did you notice anything unusual in what he said or did in the weeks or months before . . . ?"

Lines grooved her brow. She retied the shawl over her head, a nervous habit he'd noticed before. "He didn't talk about his work with me. I can't imagine all the grisly things you police must encounter, and frankly, I don't want to. He knew that. However, I do remember that he started asking me more questions."

Joe pressed for examples.

"He asked if I'd ever thought of living anywhere other than New York City. Isn't that odd? I've spent my whole life in Manhattan, and so has he. The only person I know who moved away was a dear friend who dreamed of wide-open spaces. But I've lost touch with her."

It was an odd question, coming from Connor. He'd been a proud New Yorker ever since they'd met as kids. There was something special about the neighborhood in which one grew up. Loyalty to it rivaled the fervor some folks had for the Yankees or the Sox.

It was that loyalty to one's roots that had kept Pop from pulling up stakes from Union Square and moving north, along with all his best customers. One establishment after another—from private mansions to Tiffany's jewelry store—had closed its doors and migrated away. But Joe's parents staunchly refused to go. Both could trace back two generations to this area, God rest them. They'd find a way to stay, Pop had said. But it was Mama who had found that way, by turning their four-story brownstone into a boardinghouse.

Though Joe and Connor were only teens when the Caravellos lost the restaurant, Connor had been the one to clap Joe on the shoulder and tell him things weren't so bad as long as they remained in the neighborhood.

"Then he said something about me finding something else to do, other than selling flowers," Doreen continued. "I told him the only other thing I'd enjoy would be growing them myself but selling them suited me fine. To play along, I asked if he'd ever thought of being a cop anywhere else."

"And?"

Doreen shrugged. "He went real quiet for a minute, and I thought he might actually say yes. But when he finally replied, he said this was our home, and there was no point pretending otherwise."

Headlamps cut through the dark as delivery trucks motored up to the curb at Union Square, idling while drivers hopped out and unloaded their sweet-smelling cargo. The interview was over.

Doreen bustled about, positioning huge paper-wrapped bouquets in upturned crates, while Joe lined up potted hydrangeas and chrysanthemums on the sidewalk. The air hummed with the pre-dawn hustle, the floral fragrance competing with the exhaust fumes of the trucks.

Straightening, Doreen rubbed the small of her back. "Off with you, then," she told Joe, a smile contradicting the scold in her voice. "I know Connor told you to watch out for me. I don't think he meant for you to trade your work for mine."

Keeping tabs on her might be his duty, but it wasn't work, and he told her so. He tipped his hat to her, then descended into the subway station for the ride south.

On his way to headquarters, Joe rolled the morning's conversation around in his mind before mentally filing it with everything else he knew—and didn't know—about Connor. Friends weren't supposed to keep secrets from one another. Something had been bothering him enough to consider moving. Whatever it was, why hadn't he confided in Joe?

CHAPTER

4

Now, this is a whole new level of fake." Shivering against a stiff breeze, Lauren stood with her roommates in front of a Fifth Avenue mansion several blocks from where Elsa had grown up. She hadn't come to this Halloween party because she thought it was a good idea. She'd come to make her cousin and Ivy happy.

And by the looks on their faces, they were enthralled with the spectacle before them. The front lawn was buried in sand and adorned with a canvas pyramid and a sphinx made of what appeared to be papier-mâché. Guests ambled about, some of them abandoning socks and shoes to feel the grains between their toes. Lauren and her father had not gone to the St. John estate today because the staff were setting up for a private event. No doubt it was nothing like this.

"What could be more fitting for Halloween than mummies, right?" Ivy's red-lipped smile shone beneath clustered lights casting a desert glare over the yard. It was past Lauren's bedtime, but the scene was as bright as midday. "Remember, you're here for fun, not work."

"That's a good thing, too," Lauren teased, "because there is nothing genuine about this." Live music blared from inside the mansion's doors. The melody was "Old King Tut," a popular song that made the pharaoh out to be an old man rather than the teenager he'd been when he died. She doubted anyone here cared about that fact.

Elsa hooked her arm through Lauren's and squeezed. "It's a genuine party, and I genuinely hope you'll enjoy yourself, despite any historical inaccuracies. At least the masses are excited about your field of study."

Lauren couldn't deny the pervasive enthusiasm. Products from Palmolive soap to Egyptian Bouquet Talcum Powder to King Tut Lemons to Egyptienne Luxury Cigarettes and more all claimed some connection in order to capitalize on the trend. Popular songs included "Moonlight on the Nile" and "Mummy Mine." Even the current colors available in women's fashions were named with Egyptian inspiration. Among the favorites were amulet, sand, beetle, Egyptian red, blue lotus, faience, sphinx, papyrus, cartouche, camel's hair, and mummy brown.

"I've yet to see a bird-themed party half as lively as this one," Elsa went on. "Archer said they brought in more than a dozen truckloads of sand for tonight." Archer, Elsa had mentioned earlier, worked as a preparator at the American Museum of Natural History, crafting wax flora and fauna from molds to match the native environments for the African displays. His parents were hosting this event. "What do you think, Ivy? Has the New-York Historical Society inspired anything like this?"

"Every Fourth of July," Ivy said. "No sand or sphinx, of course, but our Revolutionary New York tours always sell out. Our most devoted patron hosts a party where George Washington and his troops make an appearance in full uniform, right down to the bayonets. If I'm invited next year, you're both coming with me, I warn you."

"I'd love to," Lauren told her. "Do you suppose you'll be inducted into the Daughters of the American Revolution by then?"

Ivy's smile sagged. "I sincerely hope so. Still working on finding all the necessary paperwork."

Lauren offered a word of encouragement, aware of how important this was to her. Having lost her immediate family, it made sense that Ivy would want to join a lineage society to more firmly connect her to her roots. "Well, you're in the right place with the NYHS for genealogical records, at least."

Elsa agreed. "Oh, look at that." She pointed to a shining path resembling a river winding around the corner of the house. On it was a float made to look like a barge, bearing a woman wearing a simple white gown, black wig, heavy kohl around her eyes, and a gold headdress.

"Don't tell me that's Cleopatra," Lauren said.

Elsa laughed. "More or less. That's Archer's younger sister. Apparently she's the queen of the party. Honestly, I don't see how it would be worth it to wear that flimsy getup in this weather just for show. Come on, let's go in."

Music pulsed through Lauren as they entered and handed their coats to the butler. Potted palms edged the great hall. Across black-and-white-marble tiles, belly dancers performed to beating drums and a clapping audience.

Lauren couldn't hope to fit in with this crowd, and she didn't mind that. Most people here looked to be in their late teens or early twenties, the ladies wearing rolled stockings and sleeveless shifts tiered with beaded fringe. The men wore suits, and, for the most part, silly expressions their mothers would have been ashamed of.

During a break between dance numbers, Lauren, Elsa, and Ivy moved to the ballroom, where musicians played "Cleopatra Had a Jazz Band." Another canvas pyramid rose from the center of the floor.

"I'm looking for Archer." Elsa craned her neck. "I'd like to introduce you to him."

The song ended, and as people applauded for the musicians, Lauren spied a pair of men approaching the pyramid tent. One wore the drab linen garb of an archaeologist, the other a tuxedo and top hat. "Howard Carter and his benefactor, Lord Carnarvon?"

Elsa squinted through her spectacles. "Probably."

"Ladies and gentlemen!" the man dressed as Carter announced.

"We are about to enter the tomb of King Tut-ank-hamun!" While the band struck a moody chord, he opened a flap to the tent, and both men disappeared inside. Moments later, they emerged, looking dazed.

"Such wonderful things!" Carter said with outstretched arms.

Then the man dressed as Lord Carnarvon slapped his cheek as though to kill a mosquito and collapsed to the floor.

"The curse of Tutankhamun! Stay back!" Carter cried and dashed from view.

Lauren bit her tongue to keep from pointing out that Lord Carnarvon had not died of an infected mosquito bite until months after the tomb's opening.

Ivy stood on her toes to see what came next. "Oh, Lauren," she whispered. "You're going to love this." A coffin on rubber wheels rolled out of the opening, its decoration so ridiculous that Lauren laughed along with everyone else.

The lights dimmed, except for a beam directed on the coffin. The music stopped. Knocking and moaning sounded from within the box. With a creak, the lid opened, and a linen-wrapped hand snaked out.

As the rest of the body followed and staggered to its feet, Lauren congratulated herself for not breaking into a lecture on how real mummies had been wrapped with arms and legs bound up with the rest of the body. She did, however, whisper to Ivy, "I'll bet that your patrons who dress like colonial soldiers at least get the uniforms right."

"Down to the last button," Ivy confirmed.

"Who dares to disturb my slumber?" the mummy growled, ignoring the man lying at his feet.

"Oh my goodness, that's Archer," Elsa said, clearly amused by the Halloween joke.

He stumbled around the circle of guests, asking one after another, "Was it you?" When he came to Elsa, he took her hand in his wrapped-up mitt. "It was you!" he declared.

JOCELYN GREEN

Laughing, she played along. Light gleamed on her golden-bronze finger waves and bounced off her glasses.

"Then you're bound to me for eternity—or at least for one dance!" The band struck up the King Tut fox trot, and the mood in the room swung from ominous to hilarious. But when Archer attempted to pull Elsa onto the dance floor, her smile dropped.

"Be a sport, doll," Archer whispered through his wrappings.

"I can't." Panic flared in Elsa's voice. "Not in front of everyone."

With mounting urgency, Archer persisted, and Elsa shook her head. He might not understand her rejection, but Lauren did. She could practically feel the anxiety radiating from her cousin. Everyone was watching them now. The band replayed the same opening measures, waiting for the couple to take the floor and open it to the rest of the group. Ivy might think the gesture romantic and hope that Elsa would change her mind despite her limp, but Lauren knew better.

Elsa refused to move.

The awkward moment teetered on the brink of something sharp and painful. Lauren couldn't let that happen. Never would she have imagined that she, an assistant curator of Egyptian art for the Met, would King-Tut with a stranger swaddled in strips of bedsheets to a song that mocked a civilization she respected.

With a deep breath, Lauren swallowed her pride. "Come on, Tut. Let's boogie." Laughing at the shock and delight on her roommates' faces, she whisked Archer—and the attention that came with him—away.

43

CHAPTER

5

At last, on the third Saturday that Lauren spent inspecting Newell St. John's antiquities, she found what she was looking for. An ointment jar made of Egyptian alabaster was fake. But there was no triumph in her voice when she pronounced it.

Lawrence's head jerked up. "You found a forgery?"

She confirmed she had. "What's the provenance for this object?"

Flipping through a folder of documents, Lawrence stopped when he came to the corresponding record. "Here it is. 'Spherical jar inscribed with Hatshepsut's titles as queen, 12.3 centimeters high, with a diameter of 12.8 centimeters.' Dated to circa 1492–1473 BC. The inscription reads: 'King's Daughter, King's Sister, God's Wife, King's Great Wife (principal queen), Hatshepsut, may she live and endure like Re forever.' This jar was purchased in Luxor with other objects presumed to be from tomb 1, wadi D in the Wadi Gabbanat el-Qurud, 1917."

"Did St. John make the purchase himself?" Lauren asked.

"We'll have to ask him. But first, tell me why you doubt the object's authenticity."

She pointed to the hieroglyphs etched into one side, contained within a rectangular border. "The inscription gives it away with a few basic errors. One hieroglyph is incomplete, two are incorrectly formed. It's as if this has been copied from a photograph of an original work where some of the inscription was unclear in the image." She could see how it would happen. The thin white lines were delicate, barely contrasting with the creamy, almost translucent alabaster. "There is no way anything genuine with Hatshepsut's name on it would have a misspelling."

Lawrence squinted, then pulled out a magnifying glass to see it closer. He murmured his agreement.

Footsteps echoed across the gallery, and Lauren looked up to see Newell St. John approaching as if he'd stepped right off the cover of *Town & Country*. Apparently fresh from the stables, he still wore his riding breeches and jacket with English boots, and smelled of leather and horseflesh. His rusty blond hair had mellowed to parchment yellow with age.

"I see I've come at an interesting time. What have you found?" He addressed Lawrence.

"Dr. Westlake made the discovery, Newell. She'll explain it better than I could." Lawrence nodded for Lauren to do so.

She did, careful not to make Mr. St. John feel foolish for having been duped by what she considered elementary mistakes. "Not many collectors are fluent in hieroglyphs," she said, "so the fault isn't yours. I'm sorry this beautiful jar isn't genuine."

The man's shoulders squared. "Young lady, I have invited you into my home as a favor to your father. If I'd known you would cast suspicion on my collection, I'd have thought better of it."

She licked dry lips. "I don't blame you for not liking the news, sir. No one wants to be deceived."

"You misunderstand. It isn't that I don't like what you've told me so much as I don't believe it. At this point, all I have is your word."

Heat infused her face.

"Come now, Newell," Lawrence said. "You forget you're speaking to a doctor of Egyptology, a curator at the Metropolitan Museum of Art."

"Assistant curator," St. John corrected. "The main curator is in the field, doing the real work of discovery."

"And he trusts me to catalog and inspect every item that comes through our doors at the Met." She lowered her voice, hoping to soothe. "No one is going to run to the press about this. We only want to protect you—and others—from forgeries that would not only waste your money but also discredit the many wonderful, authentic pieces you do have. It's an impressive collection by any standard."

"There's a reason for that. I'll have you know that the piece you've singled out was procured for me by Theodore Clarke himself."

Lauren's heart sank. Clarke was a legend twice over. In graduate school, she had learned all about the American millionaire who went to Egypt for his health and ended up discovering monumental tombs. On a professional level, she knew him as an honorary fellow of the museum who had promised to donate his entire collection to the Met upon his passing. If Mr. Robinson was nervous about staying in the Morettis' good graces, he would be exponentially more so about Mr. Clarke.

"You worked with him yourself, Lawrence," St. John added. "You can vouch for him."

Her father's smile was controlled and unconvincing.

When Mr. St. John asked for a moment alone with him, Lauren tried not to feel dismissed.

By the time Joe arrived at the St. John estate in response to Lauren's phone call, the master of the mansion was waiting for him in a parlor fit for a British aristocrat. Not that Joe had ever had the pleasure of one's presence. But the mahogany-paneled walls, the fieldstone fireplace, the leather wing chairs and faded tapestry hanging behind them . . . well, it was a far cry from his parents' boarding-house.

"Detective Sergeant Caravello, NYPD," he said upon entering, showing his badge.

Lauren introduced him to Newell St. John and Lawrence West-lake, who had to be her father, but she didn't say so. From the way

Lauren had talked about him when they were younger, he'd pictured a larger man.

"Have you finished raiding all the speakeasies and arresting all the violent criminals?" Mr. St. John queried, eyes hard. "If not, I can't understand what you're doing here."

So far as first impressions went, this wasn't a great one. But Joe knew the type. Defensive. Deflecting. He could handle it.

"I understand you've been the victim of a crime, Mr. St. John. I'm here to get to the bottom of it."

"I don't believe this," Mr. St. John said. "Theodore Clarke is the most esteemed name among American explorers in Egypt. You're telling me he brought me a fake?"

"Newell," Mr. Westlake said, "Mr. Clarke is no Egyptologist. He's a rich man with good luck. That doesn't make him infallible to falling prey to forgery. It's a booming business in Luxor and has been for centuries. The shop dealers there know it's a prime location for anyone who wants to purchase a piece of antiquity. They simply increase the supply to meet the demand. I'm not saying Mr. Clarke intended to deceive you, my friend. He's a businessman, not a scholar."

"He's published books on his expeditions!" Mr. St. John protested. If he'd had a riding crop in hand to go with that fancy horse-riding outfit he sported, he probably would have given it a good whack right about now to make his point.

A look passed between father and daughter. Lauren said nothing. Mr. Westlake, however, pushed back. "He wrote the introductions. If you recall, he hired other people to take the photographs, write the chapters, and edit the work. His personal involvement amounts to very little."

A ripple passed over Lauren's brow. If she disagreed with what her father had said, she wasn't admitting it.

Mr. St. John turned his back and went to the window, where he watched his beagles chase each other over the lawn. No one said what Joe was thinking, which was that Mr. Clarke could have sold any number of forgeries to his connections in America based on his reputation alone, knowingly or unknowingly. But then, he was already a millionaire, which meant money could not be a motive.

Sensing the collector was simmering down from his previous boil, Joe began again. "I'll need to complete some paperwork here and take the piece in question back to the station for holding in evidence."

"We'll be discreet," Lauren offered.

"We?" The snooty collector mocked her. "I suppose you're on a special task force for the police department, too?"

"That's about the size of it," Joe told him. "If Dr. Westlake says what you've got is a fake, I'm taking it in. She's the expert here."

Mr. St. John rocked back on his heels. "Says who?"

The color drained from Lauren's face. The elderly man who shared her name lifted his hands to placate but was too slow in forming a response.

"Says the Metropolitan," Joe began, the Italian blood in his veins warming up. "Says a doctorate degree from the University of Chicago, decades of personal study, years studying abroad. Says the fact that she learned the German language since their dictionaries are the most advanced in translating ancient hieroglyphs. Says me, on behalf of the New York Police Department." He'd closed the distance between himself and the pale-faced collector, who probably hadn't been stood up to in quite some time. "So yeah, in this investigation, what she says goes. Clear?"

No one spoke. That left Joe with a blank form on his clipboard, a stunned collector, and two Westlakes with very large eyes.

He turned to the prettier one. "Did I get that right?"

"Exactly," she said.

Joe nodded. "So, Mr. St. John, how much did you pay for the jar and when?"

"I didn't. The jar was a gift."

Joe glanced from St. John to Lauren, and back again. "No money changed hands?"

"Not a dime."

"Why didn't you say so earlier?" Lauren asked.

"It's all in the paperwork I gave Lawrence. Somewhere in that folder is a ledger containing the date of accession and price paid for every piece, as well as the location."

While Mr. Westlake scrambled to locate the ledger and turn to the right page, Lauren inhaled deeply. "If it was a gift," she said, "this was most definitely a mistake. Clarke gained nothing from it."

"Apparently neither did I." The man's jowls trembled, and his cheeks reddened. He stalked out of the room and slammed the door.

Mr. Westlake cleared his throat. "That could have gone better. Haven't you heard that one catches more flies with honey than with vinegar?"

"I shoot straight," Joe told him. "That's it."

Lauren stepped forward. "By the way, Dad, Sergeant Caravello is also a friend of mine. I first met him during our Christmas visit to Manhattan when I was twelve. Joe, you've figured this out, but this is my father."

Mr. Westlake regarded him. "So that's why you recruited Lauren to be your consultant."

She looked away.

Joe wondered if he had any idea how insulting his remark had been. "No, I recruited her because she's the best in the city."

"Of course, of course. On that we agree. That's why I've asked for her help, as well." He turned to his daughter. "How does it feel to be in such high demand?"

"Like I have no time to waste. Did you find the entry he mentioned?"

Mr. Westlake opened the ledger and pointed to an entry dated 1917. Sure enough, it recorded a gift from Theodore Clarke of the spherical ointment jar. It changed hands in Rhode Island, well outside Joe's jurisdiction.

Joe wrote down the details. "There was no crime here. This particular investigation is open and closed. Did you find anything else questionable?"

"This is the only fake we found in the Egyptian gallery, after three Saturdays of looking," Mr. Westlake said. "We finished this afternoon, which is a good thing, since I doubt he'd let us come back next week anyway. Besides which, I have other plans."

Lauren turned to him. "The gala for the Napoleon Society?"

A nod.

"I've heard of the Napoleon Society," Joe said. "I thought it was in its infancy."

"Not for much longer," Mr. Westlake assured him, then went on to explain what he hoped to accomplish through the fundraising event a week from this evening.

"So all the private collectors in the area who favor Egyptian antiquities will be there," Joe clarified.

Mr. Westlake smiled. "That's certainly the goal."

"Then that's where I'll be, too." Joe regarded Lauren, looking for the friend she'd been to him before they'd grown up. "You coming? This is a fancy shindig, am I right? With tuxedos and lots of forks? I could use a little guidance on which cutlery goes with which course. More importantly, the folks I want to talk to would be much more willing to make my acquaintance if you were with me."

"A valiant effort, Detective Caravello. But my daughter has already refused to attend, despite my repeated invitations."

Taking a chance, Joe beckoned Lauren to the opposite side of the parlor and turned his back to her father, shielding her from view. "I know you two were never close," he whispered. "But don't let that interfere with our investigation. I need you by my side next Saturday to lend credibility and grease some stubborn hinges that might not budge for me if not for you. What do you say?"

"When you put it that way," she breathed, "how can I refuse?"

CHAPTER

6

L auren arrived early at the Hotel Astor, and yet Joe was already there, framed by the twin marble and bronze stairways as he scanned the space. Even in a tuxedo, with harp music floating in the air, he looked the part of a cop. His expression might be mistaken for on-the-job vigilance, but she recognized it as something else. The firm set of his jaw, the occasional press of his lips, the slight knitting of his brows—that's how he'd always looked when he'd been looking for her. Watching. Waiting.

The pull that drew her toward him was magnetic and automatic. Perhaps Anita and Lauren's roommates were right that she spent too much time among the dead, because by contrast, Joe Caravello made her feel very much alive. Surely the attraction she felt was only natural upon renewing a lost connection.

As soon as he saw her, he closed the remaining distance between them. "I still say you should have let me pick you up rather than meet you here. I'd feel much better if I knew you didn't have any trouble along the way."

"I'm not a little girl anymore, Joe."

"So I noticed." A smile hooked his lips and fanned a spark inside her.

She ignored it, and he stepped behind her, helping her out of her cloak.

Lauren's belted black dress with filmy sleeves and handkerchief hem wouldn't come close to matching the glamour of the other guests. At least her carnelian-and-turquoise earrings and matching hair combs fit an evening dedicated to Egyptian art.

"I assume my father is upstairs," she told him after he returned from the coat-check room. Noticing his bow tie hadn't been tied correctly, she stepped into the shadow of a potted palm tree, and he followed. "You did say I was here to help you," she whispered, pulling the ends of his tie to unfasten it.

A lump shifted behind his collar.

With only one false start, she looped and tucked until it lay right. Satisfied, she gave a light pat to her handiwork and peered up at him. "Perfect. Shall we?"

"By all means." He offered his arm, and after a brief hesitation, she took it. "Is this too old-fashioned a gesture for you?" he asked.

"Not at all. I'm as old-fashioned as I ever was." She patted her chignon and glanced pointedly to all the shingle bobs and fringed dresses on other women milling about, tendrils of smoke rising from cigarettes. "I don't even smoke."

"I believe the term you're looking for is *classic*." He kept pace by her side. "You know the great thing about classics, don't you?"

"I'm an Egyptologist. I could talk your ear off about the great things about classics."

He chuckled. "Never out of style. Tonight's gala being a case in point."

Her face heated by the smallest degree. "Egypt is endlessly fascinating," she deflected as they stepped into the elevator.

"Indeed." Joe watched the needle above the door that marked their progress as they climbed ever higher. On the mansard level, they stepped out, passed through the promenade, and headed to the banquet hall.

With buttressed ceilings, this hall was decorated in the Louis XV style and was one of many reasons Hotel Astor was known as the crown jewel of Times Square. Plush carpets patterned with medallions cushioned Lauren's heels, and fan-shaped chandeliers dripped with crystal and amber light. Around the perimeter, linen-clad tables displayed Egyptian artifacts in locked glass cases.

"You're here!" Lawrence broke away from the men with whom he'd been conversing and made his way to Lauren and Joe. "Come, you shall have a private viewing of the items we've brought before the masses arrive."

"Shall I look for forgeries among them?" Lauren teased.

"Do your worst, Doctor." Lawrence grinned. "But you'll not find a fake here. All of these came directly from Egypt after having been uncovered and procured by legal means, in full cooperation with the Egyptian government."

Joe edged toward one of the tables. "You're holding an auction with these?"

"The items on those two tables are all open to silent bidding this evening. But those three tables over there hold some of the artifacts we've been curating for the Napoleon House over the last few years. We'll not be parting with those tonight. They're too valuable not to share them with the general public as soon as the house in Newport is renovated and passes inspection. You'll pardon me, both of you, but I've got some final preparation to do. Take your time and enjoy."

While Lawrence excused himself, Lauren moved to the closest table. Through the glass, she peered at a breathtaking necklace made of teardrop beads of gold, carnelian, lapis lazuli, turquoise, and green feldspar. The pectoral, which was about eight centimeters wide and more than four centimeters tall, was backed in gold and inlaid with all the semiprecious stones present in the necklace, with the addition of garnet.

Joe stood near her. "Explain it to me. Explain all of it."

She lifted her gaze to his and found he was in earnest. "All right, Detective—"

He held up a hand. "I know we normally use our professional titles in public, but how about for tonight, you call me Joe. I don't want to put people off if they learn I'm a detective before I have a chance to make a fair first impression."

"But you will be honest with them, won't you? About who you are and what you're doing?"

"Of course. I'd just like to make it through the small talk before they decide to clam up."

Fair enough. With a nod, Lauren turned her attention back to the necklace in the case. "You can see from the card placed next to it that the pectoral—that's the pendant—is inlaid with three hundred seventy-two cut pieces of semiprecious stones. It also tells us the necklace is dated from circa 1887–1878 BC, and that it was excavated in 1914. What the card doesn't say is that the symbols of the falcons, cartouche, cobras, sun disks, and the figure holding up two palm ribs all combine so that together, it translates to 'the god of the rising sun grants life and dominion over all that the sun encircles for eternity to King Khakheperre.' This would have been worn during the Middle Kingdom by a royal woman in the king's family."

Joe studied the falcons, each row of their feathers alternating between turquoise and lapis lazuli. The tail feathers were tipped in carnelian, and everything was framed in gold. "And your father didn't want to keep this for his museum?"

Lauren tapped the glass case with one finger. "This piece will go for an extraordinary sum. Maybe he needs the money more at this point. If you were to flip the pectoral over, you'd see that the gold backing is engraved with every detail you see on the front, right down to the dozens of individual falcon feathers. This was a trademark of Middle Kingdom jewelry, especially for royals. The only person who would know about that gorgeous detail would be the wearer, and that was enough. Truly remarkable."

The next case held a charming bracelet ringed with gold-encased scarabs the size of her thumb, linked side by side. "You've seen scarabs at the Met. They are the most common amulets of ancient Egypt, so they aren't all that valuable by themselves. But these are made of lapis lazuli and framed in gold, so it will fetch a pretty price, although a fraction of what that necklace will."

They moved among the tables, and she filled in any details not written on the description cards. He took notes as studiously as though he were to be tested on the material.

"I've always thought the ancient Egyptians were obsessed with death," Joe mused aloud.

"You miss the point," Lauren told him. "They were obsessed with life."

"The afterlife, you mean."

"Isn't that life, too? It's easy to lose sight of the fact that there is more to life than the years we spend on earth. But the Egyptians never forgot it. They started building their tombs as soon as they had enough resources to begin. They spent more money on their comforts during the afterlife than they did for this one."

Ridges formed across Joe's brow. "And I've always thought that was a little sad."

"I know what you mean, and obviously, I don't share their poly-theistic religion," Lauren said. She believed in one true God, even if He had felt distant at times, especially during her turbulent teenage years. "The fact that the Egyptians believed in many things to save and protect them doesn't really set them apart from our culture today, though, when you think about it."

Joe lowered his pencil and notebook. "Go on."

"What do New Yorkers put their trust in? For some, it's wealth. Status. Others idolize happiness and use whatever means they can to achieve it, but it won't satisfy. When anyone makes their own happiness the ultimate goal, no matter the cost . . ."

"It never ends well. You're right. Most crimes are committed for selfish reasons."

"Exactly. All that to say, I've learned many things from Egyptology, not the least of which is the idea that what we do in this life matters in the next. That we should be preparing ourselves for what comes after. Death isn't the end of life—it's really the beginning of our eternity."

Lauren's mother had not been well enough to bring her to church on a regular basis, but she taught her from the Bible at home. Among the truths they clung to was that they would meet again in heaven, where there were no tears or pain or sorrow.

Joe looked at her with a compassion she'd rarely known. "I'm so sorry about your mother. You'll see her again."

Lauren wondered if she'd spoken her thoughts aloud before realizing she hadn't needed to. Joe had been there for her when her mother died, when Lauren was fifteen. Were it not for his support, the weight of her grief would have crushed her.

She squeezed his hand in gratitude and felt a measure of that comfort all over again.

Guests began to arrive, and Lauren watched for people she knew. "There's Newell St. John," she said. "Have you spoken with him?"

"I tried. He's still sore about what we discovered and with me in particular. I hope he doesn't poison the rest of the guests here against me."

"You'll need to tread more carefully if you're going to get any cooperation from others."

"You know I've always been a straight shooter."

"Yes, and you're shooting yourself straight in the foot." She glanced away, smiled at someone, and turned back. "Come, you'll want to meet Victoria Vandermeer and her husband, Miles."

"Is she the one wearing a gold arm cuff and—what is that on her head?"

Lauren smiled. "Let's call it a headband. But yes, that's the one. The Vandermeers are extremely generous with the Met, but they offend easily. So we won't lead with the fact that we're looking for fakes. Just like St. John, they'd be insulted at the insinuation."

"Touchy lot, these artsy types," Joe mumbled.

Lauren didn't deny it. "If you're going to earn these people's trust, you'll have to put in the time to listen to their small talk. Ready to be charming?"

He flashed her a dazzling smile in response, and she held back a laugh as she led him to meet the couple.

"It's so good to see you again," she began and, with practiced ease, introduced Joe to Victoria and Miles.

"When Miles and I heard about a new, exclusive society, we just had to come and learn all about it," Victoria gushed. "How many people received an invitation to this gala, do you know?"

All it took after that was a few questions from Joe, and Lauren knew Victoria could talk for another twenty minutes without stopping. Miles nodded and smiled beside her, a reflection of light bobbing on his spectacles. He was taller than his wife by five inches, but she owned the larger personality by far.

At the edge of her vision, Lauren spotted none other than Ray and Christina Moretti. With a pang of alarm, she remembered that Mr. Robinson had tasked her with smoothing things over with the couple. She'd completely forgotten. She wouldn't be surprised if they'd cut off all ties with the museum by now, but if she could do anything to salvage the relationship, she would. Holding up one finger, she signaled that she would soon return.

Forcing himself to listen to Mrs. Vandermeer, Joe angled himself so he could keep Lauren in view. She was talking to a man in his fifties with silver-threaded dark hair. The woman on his arm looked at least twenty years younger. Strands of diamonds in her ears stretched long enough to reach past her blond hair and brush her shoulders.

"What is so interesting over there?" Victoria Vandermeer turned around, then faced her husband with a knowing look before whispering to Joe, "No wonder you can't look away." She waved a fan as if something smelled. "New money. If you ask me, those people and their kind only play the fool when they pretend to prestige. How did they get an invitation, anyway?"

Joe managed a response of some kind while making a mental

note that the Vandermeers didn't like that the Morettis made their money instead of inheriting it.

By the time Lauren returned to their little cluster and the Vandermeers moved on to mingle elsewhere, he'd never gotten around to talking about forgeries with the Vandermeers at all.

"Who were you speaking to?" he asked Lauren.

She led him farther away for a modicum of privacy. "Ray and Christina Moretti. They have a huge collection of Egyptian artwork. But you don't need to waste your time talking to them."

"And why's that?"

"I've seen his collection before. Most of it he inherited from his father, although he did send a buyer directly to Cairo to bring back a few more pieces."

"So you don't think he would have acquired anything stateside in the last three years?"

She shook her head. "No. I also don't want to insult him further by suggesting he's been fooled. He's been one of the biggest supporters of the Met for the last several years, but I'm afraid that's about to change, if it hasn't already."

"Why? Did the Met not want donations of 'new money'?" He shrugged at her incredulous expression. "Mrs. Vandermeer's words, not mine."

She glanced over her shoulder, likely reassuring herself they weren't within earshot. "Mr. Moretti recently offered to give the Met a portion of his collection to put on display with the caveat that the room in which it is housed be named for him."

Joe caught himself before whistling. "That's quite a caveat."

"Mr. Robinson, our director, declined the offer as respectfully as he could, but we're concerned that Mr. Moretti may choose to withdraw his financial support, as well. So the last thing I want to do is ask to dig around in his private property, looking for forgeries."

"You're sure about this?"

She touched his arm. "I'm not letting him off the hook because I'm afraid of how he'd react. I really don't see the need for it. Trust me."

A short laugh puffed through his nose.

"Oh, that's right." Her eyes narrowed, but a smile curved her lips. "You don't trust anybody anymore. Well, trust me or not, but I'm telling the truth. Let's connect you with other collectors instead."

Lauren introduced him to several more patrons of the Met, the women sparkling with jewels, the men dripping with self-importance. After engaging in the socially expected amount of small talk, he told them he had reason to believe forgers had been taking advantage of the King Tut craze. "If you've acquired any Egyptian artifacts within the last three years, Dr. Westlake would be happy to take a look to affirm their authenticity."

It didn't prove to be a popular idea.

"Think of it this way," Lauren added. "If your art is genuine, you'll have the satisfaction of knowing for certain. If not, the police will have more evidence and clues to catch the forgers."

Her gentle prodding persuaded several couples to agree, as long as all would be done with the utmost discretion. No one wanted anyone else to know their investments were being questioned.

During the meal, Joe took cues from Lauren to follow proper dining etiquette. While the waitstaff served chocolate soufflé and refilled coffee cups, Lawrence Westlake took the podium and waxed eloquent about the date. Three years ago, he explained, King Tut's tomb was opened, reigniting a passion for Egyptology.

"And as we gather here in a great hall decorated for Louis XV," he went on, "may we not forget that one hundred twenty-six years ago this year, a French soldier discovered the Rosetta Stone during Napoleon's Egyptian campaign, the first step in unlocking the ancient Egyptian language of hieroglyphs."

Though he much preferred listening to the man's daughter, Joe took notes as Lawrence recited the mission of the Napoleon Society; named the board members, who stood in turn; and argued for the need of another educational society and museum.

Frankly, Joe wasn't convinced, but he was intrigued. The more he learned about this world and the people who inhabited it, the closer he would come to finding forgers and solving the significance of that oyster shell Connor had allegedly plunked into Wade Martin's drink minutes before the raid.

The lights dimmed, and on a screen at the front of the room, lantern slides projected the images of artifacts already acquired for the Napoleon House. Lawrence and another board member took turns narrating these, while a third member followed with descriptions of the items available in the silent auction.

Joe leaned toward Lauren, catching the fragrance of apple blossoms from her hair. "You should have been up there," he whispered. "You'd do a much better job."

The smile she sent him in return, complete with wrinkled nose, was halfway between a scold and gratitude. He quite enjoyed it. He always had.

When the lights turned on, Lawrence announced that dinner was over and bidding in the silent auction was now open. So was the dance floor. A string ensemble struck up a waltz.

Soon, Joe and Lauren were the only ones at the table, the others having left to make their bids. He took the last sip of his coffee as Lawrence approached, a twinkle in his eye.

"I'm so glad you came, Lauren. It's important to me that you understand the importance of what I'm doing." The elderly gentleman reached for his daughter's hand, and then lifted it to bring her to her feet. "What do you say? For old times' sake."

She hesitated, then agreed.

While Lawrence led her onto the floor, Joe left the table and ambled along the perimeter of the room, making mental notes about who was bidding on the items. A forger could be here tonight, studying the artifacts and the people who would buy them. If Joe was a forger, that's what he'd do.

Questions filled his mind as he watched the guests orbit the artifacts and one another. Had Joe introduced himself to a crook? Had he told him that he was on the hunt?

No matter. Forgers loved the adrenaline rush. They loved the challenge. Fooling a New York police detective and a curator for the Met was most likely a challenge a forger would be eager to meet.

Assistant curator. Joe could hear Lauren's voice in his mind, correcting him. She was far too modest. He scanned the swirling couples until he found her again. That strange hemline, cut to resemble triangles, pointed to shapely ankles as she moved across the floor.

She wasn't dancing with her father anymore. Her partner was a fellow of middling years wearing a green silk ascot. His brown hair was short but wavy, held in place with enough Brilliantine to reflect the light. Thomas Sanderson, if Joe's notes were right. Deep, deep pockets. Sanderson was smiling, but Lauren wasn't. When she turned her head away from whatever Sanderson said, she locked her gaze with Joe's.

Before he even had time to make a conscious decision, he went to her. "Mind if I cut in?"

Sanderson halted his steps but didn't release Lauren.

And Joe had asked so nicely. Before he could clarify that his question wasn't really a question, Lauren pulled free of the man and stepped toward Joe instead.

"I don't mind at all," she breathed. To Sanderson, she smiled and said, "I find it best to cooperate with the police at all times, don't you? Have a lovely evening. I do hope you win your bid."

A smile tugging, Joe resisted the urge to flash his badge. Or the sidearm breaking the otherwise smooth lines of his tuxedo.

"Yes, quite." Sanderson gave a small bow, then faded from view.

Lauren turned to face Joe, light glancing off her dangling earrings. She stepped into his hold. "Thanks, Joe."

He liked the way her hand fit into his. Liked the way her eyes crinkled at the corners when she smiled. But he had no idea what to do with the pinpricks in his chest when she directed that smile at him. It was pleasing and painful at the same time, almost like a thaw.

"You're welcome." He gave her hand a gentle squeeze, then guided her back into the dance. "How much was Sanderson bothering you?"

"You aren't going to believe this," she whispered, leaning in, "but somehow he'd heard that I found Mr. St. John's ointment jar to be a fake. He even knew it had been a gift from Theodore Clarke! I was mortified. We promised discretion."

"Who told him? Someone here?"

"No, several ladies called on his wife this past week—she's been ill—and it was one of those friends, but he couldn't recall which. I swear I didn't tell a soul about it—did you?"

"Outside of the report I had to write, no."

"Then I don't understand it. Unless one of Mr. St. John's servants let it slip to someone. In any case, I begged Mr. Sanderson not to say more about it to anyone else." Lauren inhaled deeply, apparently recomposing herself. "I do hope you haven't abandoned something important for my sake."

She was something important. "Rest easy. My priorities are right where they should be. Besides, this gives me a much better view." He looked over her head as they turned about the floor, alert for anything unusual. "I thought you were dancing with your father. For old times' sake."

A short laugh escaped her. "*Very* old times. I only recall dancing with him while standing on his feet when I was five or six years old. If he gave the impression we'd ever been in the habit of dancing, that was false."

Anger flared. Whatever emotional capital Lawrence had with her, he wanted to use. Why? "Whose idea was it for you to switch partners?"

"My father's, I'm sure. He waltzed me right over to Mr. Sanderson, but just before we reached him, my father told me to make him comfortable, to impress him, and to put him in a generous mood."

Joe almost tripped but recovered before stepping on her feet. He spread his hand over the small of her back. "He's using you."

"I know." Her tone held the edge of bitterness, but no surprise. She stayed quiet for the next few turns before adding, "So are you. That's why you contacted me again, isn't it?"

Her words were a blow, rendering him speechless for a moment.

"You're helping me conduct an investigation," he said at last. "I never tried to trick you into it, and I wouldn't manipulate your emotions to get what I want."

She lifted her chin. "You're right, Joe. It's not the same, and I want to help you. I'm sorry. I'm not irritated at you, really. I'm irritated . . . near you." A sigh swelled and released in her, and he watched the pulse in the hollow of her throat.

For a minute, Joe thought she might share with him what was truly going on behind those stormy blue eyes. She didn't.

Perhaps curving his hand to the hollow of her waist had made him forget they hadn't come here together. This wasn't a date. It was a job. He was here for clues that would lead to a forger. Clues that might shed light on Connor's demise.

The music ended, and Joe counted himself lucky that this brilliant woman had ended up in his arms, if only for half a dance. "On behalf of the New York Police Department, I appreciate your full cooperation," he teased.

"You're welcome, Joe." That smile again.

He hadn't realized until now how much he'd missed it.

CHAPTER

7

Happy birthday, Mother." Lauren laid a bouquet of gold chrysanthemums on her mother's marble headstone. The petals rippled in a breeze that skimmed her cheeks. Goldie Westlake would have been sixty years old today.

"My father should be here," she added.

Elsa shifted beside her, balling her cold hands into fists and pressing them beneath her folded arms. "Maybe he came earlier?"

"If he did, he didn't bring flowers." Lauren nodded toward the lonely blooms she'd brought, a splash of sunshine on an otherwise washed-out day. "I suppose I could have mentioned the date when I saw him last night, but I was thinking about forgeries and the Napoleon Society and Joe, who feels like the friend I remember and a man of unplumbed depths all at once."

"So you said last night. I'll bet he made a much better dance partner than King Tut's mummy." Elsa grinned.

"Anyone would be a better dance partner than King Tut's mummy."

"Touché."

Lauren sent her a small smile. "Anyway, I don't know why I thought my dad would remember Mother's birthday now when he rarely did when she was alive. It's probably better that I don't see him until I get over what he did last night anyway."

When Lawrence had passed her off to Mr. Sanderson, it triggered the emotional memory of his abandonment all over again. She thought her father had wanted to spend time with her, and then he gave her up and walked away to do something else.

It had been such a small act, and yet it brought to the surface feelings of rejection long buried.

"The last thing I want to do is argue in front of my mother's grave."

Elsa tucked her scarf beneath her chin. "You know, I've never actually seen you argue with anyone."

"Maybe I do my arguing on the inside." A rueful smile bent Lauren's lips.

"Well, if we ever do choose sides, sign me up for yours." Her cousin nudged her with an elbow.

Lauren chuckled. But there shouldn't *be* sides. If she had any interest in whatever remnant of relationship she had with Lawrence, she needed to forgive him, as often as she needed to, or succumb to a lifetime of embitterment.

That wasn't what she wanted. That wasn't what Mother had wanted for her, either.

"Both of our mothers certainly set an example for resentment against my father," Lauren murmured, and Elsa agreed. "But eventually, mine confessed the need to forgive him, and that she should have done it long ago, for her own sake as much as for his."

Before she died, she had told Lauren, *"How I wish you knew your father."* Then she'd closed her eyes and whispered, *"Redeem this."* She never opened her eyes again.

But one person could only do so much.

Footsteps crunched on the brittle grass, then stopped short. "Lauren?"

"Mrs. Foster." Something disagreeable threaded through Lauren at the sight of the hawk-nosed nursemaid who had tended Mother since before Lauren was born. Most memories that included Mrs. Foster were unpleasant ones.

Elsa greeted her, too, reintroducing herself. "You came to my house on Fifth Avenue many times. Good to see you again, Mrs. Foster."

"Call me Nancy." She was older than Lawrence by a few years and looked every inch her age. Stooping with rounded shoulders, she lay orange asters alongside the chrysanthemums.

"Thank you for coming," Lauren tried, as if this were a meeting she had called for, which it was not.

"I have never missed her birthday, not since I was hired to look after her when she was but a wee thing."

It was a wonder they hadn't seen each other here before. Lauren supposed her luck had to run out sometime.

She sealed her lips to trap the thought on the tip of her tongue. That she was jealous of the time this woman had had with her mother. Jealous that she'd known her so well before Mother ever grew ill, and that Nancy was usually the only one allowed to be with her after that.

"You knew her longer and better than I ever did." The words slipped out before Lauren could strip the facts of feeling. "I wish I'd understood her better. I don't think she understood me, either."

Nancy hobbled closer. The once-formidable woman now looked up at her and Elsa. "She understood more than you give her credit for." Her gaze narrowed. "You never read the letters."

Lauren glanced at Elsa, who only shook her head, the questions in her eyes reflecting her own.

The aged nursemaid sighed. "Maybe grief made you forget. After your mother passed into glory, Mr. and Mrs. Reisner let me stay on in the house until your father came back and settled affairs. When he did—months after the funeral—I found a small wooden chest in his fireplace when I went to light the bedroom fires. It appeared he intended for it to be burned. I wasn't about to destroy it without knowing what it held, so I looked. It was full of your mother's letters to him over the years. He was going to *burn* them. Like he had no use for her memory, just like he had no use for her in life, God rest her." Nancy's voice shook, the soft skin beneath her jaw trembling.

"I wouldn't have any part in that. Instead, I added the letters your mother had kept from him, and I left the box for you. You didn't read them, did you?"

"Did you?" Lauren snapped. She hadn't meant to, but her nerves were strung tight at the thought of her father wanting to destroy those letters.

Nancy pushed her hat back on her brow. Wrinkles bracketed her pursed mouth. "I was the one who read them to her when she hadn't the strength to read herself. I was the one who wrote her final message to him near the end. I don't mean to scold, but she'd have wanted you to know *her* better instead of chasing after a man who won't even visit his wife's grave on her birthday."

A white cloud puffed from Elsa's nose. "Pardon me for saying so, but Lauren would have known her mother better if she'd been allowed to be around her more often."

It was exactly what Lauren had been thinking, but she hadn't come here to spar with Nancy.

Turning from the woman's disapproval, Lauren knelt before the tombstone. She tugged at a weed caught in the unyielding earth, and Elsa followed suit.

"I snuck into Mother's room at night sometimes," she murmured to her cousin, willing Nancy to pay her respects and leave.

"To sleep in the bed with her?"

"On the rug on the floor beside it." Only once did Lauren crawl into the cold space her father left empty. She didn't know she'd kicked in her sleep until Mother's soft groan awoke Nancy and got Lauren sent back to her own room. "I wanted to be with her, even if it meant sleeping on the floor. But I found myself back in my own bed before morning every time. I don't remember walking back to my room, though. I told myself a fairy spirited me away."

A grunt sounded from behind. "I've been called worse."

Elsa sat back on her heels and twisted around.

Lauren stood, bracing herself for another tirade.

"What was I to do when I came in to check on her and found her, sick as she was, curled on the floor beside you?" Nancy began. "She would drag a blanket down to cover you both, but that was no bed for a woman in her state. She'd never get well on the floor with the cold seeping into her bones. Oh no, not on my watch."

Lauren's breath caught on the new information. She would give anything—*anything*—to remember the feel of her mother's arms around her.

"Your mother would only go back to her bed once you were safe and warm in yours. I'd have locked you out at night if she'd let me, but she forbade it. When I did separate you, it was for her good. Her life was my life's work."

The air in Lauren's lungs grew thick. Mother had wanted to be near her. Lauren should have tried again. Tried harder.

Elsa stood silently beside her, having risen at some point during Nancy's speech.

The lapels of Nancy's overcoat flapped in the wind, and curls of grey hair twirled beneath her hat. "Find those letters. You owe it to her to hear her side of the story." She kissed her wrinkled fingertips, touched the tombstone, and walked away.

Magenta and tangerine streaked the sky that would soon deepen to purple, then black. A chill prickled Lauren's neck. The temperature was dropping along with the sun. "Do you have any idea where a box like that could be if I left it in your house?"

Elsa bit her lip. "Sorry, I was eight years old when Aunt Goldie died. Attention to detail was not my strong suit. But it is now. If it's in the house, I'll find it."

CHAPTER

8

MONDAY, NOVEMBER 23, 1925

Lauren rubbed at the kinks in her neck before shuffling her papers together and stacking them under the Hatshepsut paperweight. Quarter past five already. It had been another full day of planning for the Met's spring exhibition on the Egyptian afterlife. She had been in talks with a few different museums around the country over the last several weeks, confirming the terms of their loans for the show. Most were cooperative, but the Boston Museum of Fine Arts required a more delicate touch. She supposed it might have something to do with the decades-long rivalry between the MFA and the Met. At least they'd agreed to host her for a visit after Thanksgiving to finalize the details. Some things were simply better discussed in person.

Standing, she put on her coat and found in her pocket the mail Anita had passed to her earlier today. She had recognized her father's handwriting and ignored it.

Drawing a fortifying breath, she opened the envelope and pulled the card free. After skimming his thanks for coming to the gala, she tossed it in her waste bin, turned out the light, and stalked away. The letters she was truly interested in were the ones Nancy had referred to yesterday. Surely the box that held them remained safely within her aunt's house. It was only a matter of finding the time to search.

Locking thoughts of her parents into a corner of her mind, she bade the security guards a good night and exited the rear of the building. Snow fell from a dove grey sky, sticking to the tops of trees and cars but melting on the sidewalks almost as soon as it landed. She blinked flakes from her lashes. Central Park would be magical tonight, but her shoes weren't made for a walk in the snow.

When she reached the narrow drive, a shiny black Studebaker Six pulled to a stop right in front of her. The back seat window lowered.

"Dr. Westlake!" Ray Moretti called, his wife waving beside him.

Lauren greeted them both, hiding her surprise at seeing them at the Met.

"Get in, would you? It's freezing out there!" Christina crooned.

Before she knew what was happening, the driver had hopped out and come around to Lauren's side. He opened the door to the far back seat and waited for her to enter.

She didn't move. "What's going on?" She tried to keep her voice light.

"I heard a rumor about you, and I want to talk to you about it," Mr. Moretti told her. "But please, don't make us get snowed on to do it. Let us give you a ride home while we chat."

Mr. Robinson's directive to repair the relationship with the Morettis echoed in her mind.

Lauren slid into the back seat. It was a six-person vehicle, so Ray and Christina were in the seat in front of her, and the driver had the front seat to himself. The couple angled sideways to see her, lights from other vehicles casting shadows from their profiles.

"Good." Mr. Moretti smiled. "I heard from other guests at the gala Saturday night that you're on the hunt for a forger."

"Well, forgeries, yes."

"Right. You've been offering to look at private collections to see if any fakes have snuck in among the genuine artifacts. True so far?"

"Yes," Lauren admitted. "I've offered to discreetly do this for our valued patrons as a service to them. I hate to think of anyone being deceived by forgery."

"And are we not your valued patrons, Dr. Westlake?"

She inhaled sharply. "I—that's not at all what I meant."

A car behind them honked, the beams from its headlamps shining in through the Studebaker's rear window. Mr. Moretti's pupils constricted in the light.

The car rolled forward, then steered into traffic. It would probably take just as long to drive all the way around Central Park as it would have for Lauren to walk straight through it as usual, but at least she was warm and dry.

Mr. Moretti turned toward her again. "And yet you didn't make this offer to me when you had the opportunity Saturday night." His tone was smooth and cool, his smile fixed in place. If this was him putting her at ease, it wasn't working. "Is that because of all this unpleasantness with Mr. Robinson? Has he turned you against me? I'd so hate to lose your esteem."

"Not at all," Lauren rushed to say. "You haven't lost my esteem. The only reason I didn't offer to examine your collection is that I was—I still am—convinced that no forgeries are among it. At the benefit soiree you hosted at your Long Island estate last year, you told me how you came into possession of all your pieces, and I saw them myself. The forgeries I'm looking for would have been acquired stateside in the last three years. I understood—or at least I thought I understood—that you acquire pieces yourself or through a personal buyer in Cairo." She was sputtering like an idiot. Making herself sound guilty when all of this was the absolute truth. "Please believe me, Mr. and Mrs. Moretti, I assumed your collection was above question. I never meant to exclude you from any service you might find helpful."

"That's quite all right, sweetie, I'm sure." Christina lit the end of a cigarette and puffed smoke from the side of red-painted lips. "That makes perfect sense."

Lauren glanced out the window as they turned east, not west. "Excuse me, but my apartment is the other way."

"I appreciate your confidence, Dr. Westlake." Mr. Moretti seemed not to have heard her. "But as it happens, I did acquire a piece fairly recently. If the forgeries are as rampant as you say, I'd like you to take a look at it. Would you mind?"

"Right now?" Their estate was twenty-some miles east of here, among the mansions of Long Island's north shore.

Mr. Moretti lit his own cigarette, and wispy curls of smoke snaked up to the ceiling, spreading throughout the car. "Well, we're here, you're here. . . . No time like the present."

Lauren tried not to cough but failed.

"But do you have time, dear?" Christina asked. "We're not going all the way to the country house. Just to the Fifth Avenue apartment."

Fifth Avenue. She could manage a detour of a few blocks. With effort, Lauren steadied her breathing and agreed.

Minutes later, she stepped inside the most opulent penthouse apartment she'd ever seen. Larger-than-life oil paintings hung in ornate frames in the entryway. The space opened into a drawing room that had been styled to resemble a German hunting lodge, complete with dark wood beams on the ceiling, a chandelier fashioned of elk antlers, more wood paneling the walls, and a taxidermy bear standing at full height beside the massive stone fireplace.

"Don't worry, Dr. Westlake, I have my own salon." Holding her cigarette between two fingers, Christina beckoned Lauren through a set of double glass doors and into what appeared to be a salon right out of Versailles. Cream-colored furniture was gilded with gold leaf and upholstered in shades of blush and pink. A pug sat on a round tufted ottoman, eating undercooked steak from a silver tray while a servant stood ready to take the remains away. Toile wallpaper depicted scenes from the French countryside between floor-to-ceiling silk drapes.

And all this inside a stately-looking brownstone. Lauren had never seen anything like it.

"Over here, Dr. Westlake. Come take a look at this." Mr. Moretti led the way into the dining room, and Lauren covered her gaping mouth. Life-sized hieroglyphs and vignettes covered the walls in bold colors that fairly leapt off the plaster. It was a landscape of stiffly posed Egyptians going about their daily tasks.

"Who painted this?" Lauren asked. It looked as though it could have been done by one of the restoration painters on the Met's Egyptian department team.

Mr. Moretti waved the question away. "I hired the work out. I used lantern slides to project the images on the walls, and painters had no trouble tracing the forms and filling them in with color. But that's not what I wanted you to see, although I'm gratified by your reaction. Look here."

The dining room table had been customized so that a glass case was set into its surface. The case was three feet long, the perfect proportions to display a two-and-a-half-foot length of the Book of the Dead, which was a common collection of spells to help navigate the afterlife. What an odd choice of art to join the Morettis and their guests for meals.

"Isn't it morbid?" Christina asked. "This is where we eat and entertain, for goodness' sake."

"That's what makes it perfectly placed," her husband countered. "It's a reminder to eat, drink, and be merry, for tomorrow we die!"

Removing her hat and gloves, Lauren leaned over to inspect it with a magnifying glass Mr. Moretti supplied.

"Well?" he pressed.

"The fibers of the papyrus look authentic. The text, too, has been written with a steady, confident hand, which is a good sign. Forgers often wobble or make other mistakes."

"Such as?" Christina asked.

She moved the magnifying glass over the figures. "The ancient Egyptians represent the human form in ways that don't make sense to us, and if forgers aren't careful, they'll 'fix' part of the body without realizing what they've done." She looked up and pointed to the wall where a woman had been painted with her hands outstretched. "You see the position of her thumbs? That's not natural, but that's how the Egyptians painted them. And the way the eyes face front even though they are on a profile. Some forgers don't pick up on the fact that men are always painted red-brown, and women are always painted yellow. Furthermore, men are portrayed with one leg forward, as if in motion, whereas women are typically portrayed with feet together."

Mr. Moretti looked from the wall to the papyrus, squinting at the figures drawn there. "I don't see any of those mistakes here."

Lauren smiled. "Neither do I. Your section here looks immaculate."

"Really?" Christina frowned. "It looks a little tired to me."

Lauren allowed herself a laugh. "If you were three thousand years old, you'd look a little tired, too. Honestly, if the ink was darker and easier to read, that would be another sign it was faked. But to my eye, this appears appropriately tired, as you say."

Mr. Moretti squared his shoulders. "Well, you've set my mind at ease, Dr. Westlake. My habit is to make my purchases personally or through my buyer in Cairo or Luxor, but when I came across this opportunity, I couldn't pass it up."

Only half listening now, Lauren leaned in closer, studying the figures once more.

"You noticed something else." Wariness edged his voice.

"It may be nothing to worry about," she hedged.

"Too late for that." Mr. Moretti's smile looked more like a grimace. "What's giving you pause?"

She straightened, gathering her wits about her. The last thing she wanted to do was cause alarm unnecessarily, especially since his relationship with the Met was already tenuous. But he was already agitated by her hesitation, so she drew a deep breath and forged ahead.

"It's the coloring in the corner. Do you see this body of water? It would have been painted blue."

He frowned at the spot in question. "It *is* painted blue."

Lauren inwardly cringed, uncomfortable with correcting him. "That's a shade of green."

"Regardless, it matches the facsimile I have in my library. The British Museum's Sir E.A. Wallis Budge's elephant folio from 1890. I believe that's the standard, is it not?"

"It is, but not many people know the story behind the printing of that book. Reproducing color illustrations of the Book of the Dead was exorbitantly expensive, you see. There were only a handful of sections in the original scrolls that had been painted blue. In order to save money, Budge's publisher decided not to add the blue ink, and to instead substitute this aqua-green already used throughout the book. The variation is slight, and not many would even notice the difference."

Christina leaned over the glass, her bob coming to points on either side of her face. "But how do you know?"

"It's my job," she said, as humbly as she could. "And I've seen an original in the British Museum."

Mr. Moretti clapped his hands, and a servant appeared at the door. "Drinks."

The servant went to the sideboard and began filling glasses. From the smell of it, he wasn't pouring grape juice. Or near beer.

"I'm sorry if I've disappointed you, sir," Lauren said, suddenly anxious to make her exit. "Everything else about this section of papyrus is so convincing, I almost didn't catch it."

When the servant appeared at her elbow, Mr. and Mrs. Moretti plucked two of the glasses off the silver tray and waited for her to take the third.

"I—I don't drink."

"Yours is only a fruit cocktail, sweetie," Christina said. "Go on."

Lauren took a tentative sip from the tumbler and found it to be as sweet as cherries.

Mr. Moretti cocked his head and looked at her with an intensity that might flay the skin from her thoughts. "So you're sure this is a forgery?"

"I wish I wasn't." She looked again at the beautiful, meticulously done piece. "But I'm sure." She took another sip.

———o———

"Maybe I haven't been clear." Gripping the telephone tighter, Joe kept his voice as cool as he could. It was exhausting, being this polite. He really didn't have time for it. "I'm not selling anything. I spoke with Mr. and Mrs. Vandermeer at the Napoleon Society gala two nights ago. We were introduced by Dr. Westlake, curator at the Metropolitan Museum of Art."

"The Vandermeers have already made their donations for the year. Their charitable giving cycle will begin again after the new year, so you may make an application after that."

Joe white-knuckled the end of his rope with the Vandermeers' secretary. Why didn't these people answer their own phones, for pity's sake? "I'm not asking for charity, either. As I said earlier, I'm calling from the police department. I want to make sure your employers have not been victim to a crime."

"I assure you, nothing has been stolen, and they are both in perfect health."

"Would you take a message, please, and have one of them call me at their earliest convenience? If I don't hear from them soon, my only recourse will be to pay a personal visit." He imagined none of that ilk would appreciate a police car at their home for all the neighbors to see. The news might even make it into *Town Topics*, the society rag their type adored.

After hanging up, Joe leaned back in his chair, hands behind his head. He'd been fighting a black mood all day, and dead-end phone calls like the one he'd just ended were only part of the reason.

Across the desks from him, Oscar McCormick ate a corned beef and sauerkraut on rye. Loudly. It didn't smell good.

"You couldn't wait until after your shift to eat dinner?"

"Hm?" He looked up, a little too delighted at having been addressed. "Have you had one of these yet? If you had, you wouldn't wonder why I'd eat one at any time of day. I'd eat it for breakfast."

"You *have* eaten it for breakfast," Joe reminded him.

"Exactly." He grinned.

Joe shook his head and bit his tongue. The kid probably had no idea that had been Connor's favorite thing to order from Katz's, the Jewish deli on Houston Street, less than a mile from headquarters. The first time McCormick had brought the sandwich into the station, Joe had smelled it before McCormick had even come in the room and plopped down at Connor's old desk. For a fraction of a second, Joe's senses had tricked him into thinking Connor was back, that it had all been one big misunderstanding and things could go back to the way they'd been. The way things ought to be.

"Hey." McCormick brightened. "Next time I go, I'll get one for you, too, okay? This is the best thing on the menu."

"Make it a pastrami with mustard," Joe muttered.

Over McCormick's protests, Joe straightened up his desk, locked the drawers, and left. He needed to let off some steam.

The police academy occupied the fourth floor of the station, including physical fitness equipment. He changed clothes in the locker room, stretched, and started running on the track.

Breathe in. Breathe out. He always thought better while he was running. Then again, right now, he wouldn't have minded not thinking at all. Frustration simmered at how little progress he'd made in the last month with the hunt for forgers.

Circles. Joe was running in circles, literally, and he was stuck in the circuitous tracks in his head. His lungs burned as he lost track of laps and pushed himself to his limits before finally calling it quits. Hitting the showers, he wished he could rinse away the foul temper he'd been soaking in all day.

By the time he was clean again, he at least felt ready to call Lauren and see if she'd had better luck arranging meetings with collectors. It was after five, though, which meant he wouldn't reach her at the Met. He looked her up in the city directory and rang her place.

"She's not home yet, Detective," one of her roommates told him. "I have to go out, but I can leave a note asking her to call you. She has your number?"

The last thing he wanted to do was spend another minute across from Oscar McCormick and Connor's old desk. "I'm leaving the station for the night," he told her. "I'll head up your way and wait for her in the lobby."

After a brief ride on the subway, Joe emerged and walked the rest of the distance to the Beresford. Wind bit his cheeks, announcing winter had made its entrance ahead of its calendar appointment, as it normally did in New York.

The rush of taxis on Central Park West filled his ears. Taillamps shone red as vehicles braked their way through the precipitation. Flakes swirled in the fan-shaped arcs of light cast by lampposts along the sidewalk. As he approached the Beresford, a Studebaker Six rolled up to the curb and parked, exhaust pluming from its tail pipe. The rear door opened, and a woman stepped out on unsteady legs, a lock of long hair tumbling over one shoulder as she slammed the door shut again.

Joe frowned. "Lauren?"

Adjusting her hat, she looked at him and smiled. "Joe!" Immediately, she put her hand to her head again and grimaced.

At once, he was at her elbow, supporting her. She reeked of cigarettes. "I thought you didn't smoke."

"I don't, although you'd never believe that by the smell of me, would you? The Morettis both smoked in the car with me. I couldn't get away from it."

Her breath carried an all-too-familiar scent. "Have you been drinking?"

"Hm? Fruit cocktail," she mumbled.

The doorman opened the door. "You all right, Dr. Westlake?"

"Fine, George. Thank you. Although . . ." She turned bleary eyes on Joe.

"I'll see you safely to your apartment," he said, fighting to keep the edge out of his voice. Something was going on.

She smiled and patted his chest. "Gentleman," she called him.

The words forming in his mind were anything but chivalrous.

By virtue of his self-control alone, he made it through the lobby, up the elevator, and down the hall to her apartment without letting any of them escape.

Inside her living room, he set her on the couch and took the armchair across from her. "What were you doing tonight?"

He didn't bother hiding his surprise when she told him the Morettis had rolled up in the drive behind the museum as she was leaving it. "How did they know when you'd leave work? How did they know you take the rear exit?"

She frowned. "When did you get to be so suspicious? Oh, I know. It's part of the job."

"Actually, my father taught me that long before I wore a badge." He found it ironic that the most valuable lesson he learned from Pop was one his father never intended to teach. As a teen, Joe couldn't help but question why his father's behavior didn't match his words. Everything was fine, Pop had said. No need to worry. But he paced instead of slept. A crate of rotten tomatoes reduced him to tears, and he exploded at Joe for taking the bus when he could have walked and saved a few cents. Pop even yelled at Mama—just once—for being too generous with portion sizes, and then stormed out of the restaurant, disappearing for hours. Joe and his brother finally found Pop and peeled him off the bar where he'd apparently spent enough money to pass out drunk. The confrontation that followed Pop's uncharacteristic behavior and binge was one Joe preferred to forget. But no one was allowed to treat Mama that way. Not even Pop.

So, yeah, Joe was suspicious, and he wouldn't apologize for it.

"Well, in this case, there's nothing shady going on," Lauren said. "I usually leave at quitting time, right around five. I'm a creature of habit, and they must have noticed. It wouldn't be hard."

"Okay, but why couldn't they pick up the phone instead? And are you in the habit of climbing into your patrons' vehicles?"

Lauren waved a hand dismissively, as though he were an over-reacting parent. Fine. If that was so, she was behaving like a naïve child. She closed her eyes and leaned back her head. "I didn't want to imply they were dangerous people by refusing. All they wanted was for me to examine a recently acquired papyrus and see if it was fake."

Nothing about this made sense. "You told me two nights ago you were sure Moretti didn't have any forgeries."

"Well, I'm sorry to say, I was wrong. We can't track it, either. He purchased it from someone who bought it in Cairo. It was forged in Egypt by a true artist, but one who we'll never meet, I'm sure. Which is why he served a round of drinks."

Joe stifled a groan. Either Ray Moretti had served genuine alcohol smuggled in from Europe, or he'd served locally distilled alcohol, which could make a person sick, blind, paralyzed, or dead. "Tell me you didn't," he said.

"I told them I don't drink, so they gave me a fruit cocktail."

"Uh-huh, and how is that drink making you feel right about now?"

"What?" Her eyes popped open. "You think—"

"Lauren, a fruit cocktail is still a cocktail. If there hadn't been alcohol in it, you wouldn't feel the way you do."

"Oh no." She covered her mouth. "Please don't tell me you're going to arrest them. I'm supposed to improve relations with them. I can't be the cause of this kind of trouble."

Lauren was far too concerned with pleasing people. Then again, she always had been. She wanted to keep the peace. He wanted justice. You couldn't always have both.

"Prohibition is a funny thing," he told her. "It's not illegal to drink in private. It's only illegal to produce alcohol, sell it, distribute it, or drink from a flask in public. So as long as you didn't pay for that little dose, I've no cause for legal action."

Still wearing her coat, she kicked off her shoes and folded her legs beneath her, leaning into the side of the sofa. "Good."

But it wasn't good. None of this was. Joe paced to the window that looked over Central Park. It was dark, with nothing to see but lampposts, traffic, and his own dour reflection. He looked older than thirty-five. He felt older, too. By a lot.

She'd surprised him tonight. He was sick to death of surprises.

They felt like deception, and deception felt like betrayal. Betrayal meant he'd been hoodwinked, and that felt a lot like shame.

"Don't drink anything if you don't know where it comes from," he said. "It's dangerous. You clearly have no idea how people are making liquor these days. The stuff they put in there isn't fit for rats."

"Okay, Joe. I won't do it again."

"And for the love of all that is holy, I don't want you going off on your own to people's homes, no matter how well you think you know them or how trustworthy they seem. Especially when you don't have your own transportation out of there."

"You're yelling at me. Stop it." She curled into the corner of the sofa, hugging a decorative pillow.

He hadn't really been yelling.

Joe looked around the apartment and realized it had no kitchen. It did, however, have a type of wet bar. He filled a glass with water from the sink and brought it to her. "Drink. The water will dilute the alcohol in your stomach. When was the last time you ate?"

"Lunch. Or—no, I skipped lunch."

Given her build and intolerance to alcohol, it was a wonder she hadn't passed out yet.

"Do you have food in the apartment?"

"Maybe?" She sat up straighter and drank. "I try to keep chocolate in case of emergencies, but I've exhausted that supply."

"Pitiful," he mumbled, more to himself than to her. "What you need is protein to soak up the sugars. I'll be back."

Having a badge had its perks. Figuring the kitchen was active since the dinner hour wasn't over, he located it, entered without hesitation, flashed his ID, and requisitioned two steaks with sides of mashed potatoes and green beans topped with almond and bacon. Then he returned to Lauren's apartment with the tray.

"Room service." He set the plates and cutlery on the table and told her to join him.

"I don't remember you being this bossy," she said as he pulled out the chair and seated her.

"I don't remember you being this reckless. You have no concept of the danger you courted."

Her eyes were closed, lashes dark against her cheeks. At first, he thought she was studiously ignoring him, but then he realized she was saying grace. "And thank you, dear Lord, for keeping me safe, despite my walking into the lion's den, if what Joe believes is true. Thank you for bringing him here to take care of me while he scolds me into oblivion. Amen." She smiled up at him, apparently unintimidated. "Let's eat."

Joe cut into his steak with more gusto than the task required. His middle clenched, but only because of what could have happened. He wasn't speaking in hypotheticals. Women disappeared in this town. They were preyed upon, sometimes by men they knew and trusted. They were assaulted. Worse.

Lauren closed her eyes and swallowed, clearly enjoying her meal. Then she turned those blue eyes on him. "I can see you've had a long day."

His hand went to the scruff shadowing his jaw. He had shaved, but that had been before four o'clock this morning. "I'm worried about you." There, he'd said it. "I pray to the same God you do, and I do thank Him that you're safe. That doesn't mean you get to throw caution to the wind."

If he wanted to put a finer point on it, he could talk about all the other victims he'd seen who most likely had cried out for divine assistance in the hour of their ultimate need. He'd never pretend to know the mind of God—why He answered some prayers and not others. But Joe did know the minds of criminals.

"You're only hunting forgeries because I asked you to. If something were to happen to you while you're doing this job, that's my responsibility. I can't let that happen, Lauren. I can't."

She stopped chewing and placed her fork on her plate, giving him her full attention. "I'm so sorry you were worried. I didn't realize you had so quickly resumed the role of guardian for my well-being."

"Yeah, well, the position didn't seem to be taken." Then again, maybe he'd gotten this all wrong. "Is it?" He took a drink of water and tried again. "That is, am I overstepping here? Is there another man already—and I'm not talking about your father."

Her eyes narrowed. "If you're asking if I'm seeing anyone, the answer is no."

"I thought you were. I heard that you were engaged a while ago."

A rueful smile curved her lips. "A lifetime ago. I was twenty-four and had recently finished graduate school. Richard had just enlisted to fight in the war in Europe. Did you go, Joe? I thought of you and wondered. I prayed for your safe return, just in case."

She had? That surprised him. "I stayed. The department needed a corps of us veteran officers to stay behind as a stabilizing force." He'd been twenty-seven years old when the US joined the fight. So many young men had enlisted right away and spent months in camps, waiting to go over. Many of them never saw action before the war ended. Joe hadn't felt like he was shirking a patriotic duty by remaining with the police. He'd been fulfilling a duty he'd sworn an oath to years prior. His service was protecting the home front by upholding law and order. He'd never regretted that choice. "What happened when Richard enlisted?"

Lauren sighed. "He wanted me to marry him before he left, but I wasn't ready. I told him I'd wait for him, and that we could chart a path when he came back. It wasn't enough for Richard. He went to war without saying good-bye."

"And that was it?"

She lifted a forkful of beans. "That was it. Never heard from him again. It's all for the best, though. My work doesn't leave much time for relationships outside of a few."

The scoundrel left her. Abandoned her. Just like her father had done. He hated to think of the heartache Richard had caused her, but if he wasn't willing to wait, he wasn't worth much.

"So the position *is* open," he said, his tone much lighter than he actually felt. "I formally accept. As the guardian of your well-being,

I'm responsible for your safety while you consult on my investigation. In all seriousness, I need you for this work, Lauren, but promise me you won't go into other people's homes alone anymore. If you're going, I'm going. Clear?"

"Clear. Thank you," she added. "For caring."

Joe didn't want to admit, even to himself, how much he did.

CHAPTER 9

Morning light filled the Great Hall at the Metropolitan Museum of Art. Outside the soaring windows, snow dusted the trees lining Fifth Avenue and draped a mantle over the great lions flanking the entrance.

Lauren carried a clipboard through the Egyptian gallery, envisioning how she would arrange the space for the upcoming exhibition. Some of the current items would need to be returned to the labyrinthian underground storage space to make room for the themed displays she had in mind.

Anita rushed up to her, cheeks pink from cold, stuffing her mittens into her coat pockets. "Have you seen her in place yet?" she asked, nearly out of breath. "How does she look?"

Lauren smiled at her assistant. "I decided to wait for you." Last night after the museum closed, the carpenter had moved a newly completed display case into one of the Egyptian galleries. "Ready?"

"Aren't I just!" Anita pulled off her wool cap, and static electricity crackled in her hair.

Together, they walked into the New Accessions room. There, on a raised dais with steps all around it, was a glass case containing the anthropoid coffin holding the mummy of Hetsumina, dated from the Greco-Roman period, between AD 90 and 100. Her coffin was lavishly appliquéd with gold-leaf hieroglyphs and painted to portray the young woman wearing a black wig and Roman-style dark red tunic with black stripes edged in gold. The coffin's lid had been removed and set aside so viewers could view the mummy.

Inscribed on the bottom of the coffin's foot were the hieroglyphs that translated, *Hetsumina, daughter of Hopikras, died untimely, aged twenty-seven. Farewell.*

Lauren had suggested saving the display for the opening of her spring exhibition, but Mr. Robinson had decided they ought to waste no time in sharing this gem with the public as a preview of the upcoming show.

She had to admit it was a good strategy, and she was happy not to delay bringing such artistry to light.

"She's the cat's pajamas, no doubt about it!" Anita sighed.

Voices and footsteps signaled that the museum doors had opened to the public for another day of wonder and discovery.

"I was right to look for you here first, I see." Lawrence's voice turned Lauren toward him in time to see him notice Hetsumina's coffin. His silence as he stepped closer was as eloquent as anything he could have said. He wasn't often speechless.

"She's the berries, isn't she?" Anita beamed. "And you're the first of the public to see her. Lucky you."

"Am I?" With a winning smile, he faced her, then glanced to Lauren, expectation in his crinkling blue eyes.

Right. "Anita, this is Lawrence Westlake of the Napoleon Society." She hugged her clipboard to her chest. "And my father."

Lawrence bowed to Anita as Lauren introduced her, as well.

"It's a pleasure to meet you, Mr. Westlake. Truly an honor." Anita pumped his wrinkled hand in her smooth one. "Sorry to scram, but I've got a meeting to get ready for. See you then, Dr. Westlake."

"Thank you for acknowledging me," her father said when Anita had gone. "I didn't expect it, and I can't tell you how nice it felt. At the gala, I didn't introduce you as my daughter because you worked hard for your titles and deserve to be known for them and not for who parented you. I also realize that my role in your life has been insignificant. I didn't feel I deserved to claim you. If people recognized that we share a last name, so be it."

"Your role was not insignificant," Lauren reminded him. "It was your passion for Egyptology that started me on this path."

"And look where it has led you." He opened his arms wide before gesturing to the new coffin. "What a thrill."

"It is." She was gratified that he understood. "Even more thrilling would be to find her twin."

"Oh?"

"According to the inscription, Hetsumina had a twin sister named Hatsudora." She walked around the coffin and pointed to the hieroglyphs that told the tale. "They did everything in life together. They were twin princesses. Born on the same day and died on the same day of the same disease. You know as well as I do that sons were prized more highly than daughters. But look at this. These twin girls were absolutely beloved." Lauren wondered what that felt like.

"And were they not buried together?"

She sighed. "That's unclear. The Met team went through the entire tomb, and Hatsudora's coffin was not there. It could be that they were buried in separate tombs, which would make sense if the young woman had married into another family by the time they died."

"Or?" Lawrence prompted, his expression suggesting he'd thought of alternate possibilities himself.

"Or tomb robbers had already been in the tomb and taken her. Hetsumina had been hidden under a mudslide that required painstaking excavation. I wouldn't be surprised if robbers took the twin they could reach without realizing the other was hidden beneath the mud."

"Any number of things could have separated this pair," Lawrence added.

"They ought to be together. Can you imagine? I do believe the Met would pay almost any price if the missing twin were ever found. It would be a highlight of my career to reunite them."

Visitors pressed in around them, and Lauren gave way. When her father beckoned her to the side of the room, she joined him. Fleetingly, she wondered about his stamina these days. He didn't complain, so she had no idea what age had done to his joints or ability to stand for long.

His knee popped as he lowered himself to the bench and patted the space beside him. "Was attending the gala helpful for your friend Joe? Did he find what he was looking for?"

Lauren sat. "He met a lot of people who might be able to help. I'll follow up with them and encourage cooperation."

"If I didn't mention it yet, I really appreciated having you there."

She nodded. "I enjoyed seeing the artifacts you brought."

"I knew you would. Just like I know you would enjoy seeing such things in the field even more. You deserve it. Please, reconsider coming on the Napoleon Society expedition with me. You've always wanted to do this. Now's your chance."

But the board wasn't satisfied with her existing credentials. They wanted more. Part of her wanted their approval. The other part of her wished she didn't care at all. Seeking affirmation was exhausting.

"You know how busy I am." She'd already spent too much time chatting with him this morning. "I'm getting ready for an exhibition almost single-handedly, and now my evenings will be occupied helping Joe. If the work I'm already doing doesn't stand on its own, then I don't know what else I could possibly do. Why are you smiling?"

He slapped his knee. "Because, my dear girl, you did not say you don't want to go. You said that, given your busy schedule, you don't know how to impress them. But I do."

Lauren waited.

"Write about your work with the detective. Outline how you can tell if an artifact is fake. Publish your articles. Write case studies of what you're already doing. How long would it take you for a five-hundred-word piece for a newsletter?"

"Whose newsletter?" The Met had its own bulletin, but her father had no say in what they published.

"The Napoleon Society newsletter," he answered. "The editor is always looking for content, and the board would get to see fresh samples of your work. At least you'll get some credit for all you're doing pro bono for the police. Wouldn't more publishing credits be good for your résumé, too?"

His newsletter was not an academic, peer-reviewed journal, so she wouldn't actually be adding to her credentials. But there were other reasons to consider. Articles would reach far more people than she could otherwise. If she could teach them how to spot forgeries before they paid for them, all the better. Still, she wasn't sure she was ready to attach her name to her father's publication. "I'll think about it."

Standing, she cradled her clipboard in one elbow. He pushed himself up with a grunt, and she supported him.

He clasped her hand. "Thank you."

She felt in his grip the warmth she remembered. The warmth she had dreamed of when he was away and clung to upon his every return.

And her father *had* returned. Yes, he'd stayed away too long and at all the wrong times, but he was here now. She could not fulfill her mother's dying wish to redeem their relationship if she rebuffed him forever.

Here was her chance to do better. To stop pushing away what she longed for most of all. "Do you, by any chance, have plans for Thanksgiving?"

His smile trembled. "I would like to spend it with my only daughter." His voice was hoarse. "For whatever you have in mind."

At the police station, Joe tipped the last of his coffee down his throat while perusing the logbook to see what he'd missed during the night shift. There'd been domestic disturbances, theft at a filling station, vandalism, drunk and disorderly behavior. All the usual nocturnal activities. There'd been another raid on a speakeasy, too, but thankfully no murders in the precinct. That was something.

But two phone calls had come in right around the same time, and both had reported a situation for the same address. One mentioned the sound of breaking glass. The address was one of the antique shops he'd visited weeks ago. Yet the owner had not called the police to report anything himself.

Maybe there hadn't been time. According to the log, Officer O'Neal had called the shop owner after receiving the complaints. That was protocol. A telephone call from the police often sufficed to put a cork in whatever was brewing. The department simply didn't have the numbers to pay a personal visit every time they received a complaint.

So whatever had happened at the shop to cause the noise, the owner could have filed a report when O'Neal called. Pushing back from his desk, Joe walked over to the clerk.

"Help you, Caravello?"

"Logbook says O'Neal made a call to an antique shop early this morning." Joe gave him the address. "Did he file a report or any notes from that conversation?"

The clerk flipped open a file folder and thumbed through a stack of papers. "Here's O'Neal's paperwork from last night. There's no report here for that address."

Odd.

Antique dealers weren't known for their rowdiness, let alone noise during the night. What he had learned of them so far, however, was that they were meticulous about their property.

"I'm going to check it out," Joe called over his shoulder, already walking away.

Twenty minutes later, he was parking a police car in the only space available in a three-block radius of his destination. He walked past a bakery, a laundry, and a bookstore before finally arriving at Feinstein's Antiques. The glass had been broken on the front door. A sheet of cardboard covered the hole.

"Hello?" He stepped inside, the bell clanging overhead. "Mr. Feinstein?"

When there was no reply, Joe stopped and listened for movement. His hand went to the sidearm holstered beneath his jacket. The lights had not yet been turned on, and the windows remained shuttered.

The soft sound of snoring drifted toward Joe as he maneuvered between tables piled too high with old things. There, in a Queen Anne chair, Mr. Reuben Feinstein sprawled with his jaw hanging open in sleep. Mismatched socks peeked from beneath the hem of his trousers. A nasty lump swelled at his temple, a cut slashing through its middle.

"Mr. Feinstein?"

He startled awake, then slid his spectacles up his nose and frowned. "What are you doing here, Caravello?"

So he did remember talking to him before. "It's good to see you again, too. Your door was unlocked, and it's normal business hours. I let myself in."

Gripping the arms of the chair, Feinstein pushed up and squinted at the cuckoo clock on the wall to his right. "I dozed off after opening the shop." He shuffled off, pulling cords and switching on lights.

"Are you here to shop this time?" Feinstein asked. "Christmas is coming, after all."

Joe schooled his features not to give away his surprise. The shop had clearly been broken into last night, and Feinstein was injured. He knew Joe was a police detective, and yet he didn't mention the crime. If anything, Feinstein seemed bent on distracting him.

"Is that right?" Joe played along, allowing him to show brass candlesticks, a silver tea service, a dresser set complete with a button hook made by Tiffany & Co. All of these were valuable.

None of them had been stolen.

Joe was finished playing dumb. "What happened here this morning around two o'clock?"

Feinstein turned away to fuss with some kind of jeweled chess set. "I already talked to the police about that. Officer O'Neal called, and it's taken care of."

"Did you file a report of the break-in?" Joe asked. It was possible the report had been misplaced.

"No, no need for that."

Right. This man was hiding something, and something big. Joe locked the front door and turned the sign so it declared the shop closed.

"Mr. Feinstein, this will go better if you tell me the truth."

"They were only hoodlums. Youths gone astray."

"So you saw them?" Joe began to fill in a form on his clipboard. "How many were there?"

Feinstein licked cracked lips. "I'm not filing a report."

"Why not?"

"I-I didn't get a good look. At least not good enough to guess, so you see, I have nothing really to report."

Joe reviewed the notes he'd made before leaving the station. "But you've filed reports before in order to claim damages to your property." He named two dates in the last five months. "The most recent was in October when eggs had been thrown at your building."

"Do you know how damaging raw eggs are?"

"I do. You told me all about it. The other report you filed was when someone had used the public trash can on the street corner to dispose of rotting meat. You claimed the stench was keeping customers away. But in neither of those cases did you see the people who had done those things. It didn't stop you from filing a report."

His composure flickered, and then he lifted his chin. "Did the police ever catch those people? No. So filing reports is a waste of time. Mine and yours, I might add."

Joe silently watched him until perspiration beaded the older man's brow. Nodding to the cut on his temple, Joe asked, "How'd you get that?"

"I fell."

Joe didn't buy it. "Here I was thinking that whoever broke into your shop last night had also struck you when you came to see what the commotion was. But if so, you'd have gotten a good look at him, seeing as you weren't hit from behind. But you already told me you didn't see anyone, so yeah, you fell. Okay."

Reuben Feinstein looked so miserable Joe almost felt sorry for him. Almost.

"What did they steal?" Joe pressed.

"Pardon?"

"Even common hoodlums don't break into places for no reason, taking a risk without any reward. I see they left those silver things behind, so what did they steal instead?"

"Only a few things. A gold-rimmed bone china teapot, the matching sugar bowl, and a few teacups and saucers that went with the set. See for yourself."

Joe followed him to the sales counter, and Feinstein lifted a box that held a creamer and three cups and saucers, all of the same pattern.

"It's little good to me now," Feinstein said. "The value was in having the complete set all together. No one will want to pay much for these odds and ends, even if they did belong to Eliza Hamilton once."

So why would any thief run off with a partial tea set, when the whole was there for the taking? Feinstein was spinning tales faster than he could stay ahead of them.

"But your shop is insured, I take it."

The color bled from Feinstein's face. "It is."

"So you can file a claim with your insurance company to recoup the cost of the tea set and the glass to replace the pane in the door."

Feinstein swallowed. "I can," he said. "Later." But Joe could tell that he wouldn't, otherwise he wouldn't have reacted so strangely.

Why would anyone not file an insurance claim for something like this?

Because there would be an investigation, and Reuben Feinstein didn't want to answer questions. Not Joe's. Not anybody's. The man looked scared.

"Why are you pushing so hard for this to be a bigger crime than it was?" Feinstein squeezed his hands together in front of a rumpled vest.

Joe wanted to ask why Feinstein was so intent on lying to him. But the terror in his eyes stopped him. Feinstein knew something but didn't want to say what. If Joe pressed much more, he might bolt.

Had someone threatened him? It seemed the only likely reason for his uncharacteristic behavior.

With a sinking gut, Joe recalled the Black Hand Society, an Italian Mafia that had held shopkeepers like Feinstein in a choke hold. They demanded kickbacks from innocent civilians and promised violence for those who didn't cooperate. The extortion ring had started off targeting small businesses in Little Italy and expanded until no one was outside their reach. The NYPD had rooted out the Black Hand Society by 1920. Had a new group stepped in to fill the power void left behind?

So far, there was no proof of that. But it was possible. If a group like that had gotten to Feinstein, no wonder he didn't want to be questioned. Maybe his shop was being watched even now to see if Feinstein would squeal.

"If you think of anything later that you'd like to share, please call the station," Joe said. "I'll see myself out."

He ambled through the store, alert for clues. Something white poked out from beneath a claw-foot tea table. Bending, he picked up a small C-shaped object. It was a teacup handle. He looked again at the tea table beside him. It held nothing but a thin layer of dust and silhouettes where no dust had fallen at all. Scallop-edged circles matched the saucers he'd just seen. Other shapes could well fit a teapot, creamer, and sugar bowl.

The cups he'd seen were all intact. But no thief would steal a cup without a handle if he were looking for monetary gain.

Pocketing the broken piece he'd found, Joe decided not to waste any more time asking Feinstein for an explanation. Instead, he bade him good day and left.

And went straight to the public trash can on the street corner. Inside, he found one answer and a whole new pot full of questions. For there, scattered over a greasy newspaper, were shards of bone china. Joe reached in and picked up a fragment that matched the pattern from the Eliza Hamilton set. There were enough pieces here to put together a teapot, a sugar bowl, and three cups and saucers.

These antiques hadn't been stolen. They'd been destroyed. Whoever had done this wasn't the same person who had swept the remains into a dustpan and deposited them in the trash can outside. Faced with one more lie from Feinstein, Joe had a feeling he'd stumbled onto a bigger problem in Manhattan than a forger.

CHAPTER 10

THURSDAY, NOVEMBER 26, 1925

The smell of bacon, eggs, and coffee filled the Beresford dining room. Lauren poured maple syrup onto her Belgian waffle and passed the small pitcher to Elsa.

"What time is your father coming?" Ivy asked her.

"He's not." Lauren's cheeks burned. "He called yesterday afternoon to cancel." Actually, he'd had a secretary from the Napoleon Society call on his behalf, but Lauren was too embarrassed to admit he hadn't even told her himself.

Elsa wiped the outside of the syrup pitcher before cutting her own waffle in squares according to its natural grid. "Uncle Lawrence doesn't want to spend Thanksgiving with you? Er, sorry, that came out wrong. I'm disappointed he wouldn't since he lives so close now." Elsa's parents, Lauren's aunt Beryl and uncle Julian, lived right across the street from the Met on Fifth Avenue, but they were spending the fall with Uncle Julian's sister in Monte Carlo.

"I thought things had improved between you and your dad," Ivy added.

A waiter dropped by to refill their coffee mugs. Once he'd gone, Lauren explained that her father was out of town, something to do with working for the Napoleon Society. "Don't ask me why it's so urgent it couldn't wait until after the holiday. But it's fine, really. I haven't celebrated Thanksgiving with him in more than twenty-five years."

Ivy's eyebrows arched, disappearing behind her thick black bangs. "But he said he would come, then changed his mind less than twenty-four hours before the holiday? That stings. But maybe he really does have some emergency."

Lauren forced a smile for her roommates. "When it comes to my father, I've grown used to disappointments," she said. She ought to have expected it. She ought not to have placed so much significance on the fact that they'd made plans together. In any case, she'd been quick to adapt and make new ones. Tomorrow, she and Elsa would hunt for those letters Lawrence had once tried to burn.

"And there's no one else besides us you'd rather spend time with today?" Elsa asked. "Perhaps a certain someone who insisted on bringing you home from the Hotel Astor even though you are thirty-two years old and perfectly capable of riding the subway alone?"

"Oh!" Ivy brightened. "You mean the certain someone who also commandeered two steak dinners from the kitchen and stayed until he was sure you were feeling better? Good gravy, Lauren, teach me your ways. Tell me where I can find a man like that."

"Didn't you know?" Elsa jumped in. "They met at the Met when she was twelve years old."

Lauren laughed at Ivy's stunned expression. "It's true," she confirmed. "I grew up in Chicago, but my mother and I stayed with Elsa's family every Christmas. That year I went to the Met by myself. My mother was sick, my aunt and uncle were busy, and Elsa, only five at the time, had no patience for museums if they didn't have taxidermy animals. That's where I first met Joe. He asked if I was lost, since he didn't see an adult with me, and immediately appointed himself my guardian. Only much later did I learn he'd been dropped off at the wrong Met, so if either of us was lost, it was him."

"You're kidding," Ivy said.

"Nope. At fourteen years old, he got in a cab and asked for the

Met. He thought he was going to a matinee at the Metropolitan Opera. But he didn't tell me that for years."

"Then what did he tell you?"

Lauren chuckled. "He told me not to talk to strangers. To which I replied that *he* was a stranger. He took care of that in a hurry by simply introducing himself."

"I'm Joe Caravello. Like Joe Petrosino, you know?" He'd puffed out his chest, squaring his shoulders. When she hadn't responded to his posturing, he added, *"Don't tell me you don't know Joe. Best cop in the city. First Italian detective on the force."*

Lauren had smiled and shook his hand. *"And I'm Lauren Westlake. Like Lawrence Westlake. Only I'm smaller than him and a girl."* She hadn't expected the skinny boy with black hair and green eyes to recognize her father's name, but she had enjoyed saying it together with hers like that. Lauren and Lawrence. Anyone could tell she'd been named for him. She'd been proud of that, and she'd hoped he'd been proud of her, too.

"Obviously, they didn't stay strangers for long." Elsa speared another perfectly cubed piece of her waffle, somehow managing to grin and chew at the same time.

"We saw each other at the Met quite a bit after that. He always knew where to find me—the Egyptian rooms."

"And so, I ask again why you're not seeing him today," Ivy pressed.

"Because unlike my father, I have no plans to work on Thanksgiving."

"Good for you," Elsa said. "Speaking of work, are you considering Uncle Lawrence's offer to go on that expedition with him?"

Digging her spoon into a section of grapefruit, Lauren excavated a chunk and let its citrus flavor burst upon her tongue. "I already told him I wouldn't go. At first, I doubted there was any such expedition scheduled. But if he was lying to me about that, he lied to the richest people in Manhattan, too. He and another board member gave a presentation about the upcoming dig during the gala."

"You don't think he's really lying about that, do you?" Elsa asked.

Lauren folded the napkin in her lap. "Not anymore." She'd read the pamphlets about the trip and even pulled two board members aside to question them. Their answers satisfied. "But that doesn't mean I'm signing up."

"It does sound like a wonderful opportunity," Ivy said. "There's time to change your mind if you want to."

In some ways, Ivy and Elsa were two peas in a pod. They worked in adjacent institutions on Central Park West, with only 77th Street between them, and walked to work together every day. They'd met, in fact, when taking their lunch breaks in the same spot in Central Park. Both being extroverts, it had been easy for them to strike up a conversation that led to Ivy's moving in.

But on the subject of Lawrence Westlake, they differed. Where Ivy maintained a determined optimism, Elsa wouldn't push. She knew too well how he'd hurt Lauren.

Elsa checked her watch. "Speaking of time, we better shake a leg."

A few minutes later, Lauren, Elsa, and Ivy exited the elevator on the main floor and crossed the lobby. A whoosh of cold air splashed Lauren's face as the Beresford doorman held open the door, ushering them onto the sidewalk.

"Lauren."

She turned at the sound of her name. "Joe!"

He wasn't in uniform today. A herringbone newsboy cap matched his brown leather coat, and the green in his plaid scarf, his eyes. His subtle smile swept through her.

It took Joe a moment to realize Lauren wasn't alone. He nodded to the two ladies flanking her. The blonde with glasses he recognized as her cousin when he noticed the limp. The other young woman wore a fuzzy grey hat over a sleek black bob. They gaped at him. "Your roommates?" He'd left Lauren's apartment before they'd come home Monday night.

"And dear friends. Ivy Malone and, you may remember, Elsa Reisner. This is Joe."

"Pleasure." He shook their mittened hands, adding, "Nice to see you again, Elsa."

"Mutual, I'm sure." She gave him a cheeky grin.

A breeze ruffled the fur on Lauren's collar. She wound a scarf around her neck and tied it below her chin. "We were about to get spots for the parade."

"Coincidentally, so was I. You happen to live along the route."

"Berries. Let's go." Elsa looped her arm firmly through Ivy's and took off marching down the sidewalk. "Try and keep up," she tossed over one shoulder with a smile.

Lauren chuckled, then looked up at Joe while adjusting her cloche. "Aren't you taking the day off?"

"Does it look like I'm working?"

"Every time I see you it's because you are."

It had taken a while on Monday night to finally get around to why he'd come to her apartment in the first place. He'd wanted to update her on his progress—or rather, lack of it—connecting with the leads he'd gained at the gala. He needed her help. Which she'd promised to provide as soon as Thanksgiving week was behind them.

"Well, this is me not working. If the topic happens to come up in conversation, so be it."

"I see." She smiled. "I must say, your timing is impeccable."

He shrugged but didn't tell her how long he'd been waiting. "It didn't take much deductive reasoning to guess you'd want to see the parade, like the rest of Manhattan. Are you meeting your father, too?"

She pursed her lips. "He's out of town on some kind of Napoleon Society emergency, and my aunt and uncle are in Europe."

"So you're spending Thanksgiving . . . ?"

"With Ivy and Elsa. The Beresford is putting on a feast for residents this afternoon."

The food Joe's parents were cooking up today was certain to be far better.

They came to the corner of 81st Street, and he tucked her hand through his elbow as they crossed it. Sidewalks teemed with parade seekers. When they reached the other side, he didn't let go of her in the crowd. He was tall enough to keep an eye on her roommates, too.

Ivy looked over her shoulder, likely to be sure Joe and Lauren were still behind her. Lauren waved.

She'd probably rather be with her friends.

Joe's impulse to see her today had felt like the right thing to do. Now he felt selfish for inserting himself. "I don't mean to keep you from your original plans for this morning," he said.

"Keep her?" Elsa turned around. "No, you can't keep our Lauren, but we don't mind sharing her, seeing as you've come all this way."

Joe looked to Lauren. "Sure?"

"If you're going to watch the parade near us, you might as well watch it with us," she said. "Besides, we might get hungry. Or thirsty." She batted her eyes at him, then sniffed the air and grinned.

Joe laughed at her not-so-veiled request. "Roasted chestnuts? Hot chocolate?"

Three feminine hands shot up in the air.

"We just ate breakfast," Ivy said, "but by the time you get back from standing in line, it may be near lunch."

"I surrender. Where should I meet you?"

Elsa pointed at the American Museum of Natural History. "The steps," she said. "We'll have a good view from there."

Joe tipped his hat to the three of them and turned to get in line.

Lauren didn't leave his side. "You'll need help bringing back food and drinks for four."

"So I will."

The street had been closed to traffic, so they darted across to a vendor at the edge of Central Park. Questions Joe had been meaning to ask Lauren rose to the surface. "I know I said I wasn't working today. But as long as we're both here, do you mind if we talk about it?"

"I really don't have anything to report, Joe. I've been totally wrapped up in my own work."

He blinked. "Is that a mummy joke?"

She laughed, and it was a musical sound.

"You might not have any updates, but I do." He shared about his visit to Feinstein's antique shop and the man's refusal to file a report for the break-in, but left out his fear of a new Mafia filling in for the Black Hand. No need to scare her with an instinct he wasn't even sure he could trust. "I've been looking at Feinstein's cagey behavior from every angle, even wondering if he could be a forger."

"Really?"

"I quickly dismissed the idea. A forger needs a steady hand and discerning eye, right? Feinstein has neither. He mentioned weeks ago that he's color-blind. But he's definitely hiding something."

"So the search continues."

"Slowly. Two people I met at that gala have agreed to let us come look at their collections. We have appointments next week, in the evenings. Are you available?" he asked.

She pushed her cloche back again and looked up at him. "I'd be happy to help you next week."

"Good. I also wanted to talk to you about the Napoleon Society starting a new museum." It had slipped his mind when he'd seen her Monday evening. "I'm still not convinced of the need for such a giant undertaking, but I'm looking at this from outside the art world. Do you think there's enough support to be had from the public to warrant this new venture?"

"I've wondered the same thing. But considering the huge success the gala was, yes, there is enough interest to support it."

"How huge is huge?"

She told him how much money was raised through the silent auction and donations. It boggled the mind.

Joe whistled. "All of that raised in one night, too. To think, my father lost his restaurant for want of a small fraction of that sum."

Ridges lined her brow. "I'm so sorry," she told him, and it was a relief that he didn't need to explain anything, since he'd already told her when they were teens.

"Nah, you weren't the one who scammed him." And that was enough said about that.

Lauren waited for Joe to say more, but he looked away, a muscle bunching in his jaw. When he turned back to her, it was with an expression so studiously neutral, she knew the conversation was over.

Just as well. They'd come to the front of the line. Joe placed an order for two bags of roasted chestnuts, one bag of mini-doughnuts, and four hot chocolates.

Moments later, Lauren took the bags of food, and Joe balanced the steaming beverages on the cardboard tray that came with them.

As they reached Lauren's roommates on the steps of the American Museum of Natural History, the rumble of a police escort on motorcycles cut through the din of the crowd. Joe handed the hot chocolates to the ladies, and Lauren distributed the bags of treats. A marching band came next, bearing a wide banner proclaiming the start of the Macy's department store's parade.

Lauren extended the bag of chestnuts toward Joe, and he pulled out a handful. Macy's staff dressed as clowns, cowboys, and knights threw candy to children lining the street. Bears from Central Park Zoo lumbered by, followed by monkeys, elephants, and camels.

Lauren watched the camels with a broad smile and couldn't help but think of Egypt. Of riding a camel herself one day, as she had always dreamed she would. Nostalgia swept over her as she recalled riding her father's shoulders as a child, pretending he was the hump-backed beast.

She'd called out what she spied in their imaginary desert: *"Sandstorm!"* Her father had lifted her off his shoulders and huddled with her on the floor under his desk. *"You're safe,"* he'd whispered and kissed the top of her head. Lauren had never felt more loved.

"Lauren?" Joe said. "I asked if you've ever ridden one of those." He pointed to the long-lashed, shaggy camel.

"Not yet," she told him. "Someday."

Joe's parents had outdone themselves. Most of the boarders had gone home for the holidays, but that hadn't stopped the Caravellos from cooking a feast with all the trimmings for themselves, Joe, and Doreen, who had brightened the dining room with vases of burgundy and orange chrysanthemums. Finishing his last bite of pumpkin pie, Joe noticed his mother looking at the empty chairs around the large dining table.

"Those should have been filled," she said softly, and Joe knew it wasn't the college girls she was missing.

Pop cast his gaze downward, clearly understanding what Mama meant, too. Joe's brother was married with children, and they hadn't come for the holiday. Pop blamed himself for the breaking up of his family.

"I did call him a few times to tell him how much we'd like to have them come," he said.

Mama's eyebrows rose. "And what did he say to that?"

The beat of silence that followed was full of meaning. Pop took a drink before responding. "He's a busy man. Perhaps he'll call later. You answer the phone if it rings, eh? Michael would like to talk to you or to Joe. It's okay."

"No, it's not okay," Joe countered. After all these years, Michael still refused to talk to his dad? Didn't he understand that hurting Pop also hurt Mama? Hurt Joe? "You made mistakes. We got past them. It's too bad he hasn't." That was putting it mildly. When Michael decided to cut ties with Pop, Joe might as well have lost his brother, too. Then there was Mama, who felt most keenly the absence of a daughter-in-law and two grandchildren she would have loved to spoil. Family was everything to Mama.

"He has his reasons." Pop rubbed at a wrinkle in the tablecloth. "If I hadn't—"

"That's enough of that, please." With a brave smile, Mama grasped Pop's hand and gave it a firm squeeze. "I don't remember inviting Guilt or Shame to the table today."

"In fact," Joe added, "I distinctly recall kicking both of them to the curb. You were swindled, Pop. A victim of a crime." It struck Joe then, as it often had, that the man who stole the Caravellos' money had probably spent it all within a few months. Yet here they were, years later, still suffering the consequences. Sure, Pop owned his decisions that made him vulnerable to a scam. He'd kept their desperate financial circumstances hidden from his family. Lied about it, even. But the real criminal had gotten away, free to prey on the next target, and the next, and the next.

It wasn't right.

Inspector Murphy's suggestion that Joe's interest in hunting forgers stemmed from his father's situation came back to Joe again. But people who could afford to spend thousands on antiquities clearly didn't need that money to live on. It was a completely different circumstance than losing the restaurant that served as their family's livelihood. Joe was after the criminals, no matter who the victims were. He just prayed he'd get a break in the case soon.

"Honestly, I can't recall a time I ate so well for Thanksgiving," Doreen jumped in, and Mama looked grateful for the change in subject. "Everything was wonderful! I couldn't eat another bite."

Patting his usually trim stomach, Joe agreed. Judging by the amount of food left in the bowls and platters, there was still enough to feed a family of eight.

"Come on, Joey, please. Here, there is pie." Mama lifted another slice of pumpkin pie and deposited it on his plate.

"I wish I had more room to spare," Joe protested, but Mama cut him off with one of her looks.

"I just said, there is pie." She jabbed the pie server at the piece as if that concluded the matter. "In this house, once served, food is always eaten."

Joe swallowed a chuckle. His little mama had come by her standards honestly. Wasting food was wasting money, and wasting either was near to a crime. Since it had been her penny-pinching that had seen them through the leanest years, he'd never disparage her everlasting frugality.

"And where is Dr. Lauren Westlake this afternoon?" Pop asked. "Dining with her father?"

With the side of his fork, Joe cut a sliver from the pie. "Uh, no, he had to cancel on her."

Three pairs of eyes riveted on him.

"*Had* to cancel?" Mama repeated. "Why does one *have* to cancel on family at such a time? Are they on good terms?"

Joe told them what he knew, which wasn't enough to satisfy. He'd often thought he'd gotten his passion for detective work from his parents, whose curiosity knew no bounds.

Doreen tsked her disapproval and shook her head. This was her first Thanksgiving without family, Joe realized. She may appreciate the food and even the company, but it wasn't the same as celebrating with her own flesh and blood. Joe wondered if the day would be different for Connor than any other.

"You should have asked her and her roommates to come here," Mama said. "We had enough food to feed three more. Or just one more, if that's better. Maybe that would be better." She gave him a pointed look.

Joe wasn't ready for this. "We work together, nothing more." He reached for the bowl of whipped cream to add a dollop to his pie.

She grabbed it first and pulled it out of his reach. "At this rate, working together is all you'll ever do. Is that what you want? If so, your strategy is a good one."

"All right, my dear, you've made your point." Barely disguising a smirk, Pop scooped a spoonful of whipped cream and plopped it on Joe's pie.

Joe insisted on cleaning up after the meal.

"Let me help you, Joe," Doreen said. "You might as well let me earn my keep around here, at least a little." She gave him a look that suggested she knew the rate they were charging her was steeply discounted.

After they cleared the table, Joe rolled up his sleeves and filled the sink with soapy water. Doreen found a dish towel and set to drying what he scrubbed. Her hands and wrists bore marks from years of handling flowers with thorns and thistles.

Joe bore his own faded scars from his childhood job of delivering flowers for Doreen. Connor had them, too. His might have healed better if he hadn't picked his scab one day when Joe had started bleeding. Connor had rubbed his wound against Joe's and proclaimed they were blood brothers. After Michael took off, years later, Connor had pointed to their scars and said, "*You still have me.*"

"Is the jail open on Thanksgiving, do you suppose?" Doreen asked. "For visitors, I mean."

"It's open." Joe had already decided that if she wanted to see Connor, he'd take her.

The woman took a shuddering breath. "I don't know what to say to him, Joe."

He leaned harder into scrubbing mashed potatoes off the inside of a pot. "He may not know what to say to you, either. But at least he'll know you care enough to see him."

She reached for a ladle and wiped out its bowl. "I hope so."

"I'll bet he misses spending Thanksgiving with family even more than you do." He rinsed the pot, set it on the drain board, and plunged his hands into the warm water for the next. "If you need to do this for your own sake, that's reason enough to go, too."

Doreen kept quiet as she dried the last of the dishes. Joe didn't interrupt her reverie as he drained the water from the sink and put everything she dried in its proper place.

At last, she hung the wet dish towel over the oven door handle and turned to him. "Then it's time, don't you think? For both of us."

Joe exhaled. "You and Connor?" he confirmed.

She took his hand and squeezed it. "You and me."

The county jail was always a depressing place to be, and even more so on a holiday. Joe led Doreen toward the row of chairs where visitors could speak to inmates through telephones connected through plates of glass.

Doreen clamped tighter on his arm when the attendant left to fetch Connor. "What if he doesn't want to see me?" she asked.

"If that's the case, he won't come forward. He does have a choice in that." He guided her to the chair and backed away, giving her privacy with her nephew.

The door opened from the other side, and Connor appeared, a shadow of the man he'd been. A beard obscured his face, but not enough to hide his pale complexion. Neither did his jail uniform disguise that he'd lost weight. A jagged lump convulsed in his throat when he saw Doreen.

With a small cry, she placed her palm on the glass that separated them.

Joe turned away, his middle twisting. How was he supposed to feel here? He could feel sympathy for Doreen without question, but was there any to be had for Connor himself? He had shot an unarmed man. He'd gotten into some kind of trouble Joe didn't understand. He swallowed, pushing down emotions that wouldn't help him do his job.

He didn't know how much time had passed while he stood with his back to Doreen. It was enough time to remember that the last time he and Connor had been here, they'd been on the same side of the glass. The same side of everything, or so Joe had thought.

"Joe," Doreen called, and he turned.

A charge went through him when he met Connor's gaze. Just as quickly, Connor looked away, but he still held the phone, waiting.

Joe closed the distance between them and sat on the stool where Doreen had been. Her complexion mottled, she clutched a handkerchief and walked away.

The phone felt heavy. Joe pressed the weight to his ear.

"Thank you for taking care of her." Connor's voice was husky through the wire.

"We'd never leave your aunt to fend for herself," Joe said quietly.

"It's good to see you," Connor said. His collarbones formed small shelves behind his uniform. His fingernails had been bitten to the quick. "You're okay, right?"

"Could be worse." Joe allowed his tone to convey much more. He didn't understand why Connor had taken the shot in a place crowded with civilians, many of them inebriated. He especially didn't understand why Connor discharged his weapon at a target inches from Joe. If the gun had been rotated slightly, it would have been Joe in the ground instead of Wade Martin.

But because he wasn't allowed to talk about the reason for Connor's arrest, he couldn't say any of that.

This was going to be a short conversation.

Connor scratched behind his ear. "Any interesting cases lately? I'm about to die of boredom in here."

"I'm doing a lot of the same old policework I always did," Joe told him. "Writing up reports for prosecutors, interviewing witnesses and suspects on several ongoing cases. Trying to stay away from speakeasy raids for as long as Murphy will let me. You understand."

Connor looked away, and silence buzzed through the earpiece. He did not say that he never meant to kill an unarmed civilian. He didn't say that he should never have discharged his weapon.

Maybe he was merely following the rules by not talking about that night at all.

An itch crept between Joe's neck and collar. "The only thing new since you were around is that I've started looking into forgeries. Found one right away, but it's really small. Dr. Westlake—you remember me talking about Lauren from years ago, right?—she's an Egyptologist at the Met now, and she says it wouldn't have been worth much anyway, even if it had been genuine. So even if someone discovered they'd purchased a fake, the amount lost would not be worth killing over, at any rate."

The hollow gaze swung back to Joe. "That oyster shell," Connor whispered. "Tell me you got rid of it."

"Does it have anything to do with your upcoming trial?" Joe asked. "If it does, then we can't talk about it."

"I'm serious, Joe. Let it go. Don't think about it again. There is other work to do. Safer work."

Joe's ire spiked. "We didn't join the police to be safe. I'm in the job to find the truth and stand up for justice. And if there's one thing I know about that shell, it's that it's loaded with secrets."

"Some secrets are better left alone."

"See, that smells like a rat to me." The stool whined again as Joe twisted to check on Doreen.

"I'm trying to protect—"

Joe's hand curled into a fist over the phone. "That's not your job," he hissed.

"I've given up on protecting *you*, Joe. But my aunt. Your parents. Every last one of those little coeds boarding at your place. That's who I'm trying to protect now."

The hair raised on the back of Joe's neck. Connor had never been given to theatrics.

"You want to put them all in danger? Keep digging around about that stupid shell." Connor made to hang up the phone.

Joe knocked on the glass, motioned that he had more to say. "How can I keep them safe if I don't know who the perpetrator is? If he's as dangerous as you say, he's a menace to society and needs to be taken off the streets."

"Drop it."

"Connor!"

But he'd already slammed the handset into the receiver and stalked away.

CHAPTER

11

D isappointment hung heavy on Lauren's shoulders. After spending all day searching her aunt's home with Elsa, they still hadn't found the box of letters written between her parents.

Elsa's limp was more pronounced than usual as she made her way to the couch and collapsed onto it. "When my parents return from their trip, I'll ask my mother. She may know where it is."

"All right." Lauren scratched Cleo under the chin. The fact that the cat wasn't standing at her food bowl told her that Ivy must have already fed her before going out tonight. "Or do they employ any servants who would have been working seventeen years ago?" Most of the staff who hadn't traveled with Aunt Beryl and Uncle Julian had been given time off for the holiday and weren't around today. "Maybe one of them knows something."

"I'll look into it." Elsa snagged the latest issue of *Bird-Lore* magazine from the coffee table and opened to where she'd left off before.

After trading her shoes for slippers, Lauren settled in at the desk in one corner of the room and fed a clean sheet of paper into the typewriter. She hadn't found the letters she'd been looking for, but she could write one of her own.

Dr. James Breasted had been one of her professors at the University of Chicago, and they regularly corresponded. She asked him for help with tricky translations from time to time, and she was more than happy to proof articles he wrote for scholarly journals. Today's message, however, would be different.

Lauren tapped out the usual greeting and pleasantries, asked after his wife, updated him on her work, and inquired after his own. Aside from teaching, he organized a group of artists, draftsmen, and archaeologists for an epigraphic survey. Together, they made high-quality copies of hieroglyphs they found in tombs and temples in Egypt and brought them back for reproduction in textbooks and journals.

Now for the reason for the letter.

Have you heard of the Napoleon Society? If so, what are your observations so far? My father's on the board, but please don't let that keep you from sharing your honest opinion. The society is organizing an expedition to Egypt, and there may be a chance for me to join it. My boss at the Met has made it clear they'll not be sending me. If you know of other opportunities for me to use my skills in Egypt, I'd be most grateful if

A knock on the door sounded urgent.

"Are you expecting someone?" Lauren asked Elsa.

"No."

"Lauren." The voice was her father's. "Lauren, there was a fire." She rushed to the door and opened it.

"Dad!" she gasped at the sight of him. She pulled him inside and vaguely heard Elsa say she would go for some ice.

"It looks worse than it feels, really." He touched a fingertip to the swelling on one side of his face.

"Your hands are all scraped up, too. What on earth happened? You said there was a fire?"

"There was, but I can't blame this on that. I'm not as spry as I used to be." He grabbed the back of a ladderback chair for support.

Noting his unsteadiness, Lauren sat at the table so he would do the same. "Where else are you hurt?"

"My knees are a bit banged up. The left shin. But it's nothing that time and rest won't heal."

"Are you going to tell me what happened?"

"Grand Central during the Thanksgiving travel rush happened. I lost my balance getting off the train, and then the press of the crowd was too much for me to fight."

Lauren's hand flew to her mouth. "Tell me you didn't fall to the tracks."

"That gap between the platform and the train is a perfect fit for me." He coughed into his handkerchief. "I was never in any danger, since the train had stopped. One of the Red Caps had a dickens of a time helping me back up again. But that's not what kept me away from you on Thanksgiving."

Lauren's heart thudded violently against her ribs. She could picture one of the uniformed men who normally carried hatboxes and luggage pulling up her father instead. She blinked back the heat in her eyes. "It could have been different," she whispered. It could have been so much worse.

"Now, now," he said. "This is the least of my concerns. I came straight here from the terminal. I need to explain why I wasn't here yesterday."

Elsa returned with a rubber bag filled with ice and slid the first aid kit onto the table. While Lawrence held the bag to the fast-growing knot on his temple, Lauren dipped cotton swabs into a bottle of hydrogen peroxide and dabbed the scrapes on his free hand.

He'd done the same for her once. She had been seven years old, and Nancy had told her again to be quiet, so she'd run outside to climb the giant maple, wishing she were a bird. Even more, she wished her father would come home, or at least that her mother would follow her to the tree like she had before getting sick. *Fly away, little birdie,* Mother would say, *but let me be your nest when you land.* And Mother would stay there, watching and waiting until Lauren was ready to climb down.

But on that particular day, Lauren hadn't even made it past the second branch before falling. If Mother hadn't been sick, she would have been there to catch her. Something fierce had risen up in Lauren that she didn't recognize, an anger so strong it shook her. A few tears squeezed free, but she bottled the rest, afraid of the fury inside.

And then, almost as if she'd conjured him, her father appeared after being gone half a year. He scooped her up in his arms and kissed her damp cheeks. The pain that made her cry had nothing to do with her fall, but she wouldn't tell him that. She wouldn't tell anyone that. In the house, Nancy had rushed forward, but her father had insisted on tending her scrapes himself, and Lauren's anger began to cool.

"Next," Lauren said now, and he switched the ice bag to his right hand so she could disinfect the left. She felt a twinge over the pale brown spots on his skin, the soft wrinkles that bunched over large knuckles. So many years had passed since she'd held the hands that once held hers.

"I would have been here if I could have," he said. "But there was a fire at the house."

"Where?" She finished wrapping his hand with gauze and tied the ends.

"The Napoleon House. The museum for the Napoleon Society, in Newport, Rhode Island. Remember?"

While Elsa put away the first aid kit, Lauren struggled to make sense of what her father was saying. "Go on," she urged. "Tell me everything."

He leaned into the ice bag and winced. "I got a phone call Wednesday that there was an emergency at the house we've been renovating into our museum. I had to go, Lauren. We'd started storing some artifacts there already, and I had to see if there was anything I could do to salvage them."

"What was the damage?" she dared to ask.

"The firefighters stopped the blaze before it reached the artifacts, thank God. It started in the attic, a problem with the electrical wiring. There was a spark inside the walls, and it spread. Much of the roof is gone, the attic open to the elements. Repairs will set us back quite a lot, but at least we didn't lose more than we did." The quaver in his voice clashed with the optimistic platitude.

"Tell me you have property insurance, at least?"

"We do." He placed the rubber bag on the table. While Elsa disposed of the ice, he folded his bandaged hands. "But there is a huge deductible we must meet before the insurance company will help, and we need to pay for the work to get done immediately, and then it's anyone's guess as to how long the insurance company will take to reimburse whatever amount they approve."

Lawrence groaned and leaned back in his chair. "I wanted to do this right, Lauren. I'm trying to build something that will last. Something that you can finally be proud of, since I know I haven't given you reason to feel anything toward me but resentment."

But resentment had made a poor companion. Far poorer, she decided, than the man before her, humbled and admitting to his mistakes.

It wasn't satisfying at all to see him hurting, no matter how he'd hurt her in the past. "This isn't your fault," she assured him. "You've had a setback, but you'll soon get your feet under you again." The idea that he valued her esteem came as a startling surprise, since she'd always craved his approval, if she could not have his love.

For the first time in years, she wondered if she might finally achieve both.

CHAPTER

12

It was already dark when Joe parked outside the Met's front entrance. Headlamps flashed in Joe's rearview mirror from a Buick idling behind him. Was the driver waiting to pick someone up from the museum, or was this a tail Joe would have to shake? If Connor's concerns were justified, Joe's investigation had likely attracted the attention of those who'd want to stop it.

Someone could be watching him. Or they could be watching for Lauren. She was the key to his entire investigation, a walking library full of clues. If she was taken out of play, he wouldn't easily be able to continue.

Sleet pinged the windshield. Lauren exited the museum and trotted down the steps, turning her collar up. She spotted him and waved.

Great. If anyone wondered which woman was Dr. Westlake, she'd just advertised herself by hailing the only cop car at the curb. Grabbing an umbrella from under the seat, he left the car and marched toward her, ready to shelter her from the elements and anything—or anyone—else.

A man in a trench coat headed straight for her from behind. A fedora obscured his face, but his movements were too quick, even for one dashing to get out of the weather.

Joe quickened his pace.

So did the man in the trench coat. He reached for her without calling her name.

Joe took the steps three at a time until he gained her position, one hand locked around the still-closed umbrella, the other ready to go for his revolver.

The man sailed past them both and tapped a different woman on the shoulder. "Miss," Joe heard him say, "I thought I saw you drop this on your way out."

Shaking his head, Joe tried to flush adrenaline from his system on a long exhale.

"Eager to see me?" Lauren smiled. "That was quite the sprint up those stairs. For a minute there I almost thought you were going to offer me the use of your umbrella." Laughter danced in eyes framed by lashes spiked with rain and sleet.

Dash it all. He snapped open the umbrella, held it over her, and linked her arm through his. "I thought . . ." What could he say? He thought a man was going to attack her? Abduct her? With all these witnesses? Nah. "I thought you'd be hungry."

She gave his arm the slightest squeeze. "You thought right. I'm starved."

"Oyster Bar?" The restaurant was inside Grand Central Terminal, a few blocks from Thomas Sanderson's home on Madison Avenue.

She agreed.

The drive down Fifth Avenue took them past the twenty-one-story Plaza Hotel presiding over the corner of Central Park. A few blocks later, they drove by the nearly-as-tall St. Regis Hotel, then St. Thomas Church, and the twin-spired St. Patrick's Cathedral. It was only two miles from the Met to the terminal, but with the weather slowing traffic, twenty minutes passed before they rolled into a parking spot.

They entered the terminal from 42nd Street and walked right into Vanderbilt Hall. While Joe kept an eye out for suspicious characters, Lauren looked up.

One hundred twenty feet above the pink marble floor, the ceiling boasted twelve constellations painted in gold on a background that had originally been sea-green but had been stained darker by cigarette smoke since then.

"First time here?" he teased.

"Do I look like a tourist?" She laughed, but her gaze never left the barrel-vaulted ceiling. At dozens of points in the constellations, light bulbs shone through, completing the effect of the night sky. "Did you know this was painted upside down and backward? But it was too late to do anything about it by the time they realized the mistake."

"I'll take your word for it," Joe said without examining it for himself. Stargazing would supply the perfect opportunity for anyone following them to slip into position undetected. "Let's eat." With a touch to her elbow, he guided her to the ramp that took them to the cellar level.

Beneath the main concourse, the Oyster Bar opened wide its arms with arched and vaulted ceilings covered in creamy terra-cotta tiles interlocked in a herringbone pattern. Lauren started toward the long counter, where they could see chefs shucking oysters at a dizzying speed. It was a marvel to behold, but Joe didn't want his back to the entire restaurant.

"I can see more from one of the tables," he told her. "Do you mind?"

Thankfully, she didn't, and they found one from which he could keep an eye on all doorways.

Red-and-white-checked tablecloths draped the tables. After placing their orders, Lauren folded her long fingers. They were smooth and fair, so different from his mother's work-roughened hands.

Different from his own.

He could still hear her aunt's voice, that day he'd gone to the Reisner mansion when he hadn't found Lauren at the museum. Lauren had been in mourning for her mother, but Joe didn't know that yet. *"You're the young man she's been meeting at the museum?"* With naked disdain, she looked at his hands. They were clean but chapped red from working at the boardinghouse and scabbed from delivering thorny-stemmed flowers for Doreen. Joe's response had revealed an accent Mrs. Reisner didn't like, either. *"You stay away from her. Stay with your own people, your own kind."* She'd made it clear that Lauren was better than Joe. But he knew that already.

Picking up a lemon wedge, he squeezed too much juice into his goblet and took a sour drink. "How's the Napoleon Society coming along?" She'd told him about the fire over the phone.

"I *almost* feel sorry for my father. The fire damaged more than the roof. Newport society—which is really New York society in a different location—associates him with what they see as gross negligence for 'allowing' a fire to harm one of their historic homes. He feels like he's been branded a failure even before the doors opened."

Joe leaned forward. "If it's image they care about so much, they'll come around again once the Napoleon House is restored and polished to a shine."

"Throwing money at a problem doesn't always make it go away."

Spoken like someone who'd always had enough of it. He huffed a laugh. "Goes a long way, though."

Understanding sparked in her eyes. "I'm sorry if that came across as insensitive. Do you want to tell me how it's been with your family?"

Joe pulled a slice of steaming bread from a basket and began slathering it with chive butter. "It's not so bad waking up before the sun to help them in the kitchen or helping clean up at the end of the day. The cooking alone is worth it." He took a bite of the sourdough and let it melt on his tongue.

"Free room and board?" Lauren asked. "Can't beat that."

"I insist on paying rent like everyone else. They enjoy having me around, and I like keeping an eye on them. When something breaks around the place, I don't want Pop trying to fix it at his age. It's a real song and dance routine most of the time, since Mama and I don't want him knowing there was anything to be fixed in the first place." He paused to take a drink. "I make it sound like I'm doing them a favor to stay, don't I? But it's no trial. It's the least I can do."

He scanned the environment again, alert to being watched. All his helping around the boardinghouse would amount to nothing if he were ever to lead danger back to their doorstep.

Unaccountably, tears lined Lauren's lashes. "You are rich, Joe Caravello. So much richer in love and family than I've ever been. You have what I always craved. A place to belong, and the people to go with it."

Joe scratched behind his ear and wished with all his might she wouldn't cry. It unraveled him when she did that.

"Please, Lauren," he whispered. "Please don't cry." That sounded more ardent than he intended. "People will blame me and throw me out before I have a chance to taste my salmon."

Her eyes squeezed closed, and she laughed silently, shaking her head.

"See now, that sort of looks like you're sobbing." He shifted on the bench, totally out of his depth here. "Your condition seems to be getting worse."

This time she let her laughter break free and reached across the table to clasp Joe's hand. "My condition?" Her smile was convincing. "Yes, that's right. It's called the human condition, Joe. Not just facts but feelings, too. You didn't used to be so squeamish with them."

His thumb grazed her knuckles. "I've grown very fond . . . of facts."

"Yes, Detective. There, there. We'll do our best to find you some more tonight." With a wink and a squeeze of his fingers, she released him and sat back as the waiter returned with their dinner.

Inside Thomas Sanderson's mansion, Joe visibly relaxed. Or at least, Lauren noted, he had stopped looking over his shoulder. Hypervigilance, she figured, was an occupational habit for any police officer.

"If you'll follow me, please." Mr. Sanderson's butler led them to a reception room paneled in dark walnut wood and appointed with chairs upholstered in aged leather. "Mr. Sanderson will be with you shortly."

Lauren warmed before the crackling fire. Marble pillars on either side of the grate were carved to look like Greek goddesses with arms stretched overhead to support the mantel. In a corner of the room was another marble statue, probably of Greek or Roman origin.

When Mr. Sanderson entered through the double doors with a manila folder, his prize-winning German shepherd came with him. "You don't mind if Governor joins us, do you?" he asked.

"Not at all." Lauren held out her hand for the dog to sniff.

Joe did the same, engaging Mr. Sanderson in small talk about the breed while Governor wagged his tail and looked up at his master with liquid brown eyes.

"But let us begin," Mr. Sanderson said, and led them out into the hall and up one side of a double spiral staircase. Governor matched his pace to theirs as they entered a second-floor gallery wide enough to hold receptions.

Lauren relished a slow walk through the chandelier-lit space. "It's like visiting old friends," she murmured. Then she added for Joe's benefit, "Mr. Sanderson was kind enough to loan some of these artifacts to us for previous exhibitions."

"That was generous of you," Joe said.

It was, though Lauren wondered if Joe realized how beneficial Sanderson's generosity had been to the collector's status among his set, not to mention his own sense of self-importance. Sanderson's name had been printed in the exhibition catalog and on description cards placed with every display of the pieces he'd loaned. Most collectors found that an enviable ego boost indeed.

She stopped short in front of a set of canopic jars made of indurated limestone. All four had lids that were human-headed. "These are among your newer acquisitions?"

After commanding Governor to sit and stay, Mr. Sanderson joined her, his polished oxfords tapping the marble floor. "Yes, I couldn't resist the complete set of all four. You see the cracks in this one, and a missing chunk out of that third one there, but given their age, I'd say they've weathered the millennia quite well. I'd considered having that lid restored, but there's a certain charm in showing the jars as they were found in Egypt."

"There is." Out of habit, she pulled a pair of white cotton gloves from her purse and put them on before picking up the lid and reading the text carved inside.

"You could restore it?" Joe asked. "How would you go about doing that?"

"Oh, not me, my good man. I'd have to find someone who has both the technical skill and knowledge of the ancient art so it could be done right. There's no one I trust more than the team who works at the Met. There's none better. Wouldn't you say, Dr. Westlake?"

"Yes, of course, but they're quite busy with museum work as it is without taking on private projects," she told him, bracing herself for the news she was about to deliver. She could only imagine what he'd spent on four matching canopic jars.

"Come again?" Joe looked at her. "The team at the Met?"

Lauren removed her gloves and slid them back into her purse. "That's right. The Egyptian department has its own underground facility to support what you see in the galleries. We have rooms for inventory that we rotate in and out of the galleries, and workshops for carpentry and minor restorations."

"But made with considerable skill and care," Sanderson inserted.

"For example?" Joe prodded.

"You've seen the little blue hippo made of blue faience, with black line drawings of lotus blossoms all over him. Only his front left leg is original to him. The other three legs were restored so he can stand properly."

"The hippo has three fake legs?"

"That doesn't make the hippo a fake," Lauren assured him. "It's a common enough practice among museums, Detective. But restorations are only done in particular circumstances. The object needs to be mostly whole already, it cannot suffer any harm during the process, and the restoration must be helpful enough to the overall work to warrant the effort."

She could see that Joe had more questions, but this conversation could take far more time than they had. Turning back to Mr. Sanderson, she said, "May I see the provenance for this set, please?"

He withdrew a document from the folder he'd been carrying and passed it to her.

It didn't take long for Lauren to make her verdict. "I'm sorry, Mr. Sanderson, but this entire set was forged."

The color leached from his face. "But how can you be so confident?"

"Inside the lids are the typical identifying labels." She waited while he picked up the first lid and stared at hieroglyphs. "That says that these jars held the remains of a woman who was a mayor's daughter during the twentieth dynasty, which was the Ramesside period. The provenance document agrees, dating these pieces to sometime between 1184 BC to 1070 BC."

"I believe you, Dr. Westlake," he said tentatively, "but I fail to see the problem in any of this."

She glanced at Joe, who was taking notes, as usual. "During the Old Kingdom, canopic jars had simple disk-shaped or hemispherical lids. Then, from the late First Intermediate Period to early Middle Kingdom, lids became human-headed, like these. But as I've said before, according to the dates on the lids, these jars claim to come from the Ramesside period. But from the Ramesside period on, the lids always represented the four sons of the god Horus. One was human-headed, another hawk-headed, another ape-headed, and the last jackal-headed."

She took a breath, waiting to see if he understood that a talented forger had made a big mistake.

His crestfallen expression said he did. "Is there any chance it could simply be a clerical error?"

"If it was only the provenance that got it wrong, I would have thought it possible. But the etchings on the lids themselves say the same thing. It's simply impossible."

"Could someone have reused the jars, centuries later?"

It was a valid question. "If that were the case, they would have modified the label, crossing out the original name and adding the new one. So no, that's not the situation here. I am certain these are extremely well-made forgeries."

Mr. Sanderson brought a handkerchief to his brow. "Well, this is why I asked you to come, after all."

Lauren caught Joe's eye and detected a hint of something approaching compassion, or at least regret for the whole situation. From all appearances, the Sandersons were fabulously wealthy. But appearances could be deceiving, every forgery a case in point. Perhaps the loss of the money invested in these fakes would hurt them more than one might imagine.

"I'm sorry, Mr. Sanderson," Joe said. "You've been the victim of a crime, and thanks to your cooperation, we have more evidence to hang on the one who did this to you as soon as we apprehend him."

"My reputation will be ruined when people find out. What will they say?" Mr. Sanderson groaned. "What will my wife say?" Moving as though the starch had gone out of him, he sat on an upholstered bench and signaled Governor to come.

The German shepherd trotted over and rested his head on Mr. Sanderson's knee. While Joe joined them and began his line of questioning, Lauren continued to walk the length of the gallery. She was pleased not to find anything else amiss.

Lauren thought again of her father's suggestion to write up her notes as an article for the Napoleon Society newsletter. With what she'd written from this visit alone, she could protect people like the Sandersons.

Suddenly, it felt selfish not to.

By the time she returned to where Joe and Mr. Sanderson were seated, they were deep in conversation.

"Daniel Bradford," Joe said as Lauren took a seat alongside him. "Spell it, please?"

Mr. Sanderson obliged, and Joe wrote it in his notebook before catching her up to speed. Bradford was the dealer who'd sold the canopic jars. At last, a lead.

"I'm sure Mr. Bradford couldn't be to blame." Sanderson rested a hand on his dog's head. "He brings art back personally from Cairo and Luxor, and supplies only the best high-end art dealerships in Manhattan, like the one I favor on Madison and 76th. It's run by Aaron Tomkins."

Joe wrote that down. Lauren wondered if the art dealer was involved in the forgeries. Tomkins almost certainly worked with more than one buyer. Were others selling forgeries through him, too?

"Bradford knew what I was looking for before he made his last trip," the collector continued. "So he picked these up and offered them to me directly without going through Tomkins. Saved me a percentage of the cost by skipping the middleman. These must have been forged in Egypt before he brought them back. He'll not suffer any consequences, will he? He's as much a victim as I am in this. Please, please, take care in how you speak with him. I'd hate for him to refuse to work with me after this."

"Of course." Lauren gentled her voice. "We only want to make sure this doesn't happen again. Only the forger himself is to blame."

"Could you describe Bradford's physical appearance for me?" Joe asked.

"Oh, he's about five eleven. Grey hair. In his sixties, I'd guess, but he somehow manages to keep himself fit and trim. Brown eyes. A gentleman's hands, with neatly manicured fingernails. When he's agitated, a muscle twitches under his left eye."

Joe looked up from writing. "You've seen him agitated? Do you recall the reason?"

Color crept up Mr. Sanderson's neck. "Too many questions."

"It could be important, sir. We're almost through here."

"No." Mr. Sanderson shook his head. "What I mean is, Bradford gets that twitch when I ask him too many questions."

This interview grew more interesting by the minute.

"I see." Joe's expression remained impressively neutral. "And what was the nature of the questions that provoked him?"

"I don't know. Just . . . questions about the artifacts. Where he found them, what they mean, what they're worth."

"All the usual questions one should be asking," Lauren said, hoping to put him at ease. "You're right to ask those things."

"You've been most helpful, Mr. Sanderson," Joe told him. "I'll take it from here. What's the best way for me to get in touch with Bradford?"

"Oh." He patted Governor again and fed him a treat from his pocket. "I've only ever contacted him by sending messages through Tomkins, and then Bradford gets back to me when he can. I have no idea how to reach him directly, and I get the feeling he likes it that way."

Deflating, Lauren locked gazes with Joe. They could only pray that Tomkins would cooperate.

CHAPTER

13

FRIDAY, DECEMBER 4, 1925

S now flurried against a sky of gunmetal grey. Giant wreaths with red bows encircled the two stone lions flanking the Met's broad entrance. It was Christmastime in New York, but Joe felt none of the spirit.

He'd paid a visit to Aaron Tomkins's art dealership yesterday morning, with a message for Bradford to get in touch with Joe as soon as he could. He seriously doubted that the dealer would pass the message along, though, and called Lauren to tell her. So on her lunch break, she'd taken a cab there and offered to at least examine the Egyptian antiquities he had in stock, to catch any fakes before they left his gallery. Tomkins threw her out.

Yesterday had been an exercise in futility. He'd called every D. Bradford in every city directory the NYPD had, to no avail. He wasn't surprised that the man's number was unlisted, but he did wonder how he got enough business to support himself if no one could reach him. Then again, if Bradford was in as high demand as Sanderson and Tomkins claimed, the work found him.

It was a long shot, but Joe even took Bradford's physical description to the Rogue's Gallery at NYPD headquarters, where five-inch by three-inch cards were cataloged in long, narrow drawers with the precise measurements and photographs of known criminals.

But Joe didn't have precise measurements or a photograph. He had one man's recollection of another.

Joe stepped in a puddle of slush and shook his shoe, grimacing. Bradford wasn't a ghost. He'd find him. But today, he had other plans.

Forgoing the main front doors, Joe cut a path around to the side of the building. For the first time in weeks, he was visiting the Met and wouldn't see Lauren, since she and Elsa were traveling to Boston today. It was just as well.

"Morning, Caravello," the security guard, Jefferson, hailed him as he entered. "Here for Dr. Westlake?"

"Not this time." He unbuttoned the collar of his wool overcoat and stuffed his gloves into the pockets. "I've got a meeting with the restoration department for Egyptian art." They didn't know about the meeting yet, but they soon would. "This way?" Joe guessed at a direction.

Whether it had occurred to Lauren or not, men employed by the most prestigious museum in the country to restore Egyptian art had the tools, space, and knowledge to create convincing fakes.

Jefferson pointed down the corridor. "Down the hall, first staircase on the right, all the way down. You'll see signs to direct you once you're in the basement."

Joe thanked him and set off.

Minutes later, he entered the Egyptian department's underground lair. He held up his badge and introduced himself. "I'm looking for a forger wreaking havoc with your patrons, and it would be helpful to my investigation if I could ask a few questions here."

A man with receding blond hair straightened a tie, tugged his jacket until it closed enough to button in place, and came forward. "Elliot Henry, Egyptian collections manager." His thick fingers completely engulfed Joe's as they shook. "How can we help?"

Joe tucked the badge away. "For starters, I imagine that certain materials used in forging Egyptian art can be hard to come by. Not the sort of thing you'd pick up at the local market. Could you give me a list of what a forger might be shopping for?" He knew the basics from what Mr. Feinstein had told him was out of stock in the tri-state area, but adding the Met's perspective would be helpful.

"A forger's shopping list?" Mr. Henry smiled, showing a row of short, straight teeth that revealed a preference for coffee. Joe judged him to be about fifty years old, if not older.

"That's the idea. Then I'll want to know where he might find those things. But first things first." Joe poised a pencil above his note-book.

"Come on back to my office. I'll take a look at our recent invoices. That should tell you what you want to know."

Gold. Pure gold.

Would Mr. Henry be so willing to divulge this information if he had anything to hide?

Maybe. Maybe he didn't know that someone working for him was a crook.

"Here we are." Mr. Henry's chair squeaked as he sat and swiveled around to a four-drawer filing cabinet. He pulled out a folder, spun back toward Joe, and slapped it on the desk. "Our purchases for the last quarter are inside. Help yourself."

Joe opened to a sheaf of papers that might as well have been writ-ten in hieroglyphs for all the sense they made to him. "I'm going to need you to translate, Mr. Henry."

"You bet." He rolled his chair closer, and the smell of hot dog relish lifted from a dark spot on his tie. "We use what the Egyptians used for paint colors." He pointed to a list of abbreviations and explained. "Lamp soot for black, calcium sulfate and huntite for white. We also tint clay with mineral oxides like the red and yellow ochres. The blues and greens come from synthetic materials called Egyptian blue, or frit. From this basic palette, we mix to get all the colors we need."

Joe scribbled all of that down, then looked at the vendor's name and address on the corner of the invoice. "And do you always buy from this art supplier? Could a person get these shades from any-where else?"

"These paints you could find almost anywhere. But the gold leaf is the best here."

The next several minutes followed in similar fashion, Mr. Henry explaining the invoices and Joe taking copious notes. When they reached the end of the folder's contents, Joe cocked an ear toward the noise coming from the other side of the wall.

"What kind of work is your team doing now?" he asked.

Mr. Henry filed the folder away. "A few different things. Our carpenter is working on display cases for Dr. Westlake's upcoming exhibition, for one. That's the sawing and drilling you hear. The other projects are much quieter. Have time to take a look? It's remarkable what they're able to do."

"I'd love to see."

"I'm not surprised there have been so many forgeries lately," Mr. Henry told him as they left his office and headed into a separate room across the hall. "Forgeries of Egyptian art have been common for ages, although I admit it seems to be spiking. Everyone wants a piece of King Tut." He chuckled. "Have you seen what we've got at the sales desk?"

Joe passed that desk often on his way to visit Lauren. "King Tut keychains, Christmas ornaments, miniature King Tut coffin paperweights . . . I didn't see one of those on your desk, by the way."

Mr. Henry chuckled. "No, although I did purchase a few of the ladies' scarves printed with King Tut hieroglyphs for my sister and mother. They have no idea what the text means."

"Could you tell them?"

"Only so far as to say it's a partial spell meant to protect the dead in the afterlife. I studied museum management, not hieroglyphs. That's one reason I'm not a conservator. Here's the other." He held up his hands. "Great for college football. Not so great for those tiny hair brushes we use for fine-tuned work. I'd fumble the job, for sure. Only took one try for me to know that's a job best reserved for the experts."

Joe believed him. Especially since a man who dripped hot dog juices on his tie—and continued to wear the tie anyway—did not concern himself with details. Elliot Henry would make a terrible forger.

Stopping at a worktable with its own special lamps craning over it, Mr. Henry introduced Joe. "This is our lead conservator for Egyptian antiquities." Henry clapped the slender shoulder of a man currently hunched over what appeared to be a delicate process.

"Watch it!" The man jerked an elbow backward toward Mr. Henry. Grey streaked the dark brown hair at his temples. Joe guessed him to be around forty-five.

Mr. Henry smiled at Joe. "Meet Peter Braun. The best in the business. He's so good, in fact, he can afford to be rude and know his job remains secure."

"Can't say the same for yours if you bump me into making a mistake," Braun muttered. He barely spared Joe a glance. "You'll pardon me for not shaking your hand."

"I see you're occupied. Can you tell me what you're doing?"

A long-suffering sigh blustered from the slight man. "Performing surgery on a shroud that happens to be more than three thousand years old, a rare example from the eighteenth dynasty." Columns of hieroglyphs covered the linen.

Mr. Henry explained that it had been sitting in inventory for fifty years and had never been unfolded. "Dr. Westlake wants to see if it would be worth showing in her exhibition. Peter is stitching the fragile textile with silk thread, right along the fold there, so that when we open it, it won't break apart."

"You're blocking the light," Braun said.

Irritation snapped in Joe's chest at the man's tone. Even so, he stepped aside.

Braun grunted. "By the way, if Henry hasn't told you yet, you won't find any fakes here."

"Ease up, Peter," Mr. Henry said. "He's on our side."

"Well, in *that* case." Sarcasm dripped from the man's words.

Joe chafed at the unprovoked hostility. "I'm aware I'm interrupting you, but if I could have a few minutes of your time, I'd greatly appreciate it."

When the conservator didn't respond, Mr. Henry cleared his throat. "That shroud has waited fifty years and thousands more besides. It can wait another ten minutes."

Still nothing.

"It's up to you," Joe said, voice even. "We can talk here, or I can bring you down to the station."

With cold precision, Mr. Braun set his needle on a metal tray, swiped off his glasses, and pinched the bridge of his nose. "What."

Pulling a stool closer, Joe nodded to Mr. Henry, who left the two alone. He sat, propping one foot on the bottom rung. "Mr. Henry said you're the lead conservator. How many others work with you?"

"*For* me," he corrected Joe.

Interesting. The hierarchy was obviously important to him. It only took a few questions about his conservation team to realize he considered them his underlings. To conclude that Braun was confident in his skills would be a vast understatement.

Behind the conservator, two young men bent over a slab of stone. Wearing gloves, they dipped cotton swab–tipped wands into some kind of solution and carefully went over the stone.

Mr. Braun sighed. "I trust them to clean without my direct supervision, but not much else."

"Then why hire them if they're so incompetent?"

"Do you have any idea how hard it is to find qualified conservators who specialize in Egyptian antiquities? Next to impossible. We have to train them ourselves."

"Did you learn on the job here, too?"

A laugh puffed through his nose while he wiped his lenses with a handkerchief. "No, I came with my résumé in perfect order, ready for responsibility. Before the war, we had more help. Bright, promising young men. But they enlisted and came back with tremors in their hands. Their careers were over. I've been trying to train up a new team ever since."

"That sounds challenging," Joe conceded.

"You have no idea." Braun replaced his glasses on his nose and peered at him again. "You've been working with Dr. Westlake, have you? I guarantee that when the upcoming exhibit opens, she, Lythgoe, and Winlock will be the ones who get all the credit. The public will be looking at my handiwork but will have no idea the time and skill it takes for the artifacts to be deemed worthy of display."

"Will your name be in the catalog?"

He crossed thin arms over an apron-covered oxford shirt. "I doubt it. The director wants to keep this work quiet, even though all of it is standard. Coward."

Joe scratched the word into his notebook. "What is he afraid of?"

"Scandal. Or even the slightest whiff of it. Don't tell me you don't know about Cesnola."

Joe racked his brain, mentally searching through all he'd read as background for this case. "The first director of the Met," he supplied at last. "Luigi Palma di Cesnola, the Italian American war hero who donated his own artifacts to the museum in its early years."

Mr. Braun picked up his needle again and bowed his head over the shroud. "His legacy haunts us."

Sleet ticked against the enormous arched windows of the New York Public Library's Main Reading Room. Beneath a ceiling mural that billowed with cloud and sky, Joe placed his pencil beside the book he'd been reading and studied the notes he'd taken. He was on to something.

Cesnola, first director of the Met, he'd scrawled at the top of the page. What kind of haunting legacy had the conservator been referring to?

It had taken Joe the better part of the day going through old books and newspaper accounts, but he'd finally pieced the story together.

The legacy, at least as perceived by Peter Braun, had been scandal. Forgeries, to be exact.

Luigi Cesnola had been accused of displaying forgeries in the Met, and even though the board of directors had given him a vote of confidence, the stain had never quite left the public's mind. Later, there were more accusations that the Met's restoration efforts under Cesnola's direction had altered the artifacts so substantially as to be classified as forgeries. Cesnola denied guilt once again but, to silence the critics, ordered the plaster noses that had been formed on broken statues be dissolved.

No doubt the current director wished to avoid attention that might lead to similar controversy.

No wonder Peter Braun felt unappreciated, though his expertise proved invaluable to the Met. The chip on his shoulder was large enough to park a Buick.

Joe turned the page in his notebook and wrote Braun's name at the top of his list of suspects as a forger.

CHAPTER

14

NEWPORT, RHODE ISLAND
SATURDAY, DECEMBER 5, 1925

W e're here." Lauren nudged Elsa awake as the train pulled
into the station in Newport, Rhode Island. It was only a
slight detour on their way home from Boston, and Lauren
hadn't been able to resist.

Elsa blinked, then pushed her glasses up the bridge of her nose.
"What is the plan, again? Are we just going to show up?"

Energy building, Lauren leaned forward to look through the window. "No, no. My father is meeting us here at the station and will
escort us to the museum. Or rather, to the old house that's being
renovated into one. He's here this weekend, anyway, and when I
told him we'd be in Boston, he insisted on showing us the place."

Elsa covered a yawn. "Is he fully recovered from his run-in with
the tracks, then?"

"Apparently." Lauren stood and pulled her valise down from the
shelf above the seats in their compartment. "You're a sport for coming with me."

"What else would I do? Miss a chance to see Boston? Newport
is a bonus."

Lauren smiled. They'd paid homage to Revolutionary War sites
and relaxed at a fine bed and breakfast, but the primary purpose

of the trip had been Lauren's meeting at the Museum of Fine Arts yesterday. She'd needed to meet with the Egyptian art team and confirm the loan of a couple of their pieces for her spring exhibit.

"I can still taste the Boston cream pie from last night. That alone was worth the trip." Elsa grinned sideways at Lauren.

The train chugged to a stop, and the doors opened. Bags in hand, Lauren and Elsa climbed down the metal stairs and crossed the platform to the station. After passing through the ladies' waiting room, they emerged onto the street.

Lauren's father waved from the front seat of a taxi. When he started to get out of the vehicle, Lauren picked up her pace. "Don't bother," she called, "we'll be right there."

She had half expected him to be late if he came at all, based on his history of breaking promises. The same distrustful side of her had also harbored doubts about the Napoleon House and the fire her father had claimed had stolen him away over Thanksgiving. Until she saw it for herself, it felt mythical, somehow, like another one of her father's stories, embellished for maximum effect.

Wrinkles webbed from the corners of Lawrence's eyes as he welcomed them into the vehicle. For the rest of the car ride through town, he spoke of repairs and renovations, barely pausing for Lauren or Elsa to say a word. Her father could make a zoning battle with the city aldermen sound dramatic. But add in a raging fire, its smoldering aftermath, and the resulting disapproval from the surrounding community, and the tale was fit for the stage. He reached its climactic conclusion right as the car pulled into the circle drive of a Gilded Age mansion.

For once, his timing was flawless.

Elsa stepped out of the car while Lauren exited the other side and gave her father a hand to support him. "Are your knees bothering you?"

He told the driver where he could warm up while he waited, then waved away Lauren's concern. "No more than any other man my age, I imagine." He pointed to the house with his walking cane. "There she is, the poor old dame."

"Oh . . ." Words trailed away as Lauren took in the ragged edge where the attic had once been. A tower climbed the outside corner of the first three levels, but its turret had burned away. The silhouette looked nothing like the photograph in the brochure. Instead of a roof, only a makeshift affair of tarps and unfinished wood covered the attic floor.

"I've made a name for myself in Newport now, but not at all the name I wanted. The old families who've been here since the Gilded Age blame me for the fire. Never mind that the faulty wiring connection would have resulted in fire whether I'd bought the place or not. I'm in charge of renovations, so it must be my fault."

Lauren could imagine the gossips dragging his name through the mud. "They should consider themselves lucky to have you fixing the place up," she said. "They couldn't have approved of an old mansion falling into decay, either."

"It's hard to tell with the roof gone," Elsa said, cocking her head, "but is this French architecture, Uncle Lawrence?"

Brightening, Lawrence confirmed that it was. "A perfect fit for a museum named in honor of Napoleon."

Mullioned windows reflected the sun on three levels.

Freshly fallen snow draped a sparkling mantle over the grounds, which rolled away from the house like a bolt of satin until it reached a lacework of bare trees, their every limb encased in crystal. The tops swayed in the wind, and branches cracked as ice broke off and fell soundlessly into the snow. If she looked past the soot-stained limestone château, the sprawling grounds reminded Lauren so much of her childhood home outside Chicago, it nearly took her breath away.

"You'll have to imagine the mansard rooftop and a large sign out front that reads, 'The Napoleon House.' Spelled in English, French, and hieroglyphs. I'll consult with you to get that right, Doctor." He winked at her.

"I'll bill you," she teased, turning up her collar against a raw, damp wind. "Shall we?" She offered her father her arm to steady his ascent up the steps.

Inside the house, he closed the door, ensconcing them all in a patchwork of shadows and the scant light coming through the windows. "The electricity hasn't been turned back on yet as a safety precaution. We need another inspection of the rewiring job they did after the fire."

"Smart." Lauren stepped into the spacious entryway. Before them was a double staircase. Beautiful, but impractical for older patrons and for moving large or heavy artifacts. "Are you putting in an elevator?"

"Already done." Lawrence walked forward, leading Lauren and Elsa past the staircase to see a shiny brass elevator. "Another gigantic headache, but that's over and done with, and here we are."

Nodding, Lauren slipped into what must have been a grand parlor.

Elsa gasped. "Lauren! Did you see this?" Still outside the room, she pointed to a spot to the right of the door.

Lauren joined her. On the wall, a brass plaque read, *The Dr. Lauren Westlake Gallery*.

"I hope you don't mind." Her father clasped his hands. "Each of us board members dedicated a room to a person of our choice. There's no one I would rather honor above you."

Lauren stepped back, feeling thrown off guard and unbalanced. "Why?" The gesture, though lovely, didn't make sense. "Isn't there a colleague or a mentor who's been more influential in your career? More deserving?" Her protest escaped her before she realized it might offend. "I hate to sound ungrateful," she added. "I simply don't understand."

"Any colleagues I had were only temporary, our relationships over at the end of a given dig. My mentors are no longer walking this earth, God rest them. This—" He spread his arms to encompass the house. "What I'm doing here is building a legacy. A legacy that will last beyond my lifetime. My only other legacy is you. In my mind, dedicating one to the other is only fitting."

Lauren didn't know how to respond. She could translate an ancient language. She knew how to tell a fake from the real thing. But she didn't fully trust herself to interpret her own father.

She managed a "thank you," then went back inside the largely empty room. It would be a giant security risk to keep items of any value in a house that was rarely in use. Still, a few crates sat on the floor, beckoning.

Elsa engaged Lawrence in conversation in the hallway, where he sat in the only chair they had seen on the first floor so far. Kneeling beside a crate, Lauren removed the lid and peeked inside at the nest of wood shavings. After trading her woolen mittens for the cotton gloves she kept in her purse, she carefully drew her fingers through the packaging material until she found something to grasp.

Several somethings, in fact.

She shifted to sit more comfortably. One by one, she placed each shabti on her lap. She had seen and handled thousands of these funerary objects in her lifetime. A single tomb could contain up to four hundred of them. But the small carved figures held an entirely different significance here, in a gallery named for her, with her father sitting outside the doorway.

Her memory scrolled backward to her as a little girl, sifting through a box of treasures her father had brought back from Egypt after an eight-month absence from her life. She'd found a set of three wooden shabti, which appeared to be a man, woman, and girl. At the age of nine years old, she knew their purpose. These objects were buried with noble Egyptians so that they could come alive and perform manual labor for the deceased in the afterlife.

But to Lauren, they looked like a family. They were even better than the paper dolls Nancy had given her to keep her quiet when her mother had lain in bed for days at a time.

Lauren turned over one of the shabti in her lap now, admiring the fine detail. *O shabti*, one read, *if I be summoned to do any work which has to be done in the realm of the dead, you shall act for me on every occasion of making arable the fields, of flooding the banks, or of conveying sand from east to west: "Here I am," you will say.*

Here I am. Those three little words called up another memory in Lauren's mind. *"Here I am!"* she had wanted to shout as a child, as though she were playing a never-ending game of hide-and-seek. But no one was looking for her. Her father found what he wanted in a country on the other side of the world. Her mother rarely left her room.

No one was looking for Lauren.

She closed her eyes and saw a much younger Lawrence enter the study, where she was playing with the shabti.

"This is a family," she'd told him, holding up the mother, father, and daughter. Willing him to understand this was the way they should be: together.

Smiling, he'd told her she could keep them.

He didn't understand what she was trying to say. How could he be so happy when she felt inside out and upside down? Buried hurts had boiled to the surface, and after keeping them corked for so long, she finally released the pressure. *"Take this one back."* She'd thrust the male figure toward him. *"He's never around. We don't need him."* Her voice had cracked on the lie. *"He doesn't want to be around these two, and I don't need him, either."*

Her outburst had not made her feel better. She'd cried herself to sleep that night. The truth was, she did need her father. She needed her father and mother both. But that didn't stop him from leaving again. Her feelings made no difference. Better to keep them locked up tight.

"Lauren?" Elsa's voice gently pulled her back. "Do you want to see the rest of the house?"

Lauren boxed up her memories along with the shabti she replaced in the crate. All of that had happened a long time ago. She and her father had both grown and changed. They were different people now.

Rejoining Elsa and Lawrence in the hall, she asked what his next steps were. The list of tasks and responsibilities he recited made her head spin. He led them to a room at the rear of the first floor and opened the door.

She knew this place. That desk with the drawers whose handles resembled little pyramids. The bookshelves with the feet carved to look like lions' paws held the same collection of books. Even the rug spreading over the hardwood floor held the same stacked fan pattern.

Astonished, Lauren crossed the room to examine the framed map of the world on the wall. "Is it the same one?" she asked in a whisper. She could not count the number of times she'd come into his office while he was away, tracing her finger between Illinois and the postmark of his most recent letter.

"It is."

Lauren turned to Elsa. "It's like stepping into our old house. His office was exactly like this." Even for all the visits she and her mother had made to Manhattan, her cousin had never come to Illinois.

"Ancient history isn't the only past worth preserving." Lawrence smiled. "Being here brings me some of my fondest memories."

"Mine, too," Lauren admitted. She was bewildered by the onslaught of nostalgia she felt in this partially burned Newport mansion.

"Do you sleep here, Uncle Lawrence?" Elsa pointed to a cot peeking out from behind the desk.

"When necessary." He sighed. "I don't like to spend money on a hotel when I have this grand house completely to myself. However, with the electricity off and the roof gone, I'm staying elsewhere while in town."

The burden of his responsibility seemed like a physical weight upon his shoulders. "How long are you staying this time?" Lauren asked.

"I won't leave until the most urgent repairs are completed. With one exception. I've got a reason to come back to New York by Tuesday. Don't I?"

Hope sparked, and his knowing smile fanned it to life. "I do love to visit the past," he admitted, "but it's time for me to live in the present."

Her birthday. He'd remembered, at last.

CHAPTER

15

Ten minutes before their weekly meeting was scheduled to begin, Joe hoisted a cardboard box onto his boss's desk. "You'll want to see this."

Inspector Murphy moved his coffee mug out of the way and stood to peer inside. "I'm listening." Frost climbed up the windows behind him in crystal fronds, diffusing the morning light.

"I had a productive visit with Mr. Rosenberg, of Rosenberg's Family Heirlooms." Lauren had accompanied Elsa to the store late last week for some shopping and noticed some fakes while she was there. She let Joe know so he could pick them up and talk to Rosenberg. "He was refreshingly cooperative."

Murphy withdrew one of several figures of the Egyptian god Horus. It was shaped like a human with a falcon head and had eyes that represented the sun and moon. "So these were forged."

Joe confirmed it. "They were delivered to Rosenberg by a fellow named Vincent Escalante. He brings Rosenberg finds from bulk purchases he makes at estate sales, or so he says. Rosenberg carries them for a certain amount of time. If they sell, both men get paid. If not, Rosenberg returns them."

Wrinkling his nose at the fake god, Murphy set it back in the box and took another swig of coffee. "How much does something like this go for these days?"

Joe told him a sum that almost made him spit out his coffee.

"So where is this Escalante? In holding?"

"It's only a matter of time." Moving the box to the floor, Joe sat, and so did his boss. "Rosenberg has no contact information since Escalante always contacts him, never the other way around." It was the same method employed by Daniel Bradford, the art buyer Thomas Sanderson named. Joe had asked Rosenberg if he knew Bradford or how to reach him. No dice. Figured.

Murphy's brows pinched together. "What if one of Escalante's pieces sold and Rosenberg had money for him? Wouldn't he like to know?"

Joe had asked the same thing. "Rosenberg says Escalante travels so much, visiting estate sales all over the States, he'd be hard to pin down anyway. Escalante sets up appointments with Rosenberg whenever he's acquired more artifacts to sell. Rosenberg has promised to let me know the next time he calls. I'll meet him there."

Murphy grunted his acknowledgment. "It's about time you made an arrest."

Joe agreed. He was tired of dead ends and zipped lips. He'd also visited Mr. Feinstein over the weekend to see how he was getting along after the break-in to his antique shop two weeks ago. *"No complaints,"* Mr. Feinstein had told him. But Joe didn't know if he believed it. Still, there was no evidence to the contrary. Joe had searched the daily logbooks for any other indications of Black Hand Society–inspired blackmailing, and hadn't found it.

Bending, Joe reached into the bottom of the box and scooped out a palm-sized oyster shell gilded on one side with gold, carved with a cartouche on the other. He slid it across Murphy's desk. "Look familiar?"

"Should it?"

Frustration swelled. They'd talked about this not two months ago. "The Connor Boyle and Wade Martin case."

Murphy's grey eyes clouded with rebuke. "I'm not on that case, Detective, and neither are you. So would you like to tell me what you're doing with evidence you have no business with?"

He'd like nothing better, in fact. A slow smile tugged at his lips. "I picked this up at Rosenberg's along with the Horus statues. It came from Escalante, who has an exclusive agreement with Rosenberg, which means the shell Martin was holding had to have come from his shop. If someone else is working this case, why haven't they made this connection already? Someone should have searched Martin's place or Boyle's for a receipt that would lead to Rosenberg. At the least, they could have canvassed the pawn and antique shops and asked about it."

Murphy gestured toward the window separating them from a city of six million souls. "Do you have any idea how many of those are in Manhattan alone?"

Joe did, actually. "But this one is within walking distance of our station. It would not have taken much effort for the official investigator to find it. Seems like it's not a priority."

"Caravello. It is not *your* priority. I told you that months ago."

Joe held up his hands in surrender. "I'm more than happy to let the assigned investigators do their job. But when breaks like this land in my lap, what am I supposed to do?"

The corners of Murphy's mouth pulled down. He picked up the shell, studying the carved interior. "Aside from the gold—if that's even real—this trinket is a piece of junk. It doesn't mean anything and has no bearing on the main charge in Boyle's arrest."

"I hear you." Joe lowered his voice. "It might be as inconsequential as Wade Martin's loose change or the smokes in his pocket. Especially since he claimed never to have seen it before the night he was killed."

As if inspired, Murphy lit his own cigarette and inhaled from it before blowing smoke from his mouth.

"But he also said Boyle dropped it into his drink that night. Now pair that with the fact that Boyle told me expressly not to look into it, and that's a recipe for—"

"When?" Murphy held the cigarette to the side, holding it aloft while ashes flaked and fell. "When did he tell you that?"

"Thanksgiving night, sir. His aunt lives in my parents' boardinghouse, and I drove her to visit him."

Murphy rose, leaned his thick chest over the desk, and pointed with the smoking end of his Chesterfield. "You're telling me that you discussed an open investigation with the accused when you knew it was strictly forbidden?"

Joe stood and faced him. "I'm telling you that I visited a man in jail on Thanksgiving, and he's the one who brought it up. Scout's honor, I even told him not to. But he was insistent on telling me to drop the oyster shell completely. If it didn't matter, why should he be concerned?"

"Caravello!" Murphy's fist pounded the desk. "Are you trying to get fired? Or is it my head on the platter you're going for? This isn't a game."

Joe picked up the shell and set it back in the box. "The way I see it, I'm giving you valuable information for free. I'll write up my report about finding this shell at Rosenberg's and what he had to say about it. You can pass the report to the official investigating team."

Murphy took another drag and blew through his nose. "Bring me Escalante," he fumed.

"I intend to." Joe heaved the box against one hip.

"Don't include in your report that you talked to Boyle," Murphy added. "And, Joe, for your own job security, do *not* talk to him again."

CHAPTER

16

Lauren's birthdays had always been celebrated quietly. But this— her father's idea—this was no humble affair.

Beneath stained-glass panels in the soaring ceiling, orchids ringed the trunks of potted palms placed throughout The Plaza Hotel's Palm Court. Mirrors doubled the cream-and-gold décor that made this hotel a French Renaissance château on the edge of Central Park.

Two turquoise-and-gold teapots steamed with the fragrances of lavender and bergamot. A four-tiered stand held cucumber sandwiches, salmon bruschetta, miniature chocolate tarts, pumpkin cheesecakes, cinnamon scones, and more.

Lauren's mother would have loved to experience this. Then again, she would also love that Lauren and Lawrence were here now, together. *"Redeem this."* Those parting words resounded in Lauren's spirit, reminding her what Mother's priority had been.

"Happy birthday, sweetheart." Smiling, Lawrence picked up a teapot with trembling hands. The bandages were gone, but faint marks remained to remind her how close she'd come to losing him.

She half rose, and her strand of pearls swayed as she took the small pot from him and poured the tea herself. "This feels indulgent."

He laughed. "Good. You deserve a little indulgence, especially on your birthday. You're only thirty-three once, after all." He sobered, then added, "My heavens, but you look like your mother."

Lauren settled on the plum-colored velvet cushion and lifted a cheesecake from the tray. When her mother was thirty-three, she was married and had a six-year-old daughter. When her mother was thirty-three, she was already sick with a terminal illness that would take her life nine years later.

Closing her eyes, Lauren tried desperately to shove that aside, to focus instead on the present. This one bite of cake. This one sip of tea. The fact that after years of feeling like an orphan, her father had come back to her. Inhaling deeply, she opened her eyes again.

There on the table were two shabti figures. A man and a young woman. Unlike the wooden set she'd found at the Napoleon House, these were made of faience, that gorgeous luminous blue substance the Egyptians loved to use.

"Your gift," Lawrence said. "That is, I thought we could try this again."

He must know that to her they would look like a father and daughter.

She picked up each one, marveling at the handiwork that created them and at the distance of time and space they'd traveled to reach her. Her father told her the story of their discovery in his typical dramatic fashion, but for once she didn't care so much about where they'd come from.

She cared that he remembered her. She cared that he was trying.

"You aren't going to give that one back to me now, are you?" He pointed to the male figure.

"No," Lauren determined. Her throat grew tight. "These two will stay together." After standing them up on the white tablecloth as silent sentinels, she reached into her satchel and pulled out three typewritten pages. "And this is for you."

He accepted it. "What's this? Do I get a gift on *your* birthday?"

"It's as good a day as any," she said. "This is my first article for your newsletter." She knew it may not guarantee her a spot on the expedition team. But the reply she'd received in the post from Dr. Breasted yesterday had encouraged her to try. *The golden age of Egyptian exploration is fast coming to a close,* he'd written. She longed to go while she still could. But even if things didn't work out that way, the simple notion of helping her father and helping others avoid fraud had blossomed into a worthwhile goal of its own.

"You may have to mention the fire on the property, but that won't be the only news you share," she went on. "Hopefully this article will be of so much value to your subscribers they'll forget all about that."

She watched him scan the lines she'd typed as soon as she'd gotten home from the trip to Boston and Newport. It was an article based on what she'd found at Newell St. John's. No names had been used, of course.

"This is wonderful," he murmured, shaking his head. "Oh, Lauren, you've made an old man very happy. I have no doubt that the board and our subscribers will be even more impressed."

"I've got at least three more articles I can easily write, based on my notes from the consultations I've been doing for the police."

"Anything I don't know about yet? Please say you won't make me wait for the articles to find out." His eyes glinted with something she dared to hope was approval.

Lauren hoped that Mother would be pleased, too.

"Aunt Beryl!" Returning from The Plaza, Lauren closed the apartment door behind her and stepped into her aunt's delicate embrace to receive a kiss that never touched her skin. She was fifty-two years old now, her upswept blond hair just beginning to fade. Her spine remained finishing-school straight. Aunt Beryl's smile, too, was perfect, but Lauren could never tell if it was genuine or forged for appearance alone.

Lauren hoped her own smile was warmer. "This is a surprise," she said.

"You have no idea." Elsa beckoned from the sofa, where she sat on the front half of the cushion, her back flawlessly straight, hands folded in her lap. One ankle crossed over the other. Even if Lauren hadn't seen Aunt Beryl yet, she'd have detected her exacting presence by her daughter's rigid posture.

Ivy sat beside Elsa. "Maybe I should leave you three alone for this."

"Oh, applesauce," Elsa replied. "Stay right here."

Lauren lowered herself into an armchair, and Aunt Beryl did the same. The fire crackled behind the grate, toasting the room and releasing the spicy scent from evergreen branches on the mantel.

"I understand you and Elsa searched my house for a box of letters on the word of that nursemaid Nancy Foster. I've kept it in a wall safe in my bedroom, in case you ever asked for it." Rising, Aunt Beryl took a box from where it had been hidden beneath a crocheted blanket and passed it to Lauren. "I think Goldie would want you to have this at last."

Lauren grasped the corners of the box, the sharp edges digging into her palms. "You've had it all this time? Why didn't you say anything?"

"Like you, I had put it out of my mind. You're not the only one who forgot about this. Maybe neither of us was ready to dwell upon what these letters might hold."

"I'm ready now," Lauren said quietly. "Thank you."

The next few minutes blurred. Aunt Beryl gave her one more not-quite-kiss to the cheek, and Elsa and Ivy hugged her tightly before Lauren retreated to the privacy of her room.

Her nerves tremored. Dropping her handbag on the nightstand, she kicked off her shoes and curled her legs beneath her on the quilted bed. The box felt surprisingly light on her lap for the weight of what it held.

At last, she opened the lid and pulled out an envelope at random. Mother had written this one to Dad in September 1902. Lauren would have been almost ten years old at the time, her mother thirty-seven, and her father forty-seven.

My sister has asked me a thousand times if it was worth it to marry you, and a thousand times, I tell her yes, it was worth it. For Lauren. I struggle to understand why you stay away from her. I don't doubt that your love for me has faded. I have lost my shine, no longer bearing any resemblance to my name, and I know it began even before I got sick.

What I can't understand is why you choose Egypt over Lauren, too. We have been through so much to have this child. She is brilliant when you are near, but you don't see how she flattens every time you leave. I am not enough for her, Lawrence, nor did I ever expect to be. She needs her father, too. Will you not come home before her birthday this year? Be here for Christmas at least?

I worry for her. When nurses and doctors come to see me, she stays in your office. She is not afraid of strangers, Lawrence. She is hiding from the truth that her mother is dying. You run to Egypt. She runs to the idea of it. It's where she feels safe. She is more like you than you realize. I'm losing both of you to the ancient past because you don't like the present and future.

A tear slipped to the tip of Lauren's nose, and she caught it with the side of her finger. Every paragraph prompted a new question in her mind. Her eyes hot and sticky, she read the letter again, and then a third time, trying to decipher the code.

Two things, at least, were clear. Nancy had been right in that Mother had understood more than Lauren had realized. And Lauren had work to do if she was ever going to grasp the full picture herself.

Swiping the back of her hand over her cheek, she drifted to the living room.

"Aunt Beryl?" Lauren lifted the letter. "Can we talk?"

At once, her aunt rose and followed her back to her room, where Lauren sat on the end of her bed, and Aunt Beryl perched on the skirted stool at the vanity.

"You have questions," her aunt said quietly, brushing Cleo's hair from her skirt.

"Three of them, actually, and all from reading only one letter." Lauren spread the looping script over her lap. "Mother said in September 1902 that she'd started to lose her shine even before she got sick. Then she says that she and my father went 'through so much' to have a child, and in the next paragraph implies that Dad was running away from something when he went to Egypt. Can you shed light on any of this?"

Aunt Beryl's spine seemed to soften by a degree. "The babies. Of course, Goldie was talking about the babies. That's your answer to all three questions."

Lauren shook her head, failing to comprehend.

Her aunt gazed at the photograph of Mother on the vanity. She picked up the frame. "My sister had trouble carrying babies to term. Before you were born, she suffered three miscarriages."

Lauren trapped the groan in her spirit, pressing a hand to the ache in her heart.

"Each baby that died took a little more of Goldie. The fourth baby was born twenty months before you. He was nearly full-term. I was there for that birth. I was there when my sister's perfect, tiny baby boy died three days later in her arms."

The pain became a fire in Lauren's chest. Four babies, four different sets of hopes and dreams wrapped in the most precious form. Four losses to grieve, with little time to heal between. Tears soaked the handkerchief balled in her fist.

"Shall I stop?" her aunt asked.

"No," Lauren rasped. "Tell me more. Tell me the truth."

"Your brother's name was Lawrence. Your father, for whom the child was named, never saw him. Can you imagine?" Aunt Beryl's voice shook with anger. "The man was off digging somewhere and never held his own son. He wasn't there to hold his wife after the death, the most devastating blow of all. Just like he wasn't there to comfort you when Goldie followed her little boys to heaven, at last."

Lauren squeezed shut her eyes, inhaled deeply, then exhaled. Again. "Why didn't they tell me?" she whispered.

The mattress squeaked, and Lauren opened her eyes to find her aunt sitting beside her.

"Your father made Goldie promise not to. It was too unpleasant, he said. He didn't even want to name the babies who came before Lawrence. But Goldie named them. William. Matthew. Isaac. And then Lawrence."

Four brothers in heaven. It was staggering.

"May I?" Aunt Beryl touched the letter, and Lauren passed it to her.

Quiet pulsed while she silently read. "'You run to Egypt,'" she read aloud at last. "That's what he did, Lauren, though it gives me no pleasure to say it. Yes, it was his work. But it became a convenient obsession. He didn't want to face his wife's grief, or perhaps his own, at home. Then once she became ill, there was even more to run from, of course. He couldn't stand to witness her decline."

Lauren felt split in two. She wanted to confront her father about keeping this secret, about leaving Mother to mourn alone. She also wanted to honor Mother's dying wish that the years of separation in their family be redeemed. Was it possible to do both?

"But this is true, too, you know." Aunt Beryl broke into her thoughts, tapping the letter once more. "A thousand times she told me she wasn't sorry she'd married Lawrence, because of you. You were a gift to her. I felt better about her being way out in Chicago knowing she had you."

Fighting a swell of emotion, Lauren refolded the letter and placed it back in the box, closing the lid firmly. That was enough revelation for now.

WEDNESDAY, DECEMBER 9, 1925

Lauren couldn't sleep for thinking of her mother. "*She had you,*" Aunt Beryl had said, surely intending to comfort.

Lauren placed the sentiment on a scale in her mind, weighing it against what she remembered of her childhood. She recalled climbing a tree to look for her father. Dashing out of the house before Nancy could scold her for making noise. Hiding in Dad's office, curling into a tight ball of loneliness. It was dark and cold, for no fire had been lit behind that grate for months.

Nancy hadn't bothered to look for her, but Mother knew where to find her that day. Sick as she was, Mother had crawled to join Lauren under the desk. Lauren's emotions had been too big to understand, too big to put into words. So all she'd said was that she was a hibernating bear, then pretended she was sleeping. Mother swept the hair off her forehead, kissed her, and said, *"All right, hide away, baby bear. Sleep through the long winter's night. I will be here when you wake."* Lauren felt Mother shivering at her back.

She should have turned around. She should have thrown her arms around her mother's neck and kissed her cheek and told her how much she loved her. She should have brought Mother back into her own warm room and put her back to bed herself. Why hadn't she?

Guilt filled Lauren's stomach with lead. But then something else, something sharp and burning, spread through her. She hated that she hadn't tried harder with Mother while she had the chance. But she'd been a child, with no idea that Mother had already lost four children. What Dad had done—and not done—was unthinkable. Unforgiveable, even, except for the fact that Mother *had* forgiven him.

After Aunt Beryl had left, Lauren had dared to look through the envelopes in the box, searching for any postmarked around the time of Lawrence's birth. She hadn't found any. All she had on the subject was her aunt's word.

Throwing back her covers, Lauren sat up and looked at the clock. Three thirty. She wouldn't be going back to sleep now. If she couldn't rest tonight, why should her father get to? She'd never be able to concentrate at work today if she didn't talk to him first. Never mind that she might have trouble focusing even after she heard what he had to say. That was a worry for later.

Lauren could bury many things for the sake of preserving peace. She could deny that others bothered her at all. With this, she could do neither.

At four o'clock, she called and woke her father. At five, she met him downstairs in the lobby.

"What's wrong? What is it?" He looked harried and alarmed, his jaw stubbled white. "Are you all right?" Through the windows behind him, light flashed in the dark from headlamps of passing taxis.

"Let's sit down." After leading him to the back of the room, she pointed to a wingback chair upholstered in ivory and camel-colored stripes.

She took the matching one beside it, a glass-topped table between them. A potted ficus tree and silk screen shielded their corner from the rest of the lobby.

"What's going on?" he asked.

Now that he was here, the lines she'd rehearsed fled her mind. She could do nothing more than blurt out, "I talked to Aunt Beryl last night."

His brow pleated. "That woman despises me."

At least now Lauren knew why. A few feet away, a Beresford staff member stoked the fire in the marble fireplace, replaced the screen, and left. Warmth bathed one side of Lauren's face. The other half felt cold.

Dad leaned back, his fingers pressing the brass nails at the ends of the chair arms. "That's what this is about?"

"She told me some things about our family that I'd never heard before." She crossed her ankles, her heels sinking into the carpet.

Lines carved deeper around his mouth. "Well, I hope you've considered the source. For goodness' sake, you might have brought me a cup of coffee for this."

It hadn't even occurred to her. She was wide awake, adrenaline charging through her. If he wasn't alert now, he soon would be. "She told me about my brothers. The three miscarried babies and little Lawrence, who died when he was three days old."

Instantly, water filled Dad's eyes, his entire composure collapsing. "My boys." A slow intake of air swelled his chest, and then deflated it.

Lauren tamped down an answering surge of emotion. "Why didn't you ever mention them? Why keep them a secret, as if they were something to hide?" Despite her best effort, her voice wobbled.

He bent forward, elbows on his knees. "We all grieve in different ways, Lauren. I'm ashamed to admit that mine was denial. I didn't know how to get away from the pain, so I—well, you know what I did. You may not believe this, but I figured that not telling you about your brothers was one way I could protect you from a sadness you shouldn't have to carry. By the time you were old enough to understand, we'd all moved on anyway."

Lauren tilted her head, wondering if that was possible. Would Mother have said she'd moved on from losing four children? Flames hissed behind the grate, a log crumbling. "But why weren't you there for Mother? Why didn't you help her through her grief? Why didn't you plan to be home for little Lawrence's birth?"

He leaned back so hard, so fast, it was as if by physical force. "So that's what Beryl told you."

Dread and doubt gripped Lauren. But whatever came next, she knew she needed to hear it.

"Did she tell you I was there when the first baby miscarried? I tried to comfort your mother, but she shut me out. She wouldn't see anyone but Nancy for weeks. The second miscarriage was the same, so when we lost the third baby while I was on an expedition, I didn't come home just so she could refuse to see me. With baby Lawrence, she didn't even tell me she was expecting. I suppose she thought she would miscarry again, and so she didn't bother. I didn't learn until weeks after his death that I'd ever had a son."

An elevator dinged, sending a jolt through Lauren. A maid stepped aside as residents exited, then polished the doors to a shine after they closed. Across the lobby, the doorman greeted early risers and opened the door to the cold day ahead. How surreal it was to sit on the edge of such ordinary routines while holding the pieces of her parents' broken hearts.

"How do you suppose that felt?" Dad went on. "Don't you think I would have moved heaven and earth to be there for the delivery of our first full-term child? I wasn't given the chance, Lauren. Your mother mourned without me, but she had her sister and Nancy. If anyone grieved him alone, it was me."

Tears glazed Lauren's eyes. She had no idea what to say but tried anyway. "I'm so sorry, Dad. I can't imagine how hard that was for either of you. Thank you for telling me your side of it, even though it hurt."

His chin trembled, and then he cleared his throat of whatever emotion gathered there. Dad passed her a handkerchief that smelled like the licorice he kept in his pocket. "There now. This is why I didn't want to tell you about all this. It does you no good." He sighed again. "This was a very long time ago. Your mother and I loved each other intensely, she loved you with her whole being, and I love you, too. That's more important than anything else I've said today. You have to know that."

She passed the linen square back to him, completely wrung out. "I do."

CHAPTER 17

Money couldn't buy happiness. But the display of it guaranteed status, and for people like Victoria and Miles Vandermeer, Joe figured that was even more important.

Luckily for Joe, Lauren had been invited to a Christmas party at their Long Island mansion, and she'd brought him as her guest. Victoria must have known the Morettis were holding their own party the same evening, on the same island. Only a social rival could bring out this level of extravagance.

Of course, the house itself had been built to impress long before the arrival of any new-money neighbors. The carved crown molding signaled hours of back-breaking work to dust it. Floor-to-ceiling windows reflected the sparkling lights inside. In this hall was a marble fireplace Lauren had said was modeled after the Vanderbilts'.

"How's my bow tie?" Joe asked Lauren.

She smiled up at him. Soft amber light from the chandeliers turned her skin to gold and burnished the finger waves in her hair. "Almost right."

Joe didn't want to be almost anything. He tugged at the ends, trying to straighten it. "Better?"

"Worse." Pivoting so her back was toward the wall, and he a shield before her, she deftly reached up and did something—he couldn't see what—that ended with a pat to his chest and a sparkling smile. "There you go."

She was in a better mood tonight than she'd been Wednesday evening when they'd visited another Met patron's house to look for forgeries. To the patron's great relief, Lauren didn't find any. To Joe's relief, she shared with him afterward why she hadn't seemed herself. What she'd learned from her aunt and father would be enough to sober anyone. But Joe was proud of her for asking Lawrence directly about it, and he'd told her so. Confrontation was not her style, but sometimes it was the only way to get at the truth. By the time they'd arrived here tonight, the weight she'd carried on Wednesday seemed to be lifting. He would take it all on himself if he could.

Lauren smiled at a passing guest, exchanging the polite greetings expected at these sorts of events. Not many of them stopped to actually have a conversation with her, even though she was easily the most interesting and smartest person in the room. And the most beautiful, without question.

"Something wrong, Joe?" she asked him. "You look like something's on your mind."

He wondered how she was warm enough, the way her dress bared her shoulders like that, and with her hair piled on top of her head, exposing the slender column of her neck.

"When do you think we'll see the Vandermeers?" he asked.

"Not for a little while yet, I expect. Typically, the hosts will make their grand entrance on that curving staircase after all the guests have had time to arrive. Trust me, we won't miss it."

In that case, he led her closer to the popping fire to warm her, and noticed her shoulders relax in its glow. "Do you see any colleagues here?"

"Mr. Robinson, the director of the Met, received an invitation, I'm sure, but he's out of town this weekend."

"No one else?"

"Not that I'm aware of. The Egyptian department really is Victoria's favorite, so I doubt other curators would be on the guest list."

"What about the Egyptian department's underground? Elliot Henry, Peter Braun? The other conservators?"

Her lips pressed into a thin line. "They deserve to be invited, but I don't think the Vandermeers would have done that. They don't care about people who remain behind the scenes, and for the most part, the restoration and carpentry staff don't care about being visible."

"Based on my interview with Peter Braun, he cares a great deal. It bothers him that he doesn't receive credit, or enough of it, for the restoration work he does."

Shadows passed over her face. "Ah, Peter. He's a prickly one, isn't he?"

"Not just prickly." Joe shared his suspicions about him, which had only grown.

Pink stole over Lauren's cheeks. "I can't deny he has the skills and supplies to create fakes, but I hate to think he'd stoop so low," she murmured.

"There's something else," Joe added. "He mentioned during my interview that his education was complete before he took the job. He hadn't needed to be apprenticed after he'd been hired. But he didn't tell me where he'd studied. Do you remember our encounter when I asked you to consult with me?"

She blinked up at him. "Of course."

"You told me all of your qualifications right away," he reminded her. "Where you studied, what you know."

"Habit," she said. "I'm used to spelling out my credentials so people—men, especially—will take me seriously."

"You wanted credit where credit was due. I don't blame you. So then why would Peter Braun, who considers himself chronically undervalued, not take the opportunity to share his résumé with me? If he was proud of his education, why didn't he tell me about it?"

"You want to know where he went to school?" Lauren asked.

"Among other things, yes. I called the human resources director to get a copy of his résumé and application for the job, but I haven't heard back yet."

"Berlin," she said. "He studied Egyptian art and textiles in Berlin. Can you blame him for not volunteering the information?"

"You studied in Berlin. You said the Germans had made the best dictionary of Egyptian hieroglyphs. Why wouldn't he—"

Lauren stepped closer to him and lifted her chin as she whispered, "He's German, Joe. Born and raised there. Came to America before the war, but he must have ties over there. Have you read the news about the German economy?"

Joe assured her he had.

"It's tragic, if you ask me, even if they did lose the war. A wheelbarrow of paper currency to buy a loaf of bread. The whole country suffers."

"So much that Peter would want to send his family whatever he could to help." That made sense. During the past week, he'd found nothing to indicate that Peter's lifestyle was beyond the means of a typical conservator.

"Careful, Joe." Lauren laid a hand on his arm. "Innocent until proven guilty, remember?"

He covered her hand with his. "I'm just thinking out loud here."

"Well, don't think quite so loud, would you? I'd hate for anyone to overhear and misconstrue the situation."

"Another scandal for the Met, you mean?"

She gave his arm a little shake. "Knock it off. We've already been hard on German Egyptologists. I don't want to heap shame on a colleague without proof of wrongdoing."

"What do you mean, we've been hard on the Germans? Wilson's armistice terms at the end of the war?"

"More than that. During the war, the British army destroyed the German House at Thebes in an act of retribution. Ever since the war ended, German archaeologists and scientists have been banished from digging in the Nile valley. Meanwhile, the Metropolitan Museum of Art team resumed excavations at Deir el-Bahri in the winter of 1919. This has nothing to do with my politics or patriotism, but my professional opinion—one widely held among

Egyptologists—is that our field of study is the worse for the loss of German contributions."

Joe stared at her, taking this in. The more she talked, the more motive she revealed for Peter to be the forger. "How interesting."

In the next moment, she seemed to realize the picture she had painted. The defiance in her expression yielded to doubt. "Oh dear." She dropped her hand to her side, and his arm felt cold where her fingers left it.

Joe could understand why she didn't want Peter to be the culprit, but for his part, the pieces were finally fitting together. "I'll keep looking and see what I find."

Nodding, she broke from his gaze and swept the room beyond him. Her eyes widened.

The host and hostess descended the spiral staircase. As he had been at the gala, Miles Vandermeer was completely outshined by the woman on his arm. Or rather, by the necklace she wore.

"That looks familiar," Lauren said.

Joe placed her hand in his elbow and maneuvered them both through chiffon dresses and coattails, until they were standing close enough for a better look.

Just as he thought. It was the Middle Kingdom necklace with the finely inlaid pectoral he'd seen under glass at the gala, the one worn by a royal woman. The lapis lazuli scarab bracelet encircled her wrist. The Vandermeers must have won the auctions for both, which meant that these pieces, at least, were genuine.

"Mrs. Vandermeer," Lauren greeted her warmly upon reaching her. "Thank you so much for the invitation. You remember Joseph Caravello from the gala?"

"Ah yes, nice to see you again."

Joe wondered if she knew he'd been hounding her secretary for weeks. He was about to ask when Lauren shot him a cautioning look.

"We'd like to pay you a visit in a few days," she told her hosts, "once you've had time to recover from tonight's event. If that's all right with you."

As if by magic, Miles Vandermeer assured her it was and gave them a time to call. "Now please," he added, "enjoy yourselves." He motioned toward the ballroom.

Joe turned to Lauren, returning her smile. "Shall we?" Only when he held out his hand did he realize how much he hoped she'd say yes.

———

Joe didn't have to do that. Now that they'd secured the appointment with Miles, they could easily blend into the crowd and then slip out to the Morettis'. But he had always been like this, Lauren realized, ever since they'd met. Surrounded by turned backs, Joe was an outstretched hand, an invitation to companionship. When they'd lost touch these past several years, the drifting away had been her doing, not his. But here he was again, offering closeness when she'd been the one to create distance.

She placed her hand in his, relishing the strength that wrapped her fingers.

They waltzed, and the chill she'd felt earlier melted away. His eyes arrested hers, sending a wave of heat right through her.

"I haven't told you what else I found this week." She hoped the change of subject would stem the tide of a rising blush.

"Tell me."

"Remember the box of letters my aunt gave me for my birthday?"

Joe winced. "You didn't tell me that was for your birthday! I completely forgot. I'm sorry."

He shouldn't be. Lauren hadn't expected him to remember it after all these years. "And is it police policy to celebrate the birthdays of their unpaid consultants?" she teased.

"Lauren," he said, his voice low, "you know that's not all you are to me. Don't you?"

She did. Of course she did, but just now she couldn't seem to speak. Not with him looking at her so intently, as if his question was of the utmost importance.

When she didn't reply, he drew her nearer. The change was fractional, and yet enough for her to imagine being held even closer. The idea fell like warm water down her back. Like relief and quickening all at once.

The corner of his lips curved upward, and she realized her gaze had slipped to rest there too long, giving her away. She marveled that her feet still moved in time with his, considering she had to remind herself to breathe.

"Okay, tell me what else you found," he said, releasing the tension between them. "Some other useful insight from the letter, I take it?"

Lauren nodded. "Remember Theodore Clarke?"

"Of course. He's the Newport millionaire who gifted Mr. St. John a forged ointment jar."

"My father worked with him in Egypt. According to the letters, it was my father who told Clarke where to dig."

Under the chandeliers, Joe's hair gleamed almost blue. "I don't remember seeing Lawrence Westlake mentioned in any news or publications I read about Clarke."

"Exactly," Lauren said. "Apparently there had been some kind of falling out between them, and my father didn't receive the credit he felt was his due. That matches up with something Dr. Breasted wrote in a letter I received on Monday."

"Your graduate school professor?"

"Right. I'd asked him what he knew about the Napoleon Society. He doesn't know much, but he did say that years ago, he was working in the same location in Egypt as my father and Theodore Clarke. From what Dr. Breasted observed, he said my father is 'best suited to entrepreneurial pursuits where he can be in a leadership position of his own.'"

"That sounds like a nice way of saying that Lawrence wants more control," Joe said. "Or maybe he just didn't play well with the others."

Lauren agreed. Whatever happened—or didn't happen—between him and Clarke must have been significant.

Joe fell quiet, and Lauren was content to follow his lead as they danced. "Interesting that he's building the Napoleon House in the same town where his rival—or former rival—lives. Is he the type of person to bear a grudge, even for years?"

"I hate to admit it," she confessed, "but *I'm* the type of person to quietly bear a grudge for years. Perhaps I get it from him. The irony."

It was a relief that she didn't need to explain. Dad wasn't there for her when Mother died, but Joe was. His shoulder had absorbed her tears, and his chest her fists.

"I'm sorry I hurt you, by the way," she added.

His dark eyebrows lifted as if in question.

"After Mother died, and after Dad came back so late and left me again. I didn't hold back when I took my anger out on you."

Joe's face relaxed. "Oh, that." He chuckled. "I could take it."

"But still, you didn't deserve that. You were in the wrong place at the wrong time, I guess."

He looked down at her, growing serious again. "I was exactly where I wanted to be. Still am."

The music slowed to a halt, and so did their feet. When they stepped away from each other, Lauren held on to his hand a few beats longer. She didn't want to let him go.

Joe gripped the steering wheel tighter, peering through the falling snow. If this kept up, it might obscure the narrow roads on Long Island's north shore. He needed to focus on driving instead of the dance he'd shared with Lauren and *The Tales of Hoffmann* opera it had set off in his head. Yes, he'd gotten over her pummeling when they were teens. But he hadn't gotten over her.

Focus, he told himself again. Getting into a wreck was not how he wanted to end the evening.

"Where *is* this place we're going to next?" he muttered. Twelve hundred mansions crowned the Gold Coast, as the north shore of Long Island was called. So far, he hadn't had occasion to call at many of them. "And why aren't these streets marked?"

"I know, it's confusing," Lauren agreed. "These estates have names, not addresses. Old Westbury, Winfield Hall, Mill Neck Manor, Eagle's Nest . . . the Moretti estate is called Château Marie."

"As in Marie-Antoinette?" he joked.

"Very likely. Mrs. Moretti is a bit of a Francophile, especially fond of the doomed queen's style."

"And Mr. Moretti loves all things Egyptian."

"Napoleon ties the two together since his invasion of Egypt opened the door to further discoveries. So for the Morettis, a French and Egyptian theme works."

"And how do the neighbors feel about it?" he asked.

Lauren sighed. "As a rule, they don't approve of new money at all. Christina seems lonely out here. She prefers to stay in the city most of the time."

She knew a lot about these people. "How close are you to the Morettis?"

"I only know them professionally. The fact that Christina has confided in me at all shows you how lonely she is. Mr. Moretti doesn't seem to mind being snubbed, but his wife feels every cut. Slow down, there's the drive."

Braking, he turned the car onto a narrow lane. Cobblestones rumbled beneath the tires. The grounds were enshrouded with darkness, but with the headlamps, he could at least see the Lombardy poplars lining the drive.

A quarter of a mile later, they approached the great house, lit up from within and by exterior lamps. The sprawling marble mansion with mansard roof looked exactly like a château. He steered the car into the semicircular drive of the forecourt, and a liveried valet in period dress approached him.

"Is this a costume party?" he asked Lauren.

"They like eighteenth-century uniforms for their staff on formal occasions." Lauren smiled. "I think it makes them feel more like old money, just like the antiques do. Sometimes families that don't have the right roots, according to society, try to make up for it by embodying history in their homes and possessions."

The bewigged valet in pink silk knee breeches rapped on Joe's window.

"Good evening," the man said. "I'll take your car."

Joe held back a laugh at the uncouth phrasing, which made it feel like a mannerly theft in progress. "I'll park it myself if you'll kindly show me where." There was no way he was going to let anyone else drive the police car.

"I'll get out here and wait for you." Lauren slipped from the vehicle while the valet gave directions to the carriage house.

Ten minutes later, Joe had parked in an old building, along with several other vehicles worth more than his annual salary, and walked back to the front entrance. A butler in a powdered wig and ruffled shirt bowed to him and opened the door, where yet another staff member took his coat from him, buckled shoes clicking across the tiled floor.

Joe couldn't believe this place.

Lauren stepped forward and took his arm immediately, eyes shimmering in the candlelight.

Candles. There was a light switch on the wall, and yet the chandelier had been outfitted with both bulbs and tapers. "Which side of the Industrial Revolution are we on here, anyway?" He spun a slow circle, taking in the two-story entryway. "Is that what I think it is?" A replica of the Arc de Triomphe spanned the vestibule.

"That was made with the same marble found in the same place," Lauren whispered. "You'll find a lot of reproductions here."

"You mean fakes?"

She swatted his arm. "We don't call them fakes if everyone knows they aren't originals. Now, be polite. We've arrived late, and I'm still trying to smooth things over with the Morettis on behalf of the Met."

"Right this way." A butler returned and guided them beneath the arch, down a corridor, and through a pair of oversized double doors. The great hall fizzed with champagne and buzzed with red-lipped flappers and their dates, cigarettes dangling from their fingers. But instead of jazz, a full orchestra played Mozart.

Ivory columns wrapped in a floral gold-leaf pattern supported a painted ceiling. Partially nude Greek gods and goddesses looked down at Joe from on high.

"Polite," he reminded himself under his breath. Unlike the Vandermeer mansion, whose dark oak and walnut panels had absorbed light and reflected it back in stately restraint, this hall dazzled with gilded cream walls and upholstery in shades of pink and gold. Even the floor was pink marble.

"That's Christina Moretti." Lauren nodded toward an oil painting hanging above a fireplace of veined blue marble. Draping the mantel were evergreen boughs sparkling with gold and crystal ornaments. On either side of the fireplace were arched niches in the wall, twelve feet high and four wide, Joe guessed. Each held pedestaled statues.

"And is that fellow supposed to be Mr. Moretti?" He gestured subtly to the fig leaf–covered marble male. He knew, of course, that the figure bore no resemblance, but he enjoyed making Lauren smile.

"You know what he looks like," she said. "There he is. Let's say hello." Lauren glided toward their host, and Joe stayed with her, declining an offer of champagne from one of the costumed waitstaff along the way.

"Dr. Westlake." Moretti smiled, hands spread wide. "You came. We are honored to have you."

Lauren returned the greeting and introduced Joe to him as her friend.

Joe shook his hand and found it firm but not bone crushing. "Quite the place you've got here," he said.

"Yeah? Thanks. My wife gave a tour earlier, but I can show you around if you like."

"That'd be fine."

"It looks like you have a great turnout, Mr. Moretti," Lauren added. "Everyone seems to be having a marvelous time."

"But not the neighbors."

"How's that?" Joe asked.

"The neighbors, the neighbors." Moretti swirled his hands in the air on either side of him. "I invited every one of them, but only a few of the other new-money folks have come so far. The old money must be allergic or something. I try to be friendly, and they go the other way. I thought they might come tonight to satisfy curiosity, at least."

Joe regarded the orchestra, which was playing "Serenade No. 13 for Strings." Definitely not a piece to dance to, more was the pity.

Moretti twisted to follow Joe's line of sight. "Mozart. Classy, right? Did you know Mozart played for Marie-Antoinette when he was a kid, and then afterward went right up to her and kissed her on the cheek?"

Lauren laughed. "I'd heard that, yes."

Moretti smiled. "I don't know if these goons are happy with a little culture, but they get enough jazz every other day of the week. A little classical never hurt anyone."

The accent threw Joe. It was a little bit Brooklyn, but if Moretti had grown up in the city, he must have at least gone to boarding school outside of it.

"What's your pleasure?" Moretti waved over a man with a serving tray of drinks. "Champagne? Gin? Bourbon? Whiskey? Don't worry, this is the good stuff."

"No, thank you."

"Dr. Westlake? How about the fruit cocktail you liked so well at the brownstone?"

Lauren's cheeks flamed cherry red. "Club soda, please, if you have it."

"Two?" he asked, looking at Joe.

"Sure."

Moretti picked up a glass and sent the waiter for the nonalcoholic drinks. "What line of work you in, Joe?"

"Law enforcement," Joe told him. "NYPD detective."

"New York's finest. Well, good for you, and thank you for your service. *Salute*." Brazenly, he lifted his tumbler and took a swig.

Joe smiled at his confidence. He hadn't missed a beat, hadn't even glanced at Lauren as if to question why she'd brought a cop to a party with alcohol. "You?"

"Management," Moretti replied. "Real estate, hotels, a couple of pharmacies."

"Big money in pharmacies these days," Joe said. Since the only alcohol legally sold was for communion services or prescribed by doctors, business at pharmacies was booming. "It's truly astounding how many ailments can be cured by liquor."

Moretti laughed deep from his belly. "Isn't that right? Astounding." The man was one hundred percent at ease.

As if on cue, the waiter reappeared, and Joe handed Lauren's club soda to her before picking up his own. He took a sip and tried not to grimace. But he hadn't asked for it because he liked it. He'd asked for it to make sure the club soda they served at the party wasn't spiked. He doubted Lauren would be able to tell.

This definitely wasn't spiked.

"Dr. Westlake!" A human version of the lady in the oil painting materialized, wearing the gown in the portrait. Aside from overdone makeup, she seemed like a pleasant lady.

She kissed Lauren on the cheek and shook Joe's hand while they were introduced. "Thank you for coming," she said. "I can't tell you how much it means to us to have you here."

Her inflection had more Brooklyn in it than her husband's, but what Joe heard even louder was a longing for . . . something. Respectability, maybe, or the appearance of it. Maybe belonging. Maybe she really was lonely here and happy to see every friendly face.

"Are you here on behalf of the Met, then?" she asked. "Have they changed their minds about our request?"

Lauren's smile pinched at the corners. "We're not doing business tonight, are we? The others from the Met extend their greetings, of course, but I'm here as a friend. Mr. Moretti mentioned a tour of the mansion. I'm sorry we missed it."

"Would you like to see it?" Christina placed a hand on Lauren's shoulder. "Of course you would. You will appreciate the Egyptian gallery more than anyone else here. Come on, I'll show you. Private tour." She swept Lauren away, leaving Joe sipping a drink with Ray Moretti.

"I can see you don't like that stuff, by the way." Moretti laughed quietly. "Come on, I'll give you a little tour of my own."

Joe kept in step with his host as they climbed a winding staircase, then entered a small, dark room that looked nothing like the rest of the house. "Are we still in the château?" Joe asked.

"You don't think old King Louis had his own cigar room?" Moretti laughed while turning to a cabinet. "You don't have to drink that stuff. What's your pleasure, really? I won't tell a soul. You're not on duty right now, are you, Officer?" He stood aside, revealing a row of bottles.

Joe moved closer and read the labels. Most were in French. Figured.

"So you've had these in your cellar since before the amendment passed, I take it," Joe joked.

"Scout's honor." Moretti was joking, too. "Go ahead, Joe. And call me Ray."

"Thank you, Ray. I don't mean to come across as unsociable, but I'm not drinking anything stronger than this tonight."

"Here's a good one you might enjoy." Ignoring Joe's comment, Ray grabbed a bottle by the neck and cradled it for a moment before opening it. With a heavy pour, he filled two goblets and thrust one into Joe's hand.

He set it on a table and drank the terrible club soda instead. Something surfaced in his host's expression, and then it was buried but not gone.

Joe got the feeling Ray didn't hear the word *no* very often.

CHAPTER 18

Two hours before the Met opened to the public for the day, Lauren took a quick walk through the Egyptian galleries, spot-checking the display cards to reassure herself they matched the exhibits.

At her side, Anita carried a clipboard with today's agenda, ready to make any notes as necessary. "Good weekend?" she asked.

"Eventful." Lauren described the Vandermeer and Moretti parties she'd attended.

"You had a date, I assume?" Anita tucked her raven hair behind an ear. "Let me guess. Your father. Or—wait, no!—a certain dashing detective."

"Good guess." Lauren allowed her smile to reveal as much as she wanted to on that score. She hardly knew what she felt, let alone how to put it into words. "My father is back in Newport overseeing repairs to the Napoleon House. What have you got for me?"

While Anita briefed her on the schedule, Lauren finished skimming the exhibit cards in the Jewelry room before passing into the adjacent Daily Life room.

"Miss Westlake," Mr. Robinson called, hustling after her from the direction of Middle Kingdom Tomb Furnishings. "A word, please."

Anita excused herself to start brewing a pot of coffee. "See you downstairs, Dr. Westlake."

Lauren smiled at her loyal assistant, then gave her full attention to her boss. "I do hope things are better with the Morettis," she began, and told him about attending their Christmas party last Friday.

"Did you? Smart. I knew you were good at this type of thing. Thank you."

Lauren nodded, then added, "I'd love to share with you some new ideas on the spring exhibition sometime."

"Sometime, yes. But right now we have a more pressing matter to deal with. An honorary fellow of the Metropolitan is in town, and we need to give him a private tour of the Egyptian rooms."

Lauren mentally juggled her other commitments to fit this in. "Who is it?"

"Theodore Clarke. I'm sure you know the name."

A jolt went through her. "Of course."

He straightened his tie, one finger pushing in a dimple. "I thought so. We do still need the Morettis' financial contributions, so keep up the friendly relations there, but the collection Clarke has promised the Met upon his death—one cannot overstate its importance to the museum. I hope I don't have to tell you how much he amassed, a sampling of all the ages and phases of ancient Egyptian art. The man discovered eighteen tombs."

"I'm well aware, sir."

"He's sensitive about the King Tut discovery eclipsing his decades of work. He knows we've lent our staff photographer and other team members to help Carter catalog the tomb as he clears it out, and I pray that doesn't affect his confidence in how we value him and his collection. We need to reaffirm the decision he already made. In other words, don't give him a reason to change his mind about the Met being the recipient of his legacy."

Heat prickled Lauren's scalp. If the stakes were this high, perhaps she wasn't the best person to give this tour after all. Then again, whatever quarrel her father had had with Clarke had been decades ago. Dad might hang on to it, but since Clarke had clearly come out the winner, perhaps it was no longer an issue.

Mr. Robinson narrowed his eyes. "You've gone pale. What's wrong?"

"My father worked with him in Egypt, many years ago."

"On good terms, I hope?"

Unable to agree, she twisted her strand of pearls around one finger.

He rocked back on his heels. "Good heavens, Miss Westlake. If there is any bad blood between them, and I mean even a drop, don't tell him who you are. I doubt your name will come up anyway. It's not important. What is important is that you show him how seriously we take the stewardship of art. We must prove to him that none do it better. Not Boston. Not anyone. Reassure him that we are the best, the only choice for his collection." He blew out a breath and smoothed his mustache.

After checking his watch, he began walking through the rooms, and motioned for Lauren to follow. "I'll be with you the entire time. I'd conduct the tour myself, but no one knows these rooms better than you. I'll help make sure the conversation doesn't derail, that's all."

"And when will this take place?" she asked.

"We're meeting him in the Great Hall now."

Theodore Clarke carried himself with the bearing of a pharaoh. In a camel-colored suit with a blue dress shirt and gold tie, he wore the colors of sand, sky, and sun. Were it not for her father's grievances against him, Lauren would be even more starstruck to meet him.

Mr. Robinson managed the introductions, calling her simply Lauren, stripping her of both her doctorate and her surname. She understood his reasons, but it still stung.

"Well, Lauren." Mr. Clarke shook her hand. At the age of sixty-two, his hair and beard were sterling silver, his skin bronzed by the

African sun. She could well imagine him in a pith helmet. "Let's see all the work you've been doing while the boys have been playing in the sand."

She smiled in appreciation of his attempt to set her at ease. "How would you like to see the most recent artifacts they sent back?" she suggested.

"An excellent place to start," Mr. Clarke agreed.

In the New Accessions room, Mr. Robinson began to relax, and Mr. Clarke's energy for all Lauren showed him served to heighten hers.

After narrating some of the smaller pieces, she brought him to the coffin of Hetsumina, proudly describing how she was discovered and the hope of finding her twin. "They deserve to be together," she said.

"Oh, undoubtedly." Mr. Clarke's eyes glinted as he slowly circled the coffin. "The race is on," he said at last. "Are you a betting man, Mr. Robinson? Who will find Hatsudora first? Your team, or mine?"

Mr. Robinson sputtered until Mr. Clarke laughed. "Never fear, my good man. Even if my team should find it, and if by some miracle we'd be able to arrange with authorities to remove it from Egypt, I would direct it this way. Over my dead body."

Clearly bewildered, Mr. Robinson laughed nervously.

"Whether she comes to us before or after your death," Lauren jumped in, "it's only right that the twins should be together again. I do hope you'll come and see our spring exhibition on the Egyptian afterlife, Mr. Clarke. Hetsumina will have a prominent place in it. I guarantee that when her twin joins her here, the two will be treated as nobly as they were in life, their stories displayed for the world to see."

At this point, Mr. Robinson reminded Mr. Clarke how many millions of people from around the globe visited the Met every year. The implication was clear: Clarke's legacy and name would reach the most people by being enshrined at the Met.

"A pleasing prospect, for any collector," Mr. Clarke agreed. "But tell me, will you banish my collection to inventory as soon as you find a way to bring in pieces from King Tut's tomb?"

"That's not going to happen." Mr. Robinson carefully addressed his insecurity, reminding him that Egyptian law declared that in the event of discovery of an intact tomb like King Tut's, it all belonged to Egypt. Unless the government made exceptions, everything being moved out of it was only traveling as far as Cairo.

"But the names of Carter and Carnarvon have traveled the world over while mine has been erased." Clarke's voice was wistful. "Did you know, young lady, that under my direction, the tomb at KV 61 was found in 1910? It was the last tomb found in the Kings' Valley for twelve years, before Tut was discovered at KV 62. My team stopped digging six feet from glory. Cairo's Egyptian Museum had a Theodore M. Clarke room, devoted to my discoveries. It isn't there anymore."

Lauren knew. "Mr. Clarke, the body of your work stands on its own. Your discovery of the tomb of Yuya and Thuyu gave scholars objects to study that previously had been seen only in paintings on the walls of looted chambers. That was only one of your landmark contributions."

His eyebrows lifted along with the corners of his lips.

"We also know that you employed Howard Carter during his season of poverty, having him illustrate many of your finds. If you hadn't kept him afloat during those years, he may not have lasted long enough to dig for Lord Carnarvon. Even if others don't know that, we do."

Mr. Robinson's nods were clipped but emphatic. "You earned your place as an honorary fellow of the Met, and nothing will take that away."

Unless it was Lauren's imagination, Mr. Clarke's chest lifted as though an unseen burden dropped away. "Onward," he said, the boom in his voice boding well.

Each passing room felt less like a formal presentation and more like a meeting of like minds. After the highlights in the main galleries, they moved below ground to show him all the work that went on behind the scenes, from their receiving and conservation rooms to the workshops dedicated to creating display cases to show the artifacts to their best advantage. Lauren would never tell her father this, but despite her misgivings, it was easy to enjoy Mr. Clarke's company.

By the time they'd circled back up to the Great Hall, the museum had opened to the public for the day, the eager crowd a fitting finish for the tour. Mr. Robinson offered to take their guest out for brunch next, and Clarke agreed. While her boss left to make a brief call to his secretary, Lauren stayed with Mr. Clarke, answering any last questions he had about what he'd seen this morning.

"Forgive me, Lauren," he said. "But there's something familiar about you. Have we met before? You must excuse an old man's memory."

"We've not met before today," she assured him.

His narrowed eyes searched hers. "Do I know your parents, then? Mr. Robinson never told me your surname. I didn't want to embarrass him by pointing that out, but please, tell me."

She couldn't ignore a direct question, and she wasn't about to lie. "My name is Dr. Lauren Westlake," she told him quietly. "I studied under Dr. James Breasted in Chicago."

"Ah! James and I have been good friends since before you were born, I'm sure. You could not have studied with a finer, more brilliant man. A true pioneer among Americans in the field of Egyptology."

Relief washed through her that her professor's was the name he landed upon.

And then, "Westlake," he said, voice softening. "Could it be that I have the pleasure of addressing Goldie Rediger Westlake's daughter?"

Lauren's heart skipped over a beat. "You knew my mother?"

To her great surprise, Mr. Clarke lifted her hand and brushed a whiskery kiss to her knuckles before folding it in both of his. "Once upon a time. Again, before you were born. Your hair is a rich walnut, while hers was a honeyed sunshine, but in your fair complexion and the charming dent in your chin, the resemblance is so strong I can't believe I didn't see it earlier. I was truly sorry to hear of her untimely passing. Forty-two was far too young."

Shock tied Lauren's tongue. Theodore Clarke loomed large in her father's letters, and here he was, speaking about Mother like he knew her, from her maiden name to the shade of her hair to her age when she died. What had their relationship been? And yet he hadn't mentioned a connection to Dad at all, though the two of them had worked together. Nothing about this made sense.

"My father—" She stumbled headlong into the blunder.

"Yes, I knew him, too." Patting her hand, he let it go and smiled as Mr. Robinson returned. In a whisper, he added, "The less said about him, my dear, the better."

TUESDAY, DECEMBER 15, 1925

Joe closed the folder on Ray Moretti and rubbed the heels of his hands against his eyes. After his encounter with the man Friday night, he'd expected to find some kind of clue in his file. All that wealth had to come from somewhere. Likely somewhere illegal.

But so far, everything checked out fine. Born in Brooklyn, he'd attended a Catholic military boarding school for most of his school years, which accounted for his accent. From there, he earned a four-year degree in business. He owned three hotels, an office and retail building, and two pharmacies. He was licensed as a real estate agent in the state of New York, current on all his certifications and permits, and he paid his taxes. For his age, he'd done well for himself, a sterling example of the new-money ideal. But was that enough money to cover a Fifth Avenue brownstone, a Long Island estate, regular contributions to the Met, and his own antiquities?

The guy didn't have so much as a parking ticket on his record. Not even a complaint by a neighbor. On paper, he was clean.

Instinct said otherwise. Nobody's file was *that* clean.

He could almost hear Lauren's voice, echoing what she'd told him last night after their appointment with the Vandermeers did not, in fact, reveal any forgeries. *"I've never seen a man so sad to find out there's been no wrongdoing,"* she had teased. But it wasn't wrongdoing he was after for its own sake. What he wanted, and needed, was progress.

"Sir." Oscar McCormick approached his desk with another folder. "I found something that doesn't make sense. I wondered if you have time to talk me through it."

Truly, it wasn't McCormick's fault that Joe hadn't taken a shine to him. The kid hadn't done anything wrong so far, aside from being a constant reminder that he was only here because Connor wasn't.

Mustering his manners, Joe motioned him over.

Before he could open the folder, however, the telephone rang again, and Joe answered it.

"Sergeant Caravello? Elliot Henry here. You called earlier looking for Peter. Did he return your call?"

"Not yet."

"I figured. Well, he'll be headed to lunch in half an hour, if you'd like to catch him there. You know the restaurant in the Met?"

"I'm on my way."

He dropped the handset into the cradle. "Sorry, McCormick. Another time. Or ask someone else." He didn't stick around for his response.

———

Joe sat across from Peter in a corner of the cafeteria-style restaurant in the basement of the Metropolitan Museum of Art. The plaster was a light cream color, but the huge square pillars holding up the floor above them were decorated with panels of scenic wallpaper.

Setting his notebook on the sea-green table, Joe noticed Peter's tray. The food was sold à la carte, and all he'd selected was toast without butter or jam, a bowl of steamed broccoli, a glass of milk, and another of water. It certainly wasn't the lunch of a man made wealthy by forgeries, or any other means. Such slim pickings would hardly fill a man's stomach.

"Not hungry today?" Joe began.

"Just because I don't eat as much as you presumably do does not mean I'm not hungry."

Curious. He was too thin to be on a weight-loss program. "Tell me they pay you enough around here to get a decent lunch." Joe already knew they did. Mr. Henry had told him Peter's salary, which was pretty average for a middle-class white male in this city.

"I have better things to do with my wages than indulge my appetite, Detective. My conscience wouldn't allow it."

"So going hungry is a moral choice," Joe said. "Care to explain?"

Peter laid down his fork and sat back. He chewed a bite of broccoli so slowly and thoroughly that at first Joe suspected it was merely to test Joe's patience. Then he realized that was a way to make food last. To trick your stomach into thinking it held more than it did.

Peter sipped the milk, then followed it with a drink of water. "Compared to what my family has, this is a feast of unimaginable proportions," he said at last. "Knowing that, I can't bring myself to eat more."

"Your family in Germany," Joe confirmed.

Shadows darkened Peter's countenance, but he didn't deny it. "They are suffering. Wilson made sure of that. Do you have any idea how it feels to live in the land of plenty while the ones you love are stranded in desperation?" His passion was understandable.

It was also motive.

"So you're sending money to family instead of spending it on yourself," Joe prompted. "Is it helping?"

"One would think." He bit the toast and took his time chewing again. "One would think that American dollars would make them rich beyond their dreams. But don't forget, there is corruption to pay for, too."

Joe frowned, sliding his notebook to his lap and making a note beneath the table. "Sounds pricey."

"You have no idea. There are bribes they must pay to get their mail. Bribes to keep them from being robbed of it. Bribes for the privilege of breathing, I suppose." He threw up his hands, his feeling of helplessness palpable. "They end up with little. But even that is better than nothing."

Joe considered this. Peter needed money, and a lot of it. That didn't mean he was forging art to get it, though. It only meant he had an immediate need for cash, in addition to the chip on his shoulder Joe had observed last time they spoke.

"What about bringing them here?"

"What about the questions you came here to ask?" Peter drank the water with controlled sips, even though his stomach growled loud enough for Joe to hear. "Surely you didn't come to ask about my family."

Joe recalibrated the conversation. The last thing he wanted to do was spook Peter, and he didn't have enough to bring him in to the station yet.

Peter's attention slid past Joe. With recognition in his eyes, he gave a curt nod.

Turning, Joe spotted a blond-haired man in his early thirties at a table for two. He opened a book and read while he ate.

"Friend of yours?" Joe asked Peter.

"Not really. It's just the registrar, and he prefers his own company, as you see. His job is unpacking everything shipped to the Met and packing up everything shipped out." Peter scoffed. "It's about the least-skilled job at the museum. Anyone with a day of training could do it."

Joe figured there was a little more to it than that but skipped ahead of that discussion. "How's work going?" He endured the expected tirade of complaints, then asked if Peter had ever worked on his own, or thought about it, since working here was so challenging.

Peter blinked. "Conserving antiquities isn't the type of work one could freelance. For steady pay, one needs to be attached to an institution. The bigger, the better. In theory."

"What about art? Surely you can do that on the side, on commission maybe. I imagine the Met has enough patrons to keep you busy that way. Unless I'm mistaken about the range of your skills."

"You wouldn't be the first."

"But you can do it, right? At least, Egyptian art? Or maybe it isn't that hard. For example, Dr. Westlake visited a patron who had life-sized Egyptian figures painted all over his dining room walls. She was impressed with the work, but this patron made it sound like it was no big deal. He'd used a lantern slide to project images on the surface and hired painters to fill in the lines."

Peter had stopped chewing. "Are you talking about Ray Moretti?"

Joe's pulse kicked up. He was on to something. "Why do you ask?"

"It was Moretti, wasn't it? I know it was, so don't pretend otherwise."

"How can you be so sure?"

"Because I painted those walls myself."

Joe watched Peter while scribbling on his notepad. "He paid you well, I hope, despite his opinion that the work was easy?"

At this point, Peter speared three pieces of broccoli at once and stuffed them into his mouth. His jaw bunched as he chewed, abandoning his earlier method of making it last as long as possible. "He paid me a fraction of what the work was worth." His brown eyes smoldered. "He reminded me of all the money he'd given to the Met so far, as if he'd personally bankrolled my salary."

"You didn't push back, Mr. Braun?"

He chugged half the glass of milk at once. "As much as I dared. He drives a hard bargain, and I realized that making him upset might put my job at the Met on the line."

Joe could picture it. Peter Braun didn't stand a chance against Ray Moretti.

"If I lose my job here," Peter went on, "I can't help my family. That's not something I was willing to risk. And what I did for that man *wasn't* easy. You couldn't hire just any painter to mix those exact shades and pigments, using the exact materials the Egyptians used. It's as much a science as it is an art, and I'd challenge him to find anyone else who could do it better. I almost chose a career in painting, by the way. But commissions are unreliable."

"Well, I'm sure he knew you were the best," Joe told him truthfully. "Otherwise, he wouldn't have hired you. As I said, Dr. Westlake was impressed enough that she remarked to me about the skill of whoever had done it."

Peter flicked a glance at Joe. "Did she find anything else remarkable there?"

"Such as?"

He pushed his glasses up his nose and finished the toast in two giant bites. "He told me he was looking for a spectacular centerpiece for the room. Said he'd make his dining room table into a display case for it if he found it."

Maybe Peter was only curious.

But maybe his interest ran deeper. Peter had been in that room, seen the dimensions, and heard what Ray was looking for. He could have forged it himself and sold it for a profit far exceeding the money he should have been paid for painting the walls. Maybe he was asking Joe about it now to see if his work had fooled Lauren. What kind of personal satisfaction would that bring a man who'd felt slighted both by Ray and by the Met?

"Detective?" Peter pressed. "Did she see the papyrus? The Book of the Dead?"

Joe studied him. "Did Ray tell you that's what he was looking for?"

"Oh, never mind," he grumbled.

"I haven't seen that room myself," Joe said, "but I did attend a couple of Christmas parties last weekend. The Vandermeers' and the Morettis'. I went as Dr. Westlake's guest."

Peter drained the rest of the milk and set the glass down with a little too much force.

Joe had stuck a nerve. He kept striking. As casually as he could, he relayed every ostentatious detail, each one seeming to stoke the fire in the overlooked, underpaid conservator who didn't eat enough so he could send money to family.

"I understand you're looking for a forger because that's your job." Peter held his voice low. "But you see for yourself how wasteful these people are. *That's* the crime, Detective."

Joe flipped his pen over and under his fingers and back again. "Spending money in ways you don't approve of doesn't break any laws."

A scowl slashed Peter's face. "You know what I mean. People like that can afford to be scammed. What difference does it make to them? A small fortune to you and me would be pocket change for their kind. They'll get more money. Don't worry about them. I certainly don't."

This, Joe believed.

CHAPTER

19

Lauren waved across the crowd to Elsa and Ivy, who wove their way back to her with freshly rented pairs of ice skates.

"Success!" Ivy declared upon reaching the bench where Lauren and her father sat. Plopping down beside him, Ivy began trading her shoes for skates.

Elsa sat and did the same. "Sure you won't join us?" Her cheeks were already pink with cold.

"Another time." Lauren sipped her hot chocolate. She needed to catch up with her father, and given his age, that was much better done on terra firma.

Straightening, Ivy adjusted her hat. "Will you be in town for Christmas, Mr. Westlake?"

"That's my plan," he told her.

"So will I." Lauren had been thinking about this for a week and a half. "You can join me at the Beresford if you like." Elsa had already invited her and Ivy to spend the holiday with her family, but she'd also made it clear that the invitation did not include Dad. After hearing his side of Aunt Beryl's story, Lauren decided she couldn't leave him here alone.

Elsa removed her fogged-up spectacles and wiped them clean. "You know, there's a lot to be said for staying home for Christmas.

The only reason I'm going with my parents to the Caribbean is for the birds. Ivy's coming along to keep me sane." She replaced her glasses.

"I can't wait." Ivy's countenance glowed as she stood. She took a wobbly step, arms lifting from her sides unevenly for balance. "You ready for this, Elsa?"

"Are you kidding?" Elsa stood. "I was made for this." With a grin, she walked stiffly to the rink and stepped onto the ice. Pushing herself from the railing, she glided as far as she could before bending her knees and skating with the best of them. Out on the ice, among so many other staggering skaters, her limp was all but impossible to detect.

Dad looked at Lauren from over the top of his steaming cup. His smile seemed cautious, forcing lines into his cheeks. "Feeling better since I last saw you?"

She felt bruised, but she wasn't angry at him. Her father had not been the villain Aunt Beryl had made him out to be. She wasn't about to call him blameless, but he wasn't malicious, either. He had his regrets. So did she. Lauren entrusted all of this to a smile and nod, which he returned.

"Good. Now then, have you found more to write about for the *Napoleon Herald?*"

"Joe and I met with three more Met patrons this week, and thankfully didn't find any forgeries in their collections. Plus, on my lunch breaks, I've been visiting various art dealerships to view their Egyptian antiquities with a goal of catching fakes before anyone purchases them. So far, Mr. Aaron Tomkins has been the only dealer to refuse me access."

"And?"

"I haven't found any new forgeries in the dealerships, but I feel better about having checked. Don't worry, Dad. I can think of at least four more topics to cover for future issues of your newsletter."

That seemed to satisfy him.

"One of our honorary fellows came for a tour of the Egyptian

Art department on Monday," she added. She'd have told him sooner, but Dad had been gone again this week, and this was a topic best discussed in person. She wanted to see his reaction. "Theodore Clarke. Didn't you work with him years ago?"

Her father scratched the side of his nose. "I did. You conducted the tour yourself?"

She told him she had, with Mr. Robinson joining them. "We started with New Accessions. I showed him Hetsumina, and he seems bound and determined to find Hatsudora, her twin."

Sunshine reflected off the ice, and he squinted into it. "Does he? Well, that sounds like the sort of challenge he'd enjoy. I hope the Met team finds it first, though."

Lauren agreed. "Although, he did say if his team found it, it would eventually come into our holdings anyway. He's willing his entire Egyptian collection to the Met upon his death, but I bet he'd loan it to us before then for a special exhibition. He's loaned so much to us before."

"Generous." He tugged his hat lower, suddenly captivated by the skaters. "Did he happen to mention working with me once he knew who you were?"

Lauren reached for a response that would be truthful and tactful. "Mr. Robinson rushed him off for brunch right after he made that connection, so there was no time to chat about it. But I'm sure he's aware you're working in the area, especially since the Napoleon House is right there in his hometown." Suddenly, she wondered if his concern about his reputation in Newport had more to do with Clarke's opinions than he'd let on. "By the way, are you still staying at a hotel when you go? Have you thought about asking if he has a guest room you could occupy instead, just for the short term?"

Dad scoffed, as she expected he would. "Utter nonsense," he said. "Neither of us would abide being under the same roof, however expansive that roof may be. Whoever said 'time heals all wounds' had never encountered Theodore Clarke. You have no idea what—" He cut himself off with a noise of frustration she'd never heard from him before. "Please, Lauren, leave it at that. Don't dig. Don't talk to your aunt, and if you can manage it, stay away from that man. Let these bygones stay buried."

A few hardy pigeons skittered along the ground, hunting for crumbs. Silently, Lauren watched them while Dad's flurry of words settled like snow upon her. The last of her hot chocolate had grown cold, and so had she.

Officially, Joe wasn't on duty. But he never stopped thinking like a cop. So when he arrived at the pond in Central Park, he took a few minutes to surveil the area.

Lauren had said he'd be able to find her here this afternoon. Hanging back by the trees, he scanned the skaters and saw children with parents or nannies. A few rowdy adolescent boys, their voices cracking, their horseplay harmless. Pairs of young women with ermine muffs must have hopped over from their Fifth Avenue homes.

And then there were Elsa and Ivy, whooping and laughing without a care what others thought of it.

Lauren wasn't with them.

His attention swerved off the ice, taking in the line at the food and drink vendor, another cluster around the skate rentals booth, looking for her signature turquoise blue coat, the one the same color as that little Egyptian hippo at the Met.

There. She sat with her father on a bench a short distance from the skating pond. Her nose and cheeks were pink, her scarf wrapped tightly about her neck and tied above one shoulder. Her chocolate brown hair was gathered in a knot, but the wind had pulled a few strands free.

Joe's gaze kept moving, analyzing, suspecting, until it snagged on a man with a newspaper occupying a bench diagonally across from the Westlakes. Who came to Central Park to read the news? It was too cold for that this time of year, unless he was waiting for a loved one who was skating on the pond.

The guy wasn't turning pages.

Moving closer, Joe confirmed his suspicion that the only thing this guy was reading—or trying to read—was lips. His line of sight was pinned on Lawrence and Lauren. He looked familiar, too. Broad shoulders. Dark hair on a small head that even his fedora couldn't disguise. Very large hands.

Joe would have enjoyed walking up to him and personally disrupting his attempted eavesdropping. But the momentary satisfaction wasn't smart for long-term strategy. If this guy knew that he'd been made, he'd run.

"Joe!" Lauren waved him over.

He could almost feel the spy staring holes into his back as he went to her. Fine. Good. Let him see that Lauren had a friend watching out for her. Let him notice the slight bulge at Joe's hip and figure that was a holstered gun.

All of this was pure conjecture, of course. And his gut had been wrong before.

Then again, it had also been right.

The Westlakes were both standing by the time he reached them. Joe shook Lawrence's hand. "Good to see you again," he said. "How are things progressing in Newport?"

"Could be worse." Then he launched into an update that lasted five minutes. "Well," he said at last, "this old man has had enough winter for one day. I'm heading back."

After he'd left, Joe pointed at Lauren's shoes. "Wrong footwear."

"What's wrong with them?" She kicked out a foot, then glanced at the iced-over pond. "Oh." She chuckled. "I needed to talk to my dad and wasn't about to make him balance on skates to do it. He managed to fall off a train platform, remember? He wasn't likely to stay upright on ice."

Joe angled to see the man with the newspaper on the bench. He wasn't there. Slowly, Joe surveyed the surrounding area and didn't see him.

Maybe he'd been wrong about the man watching Lauren.

Or maybe he'd found a better spot to hide. Joe puffed out a breath, squinting into the light bouncing off the snow.

"Do you still skate?" he asked Lauren.

"Not in many years."

"Shoe size?"

"Seven!" Ivy called out, and Joe turned in time to see her grin and wave from the rail before catching up with Elsa again. He had to admit, her timing was good.

Lauren laughed. "There's no point in you standing in line without me."

Minutes later, they'd both traded their shoes for skates and stepped onto the ice.

Joe knew his movements were a little stiff. But he wasn't trying to be graceful. His masculinity wouldn't stand for it. He did, however, intend to remain vertical. At least, if that spy was still around, he wasn't likely to follow them onto the ice. From outside the railing, he wouldn't catch their conversation, either.

With that in mind, he reached for Lauren's hand, but instead of tucking it in the crook of his arm, he simply held it and steered them both away from the edge.

They skated side by side, finding their rhythm, while Joe kept an eye on the perimeter.

"I'm really glad you came," she said. "You would not believe the conversation I had with my dad."

He looked down at her. "About Theodore Clarke?" he asked. She'd told him about the tour she'd given him the other day, including his insecurities since Tut's discovery and his comments about her parents. There was definitely more to learn there.

The wind whipped a strand of her hair across her eyes. She brushed it away, then relayed what Lawrence had told her.

"So will you leave it alone?" he asked.

"I don't know." Her brow furrowed. "Maybe I don't want to know what happened between them, especially if I'm to keep up a positive working relationship with Clarke for the Met. But I already replied to Dr. Breasted and asked him for more details about what might have caused the rift between him and Dad."

"Attagirl." In his line of work, secrets were made to be exposed.

She chuckled. "There's something else I wanted to talk to you about."

"Lead the way."

"I've been thinking about Peter, and everything you told me from your chat with him on Tuesday. He certainly seemed like the most promising suspect for the Book of the Dead papyrus, but we were forgetting one important detail. Peter couldn't have forged that papyrus. Mr. Moretti said it came directly from Egypt, so it must have been forged before it reached the States."

Joe didn't like how much she trusted Moretti's word. "Lauren," he said. "You do realize that Ray Moretti could have been lying about that, or he could have been lied to himself. A buyer says he got it in Egypt, but he didn't. Maybe he didn't want to displease his boss, which I understand. What was his reaction, by the way, when you told him his papyrus wasn't genuine?"

"No one enjoys hearing news like that, but he responded as well as any other collector in the same position. He lost a small fortune on it."

"A small fortune to us might be small potatoes to him. In any case, doesn't he want to report it to the police?"

"Not as far as I know. Maybe he didn't believe me."

He pulled her closer, wrapped his arm around her waist, and spoke so only she would hear him. "Or he might not want to get the police involved. People like him have their own ways of handling things. *Capisce?*"

She shook her head but couldn't hide a small smile. "Oh, I *capisce* plenty."

"No, no." He tried so hard not to laugh. "I say, '*Capisce?*' That means 'Do you understand?' And you say, '*Capisco.* I understand.' Except for I wonder if you really do."

"I've heard the rumors about the Morettis, Joe."

"Which ones?"

She glanced at him and skated a little faster, though she couldn't get away from him, joined at the hip as they were. "It's no secret that he owns an abundance of liquor."

No kidding.

"And he probably comes by it illegally."

"He probably does." Joe couldn't help the sarcasm. "What else?"

"I understand he owns a lot of businesses. He's successful enough to have an income that can afford both his Manhattan brownstone and the Long Island mansion. I've heard he hasn't paid all the taxes he owes. But that could just be the old money–new money rivalry."

"Looks like he has paid his taxes, actually."

"You looked him up?"

"I did my job. I wanted to check for ties to organized crime," Joe told her.

Snow fell in little feathers, landing on the apples of her cheeks and the dent in her chin. They melted there, leaving tiny droplets on her skin. He felt like they were in a Norman Rockwell painting. Except for the topic of conversation.

"Did you find any proof?" Lauren asked.

If Joe had proof, Ray Moretti would be in jail. "These guys are hard to pin down. Their strict culture of secrecy and family loyalty goes a long way in protecting them from charges that would otherwise stick."

"The Morettis have been valued patrons of the Met for years. His wife personally gives to several charities around the city."

"Do you ever wonder where that money comes from?"

"Hotels and pharmacies. Real estate—that's a big one—especially on the north shore of Long Island."

Joe wondered what it was like to be so naïve. To accept what people said, to believe the best in them, to refuse to give credence to hearsay. "I forgot how easy it is for you to give folks the benefit of the doubt," he said. Not that he had any right to complain. Lauren had extended the same grace to him when they'd been teenagers, against her aunt's advice.

191

She narrowed a sidelong glance at him through the swirling snow. "Somehow I get the feeling you don't approve."

"I approve of *you*," he said. He approved of everything about her, except her cavalier attitude toward the Morettis. Releasing her waist, he spun around to face her and held her hands instead. He skated backward, and she forward. "But sometimes you can be so focused on ancient dynasties that you don't clearly see the world you live in now."

Lauren dug her toe into the ice, stopping them short. "Are you going to tell me I'm too privileged? That I don't live in reality and have no idea how the world works?" She inched backward, changing their direction.

He didn't let her go. Other skaters faded in his periphery as he focused on the only one who mattered. "We know each other better than that," he insisted. "I care about you."

Her blue eyes softened as she squeezed his hands. "I care about you, too. I'm so glad you're back in my life. I keep wondering why we didn't do this sooner."

"I know why."

She locked her gaze with his, waiting.

"Do you remember when you said good-bye to me at Belvedere Castle, before you left for college?" Joe asked.

"Of course."

"I'd set up that picnic with a much different plan for that night. I was going to tell you how deeply I cared about you. Then you started talking about your plans for the future, and I wised up quick that I didn't fit in. I would only be in your way, and the last thing on earth I wanted to do was hold you back from your dreams."

Joe realized that he was still holding her hands, keeping her near. He released her, letting her skate backward at her own pace.

"I asked if we could write to each other, and you never did," she said. "I wrote you a couple of times, and you didn't respond."

How could she still not get it? He'd needed to get over her, and the only way to do that was to forget her. Writing letters only reminded him that she was out there, and that she'd never be his. "That's because I didn't want to be your friend anymore. I couldn't." He swallowed, and the rest of his confession stuck in his throat.

Her eyes widened. Hurt splayed across her face, and she skated faster.

"Wait, I didn't mean it like that." He pursued her, closing the distance between them. She was heading straight for a section of the pond that was barricaded with sawhorses.

"Lauren, wait!"

She didn't look over her shoulder, didn't know she was literally skating on thin ice until it cracked and gave way beneath her. With a cry of surprise, she fell through, but only up to her calves. Her right ankle buckled beneath her, but she regained her balance and held out a palm to stop Joe.

"Stay back!" she called to Joe, whose instinct was to lunge for her and bring her back to safety. "You'll break through if you come close." Her expression screwed tight. She must be in pain, or she wouldn't be standing there soaking in the freezing water, one knee slightly bent.

"Here." He took hold of a sawhorse and shoved it her way. "Use this." He hated how helpless he felt, watching her struggle to step out of the water and back onto the thin ice, balancing on slippery skates.

Grasping the sawhorse for support and to redistribute her weight, she made her way to the end of it, then accepted Joe's outstretched hand. He pulled her farther from danger, holding her steady against him. Already, she began to shake with cold.

"I can't believe I did that," she gasped. The snow that caught on her wet shins and skates didn't melt. "I twisted my ankle somehow, but now I can't feel it. My feet are numb."

"Make way, make way!" Elsa's voice cut through the crowd that was already forming around them. "We saw the whole thing."

"I've got to get her home," Joe said.

"Agreed. Come on, I'll help you get her off the pond." She and Joe kept Lauren between them while skating her to the edge and onto the closest bench. "Ivy's working on transportation, and I'll return the skates. Here." Kneeling, Elsa tore at Lauren's skate laces while Joe quickly changed back into his shoes.

Joe ripped off his coat and wrapped it around Lauren's legs, which were now without stockings, since Elsa had apparently peeled them off, too. He secured the coat in place by wrapping the sleeves around her legs and tying them. With numb feet and an injured ankle, she was in no condition to walk right now anyway.

"Get her home," Elsa said. "We'll be right behind you."

A shrill whistle cut through the air. "Joe! Lauren! Your chariot awaits!" Ivy waved at them from where she stood on the lane thirty yards away. Behind her was a horse-drawn carriage, popular with tourists, big enough for only two passengers.

"Ready, princess?" Joe lifted her arms and looped them around his neck. She held tight, and he lifted her with an arm beneath her shoulders and another beneath her knees. He carried her to the carriage and settled her inside.

"The Beresford, Central Park West," he told the driver.

"What do I look like, buddy? A taxi?"

"You are now." Joe flashed his badge case to skip the argument. "Giddyup."

Lauren wasn't sure which was more shocking. The cold that had sliced through her skates and stockings or the fact that she'd been stupid enough to skate too close to the edge in the first place.

"Can you feel anything yet?" Joe held her coat-wrapped legs on his lap as the carriage trundled through Central Park. One arm around her shoulders, he rubbed his other broad hand over the folds of wool wrapping her lower legs, careful not to touch the injured ankle.

She shook her head. "Still numb." The snow fell thick and wet, and she burrowed closer into Joe's side. She was so very cold. Without a coat, Joe had to be freezing, too. "Do you want my scarf, at least?"

"Are you kidding? Forget about it." He squeezed her shoulders. "We're almost there, anyway."

The horse wasn't pulling past a trot, but the distance between the pond in Central Park and the front door of the Beresford was less than half a mile.

A minute later, the dear old beast exited the park, clip-clopping across Central Park West and slowing to a halt at the entrance of the Beresford on 81st Street. Joe paid the driver, hopped to the ground, and gathered Lauren in his arms once more.

As soon as they were inside the apartment, he helped her into her bedroom so she could change out of her skirt, which was wet at the hem, along with her coat.

"You should take a soak in the tub to warm up," he called through the door.

"Nonsense. It's just my feet that need it."

"Then don't put on stockings yet. We'll soak your feet."

After trading her damp skirt for a dry one with a hemline that fell to the knee, she grabbed a pair of stockings for later and hobbled back into the hall.

Wrapping an arm about her waist, Joe helped her to the living room and eased her onto the couch. "I'll take care of you," he said, and she believed him.

Clearly, he remembered his way around the place from his last visit. He found the dish pan they used to wash out their mugs, filled it with water, then brought it to where she sat.

"This is warm," he told her, "but not hot enough to burn you." He guided her feet into the water.

"I don't feel much of anything yet."

"You will." Rising, he went to the counter and started a pot of coffee. The redolent smell filled the apartment with a sense of comfort and humble domesticity. With the coffee percolating behind him, he returned to her and knelt. "It doesn't look like you sprained your ankle. You must have come down on it wrong. You'll be back on your feet in no time."

Lauren agreed with his assessment. There was only a little swelling, and no bruising that she could tell yet. "I feel pretty stupid," she admitted. "I hate for you to have to go to all this trouble."

"It's no trouble," he said. "Do you mind if I—" He glanced up at her. "May I touch you? Your feet and ankles. No funny business, I promise." He held his palms up.

Her face heating, she nodded, wondering when her nerves would fire back to life beneath his touch.

Joe dipped his hands in the water and rubbed her feet and toes before massaging her ankles, too. He cupped water and laved it over her cold shins and calves, first on one leg, then the other.

"Thank you," she whispered. "For helping me."

He shrugged. "Ivy and Elsa would have if I hadn't already been there."

"You make it sound as though you're not necessary. But you are necessary. To me. And not just for this."

His hands stilled on her ankles, and he looked up at her. While she waited for his voice to surface, unsaid words seemed to ripple between them.

Then, as if remembering himself, Joe drew back from the water, went to the counter, and poured a mug of coffee. Coming back, he pressed it into her hands. "That should warm you a bit, inside and out."

Lauren wouldn't admit how warm she already felt. "Don't you want some?"

"Later." Bending a knee at the hearth, he stacked kindling among the wood. "Any better yet?"

She wiggled her toes. "Getting there."

"Good." He lit the fire and blew on the small flames.

Sipping her coffee, she tried to relax, but every sense still in operation seemed to be on high alert. The coffee smelled richer, the sofa cushions felt softer. Moments passed with the snap and pop of the growing fire the only sound between them.

"Oh." Lauren suddenly felt as though the water was far too hot for her skin. "That's enough, I think. I know the water is barely above lukewarm, but it feels like it's burning me." Setting the mug on the table beside her, she lifted her feet out of the water.

Kneeling again, Joe moved the basin aside, and spread a towel over his lap. She lowered both feet onto it, and he dried them.

"I didn't understand what you meant at first," she said. "When you said you didn't want to be my friend anymore."

"So I gathered. Words are not my strong suit."

His actions, however, spoke volumes.

Lauren leaned down and pulled her stockings back on, then patted the sofa cushion.

Joe sat with her, and she angled sideways to face him. She stretched out her legs across his lap, mostly to relieve the pressure from her ankle.

Mostly.

Pulling a blanket from the back of the sofa, Joe carefully tucked it around her legs and placed one warm hand to the bottoms of her feet. His other arm draped the back of the couch behind her. "I would have explained, but you were busy falling into the water." He twirled a wayward lock of her hair around one finger and let it go.

She felt the blood rush to her cheeks. "Try again?"

Joe looked away, as though measuring his next words. When he turned back to her, his eyes were an intense green, the color of new grass in the spring. "Ever since I met you, I wanted to be your friend. Then, when we weren't kids any longer, I wasn't satisfied with that. I wanted more. But I wasn't going to push. Your aunt and uncle clearly didn't approve of me, and you had big plans. You traveled abroad, you went to school. I joined the force. We moved on, right?"

"I suppose we did." The wedge in Lauren's throat grew sharp. "I've missed you, Joe."

He nodded, a half smile on his lips. "And then these cases threw us back together, and I told myself to be content with this miracle, that you were back in my life. I didn't even expect our friendship to pick up where we left off, and I still counted myself lucky that for however long these cases kept us together, we could be friends. That once we caught a few forgers, we might part ways again and go back to the way things were before. I've tried to be okay with that. But I can't. I'm not." His hand cupped the nape of her neck, his thumb drawing a slow circle beneath her ear.

Dusk fell outside the windows, and snow churned against the panes. Lauren's heart thumped against her ribs. "Tell me what you were planning to say that night at Belvedere Castle, when we were young and the whole world seemed at our feet."

Firelight flickered in his eyes. "I want to be more than your friend. I want to be the man who gets to take care of you, who makes you smile and sing and sigh. I want . . . you know what I want."

She could tell he was all out of words, and the fact that he was so nervous endeared him to her all the more. But he didn't need to say anything else to make himself clear. He was right. She knew what he wanted. He needed to know that she wanted it, too.

Joe slid his hand to her cheek and leaned closer. "*Capisce?*" His gaze dropped to her lips before bouncing back to her eyes, his question lingering there.

Her pulse throbbing, she looped her hands around his neck, fingers curling in the hair above his collar. "*Capisco,*" she whispered, and kissed the smile on his face.

CHAPTER 20

F igaro" had been playing in Joe's head ever since Saturday. He hoped he wasn't wearing a grin to go with it now that he was back in uniform. Silencing the music in his head, he entered his boss's office for their weekly meeting.

Garlands and bows festooned a half-sized Christmas tree in the corner. It even had ornaments on it for goodness' sake. A nutcracker on the windowsill was painted in a blue uniform with brass buttons not unlike the NYPD's. Cute.

"So who's the woman in your life?" Joe asked, dropping into a chair.

"Hm?" The inspector glanced up, then at the Christmas decorations. "Ah, that would be my mother's doing. You didn't think I had time for any other dame, did you? Here. Help yourself." Murphy slid a plate of sugar cookies across the desk.

Joe picked up a snowman-shaped treat smeared with yellow frosting, then turned it toward Murphy in question.

"My sister's kids helped decorate this year," Murphy explained. "She couldn't convince them that yellow was for stars. Whaddya gonna do, right?"

Chuckling, Joe finished the cookie in two bites.

"It's like this, Caravello." Murphy leaned back. "I'm reading your reports every week, and I'm not seeing a lot of progress on the forgery front. How do you feel about that?"

Was that a trick question? How did Murphy think Joe felt about that? "Obviously, more progress would be better. But it's a long game. Like most everything else worth doing, it takes time and patience. It took years to take down the Black Hand Society."

"You're not working on anything like the Black Hand Society. No one is being blackmailed or murdered. This is low-profile stuff. It's not the type of crime that makes headlines, and it's certainly not the type city hall funds."

"Crime is crime, right, Inspector? No one is dying in petty theft or parking violations, but we enforce those laws, too. The break will come, we've just got to be ready for it."

"Uh-huh." Murphy opened a folder of Joe's reports. "Let me see if I've got this straight. Here are the forgeries you've found so far. An alabaster ointment jar, belonging to Newell St. John. Found November 14, but determined to be forged in Egypt decades ago. Canopic jars belonging to Thomas Sanderson, found on December 2. Forger at large. Horus statues at Rosenberg's Family Heirlooms, brought in December 7—but Escalante, who brought them to Rosenberg, also remains at large. Then there's a Book of the Dead papyrus belonging to Ray Moretti, found November 23, which he isn't willing to part with." He looked up. "Did I miss anything?"

"The oyster shell Wade Martin had when he was killed."

"Right." But Murphy's expression suggested he wasn't counting that. "Not your case."

"But did anyone follow up with Rosenberg to confirm Martin bought that from his shop?" Maybe it had been Connor, after all, since neither man had confessed ownership. "Maybe whoever bought it mentioned why they would spring for it. A piece like that seems like a conversation starter. Please tell me *someone's* looking into it. It doesn't have to be me."

"It better *not* be you, and that's an order." The inspector's jaw hardened. "What is the problem here? Do you not have enough work to keep you busy?"

Joe had plenty. He was interviewing suspects and witnesses for various crimes, starting missing-persons protocols, and doing all the paperwork that came with it.

"Did you ever engage with this art buyer, Daniel Bradford?"

Frustration boiled in Joe's gut. "Not yet. Aaron Tomkins, the art dealer, told me he'd given Bradford a message for me, but that may or may not have been the truth." His neck itched beneath his collar. Decades ago, the boys in blue would have gotten information through the persuasion of brute force. Joe wouldn't resort to those tactics. But he still burned over not being able to track Bradford.

Joe changed the subject. "Did you read my recent report about Peter Braun and Ray Moretti? There's a connection there. At least one of them is dirty, and it's only a matter of time before I find out who, what, and how."

When Murphy didn't contradict him, Joe kept going. "There's something about Moretti that isn't right. His record is abnormally spotless. No one's that clean."

Murphy snorted a laugh. "Last I checked, you can't arrest someone for a spotless background check. He's the victim of a forgery and chooses to hang on to the artifact anyway. He doesn't want to press charges."

"He doesn't want me to do my job. That's what it is. This guy, nobody crosses him. So why would he be okay with a forgery? Something's wrong. We need eyes on both Braun and Moretti." As of right now, he didn't have enough on either for a search warrant, which he needed if he was ever going to get convicting evidence.

"You're reaching, Caravello. Reaching hard." Murphy broke off the head of a gingerbread cookie and popped it in his mouth. "I know you'd hoped that hunting for forgers would lead you to big fish, top dogs in organized crime. That doesn't mean you get to conjure one out of thin air so you can arrest him."

"That's not what I'm doing. Read my report again."

Murphy glowered. "You telling me how to do my job, Detective?"

Joe's lips pressed into a thin line. He knew better than to answer that.

"As for putting man-hours into watching these two, you know as well as I do that we can't spare it until Manhattan dries up or Prohibition ends. I've got a mind to pull you off this wild goose hunt."

Joe knew this was coming. "I only spend a few hours a week on this." Which Murphy could see if he actually read the reports.

"All right." Murphy slapped the folder closed. "Listen, I agreed to let you work on this as long as it isn't a drain on police resources with nothing to show for it."

"Understood, sir. I will continue to be as careful with resources as ever. I'm committed to seeing this through."

Inspector Murphy leaned forward, lowered his voice. "I get it. You're committed. No one doubts that, least of all me. It's your strength, but it's also your weakness. You don't know when to let go."

Joe held his gaze without speaking. Outside, tires squealed, and car horns blared, followed by two men shouting.

A knock pulled Joe's attention toward the door, where Oscar McCormick held up one hand. "I'm sorry to interrupt, sirs, but this is urgent. Your phone kept ringing, Caravello, so I answered it. It was Mr. Rosenberg. He said Vincent Escalante will be at his shop in twenty minutes."

Joe stood, the chair scraping the floor in his haste. "Merry Christmas," he told Murphy, and scrammed.

Eighteen minutes later, Joe parked an unmarked police car outside Rosenberg Family Heirlooms. Right on time, a man got out of his truck half a block away and pulled a dolly from the bed. After stacking three crates onto it, he rolled it toward the shop. Rosenberg opened the door for him as he neared.

Another fifteen minutes passed before Escalante emerged, his dolly and crates rolling much lighter over the slushy sidewalk this time. Patiently, Joe waited for him to pack up his truck and drive away.

Judging by Escalante's unhurried pace and his proper use of turn signals, he had no idea he had a tail.

Escalante led Joe into the Bronx, to a brick townhouse with black iron railings flanking the cracked cement front steps. Islands of snow dotted the sidewalk. Joe parked the car and strolled up to Escalante, who was unloading the crates from the back of the truck.

"Need a hand with that?" Joe asked him.

Escalante glanced at him, then past him at the stairs leading to the front door. "Yeah, sure. These aren't heavy. They're just awkward, you know? Those broken steps aren't friendly to my dolly, either."

"I figured. Load me up."

Escalante stacked two empty crates in his arms. Taking the third crate himself, he led the way up the stairs and unlocked the door. "Come on in. Set them down on the floor over there, thanks."

"You sure? Where do they really go?" Joe brushed past him, bypassed the living room, and strode down a hallway until he found a room that smelled more like a workshop than a home, with hints of paint or varnish and plaster of paris. Bingo. "This looks right." He set the boxes down. The curtains were pulled shut, but daylight seeped between the cracks. "Vincent Escalante, right?"

The man's face darkened as he stood in the doorway. "Who are you?"

"We have a mutual friend in Mr. Rosenberg. You're Vincent Escalante, correct?" He picked up a copy of *National Geographic* from one of the tables. A golden coffin mask shone from the cover. "Says here that's your name. Pleased to meet you. Thanks for inviting me in." He dropped the magazine and walked farther into the space.

"Excuse me, but I'd like you to leave now."

"Detective Sergeant Joe Caravello, NYPD." He showed him his identification wallet, then pulled one of the fake deity statuettes from his pocket. "Recognize this?"

He barely looked at it. "Never seen it."

"You might want to reconsider lying to a cop, Vinnie. Mr. Rosenberg tells me you tried to sell this through his shop. Your asking price is a little high for a fake."

"That's not a fake!"

"Yeah? How can you tell, since you've never seen it before? Don't worry, I'll enlighten you." By now, he'd memorized Lauren's notes on the subject. "This Horus statuette from the eighteenth dynasty looks pretty good, but the weight of it tells me it's all wrong. This should be made of wood, which weighs less than plaster. If it were made of wood, it would be dark brown all the way through. It shouldn't show white when scratched on the bottom." He showed him the scratch. "This faint line here, though, that's just sloppy. It looks like a seam. Wood carvings don't have seams. You could have at least had the self-respect to file that down."

"You need a search warrant to be in here!"

"You let me in yourself, Vin. Anything I see in plain sight is fair game. Know what I see?" Joe clucked his tongue and shook his head. On the table was an exact replica of the Horus statuette he'd brought with him, except for the fact that the details hadn't been painted on. He picked it up, held it next to the one he'd brought.

Escalante's face grew redder, but he seemed to have lost his power of speech. And mobility.

Joe deposited the unfinished figure back onto a layer of newspaper, then spied the plaster mold that had been used to form it. He placed the Horus he'd brought with him into the mold and closed the two halves over it. A perfect fit. The seam Joe had pointed out earlier marked where the halves came together.

"See, Vinnie, where I come from, we call this proof."

"You can't prove anything." He folded his arms in a last-ditch effort to look defiant. Confident. It wasn't working.

On a shelf behind him, another Horus stood as if looking down upon the entire scene. Joe walked over to it and picked it up. This one felt lighter. It was made of wood. There were no seams along the edges. If this was the genuine artifact, Escalante was using it as a model for the fakes.

"Do you have a provenance for this?" Joe asked.

He made a break for the door.

Joe grabbed Escalante's arm and twisted it behind him. "I'll take that as a no. You're under arrest for forgery and possession of goods stolen from a foreign country. Don't add resisting arrest to your charges." Handcuffs clicked into place.

At last.

Merry Christmas, indeed.

CHAPTER

21

Unease threaded through Lauren as soon as she saw Dr. Breasted's return address poking out from the stack of mail. She'd asked him about the feud between her father and Theodore Clarke, but now she wasn't sure she wanted to know.

Oh, how she hated conflict. She hated to have her view of either man altered by what lay inside. As Joe would say, confrontation was not her style. But truth was, aside from Joe, there was no man she trusted more than James Breasted.

Steeling herself, she dropped onto the sofa, pulled a blanket over her lap, and dove in, skimming past the opening pleasantries until she reached the part she both dreaded and needed to read.

> When the tomb in KV 55 was discovered, both men claimed the credit. This type of argument was common between them. What was unusual, though, was that the clearing of the tomb was absolutely botched, and priceless treasures were the casualty.
>
> Right away, we all saw that the condition of the artifacts within was extremely fragile. A few hours after exposure to the air, the gold inscriptions and scenes on the shrine were falling to pieces. Gold leaf peeled away and lay in drifts on the floor. Every slight disturbance in the air made it worse. Flake by flake, the inscrip-

tions disappeared before our eyes. Someone sneezed in the tomb, and his handkerchief caught six pieces of ancient gold leaf. Think of it!

Theodore hired illustrators and photographers to document everything before any attempts were made to move them. But someone touched a wooden throne, and it instantly crumbled. The sarcophagus lid suffered the same fate.

Tempers ran hot. Theodore blamed Lawrence, and Lawrence blamed a dragoman, but none of the laborers had been allowed inside—a double force of guards saw to that. Theodore and I both saw bits of the ruined pieces on Lawrence's hands and clothes, suggesting his guilt, but he denied it. Theodore suffered damage to his reputation for gross negligence in the management of the tomb. He claims that was Lawrence's goal all along. Revenge, as it were, for taking credit for the discovery. But would any Egyptologist stoop so low? That, my dear, I cannot say. If that was Lawrence's plan, it surely backfired, for Theodore fired him. Your father had a dickens of a time convincing another team to work with him after Theodore's side of the story got out.

Lauren put the letter down, lifting her gaze to the Christmas tree in the corner of her apartment. She had no idea what to make of this. There had been no proof that Dad had destroyed the throne and sarcophagus, not really. Maybe he had been sifting through the rubble after it had shattered, looking for salvageable pieces.

Then again, could he simply have made a mistake by touching those artifacts and lied to spare himself humiliation?

Worse still, could years of bitterness really have driven him to do such a thing on purpose?

In any case, no wonder the two men couldn't stand each other. Mr. Clarke had been kind to Lauren at the Met for her mother's sake alone. Why?

Lauren blew out a frustrated sigh. She'd come to realize lately how little she really knew her parents. But since Dad had warned her against looking into this piece of his past, she wasn't about to bring it up to him.

Though the rest of Dr. Breasted's letter was far more pleasant, the knots in her middle barely loosened. She reached for the rest of the mail, unfolding a thin magazine that had been stuffed into their narrow mailbox.

Her breath hitched. *Napoleon Herald: News from the Napoleon Society.* Bordering the cover were Egyptian hieroglyphs, perfect translations of the title and subtitle. The masthead was written in a scrolly font with a classic French flair, followed by the names of the board members. Lawrence Westlake's name came before the others: Daniel DeVries, Evan Aldrich, and Luke Reston. Somehow, it gave her comfort to see Dad's name with three others. Clearly, they didn't mind working with him, despite the problems with Clarke.

Her attention caught on a teaser for her article listed on the cover. Lauren flipped the newsletter open to locate it.

Reading between the Lines: Mistakes in Hieroglyphs Prove Artifact a Fake. That wasn't the headline she'd submitted with the article, but she knew editors changed things like that. Then, in smaller italicized text below the headline, *First in a series of articles written by expert archaeologist and Egyptologist Lawrence A. Westlake.*

No.

Could he have written his own article and sent it in before she had? She skimmed the body of the text for her answer. This was her work, line for line. Her pulse picked up. Had it been a mistake? Her name and her father's were so similar, a copyeditor or proofreader might have changed it without realizing the error. After all, Lawrence Westlake was already a known name in the Napoleon Society. Lauren Westlake was not.

She might have been willing to believe this were it not for the boxed text at the end of the article. *Mr. Lawrence A. Westlake is a founding board member of the Napoleon Society with thirty years of excavation field work to his credit.* A few more lines finished a miniature version of his biography. There was his picture beside it.

This was no typographical error. This was her father stealing her article and claiming the credit for his own before he passed it on to the editor.

How could he?

Had this been his plan all along?

Suddenly everything Theodore Clarke believed about her father felt like it could be true.

Anger ripping through her, Lauren covered her face and groaned. Her thoughts were too hateful to entertain, but she couldn't silence them. What he wanted all along was to make himself look better. Maybe he hadn't recovered from the incident Dr. Breasted wrote about. Maybe that was why he was so desperate for the Napoleon Society to succeed. Was he truly only interested in her knowledge of Egyptology? And if so, was he only interested in it because of what it could do for him?

If she was honest with herself, she'd already known the answers to both questions could be yes. She'd tried to make her peace with that. But never had it occurred to her that her father would steal her work and pass it off as his own.

Cleo leapt onto the fireplace mantel and picked her way between evergreen branches, candlesticks, and picture frames until she came to the bright blue shabti figures her father had given Lauren for her birthday.

With one dainty paw, Cleo knocked over the two pieces, then delicately nudged the male figure closer and closer to the edge. Part of Lauren wanted to watch it fall, this symbol of her father. This symbol of their restored relationship. If it fell and broke to pieces, it wouldn't be her doing but his.

But she wasn't willing to sacrifice these beautiful antiquities just because her feelings were hurt. Rising, she crossed to the fireplace and picked Cleopatra up off the mantel. "Go on," she said, setting her on the floor again. "You're not supposed to be up there." Lauren scooped up the two shabti figures and deposited them on top of a bookcase she doubted Cleo could reach.

Turning back to the mantel, Lauren neared the black-and-white photograph Ivy had framed of her and her father, the one taken when she was five years old. Was she as naïve now as she had been in that picture? Was her longing for her father's approval as naked? Had it made her blind?

Embarrassed, she flipped the frame onto its face and walked to the telephone. She stared at it, searching for words that could possibly contain what she felt.

Though Mother had forgiven Dad at the end, she'd had problems with him for years. Aunt Beryl couldn't stand him. Neither could Mr. Clarke. Even Dr. Breasted had seen that he didn't work well with people.

They were on to something.

Lauren locked her arms over her waist. She was too agitated to sit but too stunned, it seemed, to move. In the end, it was the Christmas tree in the corner of the room that deflated her. She had taken more care than usual decorating it this year, knowing that she'd be hosting the holiday here with her father. She hadn't even minded Elsa's precise method of evenly spaced and color-coordinated ornaments because Lauren wanted it to be perfect. Magical.

The sparkle had gone.

Lauren slumped into the armchair. The only thing magical about this Christmas was the way the spell she'd been under had broken. However her father had enchanted her, it wouldn't happen again.

Her fingers were cold as she picked up the telephone and asked for her father's exchange.

"It's Lauren," she announced when he answered, her tone as flat as she felt. This wasn't like her. It had taken every ounce of starch she had to talk to him about her brothers. Burying hurts was what she did best. After all, she'd been practicing since she was a child.

But she was full to overflowing, at last.

"Is anything wrong?" he asked. "Has something happened?"

"You gave the byline for my article to yourself. That's what happened." She curled her fingers into a fist to warm them, then rubbed them on her skirt.

"What?"

"You know what I'm talking about. The *Napoleon Herald* hit mailboxes today."

"Wait a minute." The sound of shuffling papers suggested he was riffling through his mail. "Oh!" He dared to laugh. "That's what you're upset about?"

His attitude only stoked the fire that burned inside her. It flared and leapt, and for once, she gave vent to the pain. "Why wouldn't I be upset? You hounded me for weeks to prove myself to your board, and then you sabotaged my attempt in order to make yourself look better instead. Are you so insecure after that fire that you would do this?"

"Steady, Lauren. You're way off base. I had nothing to do with this."

"I should have known better than to pass my article to you instead of sending it directly to the editor myself."

"I hate to tell you this, sweetheart, but if you hadn't gone through me, the editor may never have even seen it in time for the printing. You have no idea how busy that man is—nor can you guess how disorganized."

"You used me."

"I told you, I never intended for this to happen. I'd never take from you what's rightfully yours. Don't you know me at all?"

"If I don't, there's only one person to blame for that, and it isn't me." Lauren squeezed her eyes shut and rolled her lips between her teeth to end her outburst. She was hurt. She was angry. But she didn't feel any better for lashing out.

His sigh came through the telephone, and she could picture him easing into a chair, pinching the bridge of his nose. She imagined the crimp of his lips, a mannerism that matched her own.

"Look," he said at last, weariness fraying his voice. "I'd much rather speak in person about this, and I'd like to clear the air between us before Christmas. But I've got to dash up to Newport in the morning, and it's going to be a push to make the last train home again."

Of course. Of course he was leaving again, never mind what day it was. Dad ran. That's what he did. Mother was right about that.

If Lauren's expectations hadn't already unraveled for this holiday, she'd be painfully disappointed that she'd be alone on Christmas Eve instead of sipping eggnog by the fire with Dad, reading aloud Dickens's *A Christmas Carol* or listening to Tchaikovsky on the Victrola. Something.

Anything.

Now she was only painfully resentful. Lauren considered that her reaction to this byline was out of proportion to the incident itself, that she ought to hear him out. But he was leaving town again, exactly when she needed him to stay. She wasn't reacting only to the byline, but to what Dr. Breasted had written, and what Mother had been through, and what she herself had excused for years. For all she knew, he could have been lying to her about Mother keeping him in the dark about her baby brother's birth.

"Don't bother catching the late train," she said. "I wouldn't want you to rush back. Take all the time you need."

"Are you telling me not to join you for Christmas?"

"Do whatever is best for you," she told him, "as usual. I've learned not to wait."

"If that's the way you want it . . ."

Of course that wasn't the way she wanted it! What she wanted was for her father to keep his word, to see past the sharp words she'd hurled at him, to see the hurting daughter behind them. She wanted him to insist on coming for Christmas, or to postpone his Christmas Eve errand, or to come over right now, since it was only six o'clock. She wanted him to prove that she was his priority, even when she was prickly as a porcupine.

Lauren hung up the phone and cradled her head in her hands. Skipping dinner, she waited for him to call back or to surprise her by arriving in person. He didn't make a move.

And since she was apparently as prideful as her father, neither did she.

CHAPTER

22

THURSDAY, DECEMBER 24, 1925

When Joe arrived at the Met just before four o'clock in the afternoon, it was empty except for the staff. It was Christmas Eve, after all, and most New Yorkers were hustling to make last-minute holiday preparations.

"Here to see Dr. Westlake?" the ticket salesperson asked as he approached. A small reproduction of a Rodin sculpture stood beside the register wearing nothing but a Santa hat.

"You got it." Joe showed her his badge, but she waved him through without looking at it. By now, most, if not all, of the Met staff knew who he was and why he came so often.

Enormous fir trees perfumed the Great Hall. Oversized ornaments and giant bows adorned the branches, along with a collection of art-themed ornaments that could be purchased at the sales desk. Red and gold carpets overhung the gallery balcony that embraced the space. Through saucer-shaped skylights, the lowering sun sent its final rays of the day.

Passing between the statuary, he made his way to the Egyptian gallery where Lauren had said she'd be. He paused when he saw her, unwilling to break her concentration. There was something beautiful about seeing her here, surrounded by the objects of her passion. But the scene also embodied a loneliness.

At the Oyster Bar earlier this month, when she'd told Joe that he was richer than she was, he hadn't been willing to accept that. But when he called her office today and learned what had happened with her father, along with what Dr. Breasted had written, he understood what she'd meant.

While his home was in a flurry, the kitchen steaming with every kind of food you'd want to savor on the most celebrated day of the year, Dr. Lauren Westlake was alone among the relics of an ancient civilization with zero plans with family herself.

It wasn't right.

She looked up from her clipboard and grinned. "Am I under surveillance?" she teased.

"Guilty." He smiled and closed the distance between them.

She reached out a hand to squeeze his. "Thank you for coming."

"You sounded like you could use some company." He glanced at the mummy in the glass case. "In the form of a living human being."

"Well, she's not much for conversation, that's true, but she's a really good listener, and I know she'll never leave when I'm counting on her to be there."

Joe wrapped an arm around her shoulders and kissed the top of her head. He could only imagine how painful it was to feel betrayed by what Lawrence had done so soon after she'd worked to restore that relationship. Not only had Lawrence taken the credit for her work, but this was the second holiday in thirty days that he'd planned to spend with her and then didn't.

Joe understood why that was hurtful.

He also realized that with his line of work, he might disappoint her in the same way. He wanted Lauren to be able to count on him, but he couldn't promise that he'd always be there for her, either. Not as long as he was on the force. And he wasn't ready to quit just so he could be home every night at five and make sure he never missed a holiday.

Had he made a mistake in kissing her? If he couldn't give her the reliability she craved, was he only toying with her heart? The idea hollowed out a space in his chest.

But surely this was not the time to bring it up. Not when she was already hurting. Instead, he said, "I'm sorry things turned out this way."

She rested her head on his shoulder and sighed. Then she stepped away from him and gave him a smile though her lashes were wet. "Enough self-pity. I admit that I pushed him away the second I felt him withdrawing. I hoped he'd protest the idea of spending Christmas apart, but he didn't. The biggest surprise is that I dared to hope for anything different. Apparently I'm not worth fighting for."

"Of course you are," Joe said. "If there is ever a time I can't be here for you, you have to know that it won't be my choice."

Her expression sobered. "I understand the nature of your job, Joe," she said quietly. "I know your schedule isn't always up to you. It's different."

He nodded, even as he wondered if the result would be the same. Lauren might say she understood, but would she grow resentful over time, as her mother had? Most wives would.

"Speaking of your job," she said, "how's it going, Detective? Any new developments to discuss?"

Joe unfastened the top two buttons of his coat and loosened the scarf about his neck. "Vincent Escalante admitted to forging the oyster shells, too. But we still don't know the identity of the forger for Mr. Sanderson's canopic jars or for Ray Moretti's papyrus. Nor have I been able to locate Daniel Bradford, to my everlasting vexation. Could the same person have forged all of these? Would you be able to tell by any trademark techniques, either in the forgeries themselves or in the provenance documents?"

Lauren tilted her head. "That's an interesting idea. For example, someone could tell if two portraits had been painted by Gilbert Stuart or by John Singer Sargent by looking at their technique. Even Mary Cassatt and Claude Monet have their differences, though both are impressionists."

Joe stuffed his hands in his pockets. "The trouble is that we're dealing with various mediums within the forgeries, and the forgers are not showcasing their own technique but doing their best to imitate someone else's."

"Artists have been making copies for millennia, especially artists whose original work failed to generate a sustaining income. Sometimes, for their own gratification, they paint or etch their initials onto copies they're particularly proud of. But it would be extremely well hidden."

Joe walked to the nearest bench and sat, leaning against the wall. "Did Peter Braun ever tell you he had artistic aspirations? And I'm not talking about painting from lantern slides on a rich person's dining room walls."

Lauren came and sat beside him. "Did he tell you that?"

"He did."

She crossed her ankles. "How sad. The more I learn about this man, the more sympathy I have for him. Though I know he'd never want that. If he turns out to be our forger, I can't say that I'll rejoice."

"That's because you want to see the good in people. You want them to succeed." It was an admirable trait. Ironically, Joe's work required the opposite: detecting the bad and holding people accountable for their failings.

"From what you know of him," Joe asked, "does he have the skill to create all the forgeries we've found that haven't been connected to Escalante?"

"I don't know. There haven't been many da Vincis and Michelangelos, who could excel in multiple arts." She drummed a finger on the clipboard. "But maybe we're not looking for a Michelangelo."

"How's that?"

She stood. "Come on, I'll show you."

Setting a brisk pace, Lauren crossed the gallery to a giant tomb made of massive limestone blocks. Joe read the sign posted outside it. "The Tomb of Perneb?" This hadn't been here when Lauren and he had visited the museum as kids.

"Actually, that label is a bit misleading, since Perneb's burial chamber remains in Egypt. What the Met bought from the Egyptian government in 1913 was simply some of the aboveground chambers of his tomb. This section, which took three years to put back together again here, contains the rooms that his family would have entered to pay him homage after he died." Lauren walked inside, and he followed her.

Suddenly, they were no longer in New York City on Christmas Eve, 1925. They were in ancient Egypt, more than two thousand five hundred years before Christ had even been born. Lauren described how Perneb's family would have used this space, and their beliefs about his spirit exiting through a false door and re-entering the land of the living.

"But the really wonderful thing for us and for those who view this tomb," she went on, "is that they didn't finish decorating it in time. Perneb must have died early, and they used it the way it was."

Joe must have missed something. "How is that wonderful?"

"Because we get to see the process they used. Look here." She pointed to the vignettes carved into the wall and painted. They were life-sized portrayals of Egyptians shopping at the market, carving meat at a butcher's stall, bringing platters of food and vegetables toward that mysterious false door.

"Now come back to the vestibule." Again, she led the way, confidence in her stride. "See? All we have here are etchings, the outlines the painters would have filled in. Look at this. Do you see these horizontal lines?" She pointed to four faint bars that had been drawn across the wall.

"The finished product was not the creation of one artist, or even one group of artists who worked on these relief murals from start to finish. The first group of workers came in and simply drew lines like these across the walls. They are at waist, knee, elbow, and shoulder levels. Ancient Egyptians loved uniformity."

"That's all that first group did?"

"Yes, then the second group came in with chisels and hammers and carved away the background, so the figures would stand out in relief."

"And the third group would come in and paint," he guessed. "Right?"

"Exactly. By the end, those lines drawn by the first group were either carved away or painted over. We've known this was their process for some time, but now we have proof of it."

Joe saw the connection to the forgery cases at once. "One person is great at carving. Another paints with flawless precision. Another can sculpt. But they all work together. Is that what you're thinking?"

"I could be wrong, but to me, this makes more sense than finding one single super artist."

Joe brought out his notebook and started scribbling. He ended by writing Daniel Bradford's name again and circling it. "Daniel Bradford was involved in the sale of Mr. Sanderson's fake canopic jars, and if he's sold forgeries to one person, chances are he's sold more. If there's a forgery ring, it would not surprise me to learn that he's involved."

Lauren glanced at her watch. "It's past closing time. Security will want us to leave soon."

He could tell the idea disheartened her. As soon as they stepped out of the tomb, she had to face the fact that she was about to spend Christmas alone.

At least as far as she knew.

Joe accompanied her to her office.

"I'll just be a moment." She squeezed his arm before stepping to her desk and shuffling papers and mail around. Then she stopped so abruptly that he came alongside her.

"What's wrong?"

She passed him the note she'd been reading. In blocky black letters, it read MIND YOUR OWN BUSINESS. It was unsigned.

Joe laid a hand on the small of her back. "Where did this come from? Is there an envelope?"

She passed one to him. There was no stamp or return address on it. The only text was Lauren's name, without even an address beneath it. Someone had gotten into the building and either tucked it into her mailbox or put it on her desk.

Joe asked himself who would want her to stop hunting forgeries. Newell St. John hadn't liked it, but his concerns had been addressed more than a month ago. But Ray Moretti still held on to a forged papyrus. "Did you keep the invitation to the Morettis' Christmas party?" He'd like to compare the handwriting.

"He wouldn't have sent this. The Morettis picked me up in their car and drove me to their house, basically insisting that I *not* mind my own business, remember?"

"Humor me."

Lauren bent over her desk, riffling through a stack of old mail until she handed him a card. The envelope was engraved with her work address. The invitation inside, however, included a handwritten note.

Dr. Westlake, it would be an honor to have you and a guest in my home. Beneath it, Ray Moretti had signed his name.

It was a lucky break to have a handwriting sample. But it didn't match Lauren's four-word note.

She had the grace not to say she'd told him so as she returned it to the desk.

"So we have no idea who sent you this mild threat that fails to specify a consequence," he muttered. When the Black Hand Society sent a note, the person on the receiving end was in no doubt as to what would happen if they didn't comply.

But any threat against Lauren, no matter how toothless, was one too many. There was no way he'd let her be home alone after this.

"I'll take this and have it analyzed at the station," he said. "Let's get out of here. It's time for Christmas, and you're not going home alone."

By the way Joe's parents greeted Lauren, she could have imagined she was a long-lost member of the family. This was far better than the Beresford.

Joe had brought her through the main entrance of the brownstone, but after only a glimpse at the sparkling spruce in the living room, he'd ushered her downstairs into a kitchen bubbling over with savory aromas, including salmon, lemon, and dill.

"December twenty-fourth is *giorno di magro* in the Italian tradition," Joe told her. "No meat. But plenty of pasta, seafood, and dessert."

Joe's mother turned at the sound of her son's voice. With a smile that wreathed her face, she stopped stirring the pot on the stove, brushed a wisp of grey hair from her face, and clasped Lauren's hands. Lauren felt years of labor in the calluses. This woman worked because she loved.

"Welcome to our home," Greta said.

"Thank you for allowing me to intrude at the last minute like this."

"You're not an intrusion, my dear. You are wanted. You are making our holiday special." She sounded like she meant it. From what Joe had told her on the way here, his brother held such a grudge against their father that he and his family didn't even visit for Christmas. It broke his parents' hearts.

Lauren's throat grew tight to think of it. She knew what it was to feel left behind.

Something boiled over, and Greta turned back to stir the pot.

"Ah, *bellissima*!" Sal Caravello kissed both her cheeks, Italian style, and asked if her language studies included his native tongue, too.

"Working on it." She slid Joe a glance and smiled. "So far all I know is *capisce* and *capisco*."

"A good start." Sal chuckled. "The rest you can figure out from our hands." He gestured broadly.

"She's a quick study, Pop." Joe turned to Lauren. "Speaking of hands, ready to get them dirty?"

Eager to participate, Lauren traded her coat for an apron. "How can I help?"

With patient guidance from Sal, Lauren sliced golden-brown bread, then topped each round with smoked salmon and a dollop of some kind of herbed cheese, adding a sprig of fresh dill and a few capers to each crostini. The assembly complete, she washed and dried dishes while the real cooks did what she couldn't.

She'd never been around anything like this. Sal and Greta worked together seamlessly, proof that they'd prepared thousands of meals over the course of their decades-long marriage. Joe, she noticed, took on the kinds of tasks that may have pained arthritic hands and wrists.

"You're in charge of seasoning," he told his mother. "No one can do it as well as you."

"We'll see about that," Sal countered. "An Italian feast calls for an Italian chef, after all."

Grinning, Joe winked at Lauren, his eyes red-rimmed and watering from all the onions he'd chopped for the pasta sauce.

Greta caught sight of her son's tearful face and joined her laughter to Lauren's. "Really, Joey," his mother said, "there's no need to cry. I'm sure your father won't ruin everything."

Sal guffawed and joined in the banter. Somehow even their teasing held their love for each other.

"Here now. Lauren will be the judge." Greta dipped a clean spoon into the simmering sauce and handed it to Lauren. Sal followed suit with a spoonful of his rival sauce.

"It's a tie," Lauren declared before tasting even one.

Above the laughter that followed, Joe said, "I told you she was smart."

Smiling, Lauren sampled the offerings, each one bursting with its own tantalizing flavors. "Don't change a thing," she said. "In either one."

After she'd plunged her hands back into the dishwater, Joe stepped beside her with a spoonful of something white and creamy.

"What is it?"

He smiled, his dark lashes still wet. "Extra mascarpone. From when we made tiramisu earlier. It has to chill before we eat it."

Lauren tasted it, closing her eyes with pleasure.

"Sweet enough?" Joe asked.

She looked at him and nodded. "It's just right. Everything here is just right."

When at last the evening meal was all but ready to serve, Joe turned to his mother.

"We've got it from here, Mama," Joe said. "Why don't you get yourself ready to enjoy the feast. We'll bring it out in twenty minutes."

Greta's flushed face glowed. "Thank you. Lauren, you come out of here, too. We've wrung enough work out of you for now."

Lauren smiled. "There's no place I'd rather be."

"The kitchen?" Greta dabbed her forehead with the end of her apron.

"With you," Lauren said, surprised at how strongly she meant it. "With all of you."

This was a family. This was a home. And they'd made her feel like it was hers.

"I'm glad you invited her." Pop inclined his head toward the swinging door that led to the dining room, where Mama and Lauren waited. The soft hum of their voices revealed they were deep in conversation.

"Me too," Joe said.

Pop nodded, as if satisfied that there was nothing more to say. He added the last of the salmon crostini to the platter and declared it was time to eat. As he carried out the appetizer, Joe's stomach clamored for all the courses that would follow: risotto, linguine, pan-fried swordfish, roast pumpkin with herbs, and sautéed spinach and mushrooms.

Joe entered the dining room behind his father and lit the candles placed about the room.

"I'm right on time, I see!" Doreen announced, pausing in the doorway. Joe pulled her chair out for her, then pushed it in as she sat.

Greta warmly welcomed her to the table. After introducing her to Lauren, she added, "Doreen sells flowers at Union Square. We have her to thank for the beautiful arrangements here and throughout the parlor."

"Beautiful, as always," Joe agreed, looking at Lauren as he took his seat across from her. Whatever his mother had said to her obviously put her at ease. Her blue eyes sparkled as she admired Doreen's handiwork. The candlelight burnished her brown hair to a coppery glow. Someone must have made a joke, because she laughed. It was a light, musical laugh, as if she hadn't received a threatening note—or an almost threatening one—at all.

But all he could think of was that if anything happened to her, it would be his fault for tangling her up in this forgery business. She hadn't asked to become involved. She could have said no.

Maybe she should have.

Lauren gave him a curious smile that made him realize he'd been staring. He shook himself from his reverie and looked again at the bottles used as vases for the holly. He frowned.

He had seen those bottles before.

The labels had been soaked off the glass, but if he wasn't mistaken, those bottles were an exact match for Ray Moretti's favorite drink. The wine he'd boasted of hoarding from France before Prohibition began almost six years ago.

Joe wondered why he hadn't noticed before now. More importantly, where had Doreen gotten so many?

Adding this to his mental list of questions to pursue later, he bowed his head in time for his father's blessing of the meal shared in honor of Christ's birth.

CHAPTER

23

Lauren insisted on returning to the apartment after dinner on Christmas Eve, despite the Caravellos' invitation to stay in one of the unoccupied boarding rooms. Cleo needed to be fed, after all.

"You can still change your mind." Joe stood by the door. "Now that Cleo's had her meal, you could bring a change of clothes and come back with me."

Lauren rinsed Cleo's water bowl, refilled it, and set it on the floor next to the cat's food dish. "Is this because of that note I found in my office today? It had no bite to it," she said. "I'm not afraid to be here alone. I didn't always have roommates. Besides, this building is secure, and whoever wrote that note is surely celebrating Christmas, too. If he's planning anything else, he'll wait until after the holidays."

Joe's expression remained taut, his lips a firm line. She wished she could wipe the concern from his brow.

"Your family has been nothing short of wonderful. I couldn't possibly feel more welcome with them, but I'd prefer to sleep in my own bed tonight. You can come and fetch me tomorrow if you don't like the idea of me taking a cab back to your place."

He pulled off his gloves. "Are you sure?"

Unstrapping the heels she'd worn to work that morning, she stepped into a pair of fuzzy slippers. "I'm sure. If my father calls—I know he probably won't—but if he does, I should be here to talk to him." It would be so much easier not to, but nothing would ever get resolved that way. "I hate this fresh divide between us, especially at Christmastime." Dad was wrong, but she'd overreacted and hadn't given him a chance to explain.

Apparently convinced she intended to stay, Joe removed his coat and crossed to the cold hearth to build a fire.

The Christmas tree began shaking, jingling the silver-bell ornaments, and Lauren hurried to pull the cat from where she was climbing through the branches. After tossing Cleo to the floor with a perfunctory scold that would certainly go unheeded, she padded to the sofa and sat.

After brushing bits of bark from his hands, Joe took the folded blanket and unfurled it over her. When he sat beside her, she arranged it over his knees, too.

"I see you've done some . . . redecorating." Joe nodded toward the mantel where she'd flipped over the framed photograph of her and her father, then toward the two small blue figures peeking out from the top of the bookcase. "I'm sorry your Christmas isn't what you expected."

Cleo jumped on the couch and walked across Joe's lap and onto Lauren's. She rested a hand on the cat's back. "Expectations can be overrated," she said. "I didn't expect to spend time with your family, and I enjoyed that so much. Thank you for that."

"You're more than welcome. All of us were happy to have you, and as soon as I get home, I'm sure they'll interrogate me about why I didn't extend an invitation sooner."

She smiled but sensed something was off. He'd seemed a little distant throughout the meal. "Is something bothering you, Joe? Aside from the note and the forger we haven't caught yet?"

He scratched Cleo between her ears. But a muscle flexed in his jaw.

That was a yes.

"Did I ever tell you what I really want for Christmas?" she asked. "Honesty."

"From your father?"

"Of course. But I'd welcome it from anyone else who's brave enough to be on the level with me." Lauren held his gaze. "So what's on your mind, straight shooter?"

His mouth twitched into a smile, then fell flat again. "Yeah, you're right." He rubbed the back of his neck. He was nervous.

That wasn't good.

"I care for you deeply," he began, in a way that sounded like a caveat would soon follow. "Which is why I'm so afraid of hurting you in the long-term."

Lauren frowned. She'd known him longer than any other man in her life, except for her father and Uncle Julian. She already cared for Joe long-term. They'd known each other for two decades, for goodness' sake. "Why would you say that?"

"Your father hurt you by not being there for you when you needed him. I see how rejected you feel, even now, when his work calls him away."

"That's different," Lauren inserted, already seeing where this was going.

"I've missed dinners, birthdays, and holidays, too. For as long as I'm a police detective, there's always a possibility that something will come up at the last minute and take precedence over a plan that's been on the calendar for weeks or months. I don't want to hurt you, Lauren, but given how important reliability is to you, it seems inevitable. I will cancel plans. As much as I want to be available any time, that's not going to happen."

Lauren wasn't stupid. She knew the realities of a detective's occupation meant his hours were irregular. "I understand that. I don't need or want you to be at my beck and call. I'm not a lovesick schoolgirl so infatuated that I can't function without you. I'm a working professional trying to get to Egypt. You and I are two independent people."

"Yes," he conceded. "But when you go to Egypt, that's your choice. What I'm worried about is when we're both in the same city, and you want me to be somewhere, and I disappoint you, like your father has. It will happen again and again."

If Lauren didn't know better, she'd think he was trying to wave her off. What she didn't know was whether it was for her sake or for his.

Dread quickened. "Have you changed your mind about me? Do you want to go back to being friends only?"

"No, that's not what this is. You own my heart, Lauren. I couldn't take it back if I wanted to. And I don't want to."

She studied his face, his earnestness a balm to her ragged nerves. "Then I still say that this is different from my father's absence when I was a young girl with a dying mother. I can take care of myself now, and I have my own work to keep me busy."

"And yet you're still upset when Lawrence's work interferes with your plans to spend time together." He paused, giving her time to deny it.

She didn't. She couldn't.

"You and I have seen a lot of each other these last couple of months," he went on. "Much of that has had to do with the cases you've been consulting on. There will come a time when you're not my consultant anymore, and I'll see you less than I've been seeing you lately."

"We don't need to figure all of this out right now, though, do we?" Lauren asked. It had been a long day. Weariness lay heavy upon her. "It's not like you've proposed—" it was far too premature even to mention the word *marriage*—"anything serious," she finished.

"I'm serious about what's important to me, and that means you." His eyes shone. "I don't play games. I play for keeps. This is on the level, like you asked. Think about it. If you decide that someone like me isn't good for someone like you, I expect you to be on the level with me about that, okay?"

"All right, Joe." Sobered, she rested her head against him and stared into the dancing fire behind the grate. "I'll think about it."

He wrapped an arm around her and pulled her close. "There's a reason many detectives don't have romantic attachments," he said quietly.

"But why shouldn't you have a chance at being as happy as anyone else?"

"It's not our own happiness we're thinking of."

"Your hero, Joe Petrosino," she said. "Didn't you say he was married?"

"After years of waiting, yes, he married the woman he loved. Her name was Adelina. She was a waitress at her father's restaurant, which accounts for how often he ate there."

"Why did he wait so long to marry her?"

"Because her father objected to the match. Adelina had already been widowed young. He didn't want her to marry a policeman who could die in the line of duty, making her a widow twice over."

A chill swept over Lauren. She twisted the fringe on the blanket's edge around her fingers. "But her father relented, deciding it was worth the risk?"

"He died. They basically married over his dead body, ten years after Petrosino first fell in love with her. For ten years, he went to her restaurant to see her, since they couldn't be together any other way."

"Oh my goodness," she whispered. "He never gave up on her."

"He didn't. But he also respected her father's wishes so much that he didn't push. He could have stolen kisses or persuaded her to defy her father, but he didn't. That's because he loved her, not because he didn't."

Lauren closed her eyes and sighed. "Joe Petrosino was far more romantic than Jay Gatsby," she murmured. She'd read the novel to see what all the fuss was about but couldn't understand the appeal.

"*The Great Gatsby*?" Joe scoffed. "Forget it. Gatsby tried to manipulate the girl of his dreams into leaving her husband and running away with him. It was completely selfish. There was nothing great about him."

A log crumbled in the fire, sending up a spray of sparks. Her face warm from the blaze, Lauren turned and focused on Joe instead.

Stubble shadowed his jaw. "True love takes no for an answer. True love respects the other person's decisions, even when it hurts."

She could smell the tiramisu on his breath. He was close enough to kiss her, but she knew he wouldn't. Not when he was still waiting on her to decide whether she could accept the consequences of his occupation.

Without explicitly stating them, Joe had made clear his intentions. Now Lauren needed to figure out hers.

———◯———

FRIDAY, DECEMBER 25, 1925

The Caravello living room looked nearly the same as it had every other Christmas in Joe's memory. But with Lauren here, included in the gift exchange that followed the early morning church service, everything was different. Instead of the nostalgia of Christmases past, he found himself wondering about the future. He'd given Lauren a lot to think about last night. So much that he wondered if she wished she hadn't asked for honesty after all. But he was doing them both a favor by telling her the truth sooner rather than later.

How she responded was up to her. Like Petrosino, he refused to persuade against her convictions.

But, oh, she wasn't making it easy on him. She'd always been beautiful, but interacting with his parents and Doreen—well, she was radiant. He'd figured she was most comfortable with rich folks. In mansions, hotels, galas. Now he realized with a pang that her natural place was with family. This was where she shined. With people to love and care for. With people who cared for her.

It wasn't right that she hadn't grown up with this. He thanked God for Elsa and Ivy in her life. But roommates weren't forever, unless all of them decided to remain unmarried—a highly unlikely scenario. Where would Lauren be when Elsa and Ivy moved on?

Another man could step in and sweep her off her feet. One who was steady and reliable. Lauren would be fine without Joe. If that's what she wanted.

"I'll take that." Lauren collected cast-off wrapping paper from Doreen and Sal, stuffing it into a paper bag.

When she came to Joe, he stopped her from stooping to pick up more trash. "As it happens," he told her, "honesty wasn't the only thing I got you for Christmas." He pulled a box from under the tree, took the bag from her, and placed the gift in her hands.

With a curious smile, she returned to the armchair and withdrew from the nest of tissue paper the items he'd purchased last week. A white scarf, long and wide. A broad-brimmed hat, lightweight but sturdy enough to protect from the sun. A long, tan linen duster.

She hugged it to her chest.

"What's this?" Mama asked, looking confused yet delighted. "Are you going motoring, my dear?"

Laughing, Lauren stood, pulled on the duster and buttoned it over her dress, and settled the hat on her hair. Then she wrapped the scarf over the hat and around her face so only her eyes were visible. Those shimmering blue eyes looked straight at him.

"No, Mama," Joe said. "Dr. Westlake is going to Egypt."

"Ah!" Pop clapped, and Mama and Doreen joined in. "Brava!"

Lauren laughed again, turned to show off her expedition fashion, then returned the scarf and hat to the box with more care than they deserved. "Someday," she said. "Maybe."

"One day," Joe countered. "For sure. You'll get there, Lauren. It's only a matter of time."

"Thank you." Reluctantly, it seemed, she unbuttoned the duster and took that off, too. "I have something for you, too." She pulled a card from her pocket and gave it to Joe.

With no idea what to expect, Joe opened it. Inside were four tickets to the Metropolitan Opera. The performance was *Die Walküre* by Wagner, for this upcoming spring. He looked up, holding the tickets aloft. "It's the opera," he said.

"It's for all of you," Lauren said, "if you'd like to go. It isn't Verdi's *La Traviata*, but I figured you might still like it."

She remembered.

"The opera," Pop said reverently. "Petrosino loved the opera."

"Wagner!" Mama added. "It's perfect, Lauren, but too generous!"

"Nonsense. It's been a long time coming."

Doreen looked between them all. "There's a story here, isn't there? Is it a secret?"

Joe chuckled. "No, it's no secret. I was fourteen years old, and full of admiration for police detective Joseph Petrosino. It was common knowledge that he loved the opera and Verdi and the Italian tenor Enrico Caruso. So when I learned that Caruso was the lead in *La Traviata* at the Metropolitan Opera, I hailed a cab and told the driver to take me to the Met. I ought to have been more specific in my directions. The driver took me to the other Met. The museum on Fifth Avenue. That's where I met Lauren for the first time." He smiled at her, remembering her as a precocious twelve-year-old child in need of his supervision. Or so he had believed. "Needless to say, I did not make it to the opera that day."

Or any other. Not long after, his family's financial situation began to crumble. He delivered flowers for Doreen when he wasn't in school, but any tips he made went to his parents, not to cultural events.

"Well, you can go now," Lauren said. "I hope you all enjoy it."

Pop pushed out of his chair, bent to Lauren, and kissed both her cheeks. "*Grazie*. We will." Straightening, he began belting out a few lines from *La Traviata*. He took Mama's hand, lifted her to her feet, and spun her around before pulling her near and dancing with her among discarded bows and wrapping paper.

Mama laughed, eyes glittering. She eventually pulled away from his overtures as though she weren't charmed. Pop kissed her hand before releasing her.

Lauren watched them with something akin to wonder. Joe figured her own parents had never freely displayed affection like that. And Beryl and Julian Reisner? Forget it.

"Ach." Mama shook her head in a mock scold that no one believed. "This is what I get for marrying an Italian," she teased.

"This Italian isn't done yet," Pop announced, presenting a gift to his wife.

She untied the green ribbon and lifted the lid, then withdrew a wooden carving of a horse and rider. The details were painted in bright colors. "It's lovely, dear. What is it?"

He pointed to the box. "There should be documentation inside to explain." But his patience clearly could not withstand her riffling through the tissue paper. "That right there is a genuine Egyptian antiquity. For months, you've been talking about how interested you are in Joe's work, and Dr. Westlake's, but that you don't have time to go to the Met and look at the displays the way you'd like to. So when the opportunity came for you to own one yourself, that you can enjoy every day, I couldn't pass it up. You are holding a piece of history, Greta, and it's all yours."

Joe's stomach dropped. How much had his father paid for that piece? And how was he so confident it was real? Joe didn't share details of his cases, but his parents knew what he and Lauren were trying to do. He glanced at Lauren, whose cautious smile hinted at similar misgivings.

Mama gasped. "It says here that this comes from either the fif- teenth or sixteenth dynasty." If she was half as suspicious as Joe was, she hid it well. On the other hand, maybe she really did find Egyptology fascinating. Maybe this was the best gift she didn't even know she wanted.

Doreen's eyes rounded. "How old does that make it?"

"Those dynasties lasted from 1640 BC until 1550 BC," Joe sup- plied. He'd studied the dynasties so much these last few months it shouldn't surprise anyone he had that memorized.

"That's right!" Mama said, holding a document aloft. It must be the provenance.

Joe extended a hand, and she passed it to him. "If I'd known you were so interested in this, I would have brought you a reproduction of Egyptian art from the Met's sales desk months ago," he said. "For paperweights, they have a little black cat wearing a gold-colored collar, an obelisk that represents the one behind the museum, and I don't know what else. There's also some watercolor prints of interior tomb paintings."

"Oh no," Pop said. "That's not the same, is it?"

For Pop's sake, Joe hoped it wasn't. "Where'd you get this, Pop?"

"Don't worry." His father sat straighter. "That right there came direct from Egypt, through none other than the Napoleon Society. I knew I could trust Dr. Westlake's father." He beamed at Lauren.

She looked almost as surprised as Joe was.

"I thought the Napoleon Society was in the business of collecting antiquities, not selling them—aside from those they auctioned off at the fundraising gala," he said.

"This opportunity is for members only."

"Members only," Joe repeated, hoping to jog his own memory.

"Sure," Pop said. "Doesn't the Met offer membership levels with different benefits?"

Lauren assured him that was so.

"There you go. So does the Napoleon Society. Wait a minute, I'll show you."

While Pop left the living room, Mama passed the artifact to Joe, who inspected it only briefly before handing it to Lauren. Then he passed her the provenance, too. She seemed to relax as she studied them both. Good.

"It's a beautiful piece," she said at last. She gave the carving and provenance back to Mama, who brought it to Doreen.

"And you work with this old stuff all the time," Doreen said to Lauren. "Isn't that something? Whatever I touch in my line of work is usually dead and in a refuse pile within ten days." The florist chuckled, and Joe smiled at her self-deprecating humor. He guessed that "this old stuff" didn't really excite her. How could it, when she was likely distracted by Connor's absence?

"Here it is." Pop returned, a brochure in one hand, a cup of coffee in the other. He set the steaming drink on the table beside Mama first, then opened the trifolded paper before passing it over. "Don't show your mother," he added quietly. "It's bad manners to know how much a gift cost."

Lauren joined him on the sofa, and he held it so she could read it, too. According to this, the cost of membership to the Napoleon Society included a bulleted list of benefits: a subscription to the *Napoleon Herald*; a year-long pass to the Napoleon House, to begin from its opening day, whenever that may be; a 10 percent discount on all gift shop purchases; and a handsome, engraved wallet-sized card identifying the bearer as a Napoleon Society member. Those who donated at the highest level also received through registered mail *a carefully packaged, fully authenticated piece of antiquity, complete with its provenance document. Each item comes direct from Luxor (formerly the ancient city of Thebes) or Cairo.*

"Sal." Mama's voice was thick with emotion. "It's an extravagant gift. I don't deserve it."

"Don't you? All right, let me check." He made a show of reading the brochure over Joe's shoulder. "Sorry, no refunds. I guess you'll have to keep it. It's about time you were indulged, anyway. I'd give you a roomful of this stuff if I could."

"How about a visit to the Met instead, or even a membership there?" Joe asked. "They already have fifteen rooms of 'this stuff,' and arranged quite nicely, too. I happen to know the curator. So do you."

"Assistant curator," Lauren corrected him, as he knew she would.

"In fact, Merry Christmas, everyone," Joe said. "I'm taking you all to the Met as soon as you'd like to go."

"And I'll show you around if you'd like to go after the meal," Lauren added. "We're open today from one until six."

"What are the pair of you trying to do, outshine me?" Pop teased.

Joe leaned forward and tapped Doreen on the knee. "Do you have any interest in the museum?" he asked quietly.

She smiled, but he felt it was more out of politeness than anything else. "Of course I do. But if I had to choose one place to go on Christmas Day . . ." She shrugged. "I'd rather go to the jail."

CHAPTER

24

Lauren's heart was as full as her belly by the time the delicious German Christmas feast was over. Afterward, she and Joe had cleaned the kitchen together while his parents and Doreen rested upstairs. It was there, while he washed dishes and she dried them, that they decided that Joe would take Doreen to see her nephew, and Lauren would play tour guide for Joe's parents at the Met.

"I'll miss being with you, but this is the right thing to do," he'd said, up to his elbows in dishwater. "I hope you aren't disappointed."

If this was a taste of how things would be with him, she savored its bittersweetness. Of course she would have enjoyed his company this afternoon, but doing the right thing was who he was, and she loved that about him. She wouldn't ask him to be less, even when that took him away from her.

Lauren stood on her tiptoes and kissed his cheek. "I'm happy to show your parents the Met."

And she was. Showing Sal and Greta Caravello around made everything seem fresh and new to her, even the objects she'd known for years.

As Lauren walked with them, matching her pace to accommodate theirs, memories called out to her. *This is where Joe found me that first time we met,* she could have told them when they came to the sarcophagus in the corridor outside the Egyptian rooms.

From there, Lauren led Sal and Greta to the Tomb of Perneb, and then to her favorite exhibits in some of the other rooms. "Here is a display of jewelry worn by a pharaoh's queen," she said.

And here was the spot where Lauren had first told Joe she was going to Egypt someday. *"Just wait and see,"* she'd added, though he'd not challenged her. *"My father is coming to get me, and he's going to take me with him. He said so."*

In the Great Hall full of statuary, Lauren found the sculpture that had made Joe blush.

In the Arms and Armor collection, she showed them the knight that had been Joe's favorite. This was where he had told her all that she'd missed since the previous Christmas while she was home in Chicago. He'd told her about the Black Hand Society, the way they were terrorizing families in Little Italy and beyond, and that Joe Petrosino was a real-life knight in shining armor, the only one willing to fight them.

And right there, in the shadows beneath the grand stairway that led to the second floor, was where Joe later told her everything had changed. He had stopped talking about Joe Petrosino. He had stopped talking about almost anything at all, except the art they looked at together. Not until the following Christmas break did he admit that his family had lost their restaurant.

In the gallery of old masters paintings, Lauren had told him that her mother died, that her father was still gone, and that she wasn't ever going home. Not ever. That this would be her home now. This was where Joe had first held her hand.

In taking his parents through the galleries, she was touring her past with their son. Years of recollections were housed in this enormous museum, and she knew exactly where to find them. Yet, like all great works of art, they still managed to take her by surprise.

As Joe's parents wandered through the period rooms of the American wing, Lauren realized she was making a new memory here even now. This was where she realized she loved him.

She lowered herself onto a bench between Federal period rooms, and Greta sat beside her while Sal continued to explore.

"This has been wonderful, dear." She sighed. "I don't think I can absorb a single thing more."

Lauren laughed. "The Met has that effect on people."

"Speaking of the Met, I can't believe you got us tickets to the opera and that you remembered Joe's near-obsession with Petrosino."

"We were talking about him last night, actually. Joe told me about the long wait for his wife."

"Ah yes," Greta murmured. "Poor Adelina. After they married at last, her husband told her to keep the shades drawn in their apartment so as not to provide a silhouette for an assassin to use as a target."

With a jolt, Lauren's image of their happily ever after began to tear at the edges. "Was that necessary?"

"He thought so, and I'm sure it didn't take long for her to agree with him. She was the one who brought in the mail each day. So she saw his death threats before he did. Petrosino told her he'd been getting those for years, though, and nothing had happened to him. Yet."

Lauren flinched at the three-letter word. She knew the detective had died by now, but didn't know the details. What had Joe left out of the love story he shared last night?

"I don't know if I want to know," she murmured. "But tell me anyway."

Greta took Lauren's hand. "Joseph Petrosino was assassinated by Mafia he'd had deported to Sicily. He had a newborn daughter. He and Adelina had been married for one year."

Lauren went cold with shock and sorrow for Adelina. "No," she whispered. "Not after ten years of waiting. Not after she'd already been widowed before."

Joe's side of the conversation from last night took on a new shape as she viewed it through this lens. He had to have been thinking about this unhappy ending. "Joe didn't tell me that," Lauren said.

"Petrosino's assassination shook him more deeply than he'd want to admit." She sighed. "When he talks of Petrosino now, especially when he talks to you, he's thinking about the widowed bride he left behind to raise their baby alone. And when he's thinking of Adelina, my dear, he's thinking of you. He doesn't want her fate for you."

Tears stung her eyelids. She'd been blind not to see the full extent of what he'd meant when he'd told her he couldn't be there for her whenever she'd want him to be. All Lauren saw was a man who cared for her, might even love her, and simply had her best interests at heart. She didn't want to consider that her best interests, according to Joe, might not include him.

"Here." Greta fished a scallop-edged handkerchief from her purse and pressed it into Lauren's palm. "I didn't mean to make you cry on Christmas, dear. These are risks we don't like to think about, let alone speak of."

"I needed to hear it, though." Lauren dabbed the soft linen beneath her eyes.

Families in holiday finery shuffled past. Men in suits, women in dresses, boys in suspenders and bow ties, and girls with ribbons streaming from their hair like Clara from *The Nutcracker* ballet. When Lauren spotted Sal ambling back their way, she stood. *There is the Haverhill Room*, she thought, *and there the Baltimore. And there is the bench where I learned Joe feared that I might one day become his widow.*

Joe focused on the road as he drove Doreen to the jail to visit Connor. With the snow turning to freezing rain, he drove slower than usual over the slippery streets.

His mind, however, raced. "I never noticed those bottles you used as vases before last night," he said. "They're all the same brand, aren't they? They looked familiar, but I didn't see a label."

"Oh, I soak the labels off before using them. I know some folks like to leave them on as part of the decoration, but I find them distracting. The focal point should be the flowers or foliage, not the vessel that holds them."

He squinted through the windshield. "Do you remember what the label said?"

"It was something French. The writing was so scrolly I could barely read it, to tell you the truth. But I do remember a picture of a château above the name."

So far, she was describing the same wine Ray Moretti favored. Moretti and most likely countless others.

"Why do you ask?" she inquired.

"I think I've seen that bottle before," he admitted, "and if I could identify it, it may be a clue in a case." How that clue would help him, he had no idea yet.

"Oh! Well, why didn't you say so? If it's the label you want, I have more. Those bottles are better than the average bud vase because the broader base is sturdier. I have crates and crates of them."

Joe hazarded a glance at her, schooling his face to conceal his shock. The cost of one of those bottles—at least, when it was full of the wine—was easily a month's wages. That was before Prohibition. Now it was four times that cost. A single crate holding a dozen of those bottles would be worth four years of his salary.

"That's a lot of bottles," he said. "How did you come by them?"

A sigh lifted and released Doreen's shoulders. "Connor. He was so sweet to think of me. He knew I was always looking for special vases like that, and it certainly cuts down on my overhead expenses if I can get them at a discount. Or in this case, for free."

Joe gripped the steering wheel tighter. "Did he say where he got them?"

"Sure, I asked him the same thing, I did. He told me the bottles had all been confiscated due to the Eighteenth Amendment. Something about the Folstead Act, I think he said."

"Volstead," he corrected her.

Bottles like these would have been confiscated, all right. But Joe wouldn't have been at all surprised if they'd been emptied into some thirsty gullets instead of into the gutter. At least they weren't taking up storage space at a cost to the city. Last Joe had checked, more than $7 million worth of confiscated liquor was being stored at a cost of $20,000 per month.

Connor had never mentioned finding a cache of this wine. "Did Connor give you all the bottles at once? Or was it spread out over several weeks or months?"

"Oh, it wasn't all at once. I would say a crate or two a month."

Joe slowed the car to make a turn, then fractionally increased the speed again. "For how many months? Do you remember when it started and ended?"

"Let's see." She looked out the window again, talking quietly to herself as she sorted it out. "Started over two years ago, but at that time, it was only a few bottles a month, not a case. Then he found more, until it was two cases' worth, consistently, right up until a month or two before he was arrested."

That was hundreds of bottles. "This is really helpful," he told her. "Were the bottles always empty when he gave them to you?"

She didn't respond right away. "Now that you mention it, there was one time when I'd come to visit him in his apartment, and I saw a bottle on his table. There was no cork in it, so I assumed it was empty like all the rest, and he had set it out to give it to me. So I picked it up, but it was still halfway full."

"Was there a glass nearby?"

She shook her head. "No, he wasn't drinking it. He said he was in the process of dumping it down the sink when I knocked on the door, interrupting him."

That was one possibility.

The other was that Connor had been drinking straight from the bottle. He was no teetotaler.

"So did he finish dumping it down the sink then?" he asked her.

"I did it for him," she said. "I was the one holding it at that point, after all."

Oh, what Joe wouldn't give to have seen the look on Connor's face at that moment. "Did he seem upset that evening?"

"Something was bothering him, sure and certain, but isn't that always the case with you boys? Can't talk about work, even when it's written across your face."

Joe forced a smile. "Did you notice anything else unusual about the visit?"

"No. He was out of sorts, but I'd seen him like that before. He asked me to let him know next time I planned to visit so he could tidy up the place. But I never cared about that anyway, and I told him so."

"I bet he insisted."

Doreen chuckled. "He did at that. You know him well."

Not nearly as well as he'd thought.

"He'll be pleased to have some company tonight," she said. "I'm sure he'll want to see you, too."

"Actually, I'm just your chauffeur tonight, Doreen. I'd like to visit, but I've been instructed not to. The investigation is ongoing, and since it's not my case, I'm not to have contact with him."

"But you visited with him on Thanksgiving. . . . Oh. Did you get into trouble for that?"

"Slap on the wrist," he told her. "Nothing to worry about."

"Oh dear," she murmured. "We don't want that, now, do we? I'll pass along your greetings to him, shall I?"

By the time the visit was over and they were on their way home again, it was clear Doreen had passed along more than that. Her cheeks were flushed, and her hands shook as she clutched her purse.

"I don't understand it." Her voice warbled. "I upset him, Joe. If you'd only seen his face right before he stormed out."

Joe checked his mirrors, then glanced at the woman before slowly pulling back onto the main road. "He cut the visit short?"

"By half, I'd say!" she cried. "Every minute with him is precious, and he gave up half our time together. I'm sorry, Joe, but he's upset with you, too. More so than with me, or so he says. It was the bottles that set him off. I never would have guessed. All I said was that I'd been using those bottles he'd given me to decorate your family's home for Christmas, and how lovely they looked."

"That made him angry?"

"It made him on edge. What made it worse was when I told him you and I talked about those bottles for a good bit of the drive out here. Believe you me, I had no idea if it was to be a secret. Empty bottles used as vases! What could be more mundane than that?"

The hair rose on the back of Joe's neck. "Do you remember what he said exactly?"

"I'd be surprised if I ever forgot it. He slammed his palm on the counter and yelled, 'It's none of his business. If he knows what's good for him and you both, and for everyone he loves, he will leave it the fudge alone.' Only he didn't say 'fudge.' Swore like the drunk his father was, when he knows I don't abide that filthy talk. I do wonder now if he was trying to drive me away, knowing that I'd not stay and hear more. But he took that choice away from me when he stalked off."

Joe saw it in his mind as she described it. The flaring temper, the outburst, the red-faced cursing. Thing was, Connor only swore when he was scared. It was bravado, a last-ditch attempt to persuade when he didn't trust his reasoning to carry the argument.

"Did you know the subject would upset him so?" Doreen asked.

Shaking his head, he kept his hands steady on the wheel. "I never heard about those bottles until tonight."

CHAPTER

25

MONDAY, DECEMBER 28, 1925

D r. Westlake!"
    On the steps of the Metropolitan Museum of Art, Lauren
turned to find Daniel DeVries looking as though he were being
chased. A stab of alarm shot through her.

"Good grief, Dr. DeVries, is everything all right?" With a clutch
of dread, she added, "Have you heard from my father?"

"Yes." He'd caught up to her now, slightly out of breath. "Let's
go inside."

She hastened to lead him downstairs and into her office. If something had happened to him . . . She shuddered as their most recent
conversation played in her mind. She prayed it wouldn't be their last.

"Is he hurt?" she asked, hanging her hat and coat on the tree
behind her door.

"No." Dr. DeVries took the chair across from her desk and set
his hat on his knee. "At least, not physically. He called and told me
about the dreadful mistake in the newsletter. I'm here to accept all
blame. Your father is guiltless."

She blinked in surprise, then sat in her own chair. "When did
you speak with him? I've been calling his apartment, but no one has
answered. I expected he'd be back from Newport by now."

"He sent a telegram, which I only received late last night, since

I've been out of town myself. Apparently he's in Newport for the next few days, but the phone lines at the Napoleon House are down. Or being replaced or some such." He threw up his hands. "If it's not one thing, it's another. At least the roof has been fully replaced."

"Already?"

"A miracle, I know. Now I beg for another one: your forgiveness. The article's attribution is entirely my fault. Well, my secretary's fault, but as I am his supervisor, I should have caught the mistake before it went to print. Your father submitted the article with its proper byline. He even wrote up a short bio for you on a separate piece of paper and paper clipped it to the manuscript. Unfortunately, somehow that bio became separated from your article submission, and when my secretary scanned the name 'Dr. Lauren Westlake' at the top, he simply assumed your father had written it. You must admit it's an easy mistake to make, however unfortunate. A correction is already planned for the next issue. Beyond that, what else can I do to assure you we meant no harm? And that your father, in particular, ought to be exonerated?"

Shock and regret rolled over her in waves. "I don't know what to say." Every word she'd spewed at her father came back to her. It hadn't been his fault at all. But influenced by the story in Dr. Breasted's letter—on a subject Dad had ordered her not to pursue—she'd assumed he was guilty. She was wrong. They both ran this time, away from each other.

"I could drag my secretary in here to corroborate my story."

"No, that's all right," she mumbled. "I'm glad you came. I—I see how the mistake could have happened. Thank you for running the correction."

"Dare I hope this hasn't ended your series for us, which has only just begun?"

Lauren's mind spun. "I'll submit more articles," she said in a daze.

"Wonderful." He leaned back in his chair, exhaling through a grin. "What a relief. By the way, Agnes and I would like to invite you and your father to join us at the Hotel Astor for a late dinner on New

Year's Eve. We could stay until midnight for a rooftop-view of the ball dropping from the Times Tower."

Lauren stood. "Yes, Dr. DeVries. Count on it." For this one holiday, she and her father would be together. She pulled on her hat. "And now if you'll excuse me, I have a train to catch."

———

That afternoon, Lauren was in Newport, knocking on the door of the Napoleon House. She'd talked to Mr. Robinson about taking time off and had called Joe to tell him her plans. She'd also asked a neighbor to feed Cleo, since her roommates were still gone. Now all she had to do was fix the mess she'd made of things with her father.

She knocked harder.

The door opened, and Dad's eyes went wide.

"Dad," she said and could not go on.

With a watery smile, he enveloped her in an embrace. She could not remember the last time he'd hugged her. She shook with silent sobs as she wrapped her arms around his middle. "I'm sorry," she said. "Dr. DeVries told me everything this morning. Forgive me," she begged. "Please, please forgive me. I said such horrible things to you. I should have let you try to explain. I should have—"

"Shh. There, there." He patted her on the back as though she were still a child, when in reality, with these heels, she was taller than he was. "All is forgiven." Standing back, he glanced at the valise and hamper she'd dropped on the porch. "You're staying the night?"

"If you'll have me."

"Nothing would please me more." His thin hair was disheveled, his clothes rumpled. He looked old, a bit fragile, but entirely relieved.

She felt the same.

That night, instead of going into town for dinner, they ate from the hamper a meal of bread, cheese, grapes, and prosciutto. Since the dining room of the old house had been turned into a gallery, Lawrence took a blanket from the cot in his office and spread it on the floor. With candles and firelight instead of the chandelier, it felt like a winter picnic. A cold dinner had never tasted so sweet.

"I'll never do that again, Dad," she said above the popping fire. "I'll never assume the worst of your intentions." This was the third time she'd done that since her birthday.

"I appreciate that. I'll try harder to convince you of the truth next time you're . . . misguided."

She wasn't just misguided, she was wrong. "Here, I have something for you." It was a peace offering, a Christmas gift, and a gesture of good faith, all in one. Pulling her valise closer, she unlatched the buckle and withdrew another article for the *Napoleon Herald*, this one about the plaster statues of Horus that Vincent Escalante molded and painted to look like wooden carvings.

Lawrence accepted it with a smile that seemed to relax his entire body. "You could have submitted this directly to Dr. DeVries this morning when you saw him. He's the editor, and the one all submissions go to."

"I wanted to give it to you." Surely it wasn't lost on him that this was an act of trust. "The byline mistake wasn't your fault. I see no need to circumvent you. Besides, you may want to recommend some corrections to this draft before passing it along anyway."

Tipping the paper toward the candlelight, he read, his thin lips slanted. "Are you open to a bit of constructive criticism, dear?"

"If I've made a mistake, by all means, I'd like to correct it."

"You're not wrong. It's just that here you state that a forged carving made from plaster would be easily discovered if it is scratched or if it chips or breaks."

That was true. "A scratch, chip, or break would show the integrity of the piece inside. Plaster will be white. If a piece is truly wooden, it won't be as fragile anyway."

A deep laugh rumbled in her father's chest, and she nearly forgot that she was the one with a PhD in Egyptology. "Yes, darling, but can you imagine what a suspicious reader will do with this line? They'll take it as a suggestion that they ought to take their antiquity and bang it against the wall to see what color it is inside."

"Surely your readers are more discerning than that."

"You'd be surprised. I predict that at least a handful of our sub-scribers will misconstrue your words and end up damaging genuine antiques. Then we could have a lawsuit on our hands, and even if the Napoleon Society would win, we can't afford the legal fees." He gestured to the surrounding darkness as if she needed a reminder that restoring the house into a museum was costing them enough. "So let's avoid all of that by simply omitting that line. Leave the focus on signs that are easier to detect, such as these seams you talk about, a result of anything being molded rather than carved."

She agreed to his suggestion. "Those seams are such a telltale sign. It's amazing the clues people miss."

"It's not so amazing when you think about it," Dad said. "People see what they want to see. If they believe a piece is real, they won't even think to look for things like that. That's why your articles are so important."

Quiet settled into the space around them as they exchanged stories of how they'd spent their holiday. "You'll never guess what Joe's father gave his mother for Christmas," she said at length. "A wooden carving of a horse and rider from his new Napoleon Society membership."

"Is that right? And was she pleased?" Dad layered another slice of prosciutto atop a thick wedge of bread and cheese.

"Oh, very." Lauren described the scene and told him about the tour of the Met that followed their Christmas dinner. "Sal and Greta said it was their best Christmas in many years."

With a deep breath, she told him about Joe's gift to her. "Now all I need are dark glasses and the right shoes."

"Our expedition leaves in September," he said. "You'll ask for the time off soon?"

That seemed premature. "Not before my participation is ap-proved by the board."

"I have no doubt it will be."

Familiar resistance stirred in Lauren, a form of self-protection, she supposed, against having her hopes raised and dashed again.

Why else would she not share Dad's excitement? Why else would she not be moved by the anticipation of a lifelong dream coming true?

Logs shifted in the fireplace. Flames bobbed and nodded, then began to gutter. Lauren rose and crossed to the hearth, added more wood, then watched to make sure the fire caught. The house was beautiful, but with these high ceilings, a challenge to keep warm. No wonder the previous owners mostly used it in the summer.

"We do have central heating installed now," Lawrence told her, "but I can't justify heating the entire mansion when I'm the only one here. Or even when it's just the two of us. You don't mind, do you? It's like we're camping."

She held her hands to the warmth of the gathering flames. "I don't mind it."

"Do you remember the last time we spent a night under the same roof?" he asked from where he remained seated on the floor.

"I've been trying to recall that very thing," she told him.

"August 27, 1907. You were fourteen years old, and so desperate for my stories you insisted on staying up all night long to hear them over again."

Ah yes. But Lauren remembered it differently. It wasn't his stories she was desperate for but him. "You caught the train to New York the next day. You were leaving for Egypt again."

"That's right. I didn't mind staying up with you, though. I could sleep on the train. I'm sure I did."

Lauren, however, had fallen asleep in school three times the next day. It had been worth it for those extra hours with her father. But she did wonder now how Mother must have felt, lying alone in their bed. Had she waited for him to come to her for their last night together before another months-long separation? How many hours passed before she realized he wasn't coming? Had she cried herself to sleep?

Had she been jealous of the time Lauren had taken with Lawrence? Angry?

I'm losing both of you, Mother had written in one of her letters. Guilt needled Lauren for keeping Dad's attention all for herself.

"Clarke needed me." The irony of Lawrence's statement jarred Lauren. If anyone had needed him, it hadn't been Theodore Clarke.

"I thought you didn't want to talk about him," she said quietly.

"You need to know this about Clarke. He styled himself a great archaeologist, but what was his background? Banking. Finance. He knew nothing about excavation. If I hadn't guided his decisions, he never would have dug where he did in the Valley of the Kings. He never would have made those landmark discoveries that made him famous."

The first time Lauren had heard this story, she'd believed him. But Clarke's pioneering methods had been famous for decades. She'd learned in graduate school that he was the one who'd made a grid of the Valley and hired men to systematically work through it, long before Howard Carter picked up where Clarke had left off, famously discovering King Tut's tomb.

She crossed her arms and stared vacantly at the fire. Sparks lifted from the flames, flying erratically before turning to ash. The floor-to-ceiling windows on either side of the fireplace were bare of any coverings. Angled as they were, Lauren caught her reflection as she stood there, centered in the tall pane. Then a spark appeared at her shoulder, and she slapped at it before realizing the orange glow came from outside.

Strange.

"Do you have neighbors, Dad?" she asked. "I saw a light outside, maybe a cigarette being lit. I thought we were quite secluded in this location, but is there a gazebo or house out there that I can't see?"

He sucked in a breath. "Come away from the windows," he said.

CHAPTER 26

TUESDAY, DECEMBER 29, 1925

Nine o'clock in the morning found Joe in the gymnasium for the daily lineup. One by one, those who had been arrested in the previous twenty-four hours were led onto a stage at one end of the room. Daniel Bradford was not among them. Joe had been watching for someone matching the art dealer's description.

Most of the men brought into headquarters were between nineteen and twenty-six years of age. Three-quarters of them were drug addicts. Joe and the rest of the detectives wore masks during daily lineups, so they could get close enough to question the suspects without risking being recognized on the street by these men later.

Notebook in hand, he observed the accused. From the stage, they'd go directly to the photographer's studio, so at least he didn't need to record every physical detail. Instead, he wrote their numbers and the charges levied against them, their expressions and demeanor.

An elbow knocked his ribs. Joe frowned at the offender.

"Sorry." Oscar McCormick's voice was muffled by his mask. He tucked in both elbows and continued scribbling.

Joe moved closer to the stage and focused on the next suspect, a part-time waiter picked up in another raid last night, this one a high-class club catering to the very rich, not just flappers and two-bit floozies. Joe still considered raids an ineffective long-term strategy but had started participating again, as much to keep an eye on his own fellow officers as to enforce Prohibition. Last night, he was glad he did. Among the bottles left behind were some that matched Doreen's and Ray Moretti's.

He stepped up to the rope holding the detectives apart from the stage and named the French wine in question. "Where else is that wine sold?"

"I have no idea. I just serve the food, trying to pay my way through college."

"Who supplied the wine to the club?"

The handcuffed young man shook his head. "I told you, I wait tables. How would I know?"

"Have you seen it in the personal possession of anyone? Or is it just in clubs and speakeasies?"

"That's pricey stuff. Only a few regular customers bought bottles to take home with them."

The detective beside Joe stared at him. "Is the wine on trial? Come on, buddy. Don't drag this out."

"Do you know Ray Moretti?" Joe asked. "Was he one of the customers to purchase that wine?"

"Never heard of him."

Figured.

The waiter left the stage as another suspect took his place. It wasn't worth the cost to incarcerate him. The ones who were worth it hardly ever got caught.

After the lineup, Joe tossed his mask into his desk drawer but didn't bother refilling his mug. The coffee this morning had been too weak to deserve its name, but he had enough adrenaline to keep him going the rest of the day. Most energizing—even four days after the revelation—was that Connor had been feeding empty bottles of confiscated wine to Doreen. He had zero plans to leave it alone, as Connor had so hotly commanded.

Questions fired. The notebook he held was full of them long before this morning's lineup began.

Why can't I find a record of that many bottles of wine being confiscated over the last few years?

Was that half-full bottle Doreen caught him with an anomaly, or had Connor collected them full of wine?

If the latter is true, how could he afford it?

If he couldn't afford it, what had he done for the trade?

How did he get them if not through normal confiscation process as he had claimed?

Obviously, Ray Moretti wasn't the only person in Manhattan who favored that wine, but he was more likely than the waiter to know where to get it—without going to France.

Considering how Murphy had responded the last time Joe had brought him a clue related to Connor Boyle, Joe hadn't shared this bit during their meeting earlier this morning. Neither would he confide in just anyone on the force, given the thirsty nature of New York's finest. Who knew if others were in on this? After all, if those bottles really had been confiscated, it could have been a clerk who had made those records disappear. Joe had taken a risk as it was by questioning the waiter in front of the entire detective bureau. He had banked on them not paying much attention. Bigger fish had been arrested last night, too, suspected of violent crimes, petty theft, and drugs.

Which meant there was plenty for Joe to do without this bottle mystery. Still, he couldn't ignore it.

An incessant, repetitive noise from several feet away drew a snap of irritation. "McCormick," Joe said.

The young man jerked his head up, eyes wide, and dropped the pencil he'd been tapping. "Sorry. Habit."

Joe beckoned him over, and McCormick obeyed.

"Pull up a chair."

McCormick did as he was told. It was almost embarrassing how eager he was to please Joe, especially after the way Joe had been treating him. He'd been unfair to the new hire. Perhaps he could make up for that. "A while ago, you started to ask me about something strange you'd found. I brushed you off and had to chase a lead. Did you ever tell anyone else what you found?"

"Oh." He pushed a hand through his hair. "Yes, sir, I did. I told the Property Room clerk since I figured I was reading the records wrong. He said he'd take care of it, and that I didn't need to concern myself any further."

"That's good." Joe sounded about as convinced as he felt, which was not at all. "Well, now you've got me curious. What was that all about?"

McCormick shifted in the chair. No, he squirmed. "It's probably nothing."

Right. "If it's nothing, then there's no harm in explaining it to me, is there?" When he didn't respond, Joe tried a different tack. "I get the feeling he told you to keep whatever you found to yourself. If he made a mistake, maybe he's scared of getting in trouble. Losing his job, even. But here's a free tip. Your job isn't to look out for his. Your job, at the moment, is to answer my questions. *Capisce?*"

A small smile edged the young man's lips. "*Capisce.*"

Joe didn't bother correcting him. By now, other policemen had noticed their little meeting. Maybe they were listening, too. "Let's take a walk."

Outside, both men turned up their collars as they descended the steps from the police headquarters. After heading south on Centre, they turned east on Grand.

Whipping in from the west, damp wind carried the smell of the Hudson. The cold seeped through clothes and soaked into bones.

"How far are we going?" the kid asked.

"Not far." Joe wasn't hungry for lunch, but he always had room for cannoli.

As they approached Mulberry, Joe pointed north, toward Kenmare. "You ever hear about the Bootleggers Curb Exchange?"

Crossing the street, McCormick looked at the corner Joe indicated. "Is that where it was? Two blocks from police headquarters?"

Joe nodded. "In the early days of Prohibition, speakeasy owners and illicit alcohol distributors gathered right there, buying cases of rum and beer off trucks right in the street." He jerked his thumb toward the opposite end of Mulberry. "At 121, they would gather to discuss and plan alcohol sales."

"Wasn't there a big raid on that place three years ago?" McCormick asked.

"There was. Police found thousands of liquor bottles and barrels of rum. Thousands."

"They should have known better than to operate so close to headquarters. Right?" McCormick added, as if suddenly unsure of himself. Perhaps he'd realized that the bootleggers *did* know what they were doing in choosing such locations.

"A lot of cops were on the take to protect them," Joe said. "Looked the other way, but with open palms ready to be filled with cash."

McCormick's face shadowed. "Not you, though. You never took a dime."

"You sure about that?"

The younger man's brow furrowed, and he slowed his steps to a halt, standing in a spread of slush.

Joe decided to put him out of his misery. Smiling, he elbowed McCormick. "You're right."

"I knew it." McCormick relaxed again and resumed his stride. "I've been wondering if your moral compass rubbed off on Boyle."

"How do you mean?"

McCormick stuffed his fists deeper into his pockets, dipping his chin into the folds of his scarf. "From what I know of you, your moral compass has a true north, and his seems relative to his environment and the attitudes of those around him."

That was more articulate than Joe had been expecting. "Based on what? You never had a chance to meet him, did you?"

"Let's just say I've rubbed shoulders with those who knew him pretty well. I'd heard about that tunnel running from below HQ to Callahan's across the street so police could get their drinks without being seen entering through the front doors. I had to check it out myself."

"I bet you did." Joe squinted into the wind. "I've got a nice lecture ready to launch at you right now, McCormick, about the pitfalls of keeping the wrong kind of company. Anyone who flouts the law, especially cops who do, are the wrong kind of company. Disagreeing with the law doesn't give them license to—" Joe stopped himself before he delivered the entire speech. "I'm guessing you know the rest. So tell me. What did you learn about Connor at Callahan's? Was he a regular customer before his arrest?"

"Apparently he was, but two years ago, he stopped going completely. I figured it was your good influence on him that made him stop."

"Well, it would be news to me." Whatever good influence he'd had was obviously not enough.

Joe opened the door to Ferrara's, and warm air rushed to greet them as they stepped inside. Ferrara's smelled of sugar and yeast, and the best coffee in Little Italy. For generations, the Caravellos had loved this place. So had Petrosino, and the Italian tenor Enrico Caruso. In fact, Ferrara's had been founded as a place to relax after the opera.

With two espressos and a plate of cannoli, Joe and McCormick settled into a corner booth in the back, with a clear view of the door.

"All right," Joe said. "Now, what did you find in the Property Room?"

"It's what I didn't find that bothered me." McCormick sipped his drink. "I was looking something up in the files and came across the receipt for a raid that had been made several months ago. According to the receipt, ten guns had been seized. They were itemized by type of weapon and listed individually."

So far, all of that was normal. "And?"

"There was a photograph with the file showing all the confiscated guns laid out and tagged, but there were only nine guns in the photograph. The clerk said it was a clerical error and not to bother anyone else with it."

"A clerical error?" Joe repeated, dubious. He took a bite of cannoli, and flakes of pastry scattered to the table.

"That's a pretty big one as far as clerical errors go, right? And it happened more than once. I saw three other instances of it. There was one gun missing from the photograph. Or one extra gun listed on the receipt of seized guns."

"Did you tell the clerk about all four cases?"

"Only the first one. I found the others after he told me it was no big deal."

Joe tasted the espresso, his head filling with pressure. "Four times this happened. That's not an error, McCormick. That's a pattern, and that is a very big deal. The guns on the receipts but not in the photographs never made it into the storage chests." Wooden chests were used to hold confiscated knives and guns. When they were full, the contents were dumped into the east river.

"Then where are those guns now?"

"If whoever is doing this isn't stockpiling his own personal arsenal? Sold on the black market to the highest bidder would be my guess." Joe sat back, trying to grasp what this meant. This level of corruption was so much worse than policemen accepting bribes to ignore Prohibition violations. Supplying guns to the black market not only put weapons in criminals' hands, it stymied detectives' attempts to find them.

Joe cut his voice low. "The market for guns is bottomless," he told McCormick. "Serial criminals use a weapon once and dispose of it. Maybe they throw it in the East River. Sometimes they even wipe it off and simply leave it at the scene of the crime. The result is the same. First, getting rid of the weapon means it will never be found close to the criminal, implicating him. If we can't link a weapon to the criminal . . ." He spread his hands.

"I get it. That means they need a new one. But they're not going to walk into one of the gunsmiths on Centre Market Place to purchase one."

"You got it." He took another bite of cannoli. "Did you get a good look at the signatures on the receipts?"

McCormick brushed a crumb from his coat. "I couldn't read all of them. It's almost like they were trying not to be legible. Although, you might make them out, being more familiar with the officers than I am."

Joe grunted in agreement. A scrawl instead of a signature was a way of covering one's tracks. "Those receipts only have the signatures of the officer submitting the seized property and the clerk receiving it. We need more information than that anyway. If you can remember the dates of the raids, I'll look up the typed reports. Those will have a record of all the involved officers, not just the one person tasked with turning in the weapons." He finished his cannoli and downed what remained in his mug. "You did the right thing in telling me. I'll look into it. For now, let's keep this between the two of us, okay?"

McCormick agreed.

By the time they returned to headquarters, bells were ringing for mass from Old St. Patrick's Cathedral a few blocks north on Mulberry. For Joe, it was a tocsin of dread for what he was about to find.

The train rumbled over the tracks, hurtling through evening's darkness toward New York City. Outside the window, a mantle of snow reflected the moon's glow. But if Lauren shifted her focus from the eerie blur beyond the pane, she saw her own reflection instead.

"Come away from the windows. Come away, I said. Lauren!"

She shuddered from the memory of her father's warning last night. At first, she'd thought Dad was joking. But the fear in his eyes left no room for humor of any kind. He'd only ever yelled at her once before, when she was walking atop a fieldstone fence and about to make a misstep. He'd seen danger then that she hadn't. Was the same true again?

In the Napoleon House, she'd hurried back to his side and asked him what was wrong. But his stumbling response had been so devoid of substance she couldn't bring it to mind, even now. All she was left with was dread.

The train rocked, and her body swayed to its rhythm. In her lap, she held open *The Age of Innocence* but couldn't retain a single line. A newspaper rustled across the aisle from her. A young woman with pink cheeks and bobbed hair walked up and down between the compartments offering cigars, cigarettes, magazines, newspapers, and Hershey chocolate bars.

Lauren bought two of those, saving the one with almonds for Anita. Once the salesgirl had gone, she sank back into her own private world of thoughts.

Setting aside the novel, she peeled back the candy wrapper, broke off a creamy rectangle of chocolate, and popped it into her mouth. Was Dad's behavior unusual for him? She didn't know. How could she when up until this fall, she'd been estranged from him for years? If her father had been displaying signs of nervousness, fear, or uneasiness, she wouldn't have been around to see them.

Obviously, he hadn't been himself when he arrived from Newport the day after Thanksgiving. But that cause was plain as day. He'd just returned from seeing the roofless Napoleon House. As if that hadn't been enough, he'd also fallen from the platform onto the tracks at Grand Central. Thank goodness he hadn't been injured worse.

Lauren stared at the empty seat across from her and wished her father had agreed to come back with her this evening. She couldn't miss any more work, but that didn't mean it was easy for her to leave Dad alone in that empty mansion, knowing he wasn't at ease. Either he had no reason to fear or he did and he wasn't explaining it to her.

She couldn't decide which was worse.

Lauren did decide, however, there was no need to tell him about the note she'd received on Christmas Eve, which would only scare him further.

Ready to put those thoughts behind her, she reached for the novel again. It opened to the place where she'd tucked a letter from her mother. She'd forgotten until now it was there. She unfolded the page. This one had been written when Lauren had been fourteen years old. A year before Mother's death.

This letter was short, and Lauren wondered if Mother's strength simply would not hold on for longer. It didn't mention anything about her health or decline. She had read several other letters between her parents by now and had noticed that Dad's response to news of the disease's progress had either been dismissive, unrealistically optimistic, or absent altogether. Perhaps by the time Mother wrote this letter, she'd given up informing him about what he clearly did not want to hear.

What Lauren read in the second paragraph stopped her cold.

It's not Egypt Lauren wants but you. Egypt is just the way to your heart, and she knows it.

The words pursued and pressed against her. But it was not a weight intended to hold her down. It was a wrist to her forehead, a hand to her cheek, an ear to the wall of her chest, listening. It was her mother diagnosing the daughter she loved. It had taken nineteen years for the verdict to find her.

And Mother was right.

Truly, Lauren loved Egyptology and the privilege of working at the Met. If she had the chance to travel to Egypt, she would take it. But her quest to get there had been a quest to be close to her father, or at least to earn his approval if not his outright affection.

Maybe this was why she hadn't felt more enthusiastic when Dad had mentioned the expedition. The closer she grew to him, the less important that trip became. A relationship with her dad was more important than anything. Reconciliation and redemption, as Mother had wished, were more important even than Egypt. The hole he'd left in her life for years could only be filled with him.

And if she was going to avoid creating a similar void in her own family someday, she had to find a way to be close to him that didn't involve following too closely in his footsteps. She'd still like to go to Egypt, but she wanted to come home and live with the people she loved, who loved her in return. If God saw fit to give her a husband and children, she would not abandon them to the same fate she and Mother had suffered.

What a lonely life Dad had led. Lauren had spent so much time thinking about how his choices hurt Mother and her, she hadn't considered how Dad's running had isolated him, too. Her heart stretched and pulled to make room for a growing compassion. Was it possible that his stories and posturing were his attempt to win back Lauren's esteem? He needed to know he had that already. They needed to begin again.

Exhausted, Lauren tucked the letter away and ate another piece of chocolate, letting it melt on her tongue. She closed her eyes and leaned back. She would be in New York soon.

A soft thud announced her novel had slid to the floor. When she opened her eyes to retrieve it, she caught a quick movement accompanied by a short flash of light. Odd. She couldn't spy a camera from where she sat, but if someone had taken a photograph by accident, he or she was surely ruing the waste of film.

Twenty minutes later, the train pulled into Grand Central Terminal. Lauren gathered her things, pulled on her coat and hat, and joined the passengers shuffling off the car and onto the platform. Red Caps were at the ready, helping travelers with luggage and hatboxes.

"Help you, miss?" one of them asked Lauren, his smile bright in his dark complexion. The name on his uniform was Morris Williams.

"Thank you, but I can manage what I've brought. It isn't much." Her valise wasn't large, and the hamper was now empty. "However, I would like to thank the man who helped my father off the tracks the day after Thanksgiving," she added.

Mr. Williams tilted his head. "Here?" he asked.

"Yes, it would have been right around here, I suppose. He was on the train coming back from Newport on November 27. I wasn't here, but he told me he lost his balance in the crush of the crowd and fell in the gap. He's about my height, age seventy. White hair."

A train whistle pierced the air. Lauren and Mr. Williams began walking away from the tracks, toward the main concourse, where they could more easily be heard.

"Miss, if there's ever an accident," he told her, "even so much as a shaving kit tumbling to the tracks, let alone a human being, I know about it. I'm the assistant supervisor for all the Red Caps. They report to me, immediately. I haven't heard a single report or rumor from any Red Cap about this."

Lauren paused inside the entrance to Vanderbilt Hall. "I don't understand. Apparently my father's fall attracted a small crowd, and he specifically said it was a Red Cap who helped him out. He came home from the terminal with scrapes and cuts. Perhaps someone forgot to tell you about the incident?"

Mr. Williams widened his stance and folded his hands in front of his brass-buttoned uniform. "That's highly unlikely. When something like that happens, the passenger could sue, so I need to know about it right away. If I find out a report is delayed in getting to me, the Red Cap is fired. These are good jobs for these men. They make good money here, enough to fund their higher education. No, it's highly unlikely any of my men would risk termination by not reporting an incident like that."

By his gentle tone of voice, it was obvious he didn't relish telling her that her father's story rang false. He had nothing to gain by it, either. In fact, some would cry foul that a black man dared to contradict a white woman's claim—or the claim of her white father. Realizing that made Lauren appreciate that Mr. Williams explained the truth to her when he easily could have accepted her gratitude and moved on.

"I'm not calling you or him a liar, mind you," Mr. Williams added. "Perhaps he was confused. Perhaps he'd taken a tumble at the station of his departure, instead, inflicting injuries before he arrived at Grand Central."

Lauren summoned a smile, attempting to put him at ease. "Perhaps he did. Thank you so much for taking the time to talk to me. Good evening."

He tipped his red cap. "If ever I can be of service, you let me know."

After thanking him once again, she headed for the 42nd Street exit, walking beneath that upside-down night sky painted on the ceiling. Above the teeming travelers, cigarette smoke lifted in a mass of dirty fog, dimming the gold constellations.

A different fog gathered in Lauren's mind as she tried to make sense of Mr. Williams's revelation. She ruled out the possibility that her father had been injured at the Newport station. His mind was sharp, and he'd specifically said it was Grand Central, which was much busier than the Newport station. He wouldn't have confused that.

So if he didn't fall to the tracks, how had he been injured? And why had he lied about it?

Lauren slowed her pace. With a sickening dread, she thought again of the fear he'd displayed last night inside the Napoleon House. What was he so afraid of? And did it have anything to do with the real cause of his Thanksgiving injuries?

Footsteps echoed in Vanderbilt Hall, and cigarette smoke clogged her throat. A baby's cry yanked her attention to the left—in time to see a man with a camera aimed at her. She wondered if he was the person on the train who'd wasted a frame already.

He kept the camera in front of his face, obscuring her view of his features, shifted slightly, and took a snapshot, then another. A tourist, she thought. He was trying to capture Vanderbilt Hall, not her, and it would take several adjacent frames to complete a panoramic view.

Doubt niggled, then grew broad and deep. She teetered on its edge. Dad had warned her to come away from the window because he hadn't wanted her to be seen. Was it possible this man had truly intended to capture her in a photograph? Was it possible that he'd taken a picture of her on the train?

That made no sense. It couldn't be so.

Mr. Williams passed by her, now carrying suitcases behind a rotund gentleman, presumably out to a cab.

Activity flurried. She was surrounded by other travelers and Red Caps. Nothing could befall her here.

Adrenaline surged anyway. She tried to reason herself into a calmer state as she continued toward the exit. After all, if that man was taking a photo of her and saw that she'd caught him in the act, wouldn't he try to hide?

But there was nowhere to hide in Vanderbilt Hall, unless one ducked into the information desk in the center of the room. Other than that, there were no benches, no pillars, no columns. It was all one wide-open space, so travelers could crisscross the pink marble floor from any and all directions. If the photographer had wanted to hide, he could only do so behind the camera.

A few yards from the 42nd Street exit, Lauren made a sharp left turn. On the slim chance that her suspicions were founded, the last thing she wanted was to lead this potential voyeur out into the night after her, right to her apartment building.

Was her father's paranoia contagious? Was this how he'd felt the other night? The hairs lifted on the back of her neck, as though she could feel the man watching her. Capturing her likeness on film. Why? Was this related to the note she'd found on her desk on Christmas Eve?

She looked behind her.

He was still there, the camera still covering his face. Though his steps halted, he was closer than he had been.

And what was her plan? She wasn't about to lead him in circles around the hall all night. Instead, she went straight to the information desk beneath the four-sided clock. From there, she could see all angles of the room. Better yet, the clerk at the counter had a phone.

"Can I help you, miss?" the young man asked.

She was sure he could. But before she'd decided exactly how, Mr.

Williams breezed in from an exit and came directly to her. "Miss? Can I get you a cab?"

"Yes, please." She scanned the hall, hoping she could slip away with Mr. Williams without being noticed. She saw no camera, but the man behind it could have simply tucked it into a bag. She had no idea what his face looked like, only the black wool coat he wore, and there were plenty of those.

He could be watching even now, and she wouldn't know it.

Or she could have simply absorbed her father's fears and made them her own. There might be nothing at all the matter.

"Yes, please," she said again, venturing away from the information desk toward 42nd Street with one more look over her shoulder. She couldn't wait to be home.

CHAPTER 27

J oe wasn't Catholic, but that didn't seem to bother the priest who welcomed him inside Old St. Patrick's Cathedral between Mulberry and Mott Streets.

Rainbows spilled from stained-glass windows. Lining both sides of the nave, Gothic chandeliers hung between the cast-iron columns supporting the eighty-foot vaulted ceiling. A long table held a forest of votive candles, some of which flickered in their red glass holders.

At three in the afternoon, barely anyone else was here. A few other souls prayed or meditated in the sanctuary, and low tones drifted from a confessional booth. Joe slid into a pew polished to a high gleam. He needed quiet. Needed to think.

The police commissioner resigned today. Joe had known it was coming, but Richard Enright's parting still left him unsettled. Enright had been commissioner for eight years, since before Prohibition began. In the last couple, he'd tried to press charges against more than a dozen police detectives, deputy detectives, and captains for failing to enforce Prohibition. The charges didn't stick. In frustration, he resigned. How the new commissioner would handle police corruption, Joe could only guess.

Police corruption had brought Joe here today.

This was the pew he'd shared with Connor the day he'd followed him here, a little more than a year ago. Connor had been acting strangely, disappearing for unaccounted-for periods of time and then returning pale-faced and cagey. Whatever was wrong, he'd kept it to himself.

So one day, when Connor had been particularly distracted, he'd left headquarters without a word, and Joe followed him. All the way into St. Pat's, where Connor slumped in a posture of defeat.

Not knowing what troubled Connor, Joe had simply told him he was in the right place for forgiveness.

"Problem is, Joe, I'm not ready to repent," Connor had said. *"And I have the decency not to ask for absolution until I am."*

"Too thirsty?" Joe had asked, knowing full well where Connor stood on Prohibition. No constitutional amendment could entice him to give up the drink.

Connor had looked at Joe with red-rimmed eyes. *"Promise that when something happens to me, no matter what, you'll take care of Aunt Doreen."*

Not *if*, but *when*. He knew his sin would catch up to him.

The organist began to practice, and "Ode to Joy" unfurled to fill every corner of the sacred space. Beethoven's methodical notes led from one to the next in constant, mathematical progression. Joe's own notes progressed in the same even rhythm, only he didn't like how they were adding up.

He rested folded hands on the back of the pew in front of him and lowered his head to meet them. He had cross-checked raid reports against property seizure receipts and photographs. In addition to the four discrepancies McCormick had found, Joe had found dozens more. Just as in the cases McCormick had identified, there was one missing gun from a photograph of weapons reported as seized in a raid.

They'd all occurred between 1923 and August 1925. Even more telling, Joe noticed by the serial numbers on the guns that several had been confiscated more than once.

Of all the officers listed in the reports, the only one present at all of them was Connor Boyle.

The weight of Connor's sin hung heavy on Joe's shoulders. No, he didn't have proof that Connor had been the one to steal every missing weapon and sell it to criminals. Not enough proof for a prosecutor, anyway. But at least in Joe's mind, the evidence pointed to Connor.

Why?

Was Connor being blackmailed? Or did he have some outrageous debt he needed to pay off before harm came to him or his aunt?

Who had been killed by the guns Connor had supplied to criminals?

Sitting up straight, Joe looked at his palms and wondered if their blood was on his hands, too. If he had dug deeper with Connor right here on this church pew, all those months ago, could he have stopped what Connor was doing? Could he have turned him back toward the light, or had Connor already passed the point of no return?

Years ago, Joe used to think there was no such proverbial point. That anyone could be redeemed and rehabilitated, no matter what he or she had done. Anyone could be forgiven. These days? He wasn't so sure.

The door to the confessional booth opened and closed, and a parishioner made his way down the aisle to exit the church. Joe's gaze traveled to the crucified Christ, hanging in front of the stained-glass window. Christ forgave the thief on the cross beside Him. He forgave the ones who hung Him on that tree. Christ would forgive anyone, and as a follower of Him, Joe knew he ought to do the same.

He'd work on that.

But actions still had consequences.

Joe bowed his head in wordless prayer and let the organ music wash over him. When he rose at last, he was as ready as he'd ever be to write a report of his discoveries and submit it to the attorneys on Connor's case.

From behind the altar, wooden sculptures of the saints looked at him. Judas Iscariot, of course, was not among them. A twinge of guilt condemned Joe for betraying his friend, but he quashed it. Judas had betrayed the innocent Son of God for thirty pieces of silver. What Joe was about to do gained him nothing but a chance at justice. Connor Boyle was many things, but he wasn't innocent.

Lauren drank in the crisp, fresh air of Central Park, the long shadow of Cleopatra's Needle pointing to the museum from which she'd just come. During the new acquisitions meeting, she'd shared the news she'd received yesterday from the head curator, Mr. Lythgoe, who was still in Egypt. The coffin and mummy of Hatsudora, Hetsumina's twin sister, had been found on December 1.

Mr. Lythgoe and the Met team, however, had not been the ones to find her. As such, Hatsudora's final resting place would either be at the Cairo Museum in Egypt, or in France, if the French team that uncovered her had their way. The news had been a stinging disappointment to receive, let alone deliver to the rest of the staff in a long meeting made insufferable by cigarette smoke.

Lauren needed a break to clear her mind, and the Egyptian obelisk behind the Met was the best place for it. She thought of the inscription on the foot of Hetsumina's coffin and wondered if Hatsudora's had one to match. *Hatsudora, daughter of Hopikras, died untimely, aged twenty-seven. Farewell.*

It was not a far leap from the notion of an untimely death to all she'd been pondering related to Joe Petrosino, and then to her Joe. Lauren hadn't seen him since Christmas. They'd spoken on the phone since she returned from Newport, but there was a strain to the conversation. She could tell he was deeply troubled by something at work, but he wasn't allowed to talk about it. Keeping secrets was part of his job. But not the worst part.

With Greta's story of Adelina Petrosino fresh in Lauren's mind, she acknowledged that her own Joe's life could be cut short anytime, and the days he had left belonged to the NYPD and the city of New York for as long as he was a detective. That was a hard truth to live with.

But living without Joe, when they loved each other, seemed a criminal waste of time. After all, what relationship did *not* pose a risk? There was no guarantee for anyone's number of days under the sun. Death was a part of life, and no one could predict its coming. "Died untimely" could happen to anyone.

Loving Joe would mean bracing herself every day for the possibility of losing him. Unless she could figure out a way to live without surrendering to dread and fear.

Wind whipped the hair from her pins and brought water to her eyes. Putting her back to its chilling blast, she headed back inside the museum. Whatever she needed to resolve in her mind and heart could not be done on a ten-minute break anyway.

Smoothing her hair back into place, Lauren couldn't resist a quick visit to Hetsumina's coffin in the New Accessions room. Less than a week ago, she'd been here with Sal and Greta, confiding that she hoped to find the twin. Joe's parents had expressed more interest in all things Egypt than Lauren had ever expected. She smiled to think that now Greta owned a piece of antiquity herself, thanks to her father's Napoleon Society.

Her smile faltered, however, the more she thought of that horse-and-rider carving. Something had struck her as slightly off that morning, but Lauren hadn't been able to determine what.

But now . . .

The provenance. The provenance had identified the carving as being from the fifteenth or sixteenth dynasty. Was that right? When had Hyksos introduced horses from Asia into Egypt?

Five minutes later, she was in her basement office, looking it up in a textbook she'd kept from her studies at the University of Chicago. According to Dr. Breasted's *A History of Egypt from the Earlier Times to the Persian Conquest*, Hyksos brought horses to Egypt in the seventeenth or eighteenth dynasty, which meant that carving couldn't have been produced before then.

She rubbed at a swelling headache. Maybe she'd misremembered the date on the provenance. Or possibly it was a typographical error. She had to be certain but didn't want to alarm Greta or Sal, especially given that Sal had been swindled before.

Surely she was being paranoid. That artifact had come from the Napoleon Society, after all, and they procured items directly from Egypt. Then again, Ray Moretti's papyrus had obviously been forged before crossing the ocean.

Picking up the telephone, she dialed Joe's number at police headquarters.

"Lauren? Is everything okay?" His tone was distant and preoccupied, and suddenly she felt as though she were intruding.

"I'm fine," she told him, deciding to get straight to the point, "but I need to see that carving of your mother's along with the provenance. The sooner the better."

He paused long enough for her to wonder if they'd lost connection. At last, he spoke. "Don't tell me my father lost another sum of the family's money by buying a fake from the Napoleon Society."

Lauren bristled in defense of the father she'd been so quick to mistrust last week. Hadn't she promised she'd never jump to conclusions again?

"I don't know," she replied truthfully. "That's why I need to see it. I want to check the dates again." Dread coiled in her middle. "Can we meet somewhere?"

"I'll come to you," he said, but the words were more weary than warm. "I've got some things to take care of first. I'll be at the Beresford sometime after dinner."

She agreed to the plan, hung up the phone, and breathed deeply to calm her nerves.

If something was wrong with the horse and rider, it wouldn't be her father's fault. He'd find a way to make it right with the Caravellos, of course, and yet it would be another stain on his society.

After work, the hours piled up until "sometime after dinner" seemed as though it would never come. But he'd warned her about this. Here was a chance to practice taking his delay or cancellation in stride. When the clock struck ten, she gave up waiting, changed into her pajamas, and braided her hair into a loose plait for the night.

The knock finally came at a quarter past ten. Lauren wrapped a robe around her, resolving not to ask where he'd been as she rushed to open the door.

"I got here as soon as I could," he said. Half-moon shadows hung beneath his eyes.

After closing the door behind him, she stepped into his open arms, then quickly stepped back again, nose wrinkling. "Why do I smell gin?"

Joe rubbed his jaw, which was in need of a shave. "I was working on a case, and that's all I can tell you. Trust me."

She folded her arms over her robe and felt a small distance wedge between them. She would have to get used to this part of his job as well. It would be a challenge since Lauren's inquisitive mind wanted to know everything there was to know about the subjects that interested her.

And she was more than interested in Joe Caravello.

"I wasn't drinking," he added, "but I had to get close to those who were."

"How close?"

Setting down the box he'd carried in, he stripped off his gin-scented coat and embraced her again, one hand cradling the back of her head. "About like this," he teased, and she laughed, savoring the security of his embrace.

"A new interrogation technique," she said, pulling back to look up at him. "How innovative. I'll bet all the flappers love to be questioned by you. Lucky girls."

"The flappers aren't out this early." A smile hooked his cheek. "It's good to see you."

Lauren reached up and brushed his hair off his brow. "It's good to see you, too." They were such small words, so mundane they might have been exchanged between any two people meeting by chance on the street. But the yearning in Joe's eyes when she touched his face infused the moment with longing and restraint.

He caught her wrist and pressed a lingering kiss to the sensitive skin inside of it. "It's late. I shouldn't stay long," he said, breaking the spell with a dose of common sense.

Her face flushed and heart hammering, Lauren agreed and wrapped her quilted robe a little tighter. She reached for the item she knew would throw cold water on them both.

Bringing the box to the living room, she sat in one armchair while Joe took the other. Carefully, she pulled the horse and rider and the provenance document from within and inspected both. Her stomach hollowed.

"Oh, Joe. This is dated too early. I thought maybe the provenance was in error, but the inscription on the horse itself matches. This could not have come from the dynasty it claims because horses weren't introduced to Egypt until one or two dynasties later."

He leaned back in the chair. "Could it be that horses weren't common yet, but someone, somewhere had a few? I mean, can we say universally that there were absolutely no horses in Egypt yet?"

"I don't like it, either. But in this case, yes, we can. This is dated a few *centuries* before the first horse arrived. So there's no way this is genuine. At least we know this forger isn't Peter Braun. The Napoleon Society should have known better than to acquire this, but they did—possibly in a large batch they acquired all at once, the way the Met is bequeathed large collections with varying levels of value."

"Do you know how much money my father spent on that fake?" He left the chair and paced the living room, muttering, "What am I going to tell him? What am I going to tell my mother?"

"My father will make this right, Joe. If not a refund, a replacement, and one I'll personally inspect before it's offered to your parents." She bit her lip, ashamed that she hadn't noticed the problem with the carving when she'd first seen it on Christmas morning. When she apologized for that, Joe shook his head.

"It would have ruined the entire day to find out right then and there. No, this isn't your fault."

"It's not my father's, either," she said.

He spun to face her, green eyes blazing. "Then whose is it?" Accusation edged his tone.

Lauren stood to deflect it. "I understand why you're upset. But this is different from what happened before. This might even work in our favor."

Joe frowned. "What do you mean?" Weariness settled in the lines on his face, reminding her that he shouldered cares he couldn't speak of. They were matters of far more importance than forgeries, of that she could be certain.

"I'd like to see if the dealer who sold this carving to the Napoleon Society is the same one who sold the Book of the Dead papyrus to Ray Moretti. I'd have to go back and check with the Morettis, of course, but if it's a match, the NYPD could alert the authorities in Luxor, right? And they could investigate, potentially preventing other forgeries from being sold by that dealer." It was a small glimmer of hope, but she snatched at it.

"You're not going there alone."

"I don't have to go anywhere if he's willing to cooperate," she countered. "I only need to see the provenance document. He could send it with his personal secretary, and I could look at it in my office. If I want an answer quicker, I could call and ask for the name of the dealer. Then again, this is too important not to see it for myself."

Joe leaned an elbow against the fireplace mantel, pinning his gaze on the glowing embers. He stood there without speaking for so long Lauren wondered if he'd fallen asleep on his feet.

At last, he said, "No, we'll both go. If you can set it up, I'll come with you." Then he picked up his coat from where he'd dropped it and put it back on. "I want to talk to your father about this, too. I want to hear what he has to say before bringing this up to my folks."

Lauren swallowed. "Of course. He'd appreciate the chance to

explain how this could have happened, I'm sure. I'm eager to hear it myself."

"Is he in town?"

"He will be. My father and I are meeting Daniel and Agnes DeVries tomorrow night for dinner at the Astor for New Year's Eve. Join us. Eight o'clock. We'd love to have you, and you can get all your questions answered. Dr. DeVries is one of the Napoleon Society board members and the editor of the newsletter. But once you finish talking business, will you at least try to enjoy yourself?" She wouldn't say so, but he looked like he needed a break.

"Is this another tuxedo shindig?"

Lauren chuckled. "I'm afraid so. But don't worry. I'll be there to fix your bow tie if you still haven't gotten the hang of it."

"Is that a promise?" Grinning, Joe replaced his hat and kissed her on the cheek. "Count me in."

CHAPTER

28

Does this remind you of your homeland, Detective Caravello?"
Joe stuffed down a chuckle and smiled at Agnes DeVries.
"Manhattan is my homeland, ma'am. Born and raised here.
But this is nice. I like it." At the rear of one of the Hotel Astor lobbies,
The Palm Café was designed as an Italian garden. Twenty-two feet
above them, the ceiling had been painted Mediterranean sky–blue,
and it was partially obscured by vine-covered pergolas. Violet light
spilled from hanging lamps.

"But where were your *people* from?" Mrs. DeVries pressed. Behind her, a fern basket dangled, and Italian landscape prints covered
the walls.

"Union Square." When he saw that wasn't going to satisfy her, he
smiled again and told her what she wanted to know. "My mother's
family is German. My father's came from the north of Italy, long
before immigration waves from poverty-stricken southern Italy and
Sicily poured into New York. We've been here four generations."

"The *north* of Italy," she repeated approvingly. "There's so much
culture there! Florence, Venice, Rome!"

Actually, Rome was in the middle of Italy, but Joe wasn't about
to correct her.

Lauren sent him a knowing smile as Mrs. DeVries launched into a detailed account of who she'd seen over the holidays and what they wore. At the mention of clothes, Joe fought the urge to pull his collar away from his neck. He'd hoped that since he'd finally bought his own tuxedo, cut to his own measurements, he wouldn't feel so confined. It was better than that borrowed penguin suit he'd been forced to wear for the gala but still uncomfortable.

Lauren, on the other hand, looked perfectly at ease and stunning in a black-and-gold number that didn't hide the fact that she had a waist, not to mention other curves. He couldn't understand the current fad among young women these days. Why were dresses that looked like rectangles so popular?

He shouldn't be thinking about Lauren's figure right now, not with her father sitting right there beside her. Or how good she smelled. He definitely shouldn't think of how comforting it had been to see her at the end of a long and terrible day. Or daydream about making that a permanent arrangement so that he wouldn't need to leave her after saying good-night.

She caught him watching her and smiled before returning her attention to Mrs. DeVries, while Dr. DeVries monopolized the men's side of the table.

Stifling a sigh, Joe added cream to his cup and stirred until his coffee was the right shade of brown. *Be polite*, he reminded himself, though he was nearly bored out of his mind.

Nearby, water rippled softly from an imported fountain. With his shoe, Joe nudged the box holding the fake horse and rider, deliberately bumping it into Lauren's foot. He was here for answers, and so far, he wasn't getting them. *"Wait until after the meal,"* Lauren had warned him upon his arrival, *"or we'll all have indigestion."*

"Look at what Daniel gave me for Christmas," Mrs. DeVries was saying. Then she opened the locket she wore, revealing two small portraits, one of herself and one of her husband. "Would you believe he painted these himself?"

"But they're so small!" Lauren gasped. "We have a collection of miniatures like this at the Met. They're astonishing, painted with one horsehair at a time."

"That's how I did it, too." Dr. DeVries squared his shoulders. "It's all about using the right tools to achieve the desired effect."

"Here, Detective, you must take a look." Her voice dripping with pride, Mrs. DeVries unclasped the locket and passed it across the table to him.

Joe almost couldn't believe what he was seeing. "This detail is incredible," he admitted. It looked as though a life-sized portrait was simply shrunk down to fit this locket, while retaining every brushstroke. He handed it back. "You're very talented, Dr. DeVries."

"Oh." He shook his head a little. "I dabble."

"He's being modest." Mrs. DeVries refastened the locket. "He's a surgeon, and a right fine one, too. But sometimes I think he missed his calling, although his patients are better off for it."

"So are you, dear," he added.

Finally, this was getting interesting. "How's that?" Joe prodded.

"Oh, let's not get started on that old tale, shall we?" Lawrence said with a familiarity that attested to years of friendship. "We'll bore the young people silly."

"When we first met, he was an art student in Florence," Mrs. DeVries said, ignoring Lawrence.

"And then I came to my senses, lucky for you, since my paintings would have never afforded you the lifestyle to which you've grown accustomed."

"And how would you have known that way back then?" she asked.

"Let's just say your 'trappings' while you were on your grand tour made an indelible impression."

"It was the Gilded Age, after all," Mrs. DeVries insisted. Diamonds sparkled in her hair combs. "Besides, it isn't fair to place demands on art, anyhow, is it? Isn't that what you always say? Art isn't cranked out in a factory to pay the bills. We can't all be Vermeer."

"Not even Vermeer himself," Lauren interjected. "That is, he was recognized as a master painter and the head of his painter's guild, but his art was even more broadly celebrated and valued after his death."

"And now the Met pays untold sums for his canvases." Lawrence's voice pitched higher. The look he directed at Lauren was that of one demanding a confirmation, even though she had nothing to do with European paintings. "Right?"

A ridge formed between Lauren's brows. "Well, as I don't happen to know the figure paid for our few Vermeers, then yes, the sum is untold, at least to me."

"Millions," Dr. DeVries muttered into his coffee. "Millions."

Joe schooled his features to remain neutral, despite his growing fascination with the staid-looking surgeon. He wished he could stay here until midnight to catch any other stories that would shed light on who Dr. DeVries was, and more importantly, what he was capable of. But Joe had somewhere else to be.

Lauren could tell Joe was getting restless. To be fair, he'd waited from the crab cake appetizers all the way through the cheesecake dessert, all shared at a small round table ideal for four people, not five. She couldn't put it off any longer. At her signal, Joe lifted the box from the floor and set it on the celadon-green table.

So much for avoiding indigestion.

A hand to her churning middle, she said, "Speaking of art, I need to show both of you something." Briefly, she explained that Sal Caravello had become a member of the Napoleon Society and had been sent an artifact in accordance with the level that he'd paid.

"And this is your father?" Agnes asked, looking at Joe.

"He is." He removed the lid, and Lauren lifted out the horse and rider.

"It wasn't until yesterday that I realized there was a problem. This is dated a few hundred years before horses were introduced into Egypt." She pointed to the inscription and passed out the provenance as well. "If it hadn't been for the dating, I never would have guessed this wasn't genuine," she added, hoping to soften the blow.

Her father's experience was in exploring and excavation. She didn't expect him to have memorized every point of Egyptian history. Lauren had a doctorate in this, and still it had escaped her notice at first. Truly, she didn't blame Dad or Dr. DeVries, whose knowledge of Egyptology was even less.

No one spoke, and the fountain's murmuring magnified. Her father's complexion paled.

Dr. DeVries turned pink. "What are you saying, young lady? Are you questioning the integrity of the Napoleon Society?"

The quiet words trumpeted his doubt, jarring Lauren. It was the opposite of the deferential stance he'd taken days ago, when apologizing for his secretary's mistake with her byline.

She felt Joe tense beside her and placed a hand on his knee to stay his temper.

"With respect," she said, "I am only calling false the integrity of this one particular piece. We haven't informed its owner yet because we wanted to give you a chance to determine your response."

She hazarded a glance at Dad, who seemed at a loss for words and dwarfed by the veined marble columns behind him.

"Are you going to let your daughter make this accusation against the society?" Dr. DeVries asked. "I, for one, won't take a woman's word quite so easily."

Lauren felt as though she'd been struck, though reason told her the man was reacting in shock to the news that they'd been fooled. He was upset at the situation, she guessed, not at her.

"Dr. DeVries," Dad said, "I trust the assistant curator of Egyptian art implicitly, and so does the New York City Police Department. That is why she's been their consultant on forgeries for months, and why I commissioned her to write a series of articles for the good of our subscribers. The fact that she happens to be a woman, who happens to be my daughter, plays into it not at all. In fact, knowing how much she supports me and my work, I trust her opinion on this matter all the more. She would not bring this to us if she were not certain. Now, I wish this hadn't happened, but it has, and we have the opportunity to make it right for Mr. Caravello."

Lauren bowed her head in gratitude. Beneath the table, Joe covered her hand, apparently understanding how much it meant for her father to defend her.

Joe laced his fingers with hers. "Dr. DeVries, Mr. Westlake, obviously you're not under arrest. You're not who we're after, here."

"I should say not," Agnes exclaimed behind the fan she pumped. Fern fronds quivered in the basket hanging behind her.

"But we would like to hear what you have to say on two points," Joe continued. "The first one is simpler. How do you propose to resolve the fact that one of your members spent a large sum of money on a near-worthless carving?"

Dad looked at Dr. DeVries. "We're cash poor right now, Daniel, with the ongoing renovations in Newport. I suggest a replacement artifact. One that Dr. Westlake verifies before we offer it. Perhaps we find two, and let our member choose which suits his fancy best."

Dr. DeVries nodded his assent. "Fine. The other point?"

"We'd like to have that in writing, by the way," Joe added. "A simple letter to Mr. Caravello informing him of the mistake and how you'll make it up to him will suffice. Please make a carbon copy for my own records and mail it to me at 240 Centre Street."

Dad agreed.

Lauren squeezed Joe's hand, satisfied with their cooperation so far. "The other question we must ask," she began, "is how you acquired this in the first place. What is your process?"

The narrative that followed revealed nothing out of the ordinary. The Napoleon Society relied heavily on Sayed Mohammed, a dealer in Luxor, and upon artifacts board members had picked up on their own personal excavations from years ago.

"Our members are getting antiquities for an enormous discount," Dr. DeVries added. "They have no idea how much these items are really going for these days. That's a benefit of membership that can't be found anywhere else. It's what makes the Napoleon Society inimitable. Member investments in the society are indelible, both for our educational purposes and for their own long-term security."

Joe cleared his throat. "Well, it's a benefit when the artifacts are genuine."

Dr. DeVries's expression soured. "Indubitably. This unfortunate incident with your father's artifact is an isolated one."

"And we'll fix our mistake at the earliest possible opportunity," Dad added, looking from Joe to Lauren.

She reached across the table and gripped his hand. "I know you will. Thank you. The Napoleon Society will come through this none the worse for wear." She smiled.

Joe didn't.

Joe could picture it. Right now, while he swayed on a smoke-filled subway car, Lauren was still warm at the Hotel Astor, navigating another round of small talk with Agnes DeVries while Lawrence and Dr. DeVries swapped more stories from their long-lasting friendship. In fifteen minutes, they would all bundle into their furs, go to the roof, and join in the countdown until the ball dropped from the top of the Times Tower.

Couples would kiss and cheer in the new year.

Ah well. Joe wouldn't have been able to kiss Lauren like he wanted to with her father present anyway.

Instead, Joe had dropped off the horse and rider at headquarters, changed clothes, then caught the subway at Spring Street to get out of the cold for the four more stops to city hall.

Canal Street.

Worth Street.

Brooklyn Bridge.

At each station, more passengers boarded, smelling of gin rickeys and cigarettes as they squeezed around Joe. When the train ground to a halt under city hall, the doors clanged open, and everyone spilled out.

The lead-glass skylights were dark, but exposed electric bulbs shone from green-and-white-tile arches, and chandeliers hung from vaulted ceilings that resembled those in the Oyster Bar at Grand Central.

Emerging into the cold winter night, Joe maneuvered through a teeming throng to the southwestern point of City Hall Park. A few hundred feet to his northeast stood the domed, Federal-style city hall, completed in the 1800s. In the opposite direction, across from the southern tip of the park, a single spire rose above the colonial St. Paul's Chapel, where George Washington had worshipped. And just across Broadway, the world's tallest building—the Woolworth—scraped the sky. Not a bad view, if one knew how to read silhouettes in the dark.

But Joe wasn't here for architectural history. Here, he'd promised to meet with Big Red, the informant he'd talked to last night at Callahan's, in the meeting he couldn't tell Lauren about. Murphy would say it was a meeting he shouldn't have had at all, since it had to do with Connor. But he had to know. He had to ask.

Joe searched for Big Red among the half-lit faces beneath the streetlamps. Last night at Callahan's, Joe had confirmed Oscar McCormick's story with the bartender, that Connor had suddenly lost his taste for whatever Callahan's was serving. Then when Big Red arrived for a drink at his usual time, Joe beckoned him into a shadowy booth and gave him a list of the guns that had gone missing when Connor was supposedly turning them over to the Property Room. He'd listed their types, their serial numbers, and the dates they'd disappeared from police control. If anyone could find out what happened to them, Big Red could.

At least, that's what Joe was here to find out.

It must be getting close to midnight. More boisterous than the folks in Times Square, this crowd gathered to ring in not only the new year, but the new mayor, recently elected. Jimmy Walker was a known opponent of Prohibition, and these thirsty New Yorkers were here to celebrate what they believed would be the end of Prohibition's enforcement in Manhattan.

There. Joe spotted Big Red in a black stocking cap but didn't wave.

The man would reach him in his own time, and the less attention they attracted, the better.

At five feet seven, Big Red had to crane his neck to look Joe in the eye. "No dice," he said.

"Come again?"

"You heard me."

"Figured that was a joke."

Big Red cupped his hand around a cigarette and lit it. "Those guns didn't enter the black market. I talked to the dealers on Centre Market, too. Nobody brought in a single one of those guns for resale." Smoke puffed from his mouth.

"You're telling me they vanished?"

"Nah, guns don't vanish. What I'm telling you is that they went somewhere I couldn't follow. Sorry I couldn't help this time."

Joe watched him walk away, cigarette smoke leaving a ghostly wake. What on earth had Connor done with dozens of guns if he hadn't sold them?

Laughter and shouts rang in his ears as Joe made his way back to headquarters, less than a mile away. The brisk walk north on Centre Street would clear his head, he hoped.

Upon reaching headquarters, he jogged up the five stairs and pushed through one of the doors as the clock tower struck midnight. The roar from the crowd down the street at city hall followed him inside until the door shut behind him.

Happy birthday, 1926. What secrets would the new year keep, and which ones would finally be unraveled?

Joe unwrapped his scarf as he made his way through the marble lobby. Passing the stairs to the basement, he heard a few jailed men ushering in the new year by rattling their mesh steel cages. Before the night was over, every one of those cells would be full. They always were on this night.

At his desk, he removed his coat. Slapping his notebook on the blotter, he wrote in it what Big Red had told him, then flipped back through his notes from the Hotel Astor.

Then he pulled out the desk drawer and thumbed through the files until he came to the ones related to the forgeries. After rewriting his notes from tonight and tucking them into a folder, he flipped back to the first reports he'd filed once Lauren had started consulting with him.

Frustration surged that he still hadn't found the art buyer Daniel Bradford. Bradford had to be an alias not yet registered with the police. Joe withdrew another file folder, this one containing all the information he had on Bradford, scant though it was.

—*Buyer who supplies pieces for Tomkins.*
—*Private dealer for Thomas Sanderson, who purchased from him the set of four canopic jars.*
—*Physical description, given by Mr. Sanderson on Dec. 5, 1925:*
About 5'11". Grey hair, brown eyes. In his sixties. A gentleman's hands, manicured fingernails. Muscle twitches under left eye when agitated.

Joe stared at the description. How many men in Manhattan were in their sixties and had grey hair, brown eyes, and trimmed fingernails? That nervous twitch wasn't something that would show up in a photograph or measurement, even if they had that. He could be any one of the men Joe saw a hundred times a day. He could be Dr. Daniel DeVries, for pity's sake, were it not for the fact that Joe already knew he was a surgeon.

A surgeon who, like all other surgeons, had a gentleman's hands and neatly manicured fingernails.

A surgeon who'd studied art in Italy and continued to paint with those long, steady fingers.

A surgeon who happened to be on the board of an organization that had sold a forged antiquity.

Whose first name happened to be Daniel.

That was a lot of coincidences.

Unbuttoning his cuffs, Joe rolled up his sleeves and pulled out the provenance documents for the forgeries owned by Thomas Sanderson, Sal Caravello, and Newell St. John. The latter had never been under investigation, but Joe was nothing if not thorough with his paperwork, and he had made a copy of it just in case. All three documents indicated that their respective artifacts had come directly from Egypt.

He reread the narratives describing all three, looking for something that could tie them together. Years ago, before the Italian Squad had taken down the Black Hand Society, copycat criminals sent notes to citizens, claiming to be the Black Hand and trying to extort them. But the detectives could tell the difference. Though it could have been different members of the Black Hand Society who had written their notes, the same speech patterns, the same wording, and the same symbols were in each one.

These provenance documents had no symbols, but Joe studied them afresh for similar speech patterns, wording. Words.

On the document for the horse and rider that came from the Napoleon Society, Joe read, *The carving of this horse and rider creates an indelible impression of movement, power, and strength so associated with the Egyptian people.*

Indelible. He'd heard Dr. DeVries use that word twice tonight. Everyone had their favorite words, Joe supposed, and this one was obviously one of the doctor's. Finding it in this document wasn't a revelation, since it was no secret this artifact came from Dr. DeVries's Napoleon Society.

He moved on to the other provenance documents. One called Mr. Sanderson's particular canopic jars both *indubitable* and *inimitable.* He checked again the document for St. John's ointment jar and found none of these words. The style and vocabulary were completely different.

Indelible. Inimitable. Indubitable. These were uncommon words, and yet he'd heard Dr. DeVries say each of them in one night. Did that make him the author of both provenance documents? Did it mean the surgeon had a double life as an art dealer named Daniel Bradford?

That seemed like a stretch, but it wasn't outside the realm of possibility.

Joe blinked at the documents splayed on his desk. He unearthed his notebook and began writing.

> *Why would DeVries masquerade as an art dealer? What does he gain?*
>
> *Is he knowingly working with a forger and profiting financially?*
>
> *Why resort to illegitimate means of income when a surgeon's salary ought to be more than comfortable?*
>
> *Is he not just an art dealer but a forger, too?*

After all, it wasn't the art dealer's job to write up the provenance documents. Those documents were provided by the seller, and the dealer simply passed them on to the buyer.

> *If DeVries forged the horse and rider for financial gain for the Napoleon Society, or even if he simply knew it was fake and sold it anyway, could he have done the same thing to other new members that he's done to Sal Caravello?*

Anger smoldered at the notion. But all of this was speculation. He had no proof, just a hunch, based on three uncommon words. Yet his thoughts continued to spin at an almost reckless speed. If DeVries was committing fraud, he wondered if Lawrence Westlake knew about it.

Was he in on it?

Was Lauren?

Joe's blood pumped hotter, faster. He tossed down his pencil, his thoughts falling into the dark trench that held memories of people close to him, their secrecy and deception. His father had betrayed the family by secretly letting them crash into financial ruin. Connor had betrayed the entire police force, it seemed. But that didn't mean that the only woman he'd ever loved was lying to him, too.

It didn't mean that Lauren was covering for her father because she was desperate for his approval.

In fact, all of his suspicion could amount to nothing at all. But would he still investigate?

Indubitably.

CHAPTER 29

SATURDAY, JANUARY 2, 1926

Sunshine streamed into the Main Reading Room at the New York Public Library, gilding the dust motes that danced in the beams. It was far closer to the Caravellos' home than the Metropolitan Museum of Art, which made it a better location for this meeting that Lauren was eager to get underway.

"I don't understand why it's necessary that I be here, too." Dr. DeVries twisted his tie tack, ensuring it was absolutely straight. "Lawrence could have handled it on behalf of the society."

"Having two board members here in person, instead of one, communicates that you take this mistake seriously." Lauren kept her voice low so as not to disturb the dozen or so people reading. "This is your chance to make your member feel valued. To reestablish rapport that at this point is rather tenuous. What you want is to inspire loyalty in each of your members. Trust me, a good relationship with your patrons is worth more than gold."

"You've experience in this area, do you?" the doctor asked.

"I do. Patrons can become dissatisfied for any number of reasons. But earning our way back into their good graces, whenever reasonably possible, is a priority. It's easier to retain a member than to recruit a new one."

"Well." Dr. DeVries nodded toward the door. "Here we go, Lawrence. Time to put on a show."

Lauren frowned at the doctor's sentiment. Setting that aside, she waved to Joe and his parents, then walked closer to greet them. Joe had already shared with her that Sal had taken the news of the forgery hard yesterday, but that Joe and Greta had helped him see that he wasn't to blame. Greta, Joe had said, had been confident things would be made right.

"I'm so glad you could meet us today," she told the Caravellos, adding how sorry she was for the reason.

"You must not blame your father, you know," Greta said in low tones. "You won't hold this against him, will you? We all make mistakes, but life is too short to hold on to them."

Lauren nodded, speechless that her concern was Lauren's relationship with her father.

Then Sal, who Lauren had worried over most, gave her a smile so full of meaning that it untied the knots in her chest. "There is nothing more important than family." In the crack in his voice, Lauren heard the rift he still suffered in his own.

"Thank you," she breathed, awash in their grace.

Eyes rimmed in silver, Greta embraced Lauren, and then Sal kissed her cheeks.

"I'll wait for my turn later." Joe winked at Lauren, and she laughed along with his parents.

Grateful for that moment with the Caravellos, she ushered the family to where her father and Dr. DeVries waited.

"My dear Mr. and Mrs. Caravello," Dad said, shaking their hands in greeting, "I cannot tell you how pained I was to learn of our error. How pained we both were."

Dr. DeVries shook their hands as well. "Yes, quite. We value our members and want to make it up to you by offering to you your choice of a replacement artifact."

"And these have both been guaranteed by Dr. Westlake?" Joe asked quietly.

"They have." Dad bowed almost deferentially. "The artifacts and the provenance documents have both been verified."

A bloom of pink crept above Dr. DeVries's collar. Obviously, he didn't appreciate the implication that they needed the confirmation. "An extra measure of diligence."

Joe looked at him. "Not extra. Necessary."

Lauren's eyes rounded. As Dad explained the choice of amulets to Sal and Greta, Joe and the doctor continued to stare at each other. It was like some sort of primal challenge. She couldn't understand why.

A false smile jerked up Dr. DeVries's lips. "If you say so. As you see, we're both here, cooperating as you've insisted."

Joe's smile was natural, perhaps deceptively so. "I'd expect nothing less of board members who have their members' best interests at heart."

The words exchanged between the men were civil. Even the tone was quiet and controlled. But the energy arcing between them was nothing short of electric. If she stood too close, she'd be singed.

"Of course we do." Dr. DeVries turned his back to Joe, paying attention instead to the transaction taking place.

"May I see the provenances, please?" Joe asked.

Lauren passed the papers to him, and he studied both, apparently reading every word.

"I assure you, everything is in order," Dr. DeVries said.

Joe handed the documents back to Lauren. "Indubitably." He smiled.

A muscle twitched beneath the doctor's left eye.

"Do you have any questions for any of us about these two items?" Lauren asked Sal and Greta, redirecting the attention to the senior Caravellos.

"Your father has been doing an excellent job of answering them," Greta said. "Sal? Do you have any questions?"

Lauren feared he'd ask how the Napoleon Society had sold a fake to begin with. He had every right to inquire. Instead, he simply laid a hand on his wife's shoulder and reminded her this was a gift for her. The decision was hers alone.

All tension diffused. In the breath of relief that followed, Lauren could hear pages turn at nearby tables, the muted footsteps of readers coming and going, the murmur of a librarian offering guidance at the carved wooden service desk.

The click and whir of a camera.

Lauren scanned the room until she found where the sound had come from. A man pointed a camera at her and took another photograph. Her scare from a few days ago at Grand Central rushed back to her.

"Joe." Pulse trotting, she touched his sleeve and whispered. "That man over there is taking pictures of me."

"No, he isn't," he told her.

She frowned at him. "You didn't even look. He's twenty feet behind me."

Joe barely glanced at the man. "I see him. You're safe, I promise."

"But how can you be so sure? I'm telling you—"

"Trust me." He squeezed her hands. "Please."

For the sake of his parents, she bit her tongue before she told him how it felt for him to dismiss her concerns without even hearing what she had to say.

Making a show of looking at his watch, Dr. DeVries begged leave to go prepare for his next patient.

"On a Saturday, Daniel?" Dad asked.

"Health emergencies are no respecter of time, I'm afraid."

Sal announced they'd made their selection and said he and Greta would gladly walk out with him. Lawrence bade them farewell and stayed behind to pack up the other artifact.

The man with the camera left, too. Somehow that didn't make Lauren feel much better. She drew Joe a few tables over from Dad. "This has happened before. When I was at the Napoleon House with my father in Newport, he told me to come away from the window, but he didn't tell me why. But he was scared of something, or someone. Then on the train on the way home, I thought someone might have taken a picture of me, but I quickly dismissed the idea."

Finally, Joe was paying attention. "Go on."

"Then at Grand Central, a man, perhaps the same one from the train, followed me with his camera, taking more pictures in Vanderbilt Hall. I'd thought the man had broader shoulders than the one here today, but nonetheless. He'd disappeared by the time I had a Red Cap escort me to a cab."

His face hardened to granite. "Lauren, why didn't you tell me?"

"I convinced myself I was being paranoid. Then after getting home, it was easy to forget about it, especially with the distraction of discovering the horse and rider was a forgery. In fact, I hadn't given it another thought until about two o'clock this morning. I awoke to the sound of someone entering the apartment and almost called the police before realizing it was Elsa and Ivy arriving home from their vacation. That only made me feel more paranoid, but now I know I'm not."

"Did you get a good look at the man who was taking photos of you?"

"I only wish I had. He held the bulky camera in front of his face the entire time, so no, I never saw his face."

Dad approached, concern etched into his features. "Did I hear that right, Lauren?" He set his satchel on the table. "Were you followed home from Newport, and you didn't tell me?" Fear expanded in his eyes.

She took a deep breath. "I didn't want you to worry. I wasn't even sure of my own interpretation of events. I thought maybe I'd absorbed your suspicions from the night before when you urged me away from the window. You never explained that, either, you know."

Joe pulled his leather notebook from his pocket and began taking notes. "All right, you two. Have a seat, and let's start from the beginning. What was the date?"

Sliding into a chair, she told him.

Dad deflated into a seat of his own, lips pressed flat, as though determined not to share anything.

"I'm not the only one keeping secrets, Dad. If there's something you're afraid of, you ought to tell Joe about it, even if you don't want to tell me. I can leave the two of you alone for a while."

"I have nothing to say." Dad shook his head. "It's simply prudent not to display yourself in front of an open window where others could see you. I ordered window coverings, but they've not come in yet."

"Was someone outside the house that night?" Joe asked. "Did you have reason to believe someone might be surveilling you?"

"I thought I saw someone with a lit cigarette," Lauren told him.

"Did you happen to go outside later and look for ashes or the butt? Footsteps in the snow?"

"I would have," Lauren said, "but a fresh blanket of snow fell that night, so there was no point."

"We're wasting the detective's time." Dad stood. "Maybe both of us are imagining things, sweetheart." But his hands shook as he tightened the buckle on his satchel and tried to button his coat.

"You didn't fall on the tracks," she said.

Her father sank back down.

Joe raised his eyebrows, pencil hovering over his notebook, waiting for her to explain.

"I talked to the assistant supervisor for the Red Caps at Grand Central. I wanted to thank whoever it was that helped you when you fell the day after Thanksgiving. The man I spoke with said that no one fell to the tracks that day."

Dad opened his mouth and closed it again. "How could he possibly know everything that transpired?"

"Accidents are always reported. What you described was not filed for that day. So maybe it's time you tell how you really sustained those injuries."

He tugged at his scarf. "It's so hot in here. Why do they keep it so hot in here?"

"Mr. Westlake." Joe kept his voice low. "It will help all of us a great deal if you simply tell the truth."

Color leached from Dad's face. "Is that photographer still here?"

"He left," Lauren said.

His gaze roved the room, as though afraid they were still being observed. Or listened to.

Breathing in shallow pants, he pushed himself up again, his chair scraping back from the table. "I must get back to my work. If you want to help, Detective, don't follow me."

Dumbfounded, Lauren watched him go. Whatever her father was afraid of, he was determined to face it alone. "Something is wrong, but I have no idea what," she whispered. "Do you?"

Joe reached for her hand, and she grasped his fingers. "I don't know what happened to your dad. But I do know the photographer here this morning wasn't here for you. His name is Oscar McCormick, and he's a police officer. I asked him to come and take photos of Dr. DeVries."

"Why?"

Joe opened his notebook, revealing pages that were dated at the top. He pointed to what he'd written on January 1. The phrase *Daniel Bradford = Daniel DeVries?* had been circled in dark pencil lead.

"The art dealer?" Lauren whispered. "I hardly think . . ."

Joe brought a finger to his lips and turned the page, tapping it. There, she followed the progression of clues he'd put together based on the provenance documents, the doctor's distinctive vocabulary, and the physical description offered by Mr. Sanderson.

Her mouth went dry. "You were irritating him on purpose today," she guessed.

"So you saw it, too." He pointed to the note about the agitated twitch beneath his left eye.

She admitted she had.

"Let's take a walk." Joe put on his overcoat and led her out of range of listening ears. Their footsteps echoed across the marble as they exited the reading room and began descending the double-wide staircase.

"Mr. Sanderson has seen Daniel Bradford," he continued quietly. "I asked McCormick to take the photos so I can show them to him and see if he can identify him that way. Then we'll know for sure if he's been working with this alias."

Lauren buttoned her fur-trimmed coat and focused on the step in front of her, and the next, and the next, as she descended. If Dr. DeVries was indeed Daniel Bradford, that meant he'd played an active role in at least two forgeries. And this man was on the board of the Napoleon Society with her father.

"There must be another explanation," she whispered. Reaching a landing, her skirt flared at her calves as she turned to walk down another flight. Through the arched opening, she watched well-bundled library patrons trickle through the entrance and into the grand lobby below. "They've asked me to write articles about how to identify forgeries to print in the society newsletter."

"Your father asked you to do that. Correct? Not Dr. DeVries."

"True, but DeVries is the editor. He didn't have to include the article. You're suggesting that Bradford is somehow involved in forgeries, either by selling them or by creating them as well. But if Bradford is DeVries, why would DeVries also print an article about how to tell the difference between fake and genuine? It would be counter to his purposes."

"Maybe. Maybe not. Didn't you tell me that his secretary was the one who actually put the newsletter together on the doctor's behalf? Maybe the editor isn't as involved in the process as we think. Maybe he didn't even know about the article until after it was printed."

Lauren forced herself to consider this possibility. Her footsteps slowed, her mood sinking with every lowering tread. "If he's found to be guilty of anything illegal, it will be far worse for the Napoleon Society than the small matter of the fire at the museum. It could put an end to everything my father's been working for. The society would never recover."

Joe took her hand and walked beside her, matching his pace to hers. "Let's take this one step at a time. If what you describe comes to pass, you will get to Egypt another way. A Napoleon Society expedition is not your only ticket."

She nodded. "My concern is more for my father. Shouldn't we warn him?"

"No." His answer was immediate and firm. In the next breath, they reached the main lobby on the first floor. He drew her around the corner of an enormous pillar so they stood in the shadows beneath the staircase. "You can't say anything about this to him. If DeVries and Bradford are the same man, he is already on edge because of this incident with the horse-and-rider forgery. We can't risk your father hinting anything else to him. We don't want to give DeVries a reason to run or destroy evidence. So it's imperative that we keep this to ourselves for now. Understand?"

She ached with the weight of this burden. "I hate secrets." Her voice was small, and she felt smaller still, especially here, surrounded by cold white marble vaulting high above her. "Secrets expand between people, pushing them apart."

Joe pulled her closer, until their foreheads were almost touching. "It doesn't have to be that way. Secrets are part of the job."

"Part of *your* job," she corrected. A couple passed by but paid Lauren and Joe no mind.

"You are a consultant on this case, Dr. Westlake. I need you to promise me you'll do nothing to sabotage it. I know this is hard for you, but that means you won't breathe a word of any of this to your father. Remember, he is keeping secrets from us, too."

She wrestled with his words, not wanting them to be true. But her dad had lied about falling onto the tracks. He was afraid of something, or someone, and wouldn't tell her what. Besides which, she recognized that Joe could have kept this from her, as well, for fear that she'd tell her father. But he'd trusted her enough to be honest. The last thing she wanted to do was make him regret it.

Lauren buried her dread. "I trust you, Joe. And I promise."

MONDAY, JANUARY 4, 1926

Cold sliced through Joe's open coat, but he kept it unfastened so he could reach his gun in an instant if he needed to.

He prayed he wouldn't need to. Not here, following Lauren on her walk to work through Central Park. But her description of the man with broad shoulders taking her picture at Grand Central had jogged his memory of the man spying on her the day they ice skated.

Joe had spent the rest of the weekend surveilling her, or rather, watching to see if anyone else was watching her. If there was any chance she'd been right about a man stalking her from Newport to New York City, Joe wanted to know about it. Lauren had agreed to his plan.

Snow settled like powdered sugar on her hat and coat. Methodically, he scanned the environment and backed off when Oscar Mc-Cormick walked past him, taking the lead. The young man had been only too eager to help. Switching places every so often gave them a broader perspective on the area. It also lowered their chances of being noticed.

Half a mile from where she'd started at the Beresford, Joe saw Lauren safely enter the rear doors of the Met. Trusting the museum security guards would do their job from there, he wound his way back to where he'd parked the police car and drove to a café to wait for McCormick.

Ten minutes later, the young officer arrived, a paper envelope beneath his arm. His cheeks were ruddy as he slid into the booth and slapped it on the table.

Joe poured him a mug of coffee from the carafe the waitress had already brought. "Did you look at them yet?"

"No, I just picked them up on the way here."

Joe tasted the coffee—Ferrara's it was not—and set the mug down. "Let's see."

McCormick opened the flap and withdrew the photographs he'd taken Saturday morning at the library.

Joe flipped through them.

"Will they work?" McCormick asked.

"These should." Several photos were of the doctor's back, but one was in profile, and a few others captured his front. "I'll meet with Mr. Sanderson and ask if he recognizes anyone in the photos. I suspect he'll be able to ID him as the elusive Daniel Bradford." Joe had considered inviting Mr. Sanderson to Saturday's meeting in person, but if Dr. DeVries spied him, he might have bolted before a positive ID could be made. The photos would be better. Besides, McCormick's presence had prompted Lauren to share a few more pieces to the puzzle.

Joe slid the photos back into the envelope. "I owe you one, kid."

"Uh, sir? Make that two. I found another photo you need to see. But this one, I didn't take." From inside his jacket, McCormick pulled an envelope and slid it across the table to Joe. "I mean, I *took* it, from my desk where I found it stuck inside a city directory, but I didn't, you know, *take* the picture." He mimed holding a camera.

"I get it, Mick."

He grinned at the abbreviation of his surname. "Mick. Yeah, I like it. Does that mean I can call you Cara?"

"No."

Joe's smile vanished when he slid the photograph out of the envelope. In it were a few people on the street in front of a brick building. One of them was Wade Martin. Someone had drawn an X in black marker over his head. On the back, Martin's name had been written.

Blood turned to ice in Joe's veins. He looked around the café, but other than the waitress smoking behind the breakfast counter, they were alone. From somewhere in the kitchen, a radio played the song "There's Egypt in Your Dreamy Eyes," its mood discordant with his own.

"Has anyone else seen this?"

"Just you so far. I figured you'd know what to do with it."

Joe nodded. "Tell me again where you found it."

"Like I said, I was going through one of the city directories and found it wedged right up into the spine in the M section."

"A city directory in your desk," Joe clarified. "The desk that had been Connor Boyle's."

"Bingo."

Joe dropped the photo on the table and looked at it again. That building in the background was the waterfront-warehouse-turned-speakeasy where Wade Martin had been killed. In the photo, he was exiting the building. Joe looked closer and saw that the frame had been stamped with the date. It was taken four days before the raid.

Wade Martin's death wasn't an accident, and it wasn't self-defense. It was premeditated murder, and Connor had been the trigger.

McCormick returned to the station long before Joe was ready. Questions clamored faster than he could pen them to paper. Who wanted Wade Martin dead? Who would benefit from Martin's death, or stood to lose something if he lived? And why on God's green earth had Connor been the killer?

On a fresh page in his notebook, Joe listed the facts he did know in chronological order.

> *In June 1923, Connor stopped frequenting Callahan's.*
>
> *From June 1923 to May 1925, four guns went missing every month from the property seized by the police. Connor Boyle was involved in every raid that had seized those guns. According to Big Red, those guns were never sold on the black market.*
>
> *In June 1923, Connor began giving Doreen empty wine bottles. Connor said they were all confiscated on Prohibition raids. I couldn't find them in the records.*
>
> *In November 1924, Connor said at St. Pat's that he wasn't ready to repent. Told me to take care of his aunt when something happened (not if).*
>
> *In April 1925, Connor asked Doreen if she could imagine a*

different life in a different city, but then resigned himself to the status quo.

In August 1925, only three guns went missing from police evidence. Connor was involved in those three raids, too.

On September 28, a photograph was taken of Wade Martin exiting a speakeasy. His face was marked with a black X.

Before October 2, the photograph was delivered to Connor.

On October 2, Connor and I participated in the same speakeasy raid. I was arresting Wade Martin, saw him drop the oyster shell. He denied knowing about it and told me to ask Connor, who had allegedly dropped it in his drink. Connor shot and killed Wade.

On November 26, I asked Connor about the oyster shell, and he told me to leave it alone for my own good.

On December 25, Doreen mentioned our conversation about the bottles he'd given her, and he got angry.

Joe stared at the timeline. If Connor had been paid for those guns by someone, it hadn't been in cash. He'd been paid with crates of the most expensive French wine smuggled into the country. It was time to share this, along with the photograph, directly with the new police commissioner, but since McLaughlin had just taken office on January 1, he'd be in meetings all week at least. So until Joe could put this in the commissioner's hands himself, he would keep quiet.

What happened with Connor in August and September? How was Wade Martin involved in all this? He hadn't forged the oyster shell—that honor had been Escalante's—and it certainly was not worth killing over. But if it held zero significance, why had both Connor and Wade tried to deflect attention from it?

Joe wouldn't find answers in the burned grounds at the bottom of his mug.

He might, however, find some over a pastrami on rye.

Forty minutes later, Joe sat in a bentwood chair at a table against the wall at Katz's Delicatessen. According to one of the owners, the antique dealer Reuben Feinstein always came on Mondays before the lunch crowd. While he waited, Joe took a bite of the best sandwich in town. If the glistening meat was piled any higher between these slices of rye, he'd have to eat it with a fork and knife. The pastrami melted in his mouth, erasing the leftover taste of the scalded swill from this morning.

When Feinstein entered, Joe watched him take a ticket and stand in line before bringing it to the counter. They punched the slip of paper with his order, loaded a tray with matzoh ball soup and potato latkes, and sent him on his way.

Swiping a napkin over his mouth, Joe waved him over. "Saved you a seat."

Feinstein's expression fell when he spotted Joe. But after looking over his shoulder, he joined him anyway. "I assume we're not meeting by chance."

Joe took a bite of the pickle spear that came with his sandwich, then pushed his tray to the end of the table. "You assume right." He wiped his hands again. "Have you had any more trouble with hoodlums breaking into your shop?"

"Not since you came to visit." Feinstein ducked his head and slurped a spoonful of soup.

"Listen, Mr. Feinstein." Joe leaned forward, dropping his voice. "I know you didn't file an insurance claim after that break-in. I know you're hiding the identity of whoever was responsible, and I'm guessing that's so no more harm comes to you or your shop. I get that. They probably warned you—strongly—against involving the police." He paused, studying every shift in the man's expression.

So far, Feinstein's breathing was steady, and so was his hand as he ate the soup. He made no reply, and no denial.

"But if they were extorting you for money, meeting their demands only feeds their power. Next time they'll come back for more. No matter what they told you, you're better off cooperating with me. The police are here to help law-abiding citizens like you."

Feinstein cut the fist-sized matzoh ball with the side of his spoon. "They didn't want money."

"Information, then."

No reply.

"All right." Joe sat back. "You don't want to talk. I get it. You eat, I'll talk, how's that? I've been looking into forgeries all over Manhattan. I caught one forger; his name is Vincent Escalante. You probably saw that in the paper."

Feinstein kept eating, unperturbed. "That sounds familiar, yes."

"Last October, a man named Wade Martin was killed while in possession of an oyster shell pendant forged by Escalante."

Feinstein shrugged. "I read that Martin was shot by a policeman in self-defense. The article didn't say anything about a forgery or piece of antiquity."

"Allegedly," Joe said quietly.

"How's that?"

"The policeman who shot him is awaiting trial. The jury will decide whether that was an accident or self-defense. I'm trying to figure whether the forgery had anything to do with Martin's death."

The antique dealer stared at Joe. "I've never met Wade Martin or this Escalante fellow in my life. I've never spoken to either on the telephone. I certainly never carried any of Escalante's forgeries in my shop."

"I believe you," Joe said. But that wasn't all he wanted to get a line on. "You sell higher-end antiques, don't you? In fact, I bet some of your items come from an exclusive, in-demand art buyer named Daniel Bradford."

Feinstein tugged his collar.

Joe opened the binder he'd brought with him and pulled out one of McCormick's photographs from yesterday morning. He still planned to meet with Mr. Sanderson and have him ID Dr. DeVries, but two positive identifications would be even better.

After wiping off the table in front of him, Joe spun the photograph to face Feinstein. "Do you recognize anyone in this picture? Besides me, that is." In this shot, McCormick had captured everyone who'd come for the artifact exchange.

Soup dribbled from Feinstein's spoon. Without taking a bite, he set it down. Sweat shone on his skin. His glasses slid down his nose, and he removed them, then mopped his face with a handkerchief.

Joe had hit a nerve. "You see someone you know, don't you?"

"Yes," he whispered.

"Mr. Feinstein, I'm on the verge of catching a forger who has cheated countless people and roped upstanding businessmen like yourself into the deception. It's not your fault. You don't deserve this misery. Help me catch him."

"None of these people broke into my shop."

Not surprising. "Let's put the break-in aside. Point to the person you recognize and tell me who he is."

"I never asked for any of this, you know."

"But you can help put an end to it."

Behind Feinstein, people shuffled through the lines with their tickets, and the place filled with the smell of enough cured, smoked, and steamed meat to feed half the borough, it seemed. As soon as one table opened up, a busboy would clear it and wipe it down as more diners would claim it. Bells dinged as satisfied customers brought their tickets to cash registers to pay at the end.

All of that faded to a meaningless blur when Reuben Feinstein finally pointed to a man in the photograph.

Lawrence Westlake.

"This man?" Joe tapped Lawrence's likeness.

"That's right."

Blood pounded in Joe's ears. He took out four more shots from what McCormick had given him and spread them on the table. Perhaps a different angle would help Feinstein identify Daniel DeVries instead. "Take another look," he urged.

Huffing a sigh, Feinstein pointed at Lawrence in all five pictures. "I may be color-blind, Detective, but I know who I saw. One doesn't forget the man who brings in the antiquity he did."

Joe would get to that later. First, "What's his name?"

"He never told me, or if he did, I honestly don't remember it." Sweat trickled from Feinstein's temple. "All I know is, this man came in one time to deliver an antique that I'd agreed to sell on spec when Daniel Bradford told me about it over the phone. I was expecting to meet Bradford, since he'd been the one to call. But this man showed up with it instead. Didn't introduce himself, but his voice wasn't like the one I remembered on the phone. When I asked him who to write the check to once the item sold, he said to make it out to the Napoleon Society." He heaved a great sigh. "When was this photograph taken?"

"Saturday morning."

"Which Saturday morning? This past one?"

When Joe confirmed it, Feinstein exhaled. "Thank God, thank God he's okay." The man's relief was palpable. Then his lips pursed, and his mood shifted into one Joe couldn't quite read.

"Mr. Feinstein, when did this man come in with the artifact? What was it he gave you, and who purchased it? Do you have a copy of the provenance?"

"I have to go. I've said too much. Please, if you want to help, don't follow me," he said, an uncanny echo of Lawrence's parting words. His tray full of uneaten latkes and tepid soup, Feinstein rushed off to pay his ticket and leave.

Nerves firing, Joe scooped the photographs back into the envelope and tucked them away. It was time for yet another fresh sheet in his notebook.

> *Date unknown: Daniel Bradford called Reuben Feinstein about a potential item to sell on speculation. Feinstein agreed.*
>
> *Date unknown: Lawrence Westlake brought the antiquity to the store and told Feinstein a check should be made out to the Napoleon Society in the event of its sale.*
>
> *November 24, 1925. Feinstein's Antiques is broken into, but not reported to police. No insurance claim filed. Whoever broke in wanted information, not money.*

November 25, 1925. Lawrence learns there has been a fire at the Napoleon House in Newport. Travels to Newport that night.

November 27, 1925. Lawrence arrives back in New York City with injuries to his head and hands and, allegedly, his shins. Claims he sustained injuries by falling to tracks, but this has been proven false. Refuses to offer another explanation.

January 4, 1926. Feinstein still refuses to name the person or persons who broke into his shop on November 24. Expresses relief when learns that Lawrence Westlake, who he has met only one time, is all right. Implied: Feinstein had feared harm had come to Lawrence.

In a daze, Joe gathered his things, including the half-eaten pastrami wrapped in paper, and paid for his meal at the register.

Back at headquarters, he barely returned McCormick's greeting and picked up the telephone without taking off his coat. "Put me through to the fire inspector in Newport, Rhode Island," he told the switchboard operator.

The call went through. After introducing himself, Joe said, "There was a fire on the roof of the Napoleon House on November 25, the day before Thanksgiving. I don't have the address, but it's an old house they're turning into a museum."

"Yeah, we know it. There was only one fire that night."

"What was the official cause of the fire? Faulty electrical wiring?"

"No," the inspector replied. "It was arson."

CHAPTER

30

Christina Moretti greeted Lauren like a long-lost friend when she and Joe arrived, even though Lauren wasn't a friend, and this wasn't a social call. Still, Christina insisted they share hot chocolate and French macarons in her Marie-Antoinette salon. The lonely woman carried the entire conversation herself.

For all her wealth and fashionable address, she clearly missed her former Brooklyn neighborhood and was hungry for the companionship she'd left behind when their social status moved them up and away from her roots. The Fifth Avenue mansion wasn't nearly as isolating as their Long Island estate, but whether here or there, the old-money neighbors persisted in pretending they were superior in every way.

It wasn't right, valuing and devaluing people based on where and when their money came from. That wasn't class; it was arrogance. Lauren was so weary of people who pretended to be superior. Of people pretending to be anything other than who they really were.

Joe had called yesterday and confirmed that upon seeing the photograph, Thomas Sanderson had named Dr. DeVries as the secretive art buyer, Daniel Bradford. But what did that mean for Lauren's father? She had no idea yet. It was good that they hadn't seen each other since Saturday. Since she had to pretend to know nothing, Lauren felt like a fake herself. Surely, Dad would notice.

"Thank you for the refreshments, Mrs. Moretti." Joe laid his napkin over the gold-edged china plate before him. "If you don't mind, we'd like to take a look at the provenance for that papyrus now."

"Of course." Christina stood, her snuffling pug close at her heels. "But first, you must come take a look at the papyrus itself. Dr. Westlake says it's quite magnificent."

Lauren blinked. The papyrus was magnificent. As a forgery. "Do you keep it on display?"

"Oh yes, none of our visitors would ever be able to tell the difference."

She led them into the Egyptian-themed dining room. Joe's eyes widened at the tomb-inspired wall paintings, courtesy of Peter Braun, before he directed his attention to the glass-covered Book of the Dead fragment built into the table.

He bent to inspect it. "If this is a forgery, it's the finest work I've ever seen."

"Then maybe it's not a forgery after all." Ray Moretti entered the room and immediately owned it. He exuded a confidence that fast eluded Lauren.

Her face warmed at his suggestion that she might have been wrong. On the other hand, if this was truly genuine, how could she not be happy?

"It's all right, Dr. Westlake." He flashed a dazzling smile. "We all make mistakes." He glanced at Joe. "Don't we?" He was shorter than Joe by two inches, but there was something about the older man's presence that took up more space in the room.

Joe's shoulders squared. "Nonetheless, we'd like to see the provenance."

Mr. Moretti unbuttoned his blazer and slipped a hand into his trouser pocket. "Have you got a search warrant for it?"

"Ray!"

He turned to his wife. "You should have told me to expect company, dear. I would have been home sooner."

Tension crackled like static electricity between Mr. Moretti and anyone he looked at. Then, that smile again. It was disorienting. "Search warrant," he repeated, chuckling. "I'm only kidding. Of course, Dr. Westlake. For you, anything. You didn't even need to bring the police. Christina, you know where it is." He waved her away.

When she returned, she handed the provenance to Lauren. Joe stood beside her, so he surely saw what they'd both been looking for. The papyrus was purchased from Sayed Mohammed. It was not the man from whom Bradford had acquired the canopic jars, but it was the same dealer from whom the Napoleon Society had acquired the forged horse-and-rider carving.

"You look worried," Christina said. "What is it?"

Lauren passed the provenance to Joe for his closer inspection. "I identified another forgery over the holidays, and it came from the same dealer as this papyrus."

"What are you saying, exactly?" Mr. Moretti cradled his goblet in one hand, swirling the contents.

"I'm saying that the person who sold this in Egypt has sold at least one other forgery. It stands to reason that wasn't the only one." She paused, allowing the Morettis to draw the only logical conclusion for themselves.

"You're saying my Book of the Dead isn't real again."

"It's more than possible, yes."

"But the guy who's responsible is in Egypt. I don't see that anything can be done about it, even if you're right."

"If this is a fake, and I believe Dr. Westlake's assessment that it is," Joe inserted, "we'll need to take it into evidence."

"That won't be necessary." Mr. Moretti sipped his wine, and Christina went to stand beside him. "I'm not concerned about this piece's authenticity. You have looked at it twice, Dr. Westlake, and I've been living with it, studying it for months. It is as real to me as I could hope. You will not seize my property."

If he didn't want to pursue justice and was happy to keep what he had, there was nothing else Lauren or Joe could do.

————

"Well, that was informative." Joe tucked Lauren's hand in his elbow as they walked down Fifth Avenue toward the Met.

Lauren looked over her shoulder. Joe hated that she felt the need to do that, even with him beside her. Even more, he hated that her insecurity had only started after consulting with him on these cases.

"But it doesn't do us any good, does it?" she asked. "Knowing that Sayed Mohammed was the same dealer responsible for passing along—if not forging himself—at least two fakes. If Mr. Moretti doesn't care, then . . ." She shrugged.

"I can still send word to the authorities in Luxor and let them know what we learned. They'll want to check things out. It may be enough to send them photographs of the horse and rider." After that, the outcome was out of his hands.

When they arrived at the Met's front entrance, Joe expected to simply cut through the building and exit through the rear doors to cross Central Park and reach the Beresford. Naturally, he'd escort her until she was safely home.

"Do you mind if we make a quick detour?" She pulled off her hat as they entered the building, her nose still pink from the cold. "I want to pick up the mail Anita placed in my office this afternoon."

Joe didn't mind.

In the basement, the lights were dim in the corridor that led to Lauren's office. Unlocking her door, she stepped inside and something crunched beneath her shoe.

She punched on the light and gasped.

All over the floor were the shattered remains of some kind of artifact. She sank to her knees in the rubble and groaned.

Adrenaline spiking, Joe darted into the hall, alert for any sign of the intruder. But the door had been locked. Whoever had gotten in either had the key or coerced someone who did.

Lauren's muffled cry drew him back from the empty hall. Kneeling beside her, he read the note in her hand.

> *Dr. Westlake:*
> *Mind your own business, I said. If you don't start listening, the loss of this one priceless artifact is only the beginning. You have more to lose than statues.*

Behind the note were photographs of Lauren. On the train. In Grand Central Terminal. Sitting with Lawrence at the park. Whoever sent this was showing her how close he'd gotten to her, again and again.

Joe trapped an unholy oath in his throat.

"No, no, no," Lauren whispered, spreading her fingers through the dust and shards on the floor. "He must have grabbed something from one of the storerooms. If he had a key to get into my office, it's as likely he grabbed an item from the inventory." She moaned again. "How many thousands of dollars—tens of thousands, perhaps hundreds of thousands—have I cost the Met?"

"This wasn't your doing," Joe told her. "We'll find whoever did this and hold him responsible, not you."

"It doesn't matter. This—whatever it was—it was irreplaceable." She covered her eyes. Her chin trembled. "What has been destroyed today? And what will be next? I'll lose my job over this and my entire career."

Not if Joe could help it.

"Lauren." He put his arm around her, holding her to his side. "Didn't you used to have a statue paperweight from the sales desk?"

Her gaze jerked to the desk. Then she sorted through the mess until she found enough slivers to piece together again. She swiped her finger through some dust and rubbed it against her thumb.

The lines in her face relaxed. "It's fake. That statuette of Hatshepsut was nothing more than plaster. Whoever wrote this note must have no idea about Egyptology if he thought this was a priceless antiquity. Even a hobby collector should have known better. Which means whoever wrote this could not have been the forger we're looking for."

"I don't think we can rule that out yet." Joe shut the door behind them, then shifted to sit on the floor with Lauren. "He could have meant to throw us off by calling this reproduction priceless. Either way, it's an escalated warning. The statue is fake, but the threat is real. Let's see that invitation to the Moretti Christmas party one more time."

Shadows dimmed her eyes as she looked at him, then pulled the invitation from a pile on her desk. She withdrew the card and held it beside today's anonymous note.

The handwriting was distinctly different.

Lauren released a breath. "Mr. Moretti knows his Egyptology," she admitted. "Shelves in his personal library are devoted to the subject, including several volumes that I studied for my doctorate degree. If he'd wanted to threaten me, he wouldn't have smashed a fake—or at least, he wouldn't have called it priceless."

"Hang on." Dread lined Joe's gut. He reached inside his jacket pocket and withdrew the photograph he still carried of Wade Martin with a black X over his face.

His heartbeat pounding, Joe flipped the picture over to see *Wade Martin* written on the back. He looked from it to the note they found today, comparing especially the capital letters from *Wade* and *Westlake,* and from *Martin* and *Mind your own business.*

The handwriting was a match.

God in heaven.

All breath left his lungs. He looked to Lauren, unnaturally still beside him, eyes wide. Her pulse was visible in the hollow between her collarbones.

She'd seen. She knew what this meant.

Lawrence hadn't been paranoid in Newport. He must have known the cause of his fire had been arson, either a punishment or a warning of greater harm to come. Lauren hadn't been imagining things on the train and at Grand Central. Someone had been taking her photograph, and now they knew why. If she didn't stop consulting, she'd be next.

"Joe," she rasped, looking to him for answers, for help, though he'd been the one to lead her into danger.

He gathered her to himself, lifting her onto his lap as she threw her arms around his neck. "I'm sorry," he whispered. Her aunt and uncle had been right about him. They'd been right that she'd be better off cutting all ties and that spending time with Joe would only lead to trouble.

"You're not the one who's threatening to hurt me."

But if she was hurt by anyone, it would be because of him.

Her tears wet his neck and undid him. He longed to keep her safe, whether that meant holding her close or pushing her far away from him and the world of crime he lived in. Would she understand that? Could he survive it? He buried kisses in her hair and held her tighter.

"What do we do?" she asked him.

If only he knew the answer. "Be careful," he began anyway. "Don't tell anyone your schedule who doesn't need to know. Mix up your routine. If there's a place and time you usually have lunch, for instance, change it. Take a taxi to work. No more walking through Central Park."

She agreed.

"I shouldn't be seen with you, either, unless absolutely necessary. But McCormick and I will be watching as much as we can to make sure you're safe."

She leaned back and twisted to face him. "What about my father? I think he's in trouble, too."

"We'll get a patrol on his place, too, but you are my priority." He pushed the words past a growing wedge of anger. "The threats should be for me, not you. You don't deserve this. This wouldn't be happening if it weren't for what I've asked you to do."

Lauren shook her head, and a tendril of hair coiled beside her face. "You didn't force me into anything. Everything I've done has been because I wanted to. I don't regret a single moment I've spent with you."

His throat contracted. "Lauren, if you decide to walk away from me after this, I will understand. Find another man to be happy with, and live a long and peaceful life. I will let you go because I love you."

She smiled through glittering tears. "I will stay by your side, Joe, because I love you, too."

The salt on her lips was the sweetest thing he'd ever tasted. He kissed her with a hunger he'd long denied, and she matched his passion with her own. He couldn't lose her now.

He wouldn't.

CHAPTER

31

Almost two weeks had passed since Lauren had last seen Joe. So when he surprised her by coming to her apartment, she was overjoyed to see him and afraid something was wrong all at once.

Judging by the way he kissed her before even taking off his coat, he'd missed her as much as she'd missed him.

Giggling drifted toward them from the direction of the living room, and Lauren placed a hand on his chest, gently pressing him away. "Not in front of the kids," she teased, turning around and winking at Elsa and Ivy, whose girlish behavior totally earned the remark.

"Ooh! What's in the bag, Joe?" Unfolding her legs from beneath her, Elsa scrambled from the couch.

Ivy quickly followed. "What'd you bring us, huh? Huh?"

"Anyone here like cannoli?" Joe held a paper bag aloft, resembling a father who stayed away too long and won back affection with treats. Lauren would have laughed had she not been staring at a variation of her childhood.

But this was Joe. And cannoli *was* cannoli. Her mood lifted again as the pastry flaked apart in her mouth, releasing the sweet ricotta.

"Oh, Ferrara's," Ivy sighed around a mouthful. "It's good for what ails you, that's what. Here, kitty." Ignoring Lauren's protests, Ivy let Cleo lick her fingers clean.

Minutes later, Elsa announced that she and Ivy had somewhere they needed to be. "We'll be back *any moment*, you two, so don't get too used to the privacy." She grinned.

As soon as the door shut behind them, Joe's expression sobered. "I've been looking into some potential forgeries these last couple of weeks, meeting with people and taking photographs of their items. Would you take a look at these and see what you think?" He sat on the couch, and she joined him.

"Of course." They had agreed she would stop consulting on forgeries in person, but looking at pictures at home seemed a low risk, indeed. Joe wouldn't ask if it weren't important.

He handed Lauren a stack of photographs.

Every one of them showed some angle of a scarab. "Are these images duplicates?" she asked.

"No, that's the front and back of six different scarabs from six different owners."

She looked closer. "Then we're looking at six different forgeries, all made by the same forger."

"You're sure?"

"It's the same mistake in the hieroglyph text in every one of them. I'll spare you the finer points of translation, but trust me, these are fakes."

Joe passed her three more photographs, each showing a section of a papyrus. "And these?"

"The same mistake is in all three photos. Is it the same papyrus?"

"Three."

The cat twisted between her ankles, likely hungry for dinner, but Lauren ignored her. "I'd bet anything the forger of the scarabs forged these as well. The articles don't match the pronouns. In the Egyptian language, articles are feminine or masculine according to what they're referring to. These don't match. No literate Egyptian would have made such a mistake."

"That's what Peter Braun said, too."

Lauren blinked. "You asked him?"

"I wanted to see what he would say when I showed these to him. He wasn't as quick with his verdict as you were, but he landed on the same one. I've ruled him out as a suspect. The forger wouldn't tell me his workmanship was fake."

"I agree." She exhaled, somewhat relieved. "But how did you find nine forgeries in less than two weeks, especially if they were all owned by separate people?"

Joe pulled from his pocket his father's brochure from the Napoleon Society and pointed to a list of charter members on the back panel. "I met with as many as I could. Every one of these artifacts had been given to them as part of their membership package."

"Oh no, are you sure?" But of course he was sure. She held her head in her hands. That made ten forgeries that the Napoleon Society had channeled. "This is terrible. Did you check the provenance? Was it the same dealer in Luxor? He must have sold the society a large batch of artifacts all at once. How embarrassing."

"You mean, how criminal."

She straightened, heat creeping up from her collar. "The board certainly didn't *mean* to pass off forgeries. The Napoleon Society is as much a victim as any of its members."

"The provenance documents vary." He gave her a stack of paper to look through while he explained. "Some of them say the scarabs were purchased from Sayed, while others say they were excavated by a Napoleon Society board member. But every document uses the same language to describe the finds. How is that possible unless Dr. DeVries is behind it? There's no doubt that he's lying when he says some of these fakes were uncovered in Napoleon Society digs. Forgers don't bury their fakes. They sell them."

He was right.

Lauren paced the living room, trying to wrap her mind around this information.

"The Napoleon Society could be a front," Joe said. "The entire organization may be a fraud."

"No, not entirely." She hated that her voice sounded like she was pleading. "I admit Dr. DeVries seems to be guilty, but Dad would never be part of something like this. He was the one who invited me out to Newell St. John's house on Staten Island so I could look for forgeries."

"And where did Newell's forged ointment jar come from? Your father's old rival, Theodore Clarke. Is it possible he already knew that? Could he have found satisfaction in your discrediting him? Or could your father have planted a fake jar in place of the real thing for this express purpose? Maybe he knew that word would get out about it. Maybe that's what he wanted. Maybe he leaked that himself."

"No! Joe, you're going too far. He'd never—he wouldn't do that. Dad practically begged me for those articles on forgeries, but we didn't print anyone's names, least of all Clarke's. His goal was only to protect his members from forgery."

Joe stood, placing himself in her path. "Can you think of any other reasons Lawrence might have wanted you to write those articles based on your findings with me?" The way he asked, the way he looked at her, made her think he already had an answer. All these questions bewildered her. There were so many, and they were coming so fast, she scarcely could keep up.

"He—he wanted to work with me," she said. "He wanted me to gain credibility so the board would approve me as a member of their upcoming expedition. But that wasn't the only reason I did it. It might have started that way, but I wanted to help. I wanted to be close to him, Joe. You, of all people, should understand that."

"I do." He wrapped her hands in his. "But this isn't about your motivation and purpose. It's about his. So let's talk about the articles you've already given him. What was the subject of the first one?"

"I wrote about the St. John forgery *without* smearing Theodore Clarke."

"Right, that had nothing to do with the Napoleon Society, and he already knew that. And the second article?"

"That's at the printer right now, but I saw the proof last week. It's about plaster molds being passed off as wooden carvings."

"And that was based on Vincent Escalante's forgeries. Again, it doesn't point to the society. Have you written others?"

Unspoken questions loomed in Lauren's mind. She forced herself to answer only the one Joe had voiced. "When my father stopped by to show me the proofs, I mentioned I'd finished another article but submitted it to the Met's *Bulletin* instead. The content focused on hieroglyphic errors and seemed rather academic, so I thought it better suited to my employer and colleagues than the *Napoleon Herald* subscribers."

"Hieroglyphic errors. Such as feminine and masculine articles?" She nodded.

"How did he respond to the news?"

Lauren sat in the armchair behind her. "He lost his temper," she said quietly. "He said he was upset because I'd promised articles to him, but I reminded him that I am employed by the Met, not the Napoleon Society. I even said he could reprint it later if he really thought it matched his newsletter's demographics. But that wasn't good enough for him. I couldn't understand it."

Joe knelt before her, still holding her hands. "Sweetheart, remember when you brought me to the Tomb of Perneb on Christmas Eve? You explained how three different teams of people worked together on the murals and suggested we may be looking not for one master forger but for a team whose combined skills could include painting, carving, sculpting, and more. I think you were right."

She blinked back the sting in her eyes. "You think the team is the Napoleon Society."

Gently, he pressed kisses in the valleys between her knuckles. "I do. I think they've been using you to train them on how to make their forgeries more convincing. But we don't know how the other two members of the board feel about it. There might be an internal power play among the board."

Everything in her railed against the entire idea. She jerked her hands from his and folded her arms. He was taking away what she had so longed for—the trustworthiness of her father, and the relief it had been to know that, at long last, she was redeeming their relationship, as Mother had wanted. As *she* wanted now, too.

Over the past few months, Lauren had taken down, stone by stone, the wall she'd built to protect her heart from further hurt from her dad. She felt every one of those stones where they still lay in a pile in her chest. She felt them shift. But she would not build that wall again, could not jump to another conclusion that could shut Dad out forever. Against her will, however, doubt stacked upon doubt, past hurts the mortar between them. The wall grew.

With all her strength, she kicked at it. "How could you say such a thing? How could you, Joe?"

Then she realized she already knew. Joe's father had deceived his family in the past. Joe had felt betrayed by that, and if her hunch was right, by his friend Connor, as well. He never talked about it, but Greta had mentioned on Christmas Day that Doreen's nephew had been Joe's friend. They'd worked together on the force, and now he was in jail. That was all she knew, but it was enough.

Joe was trying to protect her from what he'd experienced. But he was wrong.

"My dad is not your dad," Lauren said.

A spark of understanding flared in Joe's eyes. "You're right about that. Pop was a victim." He left it there, but the implication swung between them, too bright and harsh to look upon directly.

"You're so sure my father is at the core of a forgery ring? Without even giving him the chance to explain himself? I don't know why this happens over and over, but somehow, he is made to look like a villain. He's misunderstood. When he's allowed to share his side of the story, we always find him not guilty."

Joe sat back on his heels. "One or two forgeries might be a mistake. But all of the ones I showed you tonight—that's a pattern. It points to intention."

Lauren stood. If Joe stayed here any longer, said any more, she'd come apart inside. "Leave," she whispered. "I can't do this, Joe. I can't believe this of him."

He rose. "You can't? Or you won't?"

Unable to bear his searching eyes, she looked past him to the fireplace mantle. "Don't do this to me," she said to the father staring back from the photograph.

TUESDAY, JANUARY 19, 1926

The Brooklyn Bridge passed over Joe. Or rather, he passed beneath it. Through the web of steel cables and Gothic arches, a full-bellied sky promised snow.

The chests of confiscated guns and knives kept in the Property Room were full again, which meant they needed to be disposed of to make room for more. Joe had volunteered to escort the weapons on the city's tugboat *Macom* on their way to the Narrows, the strait between Brooklyn and Staten Island. Oscar McCormick had come with him.

At the moment, Joe's thoughts traveled over the bridge, back into Manhattan, and landed at the Met, with Lauren. He had known she'd be upset when he told her his theory about the Napoleon Society and her father. He wasn't surprised she'd put up a fight. But he hadn't expected her to throw him out.

Lauren needed time, he reminded himself. Joe had been uncovering evidence of her father's betrayal without her, piece by piece, and she'd learned about it all at once. That was a shock. He got that. How long had it taken Joe to get over Connor's betrayal?

Maybe that was the wrong question. One didn't get over something like that. The best one could do was get through it.

"What did the new commissioner say?" McCormick's voice

brought him back to the main deck of the tugboat. Joe knew he was asking about the meeting he'd had to discuss everything he'd learned about Connor, the guns, and the wine.

The pilot inside the wheelhouse couldn't possibly hear them. With the tug chugging down the East River, they could barely hear themselves. It was a luxury to speak freely. As reluctant as Joe was to trust other policemen, the kid hadn't been around long enough to turn. Maybe he wouldn't. Maybe he'd learn from Connor's example and take a stand for what was right and good.

"He took it seriously," Joe told him.

"You didn't get in trouble for looking into it?"

Joe shook his head. Wind chapped his face, and the smell of exhaust from all the river traffic clung to him. "McLaughlin said that since Moretti's connection to Connor's case isn't yet proven, I'm free to watch for anything suspicious where he's concerned. His file is clean, but his brother's isn't."

McCormick sniffed and ran a handkerchief under his reddened nose. "He has a brother?"

"Tony." Joe wondered if he'd seen him. Had he been at the Christmas party? If so, had he been wearing normal clothes or disguised in French silk and powdered wig? "No convictions, just charges, but none have stuck."

"Like what?"

Joe shifted his weight. A wooden chest did not make a comfortable chair. "Mostly accomplice and accessory type charges. But combined with all these other loose ends, it's enough to warrant keeping an eye on him."

"Four eyes are better than two," McCormick quipped. "That is, if you're planning a stakeout. I don't think you're supposed to do those alone."

Joe chuckled. "Yeah, Mick. Okay."

They stared out over the tug's wake, since the wheelhouse blocked the view forward anyway. All Joe could see was where he'd been. Snowflakes formed and flurried, disappearing in the dark grey river.

Finally, nine miles south of the Brooklyn Bridge, the tugboat reached the Narrows. As it slowed and made a wide turn, Joe and McCormick shoved a wooden chest to the rear of the deck, opened it, and dumped the contents into the drink. The East River splashed as they emptied one chest after another.

He tried again to imagine what Connor had done with guns like these, and why.

Maybe Murphy was right that Joe didn't know when to let go. Of this, of the forgery cases, of Lauren. If anything, he held on tighter.

CHAPTER

32

FRIDAY, JANUARY 22, 1926

All week long, Lauren had tried to convince herself that what Joe had brought to her Monday night was simply his own wild imaginings. His boss pressured him for answers, and Joe was supplying them from speculation. The Napoleon Society couldn't be a forgery ring. Dad couldn't be involved. Her name could not be attached to the newsletter of criminals. Besides that, there was no way Dad would hurt her this way or prey on countless others.

But the photographs Joe had brought had been impossible to reconcile. She had studied them this week, along with the copies of the provenance documents. The mistakes were identical, even though the provenance said the artifacts had been procured at different times and places. But these forgeries were the work of one or two people, not several.

"Knock, knock." Anita entered Lauren's office, smelling faintly of the cigarettes she preferred, and extended a stack of mail.

Thanking her, Lauren tossed it on the desk.

"It's not all junk this time, Dr. Westlake. Something from the Van-dermeers." She paused. "You need anything else? Coffee, water?"

Lauren looked up at her assistant. "I don't think even coffee would give me what I need right now."

"That sounds serious." Anita slapped a Hershey bar on Lauren's desk. "Chocolate, then. It never fails to soothe and fortify. The almonds are protein, and your body needs that anyway."

There were worse ways to cope. As Anita whisked away, Lauren unwrapped the candy bar and took a bite, summoning the nerve to open what Miles Vandermeer had sent her.

It had occurred to Lauren on Wednesday that she had never truly inspected the jewelry Victoria had won at the gala in November. It had been displayed in glass cases at the Hotel Astor, and then she'd seen Victoria wearing the pieces at her Long Island Christmas party. But she hadn't looked at the back of either the necklace or the bracelet.

Dad had vouched for their authenticity.

She ought to see for herself. But after the threat she received two weeks ago, she couldn't risk being seen visiting collectors anymore.

After one more bite of chocolate, she drew a piece of Vandermeer stationery from the manila envelope.

Dear Dr. Westlake,

My secretary informed me of your request for photographs of the front and back of my wife's newest pieces of Egyptian jewelry. As it happens, I'd already had photographs taken for the purpose of filing them with our insurance company. One can never be too careful about safeguarding one's investments. I've enclosed copies of these photographs and hope they are sufficient for your purposes. If they are to be used in some kind of publication, we would be grateful to be named as the owners.

Yours very cordially,
Mr. Miles Vandermeer, Esq.

Careful to handle only the white borders of the glossy photographs, Lauren pulled them out and felt herself begin to relax.

The workmanship on the pectoral, with the three-hundred-some pieces of inlaid stones, was breathtaking even in black and white.

The photographer had expertly captured every detail. The next photograph showed the pectoral in context of the entire necklace. The next one showed the back.

Heat singed Lauren's face. The back of the pectoral was a smooth, flat surface of gold.

This was no royal woman's necklace from the Middle Kingdom. If it had been, the back would have been chased in gold—an outline of every detail on the front. She could not pretend the fault lay in blurry photography.

There were no lines. If this was real gold, and real semiprecious stones, it had not been made during the Middle Kingdom. It had never graced the neck of royalty.

Eyelids stinging, she flipped to the photographs of the bracelet, and stopped on the image showing the underside of the scarabs. She covered her mouth. The mistakes on every one matched the mistakes on the scarabs Joe had photographed and shown her on Monday.

Was nothing real? Was nothing as she had thought it to be? These were no token pieces, either. The amount the Vandermeers had paid to win them would have more than covered the cost of replacing the roof on the Napoleon House. So why had he seemed so concerned about the cash to get it done? Would Dad be able to refund the sum in full?

The implications made her light-headed. Then she turned to the last photograph, which showed the provenance documents. No dealer was named for the necklace or bracelet. According to this, Dad had found the pieces himself during an excavation in 1898. She struggled to believe that given the mistakes in workmanship. Besides, if these pieces were real, especially the pectoral, they would have been a glorious find. Surely something to write home about.

After work that evening, while Elsa and Ivy were out, Lauren brought the box of letters to the living room and searched them until her eyes grew bleary. Dad never mentioned finding a pectoral in the year 1898 or beyond it.

Sighing, she leaned her head back on the sofa. She hadn't really expected to find a record of it. If that piece had been in his possession all this time, he would have shown it to her. That's what he did. He missed birthdays and holidays, and never apologized for any of it in all the letters she'd read. In fact, he'd only apologized about all of that to Lauren after she'd been hired at the Met. But he did show Lauren the treasures he'd found. Except this one.

"I need to ask him about it," she said aloud, trying to convince herself. She had no desire to call him tonight.

A honking horn from outside snapped her circuitous reveries. Sitting up, she looked through the box again. She'd only read letters her dad had written from 1898 on. Maybe she ought to read those written by Mother. The chances that she would be the one to mention a specific find of his seemed small, and Lauren thought she'd already read through all of them, anyway.

She pulled all the letters out of the box to sort through them again and found one that had been lying flat on the bottom. It was from 1898, in her mother's hand. Lauren skimmed the first couple of paragraphs. Then,

> I wanted to wait until your return to tell Lauren about my diagnosis. She deserves to have both parents here to support her. But now you tell me you're extending your trip indefinitely, and for all your words, I could not decipher the real reason why. Do you realize I have yet to feel my husband's arms around me since I learned I have cancer?
>
> Lauren knew something was wrong. I had to tell her, Lawrence. As soon as I did, she ran into your office and locked the door. She locked me out, as you have done. I don't blame her—she's a child of five and doesn't understand. Perhaps in your office with its maps and pictures of Egypt, she can be far away from here, and far away from the news she is too small to carry.
>
> I wish you were here to comfort your daughter, even if you won't come home for me. My only recourse was to go outside and climb

the tree outside your office so I could climb through the window. I pulled on a pair of your trousers under my dress—let it never be said that you're the only Westlake who loves an adventure—and did my best to climb that tree. I would have succeeded, too, if only I'd been two inches taller to reach the branch I needed. Next, I went to the carriage house for reinforcements but found the ladder had all but rotted. By this time Nancy found me, and I was so exhausted from my failed attempts I hadn't the strength to fight her off when she brought me back inside. I suppose it was the sight of blood that made her a little hysterical. It was only my hands from the bark. And perhaps my knees. I'm afraid your trousers will never be the same.

Neither will Lauren.

Tears coursed down Lauren's cheeks. She remembered that day. She remembered running from what her mother had told her and doing her best to hide from it. She remembered Mother knocking on the door and calling her name. Lauren had covered her ears and rocked back and forth under Dad's desk. All the while, Mother had been trying to reach her, sick as she was.

Why hadn't Dad come home? Why had he left his wife with such a burden to carry on her own? Anger bubbled and steamed, the pressure building inside Lauren. Swiping the tears from her face, she read on.

You'll never guess who paid us a call here today. Theodore Clarke was in the area visiting his good friend Dr. James Breasted, who teaches at the University of Chicago. The last time Theo called on me I was a young woman living in Manhattan under my parents' roof.

You must have told him about my diagnosis—did you?—because he arrived with the most gorgeous flowers. Glorious roses in every shade of pink and yellow, with green hydrangea blooms, bursting with life and beauty and fragrance. He brought five vases full, which kept Nancy busy placing them throughout the house. Anyhow, he came when Lauren was romping about outside.

It felt so good to speak with another adult, aside from Nancy. I'd have rather spoken to you, Lawrence, but you weren't here. He was. I can't tell you how refreshing it was to have someone to talk to, who listened to me. We didn't get more personal than propriety allowed, I assure you. He didn't stay overlong—not even long enough to see Lauren, for he had another appointment to keep. But I shall enjoy the flowers as long as they live, and remember that on this day, I felt cared for, or at least noticed. By someone.

The letter fluttered to her lap. That explained how Mr. Clarke had known Mother. Had he previously been a suitor? Aunt Beryl would know. In any case, Lauren was touched to hear of Mr. Clarke's attentions when she needed the comfort of kindness, but Dad could not have enjoyed her referring to him as Theo. Had he been jealous? If he had said so in a reply, that letter had not survived. But she couldn't help but wonder if this played into the rivalry between them. Did Dad feel replaced? Threatened? He shouldn't, but sometimes people felt what they feared.

Cleo jumped on the mantel, threaded between the picture frames, then leapt to the bookcase. Before Lauren could stop her, the cat had found the shabti figures and knocked them to the floor.

"No!" Lauren lunged from the sofa but stopped when the two pieces broke into six. Dad had said they were made of faience. He said he'd excavated them himself years ago and kept them with her in mind all this time.

She'd never questioned whether they were real. Never questioned whether her father himself was a counterfeit.

Sometimes people felt what they feared. And sometimes they saw what they wanted to see.

Lauren scooped up the broken figures. The insides of the pieces were white.

"Plaster," she whispered. "Painted plaster." She hurled them back to the floor and watched them shatter.

Through the haze of white dust, she saw in her mind's eye the photographs Joe had brought of the forged papyruses and scarabs.

In her second article, she had written that plaster would show white if an artifact was scratched, chipped, or broken. Dad omitted it. Now she knew the real reason why. Even if those scarabs Joe had shown her didn't have the errors in the text, she'd bet they'd been made of painted plaster.

If Dad was fake, so was their so-called restored relationship. The dream she'd cherished, a mirage. A hole ripped open inside her where the love of her father should have been.

Joe was right. Dad was as guilty as Dr. DeVries. The photos she'd seen from Mr. Vandermeer today only added to the evidence. What a fool she'd been to let him back into her life, to place so much attachment on a man who only wanted to use her.

Mechanically, she swept up the mess on the floor. But the mess her father had made was so much bigger than she could manage.

Hands shaking, she stuffed the letters back into the box and retired to her room for the night. She fell into bed, burrowing into the covers, and begged for a deep and dreamless sleep.

"What does Tony Moretti do on a Friday night?" Oscar McCormick looked even younger in the plain clothes he wore for the stakeout. Headlamp beams from oncoming traffic flashed over his smooth-cheeked face.

Joe swiped a hand over the stubble that said he hadn't shaved since four o'clock this morning. Then he turned the wheel, steering the unmarked police car onto 6th Street, heading southwest. "We're about to find out."

They'd waited outside Tony Moretti's known place of business— an office building in Midtown—long enough for their worst enemy to be boredom. You lose focus, you look away, you miss the thing you're waiting for. Then they'd spied Moretti getting into a black Rolls-Royce. Now they were on the move.

McCormick was obviously trying not to look excited. "Do you think we're going to Little Italy? The Bowery?"

"I think we should concentrate on following their tail without getting noticed," Joe muttered.

"Right." After that, the kid was quiet, the cords in his neck visible as he craned to keep an eye on Moretti's car. Joe kept at least one vehicle between them at all times, sometimes more.

The drive was easy. One straight shot down 6th Street, for about two miles. If Moretti's driver had suspected a tail, they'd have turned a few times in an attempt to shake it off. Instead, the Rolls pulled to a stop in plain sight across from 77 MacDougal Street, in the Italian South Village.

"Italian Rifle Club," Joe said as he parked the car about half a block away. He pointed at the three conjoined Gothic Revival rowhouses adorned with full-height cast-iron balconies on all three levels.

McCormick peered through the windshield. "I don't see a sign."

"Trust me."

"I do."

The young man was growing on Joe, that was sure. "It doesn't have a sign out front, but it's been in this location since last year. Its official name is *Tiro A Segno*, which means 'Fire at the target.'" He paused to watch Tony Moretti enter the building. "It's members only in there. This is as close as we get until he comes out again."

"If it's a club with membership, we can find out who the other members are to see who his associates might be."

"But we're not about to waltz in there and ask for a list," Joe added. "We don't want to risk Tony getting suspicious."

A bang on the roof of the car shot adrenaline through Joe. In the next instant, a hand gloved in black was knocking on Joe's window.

"Can I help—Mr. Moretti." Joe rolled down the window. "Nice to see you again."

"Hey, Joe." Ray Moretti laughed. "I thought that was you. Are you here for the club? You're Italian, right? Caravello?"

"Half Italian."

"Can't half Italians be members? They got a thing for purebreds or what?"

Joe shrugged. "I'm not a member yet. My friend here is definitely not Italian, so . . ."

Ray leaned down and looked at McCormick. "Nice to meet you. This is the first time I've seen you without Dr. Westlake. You two still working together?"

"No," Joe said truthfully. "She has enough to do with her own job. I released her as a consultant."

"Well, win some, lose some, right? Say, I don't want to be rude, Joe, but I'm freezing out here. Why don't you boys come in and be my guests. Get a coffee, read the paper." When Joe hesitated, Ray added, "It won't be a problem. I'll vouch."

Joe smiled.

Inside the rifle club, a warm glow pervaded an atmosphere of newsprint, roasted coffee, and men's cologne. Newspapers in English and Italian draped a rack near the front door. Loud conversation grew louder as it ricocheted off wood-paneled walls. Framed photographs celebrated famous members, past and present. There was Enrico Caruso, the opera tenor. There was Fiorello La Guardia, formerly on the New York City Board of Aldermen, currently serving in Congress.

Tony Moretti wasn't in sight.

While Ray vouched for them with a stocky Italian wearing a shoulder harness beneath his jacket, Joe glanced at McCormick and sent him what he hoped was a reassuring nod. A nod that said he hadn't planned on dragging the kid into this place, but he'd safely see him out again.

They went deeper inside, passing through smaller rooms with round tables lit by votive candles and wall sconces. Hearty greetings followed Ray. This was gold. Joe studied and memorized every face. It could be Joe had seen them before in a daily lineup. But they wouldn't recognize him. That's why the detectives wore masks. He couldn't ask for a better in to see who Ray's friends were. The assignment for tonight had been to watch Tony. But friends of one brother might be friends of the other.

"So, Joe, what's your pleasure?" Ray turned a broad smile on him. "You're not going to raid the joint for booze, are you?"

"That's not why I'm here." But he didn't doubt that a little gin, if not something stronger, made its way into the coffee mugs.

"Didn't think so. Say, how about a little target practice for you and your friend?"

So far, McCormick had not been named, and Joe didn't mind keeping it that way. The less the Morettis knew about the young officer, the better. Call it paranoia, call it instinct. But Joe didn't like the idea of these brothers getting familiar with such a young, impressionable cop.

"Come on. You'll blow off some steam." Ray led them down the dark stairway, toward the percussive sound of shooting.

In the cellar, it was a strange thing indeed to have Ray Moretti give Joe a weapon. But when he placed a rifle in the open hands of Oscar McCormick, the hair on Joe's neck lifted.

"How about you, Ray?" Joe asked. "Join us?"

"Not my style." He wrinkled his nose. "My tastes are more refined, remember? I come for the conversation, the camaraderie. My brother, though . . ." He tilted his head and pointed to a man halfway down the range. "Just watch."

Joe did. Straight from the shoulder, Tony Moretti fired his weapon into the circular paper target downrange. Then the target moved back twice as far, and he finished unloading his weapon.

Hanging from wires on a pulley system, the targets came back to Moretti, who plucked them from metal clips. As if he sensed his audience, he turned the target to face Ray, Joe, and Oscar. With an eerie grin, Tony poked his little finger through the hole his bullets had made at the center of it. He'd been as accurate at one hundred yards as he had been at fifty.

"Bull's-eye." Ray shook his head in obvious admiration. "Practice makes perfect." When he faced Joe again, the smile he wore matched his brother's.

CHAPTER

33

Lauren didn't want to be a coward. She didn't want to run from the truth anymore, the way she had as a child, and the way her father had throughout his life. So she'd shared everything with her roommates this weekend and grieved as though Lawrence Westlake had died. Indeed, she had lost the father she thought she had. It was a different kind of pain, to mourn what she'd never had in the first place.

When Lauren returned to work this week, she immersed herself in ancient Egypt only because it was her job, and not to escape from the hard realities of the present.

She needed to notify the Vandermeers they'd purchased forgeries, but there would be no containing that news once Victoria learned it. Lauren needed to connect with Joe first and see how best to proceed. She'd called over the weekend but had missed him. He'd returned her call, according to Ivy, but Lauren had been out with Elsa. With every delay, the evidence she held grew heavier. Joe would have enough now to arrest her father. His denouement, and by association, her own, was inevitable.

Beneath the Egyptian rooms, in the basement of the museum, Lauren took her lunch break without eating. Her appetite had vanished with her hope of reconciliation with Lawrence. She would not think of him as "Dad" anymore. He'd betrayed the closeness that title suggested.

Organizing the stacks of paper on her desk, she came across the letter from Miles Vandermeer. The poor man had no idea he would soon receive some very bad news about the jewelry in the photographs he'd sent to her. *If they are to be used in some kind of publication,* he'd written, *we would be grateful to be named as the owners.*

Not even close.

Although . . .

She pulled one of Mr. Clarke's books from the shelf above her desk. This was one of the volumes he'd had published on his finds from the years 1915–1917. She didn't care one whit that he'd had others write the chapters. She wanted to see the photographs.

She flipped to the chapters about digs from 1917 and found the image she was looking for. There it was: the ointment jar made of Egyptian alabaster, inscribed with Hatshepsut's titles as queen. The jar Mr. Clarke had gifted to Newell St. John, the first fake she had identified last fall. The provenance had declared it had been purchased from a dealer in Luxor.

Then why would it be included in a volume of Mr. Clarke's excavation finds?

She searched the text for an answer and found it. The ointment jar was uncovered from tomb 1, wadi D in the Wadi Gabbanat el-Qurud. Along with several other artifacts from this site, it was snatched by a tomb raider when the guards fell asleep and turned up in a shop in Luxor the next day. Upon finding it there, Mr. Clarke purchased the artifact to recover it, adding to his personal collection.

The provenance document was not wrong. It just hadn't explained the whole story.

Pulling a magnifying glass from her drawer, she enlarged the hieroglyphs etched into the jar.

They were perfect. This was genuine. It was most decidedly not the same jar she'd pronounced a forgery.

Joe's suspicions weren't wild imaginings. Based on everything else she'd learned about her father recently, it was easy to believe he'd swapped out the genuine jar for a lookalike he'd forged, just so she would find it. Just so he could tarnish Mr. Clarke's name, even if only a little bit.

How petty. How cruel to Mr. Clarke and Mr. St. John and her. Lawrence had probably been coming out of his skin waiting for her to find the fake.

There was no doubt in her mind that her father was a crook. When it came to light, she could only imagine her career would be finished, too. Not by a court of law. No, she was confident she would not be convicted as an accomplice to this ring. But in the court of public opinion, especially among those in the art world, she'd be cast as guilty, like Luigi Palma di Cesnola, the first director of the Met, accused of forgery and only technically exonerated. The detail of where the guilt truly belonged wouldn't matter. The scandal would be enough.

That wasn't enough to stop her.

Taking a deep breath, she reached for the phone to call Joe.

It rang beneath her hand.

She answered it.

"Dr. Westlake? Theo Clarke here."

"Mr. Clarke?" Lauren flashed hot, then cold. This legendary Egyptologist had been to her house and brought her mother flowers. He might even have courted Mother once upon a time. He'd never mentioned hearing that Lauren had called his ointment jar a fake. She wondered if he knew.

"Yes, hello! I hope you're sitting down, my dear, because I have news that will sweep you off your feet."

Lauren racked her brain for what might be coming next. "Yes? I'm sitting down, go ahead."

"It's Hatsudora, Dr. Westlake. Your Hetsumina's twin. We found her."

She nearly dropped the phone. "I'm sorry, can you repeat that?"

A warm chuckle carried over the wire. "You heard me correctly, I daresay. My team has found Hatsudora's coffin."

Lauren struggled to make sense of what he was trying to say, and why he was so excited. It was a French team that had found Hatsudora, and she was most likely reposing in the Cairo Museum now. Lauren had practically memorized the letter from Mr. Lythgoe about this. They'd found her on December 1, but the news hadn't reached her until December 30.

"Hatsudora. In Cairo, you mean? In the museum?"

"No, no. A member of my team was on the spot when it appeared for sale in Luxor. This was three or four weeks ago. After my tour with you at the Met, I gave my expedition director the challenge, granting him the authority and resources to pay any price for her recovery. Now he is quite literally delivering."

Impossible. "I don't understand."

"Well, seeing is believing," he said. "Prepare to do both on Friday. I know how important this find is to you, so my instructions are to have the crate with Hatsudora in it delivered directly to the Met's receiving room. We'll open it together, all right?"

"What makes you so confident it's Hatsudora?"

"They're twins, aren't they? I've seen the photographs. It's a remarkable match for Hetsumina's coffin. What a thrill it will be to open the crate at the Met. We can view both sisters. If not side by side, close enough. Is Friday agreeable?"

"By all means," she managed to say, making a note to arrange it with Mr. Klein. "I'll add it to our registrar's schedule. Nine in the morning?"

Mr. Clarke agreed. "We'll enjoy the discovery together. Then we can haggle about whether the Met would like to purchase her from me before your spring exhibition or simply wait it out. You know you'll get it eventually."

"Oh, Mr. Clarke." She never knew how to respond to his references to his death. "Let's hope 'eventually' is a very long time from now."

He laughed. "Between you and me, if cash flow is a problem for the museum, I may be persuaded to let you have it on loan for the duration of your show. But never mind about that now. We'll see you soon. Take care."

Lauren placed the receiver in its cradle.

If her instinct was right, the millionaire was about to deliver the biggest forgery they'd ever seen. Big enough to make what the Napoleon Society had done seem like child's play.

She picked up the phone again.

"Joe." Relief broke her voice on his name when he answered. "You were right about everything. I'm so sorry for the hurtful things I said to you. Please forgive me." Saying it didn't feel like enough, especially not through a telephone wire. She was gutted, and all she could give him were a few paltry words and the pauses between while she pushed through the burning in her throat.

"I do, of course I do. I hated bringing that evidence to you, Lauren. I hated hurting you that way."

She pulled in a steadying breath. "You weren't the one who hurt me. Deep down, I think I knew that even before you left my building."

"What's happened since then?"

Lauren stared at Mr. Clarke's book still open before her. "I'll tell you everything. In person."

CHAPTER

34

Joe stood with Lauren in the dark, empty corridor outside the Met's receiving room. "We need a confession." He didn't have to tell her that again but did anyway. They'd gone over the plan plenty of times before this moment. But this was the moment that counted.

They'd decided it would be best if no police were in the receiving room when Mr. Clarke arrived with his crate. He should be relaxed and willing to talk. The only people present would be Lauren, Mr. Clarke, and the registrar, who would unpack the box. They would tell Mr. Clarke that Mr. Robinson would be called as soon as the coffin was free of its packaging. Joe and Oscar, who was currently parking the police car where it wouldn't be seen by Clarke, would stand by, ready to move in and make an arrest.

"Are you all right? You ready?" Joe cupped his hands around her shoulders, resisting the urge to draw her close. The betrayal he'd felt from his own father was nothing compared to what she suffered from Lawrence Westlake. He'd take this pain upon himself if he could spare her.

He couldn't do that, but he could see that justice was done, at least in the legal sense. Joe would have arrested Lawrence by now had it not been for Mr. Clarke's delivery today. He didn't want to risk other forgers going underground. They needed to see how Clarke would explain Hatsudora's coffin.

Lauren double-checked the small microphone clipped to the back of the necktie she wore over her blouse. The wire had been carefully stitched in place all the way down the tie so that when she buttoned her suit jacket, no one could tell it connected to a recording device attached to the waistband of her skirt. "Ready." Her beautiful face was stark and pale.

But she was stronger than she knew.

Lauren's nerves tangled while Mr. Klein tapped the mallet to the crowbar around the edges of the crate's lid. Mr. Clarke looked on, his eyes glowing. Stroking his silver beard, he leaned toward her.

"The old ticker is thumping now, I can tell you."

She managed to smile. Her pulse raced, too, but not for the same reason. She'd sent a telegram to Mr. Lythgoe and Mr. Winlock, asking them to confirm the final destination of Hatsudora's coffin. If the French team had gained ownership, there was a small chance they'd sold it to Clarke's team for a price impossible to refuse. But the answer had come back definitively: Hatsudora was enshrined in Cairo's Egyptian Museum.

"Knock, knock!" Anita's voice echoed in the cavernous room.

Lauren turned and felt the blood leave her face. There by her side was Lawrence. Tension ballooned in the room.

"Mr. Westlake said he needed to see you," Anita explained. "I told him you'd be a while, and he said it was urgent. I hope that was okay." The crimp in her brow hinted that she sensed it wasn't.

Her mouth in a tight line, Lauren nodded to show her assistant she wasn't upset with her, and Anita slipped back into the corridor. The sound of her footsteps faded into nothing.

Lawrence approached. "Don't let me interrupt you."

She couldn't find a single word to say to this man. She wasn't ready for this. She was barely ready for the confrontation she'd planned on.

Mr. Clarke set his jaw but thrust out a vein-crossed hand. "Lawrence, it's been many years. You must be so proud of your daughter."

A pounding entered Lauren's skull as the two men exchanged barbed courtesies. Even Mr. Klein paused to glance between them before resuming his work.

This was not the plan. She didn't want Lawrence here to see Mr. Clarke's humiliation. He would only rejoice in it, she knew, based on his little stunt replacing that ointment jar with a fake. Lauren would have to deal with him later, but not now. *Please, God, not now.*

"Actually, we are in the middle of something." Lauren motioned to draw him away. "Tell me what's so urgent, and then you'll have to leave." She bit the inside of her cheek. She ought to have sent him away, full stop.

"I don't mind, Dr. Westlake," Mr. Clarke inserted. "Lawrence would like to see this, I'm sure."

"And what's that?" Lawrence put his back to Lauren, and she felt it with the force of a slap.

The air cracked as nails popped free of the wood. Mr. Klein pried off the boards, and sawdust spilled onto the floor, some peppering the air before settling. Sweeping it away, the registrar set to work on the interior box the dust had insulated.

"You know Hetsumina," Mr. Clarke replied to Lawrence, "the twin whose coffin now graces the New Accessions room upstairs? My team found her lost sister, Hatsudora. Stay, and you'll be one of the first to meet her on this side of the ocean."

"Is that right?" Lawrence asked. He knew how much this would mean to Lauren, and yet he did not turn to her with delight. He didn't ask her why she hadn't told him of the find he knew she most longed for. With Mr. Clarke in the room, it was as if Lauren were as inanimate as the artifacts unpacked here, and less important.

She knew it wasn't Hatsudora in the crate, and yet she remained as transfixed as the rest of them as Mr. Klein removed layer after layer of protection. At last, he cut away the muslin sheet wrapping the coffin.

Lauren gasped at the impossibly perfect likeness to Hetsumina's coffin.

Mr. Clarke exclaimed. Mr. Klein brushed the sawdust from his knees, caught Lauren's eye, and smiled before backing out of her way. Lawrence's mild reaction barely registered.

Lauren's hand went to her pocket, which held Mr. Lythgoe's letter and telegram about the real Hatsudora. She touched them to remember the truth as she knelt beside this coffin that looked so real.

Carved from wood, it was painted in the exact colors to match Hetsumina's and appliquéd with ornate gold-leaf hieroglyphs. The young woman portrayed in the funerary mask wore the same fashions, too. The inscriptions all around the coffin contained no errors. In fact, they were a perfect replication of her sister's, with the exception of her name. If Lauren didn't have proof in her pocket that the real coffin rested in Cairo, she'd have declared this genuine.

"*Mummies don't lie*," Lauren had once told Anita. But coffins did.

"Marvelous," Mr. Clarke breathed. "She's simply amazing, isn't she? Let's call Mr. Robinson down, shall we? I imagine he'll be as excited as we are."

Lauren rose and brushed off her skirt. "I'm not so sure you'll want him here for this," she began. "This coffin is unbelievable, Mr. Clarke. Truly, *literally*, unbelievable."

"Indeed," Lawrence said gruffly. "The occasion demands the director of the museum. He may even make you an offer on the spot, Clarke. Bravo."

It was as if he hadn't even heard what she'd said. She narrowed her gaze at her father, wishing she could see past his façade into the hidden depths and motivations that made him who he was. That made him ignore her, congratulate his archrival, and insist on inviting an audience.

She wiped her palms on her skirt. "What was so urgent you needed to see me right away?" she asked him.

Lawrence waved a hand. "Not important."

"Why are you here?"

343

Seconds ticked by.

"All due respect, Dr. Westlake, but it's clear the matter can wait," Mr. Clarke said. "Shall we call Mr. Robinson?"

"Mr. Clarke, this coffin is not what you think it is. I'm willing to bet there's no mummy inside. Or if there is, it's not Hatsudora." She motioned for Mr. Klein to help her remove the lid.

He did. Just as she thought, the coffin was empty. Except for an envelope addressed to Clarke. She handed it to him.

Mr. Clarke's face paled, then darkened as he read it. "This says that Hatsudora, the mummy, was stolen right out of the coffin before my team packed it for shipping. Why didn't they send me a telegram, rather than surprise me like this? I'm sorry, Dr. Westlake, I don't know what to say. I do hope the coffin will still be of some use for you. What a disaster. I can't understand it."

"I can." Removing the letter and telegram from her pocket, she explained how. "This is the finest forgery I've ever seen," she said.

Confusion lined Mr. Clarke's face, but not horror. She was certain that whatever amount of money he'd paid for this, he'd be all right even if he never recouped a dime. "I don't understand how this could have happened. My own team . . ." He muttered in broken phrases as he tried to sort out this elaborate hoax.

Lawrence did not come closer to look for himself. All he looked for, it seemed, was satisfaction. But he did not appear to be surprised. It was as if he had known this would happen.

A glimmer of understanding knocked the breath from her lungs. "You knew, didn't you?" she whispered, but again, he didn't hear her. He more than knew. He'd arranged this entire deception. He'd known she was hoping to find Hatsudora ever since she'd shown him Hetsumina's coffin in November.

Lauren walked toward him, remembering that her every word and his were being recorded. "You called me in to look for forgeries at Mr. St. John's house last November. You'd already been there cataloging his collection before I got there. Do you remember that?"

"Of course I do, but I don't see what—"

"I found an alabaster ointment jar to be fake. The hieroglyphs were wrong. Then I learned that jar had been a gift from Mr. Clarke. But you knew that, didn't you? You knew that before I arrived. In fact, I think you took the real jar out and swapped it with an alabaster jar you—or someone else—carved to look the same. Except for the mistakes in the inscription."

Mr. Clarke glowered at Lawrence.

"Why would I do such a thing?" he sputtered.

"You hate Mr. Clarke. You're jealous of his legacy and feel that you've been wronged. You were probably jealous of the way Mother wrote about him in her letter."

Lawrence's complexion turned ashen.

"Nancy saved the box of letters you left in the fireplace, and I read them. You saw an easy way to taint Mr. Clarke's name, so you took it. Am I right so far?"

"This is ridiculous." Lawrence glanced from her to Mr. Klein.

The registrar ducked his head and made to leave as though to give them privacy.

"Stay, Mr. Klein," Lauren told him. All of this would come out in tomorrow's newspaper anyway. "I need you to pack this up again, please. I want it out of here."

He began to comply but in no hurry.

Lauren addressed Lawrence again. "The rumors about Mr. Clarke's little alabaster-jar forgery didn't do much to harm him, did they? Then there was that nasty business with the Napoleon House roof burning in his hometown, and you couldn't stand to be humiliated like that. You could imagine him in his mansion on the shore, laughing at you, along with his set."

"Dr. Westlake!" Mr. Clarke stopped her. "I did no such thing, Lawrence, I swear. I didn't even know about a Napoleon House in Newport. I don't understand what this is about."

Her father blanched. To be mocked was one thing. To be invisible, for his so-called legacy to go unnoticed, was something altogether different.

Hatred crystalized in Lawrence's eyes, and the rest of his face hardened, too. "You should have left my wife alone." He shoved a finger toward Mr. Clarke. "What were you about, visiting her when I wasn't home?"

"And what were *you* about, leaving her to die alone?" Mr. Clarke spat back. "For what? What were you doing that was more important than Goldie? Than your own daughter?"

"Is she?" Lawrence asked with deadly calm. "None of my other children lived. What's different about this one?"

"You aren't suggesting—"

"Only what I have often suspected over the course of the last thirty-three years and more."

The words came at her with the sharpness of blades. Mother would never break her marriage vows. Would she? Had she? *"How I wish you knew your father"* were among Mother's final words. But surely she was referring to the husband who had been so absent in both of their lives. Lauren was Lawrence Westlake's daughter. But at this moment, she was too ashamed of him to say so.

"Stop." She scraped the scattered pieces of her courage together. Could they see that inside she was cut and bleeding? Was that Lawrence's intention? To hurt her in order to derail her? It pained her to realize he wasn't above such a move.

"This isn't about Mother," she said. "This is about you and the Napoleon Society. About all those fakes you sent your members, the fake canopic jars you sold to Sanderson, the fake jewelry you auctioned off at the gala. Daniel Bradford is Dr. Daniel DeVries, isn't he? That's why Aaron Tomkins threw me out of his shop before I had a chance to verify the authenticity of his stock. After Joe's visit, when he asked to be put in touch with Bradford, Tomkins must have reached DeVries and been told not to have anything to do with me or Joe."

Mr. Clarke sat down on a stool, stunned into silence.

"You don't know what you're talking about," Lawrence told her.

"I do know what I'm talking about. That's why you wanted me

to write articles for you. But you wanted them so you could learn how to get better at your craft. I must say, whoever worked on that coffin got it right. The only other forgery that came close to fooling me was Moretti's Book of the Dead. Mr. Clarke has no reason to sell forgeries. This is the work of the Napoleon Society."

"Lawrence!" The strangled voice came from Mr. Klein. "I warned you!" Sweat darkened the hair at his temples.

Shock rippled through her as she stared at the registrar. "You're one of the forgers."

"I'm not just *one* of the forgers," he sneered with a German accent. "I'm the best. Lawrence and Daniel had the right connections, but none of what you described would have been possible without me."

Faster than thought, he jerked her by the arm, spinning and pinning her against him. She felt his heartbeat at her back, his hot breath near her ear, and a circle of cold metal at her head.

CHAPTER 35

Joe burst into the room, Oscar behind him, weapons drawn. Fred Klein clutched Lauren to himself, a pistol pressed to her temple.

"NYPD! Put the gun on the floor and your hands in the air!" Joe shouted.

Oscar circled around, keeping his firearm trained on Klein from a different angle.

Klein only squeezed Lauren harder. Joe couldn't look at her. He couldn't face the terror in her eyes, nor the fact that he was to blame for pulling her into this hunt in the first place. He channeled every ounce of concentration onto the gunman.

"I can't go back," Klein shouted. "I won't!" The accent brought to mind every conversation he'd had with Peter Braun. Klein was desperate not to be deported to Germany. Desperate men did desperate things.

"Put the gun down, and we'll talk about it," Joe said, his senses razor sharp. "This looks bad for you, Fred, but if you cooperate, I'll see that you have an easier time. Drop the gun."

"I can't do that."

"Then start talking if you want me to hear your side of the story before I shoot you."

"You wouldn't," Fred scoffed, maneuvering so that Lauren's body more fully shielded his.

"You willing to bet your life on it?" Joe's hand was steady and so was his voice. But there was no way he'd take a shot that might hurt the woman he loved. Unless hurting her would save her life. *Please, God, don't let it come to that.*

"Is this about money?"

Joe didn't look, but he recognized Theodore Clarke's voice.

"Name a figure, young man, and I'll pay it," the millionaire offered. "In cash, if you prefer it. Just let her go, nice and easy."

"Cash," repeated Fred. "Now, there's a smart idea."

"But don't you have enough of Mr. Clarke's money already?" Lauren dared to ask. "He already wired the funds for this coffin you forged. Even if you split that sum three ways, or four or five, you'd still have—"

"A lot of money?" Fred laughed darkly. "One would think so. But I haven't been paid what I've been promised in months. I certainly haven't gotten a fair cut for the work I've done."

Joe had checked Lawrence Westlake's bank accounts recently, as well as the account connected to the Napoleon Society. Neither had taken in the large sums he would have expected for a forgery ring.

"Where has the money gone?" Joe asked.

Lauren struggled to breathe, even though Fred's grip had loosened some. His frenetic moving behind her dislodged some pins from her hair, which tumbled to her shoulder. While the barrel of one gun bruised her temple, two other revolvers pointed at her. Well, pointed at Fred, but there was no separation between them. Joe kept him talking, and she prayed the microphone she wore caught every word.

Lawrence hadn't said a thing. Not a single word in his own defense. Nor did he warn or plead with Fred to leave his daughter alone. While Joe and Fred talked, Lawrence was slipping away. Mr. Clarke remained, though she wished he would flee to safety, and call more police. But he stood frozen, unwilling or unable to leave. Oscar kept his gun pointed at Fred so intently she detected a tremor in his arm.

No one saw Lawrence but Lauren.

He was behind Joe now. He looked right at Lauren, and the look in his eyes was not that of a father gazing on a daughter in danger. It was one of cold calculation. He wanted to know if Lauren would keep quiet. That was all.

He was running again. He was running away from her. He would leave not knowing whether the next moments would hold life or death for the only child he had left. He would disappear from Manhattan, from her life, for good. If it weren't for all the people he'd hurt, the crimes he'd committed, she would let him. How could she ever again be in the presence of a man like this? All her life, he'd presented himself as one kind of man, like a painted and gilded funerary mask. That mask had cracked open to reveal the rotten soul within.

Tears traced her cheeks and wet her lips. They tasted of a sorrow, fury, and grief deeper and darker than she'd ever known. She didn't want to care. But her heart was still beating, and so she did.

Lawrence turned.

"He's running!" Lauren cried, and Oscar gave chase while Fred swore at Lawrence for abandoning him.

Joe stayed. "Fred, if you fire your weapon, I will shoot to kill. If you let her go and submit to arrest, I won't shoot you. It's that simple."

But maybe that was what Fred wanted, Lauren realized. Not to run but to escape. He might shoot himself, or he might shoot her, counting on Joe to end his life for him.

Fred's hand shook. He grew more unpredictable by the minute. "Your father told me it would all be fine! I was the one taking the risks. Lawrence told me the names of Clarke's team in the field, and I forged telegrams and letters about Hatsudora, making it look like they had come from his people in Egypt. I crafted the coffin, took the photographs, sent them to Clarke as if I was someone he trusted. The only thing I couldn't fake was a mummy, but Lawrence said that would not be a problem, as long as I faked one last letter."

His words blurred in Lauren's mind as he rattled on about the grand scheme to deceive Mr. Clarke. Even the fragments that filtered through didn't make sense to her—something about Lawrence, while in Newport, paying someone to pose as a telegram carrier to intercept the messages Clarke thought he sent to Egypt.

"And now Lawrence has left me here to face this alone!" Mr. Klein yelled into her ear.

She fought the rising panic and wondered vaguely if the microphone was picking up her racing heartbeat.

The microphone. If Fred saw no way out of this room, he had no reason to keep secrets anymore.

"He left us both," Lauren told him. "What did he do to you? Where did the money go?"

"We were blackmailed. Someone found out about what we were doing and threatened to tell the police if we didn't cut him in on the profits."

"Who?"

"Ray Moretti."

Lauren closed her eyes. How many times had Joe tried to warn her that something was off with Ray? She hadn't wanted to believe it. She saw what she wanted to see and turned a blind eye to what she didn't.

"And the percentage he demanded kept growing. We sold him that papyrus for as much as a year of my salary. That coffin over there? Took me months to complete, but I thought it would be worth it. It's five times the value of the papyrus. We could have all been rich, but no."

"We?" Joe prodded.

"Daniel DeVries, Lawrence, and myself. The other two board members of the Napoleon Society had no idea what we were doing. They wouldn't have liked it. A house divided, no? Ray and his brother, though, those two stuck together."

Lauren's eyes popped open. "What do you mean?"

"Ray got nervous about you and the detective hunting for forgeries. But Lawrence couldn't be the one to tell you to quit, could he?

So Tony tried to scare you into stopping. Photos, a note, a smashed statue—sound familiar? That was me who let him into your office, by the way. Otherwise he would have broken down the door, and I figured I'd spare you the headache."

"He smashed a reproduction, a paperweight."

Fred's chuckle was breathy, sticking to her ear. "Tony has no concept of art."

"But why did you even start?" Mr. Clarke asked. "How did it all begin?"

"Enough talking!" Fred spat. "Just let me leave, and I won't shoot her. I'll let her go once I'm far enough away."

"Not a chance." Sweat rolled into Joe's eyes, and he blinked it back. "This is the end of the line for you."

Mr. Clarke stayed quiet, but she knew he was there, a silent witness keeping vigil. His lips moved in what she could only hope was prayer, because there was no way Joe had a clear shot. When she moved, so did Fred, pressing himself closer to her back. His body odor was overpowering.

Footsteps pounded down the corridor, but instead of hearing the distinctive shout of the NYPD, she heard German. Red-faced, Peter Braun rushed in through a side door.

In that split second of distraction, Fred angled toward it, exposing to Joe the hand that held the gun.

A shot exploded and blood sprayed Lauren's face. Fred's gun hit the floor. Lauren broke free from Fred, lunged forward, and kicked the gun to Mr. Clarke while Joe and Peter rushed Fred and tackled him.

At last, Fred Klein was under arrest. By the looks of his mangled hand, he'd not be forging with it again. As for Lawrence Westlake, he'd gotten away without confessing to anything.

Joe had blood on his hands. Thank God it wasn't Lauren's.

He gripped Fred's upper arm, and Peter held him fast from the other side. They'd wrapped Fred's injury with strips torn from muslin sheeting, but the wound soaked through.

"Go ahead," Peter said, glancing toward Lauren. "See to her before you go."

Mr. Clarke passed Joe a couple of handkerchiefs and took his place, keeping the criminal secure.

After cleaning his own hands, Joe hurried to where Lauren sat near the coffin bearing Hatsudora's name. Half of her hair remained loosely pinned while the other half curtained one side of her face. Kneeling, he brushed it behind her shoulder and wiped Fred's blood from her cheek. Her eyes were vacant, as though she'd shuttered the world from view.

He took her cold, shaking fingers in his and pressed a quick kiss to them. "You are so brave. And I'm so sorry you had to be," he whispered. She deserved more words than that, but there was no time for that now. "I've got to go. I need you to come to headquarters, you and Mr. Clarke and Peter, too, to give your statements about what happened here this morning."

She nodded.

"Oscar and I will take Fred and Lawrence in the police car."

"You found him?"

"Oscar caught up with him. Mr. Clarke has a car here and will take you and Peter to headquarters after we take the prisoners in. You can wait about ten minutes or so after we leave. Wish I could give you more time to recover first, but it's best to get statements while the event is fresh in your mind."

Another nod.

"I'll see you soon."

Returning to his prisoner, Joe told Peter and Mr. Clarke where to go when they reached headquarters, then hauled Fred Klein into the corridor.

Jefferson, one of the Met security guards, stood guarding a handcuffed Lawrence Westlake. "McCormick went to pull the police car up to the door," he said. "Told him I'd handle this one."

Joe thanked him for his part in helping Oscar catch him.

"Just doing my job," said Jefferson. "He hasn't said a word, Sergeant."

"He will." As soon as Lawrence heard everything Fred confessed to, Joe was sure he'd crack and confess, as well. For the time being, both prisoners were silent, aside from Fred's moaning about his injury.

"Our NYPD surgeon will tend it as soon as we get to the station," Joe told him.

A few minutes later, he and Jefferson marched their prisoners to one of the more obscure exits facing Central Park and out into the glaring light of a January morning. The bracing cold cut through Joe's wool uniform and chilled the sweat on his skin.

Oscar opened a back door to the car and watched, his hand hovering near the gun in his holster, in case either prisoner tried anything. Joe doubted they would, but vigilance was always a good idea.

The sidewalk from the rear museum exit to the narrow avenue had never seemed so long. But it was far preferable to parading them through the museum and out the main Fifth Avenue doors. This wasn't the kind of publicity the Met wanted.

Keeping his grip on Fred's arm tight, Joe surveyed the surroundings as they walked. There were half a dozen vehicles parked in the secluded lot to the right, service vehicles for the museum or the grounds keepers of Central Park. Around the lot, maple trees stretched their bare arms to the sky.

Joe looked again at the lot, sensing that something wasn't right. Fire danced over his nerves. Then he realized what had struck him as odd. Sunshine bounced off all the windows of the vehicles—except for one.

The first body dropped at the same time Joe heard the shot.

Lauren couldn't understand what Mr. Clarke was saying to her. She told him to try again. She fumbled to repin her hair. If she could steady her hands, if she could only repair what this morning had done . . .

Then Anita was there. She took the pins from Lauren and fixed her hair.

Peter stood at the doorway of the room, talking to two security guards, or maybe they were policemen, but she didn't know what they were saying.

"Lauren!" Mr. Clarke gripped her shoulders, and his voice broke through at last. "Your father and Mr. Klein have been shot. An ambulance has been called, but it will be too late. Lawrence is asking to see you."

The words reached her by degrees, as though coming from a great distance. A sickening awareness rolled over her. She stood from where she'd been sitting near the coffin, realizing that the man who'd forged it and the man who'd arranged it all each had need of one now.

Black spots dotted her vision. Lawrence had already been dying to her in pieces small and large. This new death, the physical one, could not be more painful than when he had abandoned her to a gunman this morning. It would only be more final. "Take me to him."

Anita offered to run for her coat, but Mr. Clarke said there wasn't time. Lauren couldn't feel anything anyway, not even the wind she supposed was cold.

Mr. Clarke held her up and walked with her outside. Maybe Anita went with them, maybe she didn't. Lauren's vision narrowed to one thing. Two bodies lay on the sidewalk. One was covered with a blanket over his face, but his blond hair showed. The other was Lawrence, covered up to his neck.

"There's no hope of saving him," Mr. Clarke said of her father.

"I know," she whispered. "I know."

And then she was alone, on her knees beside him. The blanket that hid his body didn't cover the thick, metallic smell of blood.

Eyelids fluttering, he looked at her. "I have . . . to tell you," he struggled to say. Something gurgled in his chest.

Pushing down the bile that threatened, Lauren leaned closer to hear.

"Tony Moretti did this," he said. "I kept records and proof of everything." He whispered where to find it. "It's all there."

Lauren watched his life fade. Time stretched between his breaths. "What else?" she asked. "Is there anything else you want to tell me?" This was his last chance, and they both knew it. Which words would he choose to give her, knowing she'd carry them forever, as she had carried Mother's?

Lawrence coughed, and blood dribbled from his mouth. "It's not . . . my fault." On that rattling exhale, he died.

CHAPTER

36

Night had fallen on Manhattan. Joe sat in the small, cold room in the jail with the attorney prosecuting Connor Boyle for the murder of Wade Martin. With thick blond hair, smooth cheeks, and an unlined face, Mr. Radcliffe couldn't have passed the bar exam more than a handful of years ago. Most criminal lawyers had reputations as bulldogs, but Radcliffe resembled a golden retriever.

While the attorney reorganized paperwork, Joe silently prayed again for Lauren. In the aftermath of the double homicide, Mr. Clarke had brought her to the station, where both their statements had been taken, and then he'd seen her home with a promise to Joe that he'd take care of her every need. What she needed, Joe thought, was a mother, so he had asked Clarke to bring Lauren his. Mama would wrap her in love until Elsa and Ivy could get to her. She'd stay as long as Lauren wanted. Joe would return to her as soon as he could.

He tapped his pencil on the notebook splayed open on the table. Beside it was the recording Lauren had captured on the microphone she'd worn. Next to that was a box containing all the evidence and notes Lawrence had promised in his final breath. It was exactly where he'd told Lauren it would be in his apartment, hidden inside a reproduction bust of Napoleon. It corroborated what Fred confessed, but it went further than that, too.

Mr. Radcliffe cinched his paisley necktie tighter. "Let me make sure I understand this all correctly." He'd requested that Joe help lay out all the evidence, but the attorney needed to have a firm grasp on the story, too.

"Lawrence Westlake started the forgery ring to get the cash he needed for the Napoleon Society venture," he began. "The museum in Newport cost a fortune, to say nothing of the cost of filling it with actual antiquities. That had been his aim, at least at the start."

"Right," Joe said. "His goal had been to have a legitimate museum with genuine artifacts. From what I could gather, the forgeries started as a means to an end."

"And this Fred Klein, the registrar at the Met? How did Lawrence meet him?"

Joe told Mr. Radcliffe that according to the explanation Lawrence had left behind, Fred had been a connection of Dr. DeVries's, alias Daniel Bradford. The doctor and his wife weren't at home when Joe sent officers to pick them up. Joe figured they were long gone and wouldn't be coming back.

At some point after the Napoleon Society began selling forgeries, the thrill of deception had become its own reward, or so Joe supposed. Lawrence had been running the ring since he'd moved to Manhattan seven months ago. Which meant that when he approached Lauren last October, his only goal was to use her. The expedition he'd invited her to join would have been funded by selling forgeries.

Mr. Radcliffe made a note in the margin of his legal pad. "The situation escalated after Dr. Lauren Westlake declared Mr. Moretti's papyrus a fake. Ray decided that if it had almost fooled Dr. Westlake, it would fool anyone else. He didn't want the forger to get caught. He wanted to go into business with him and take a cut of the profit, as repayment for the money Ray had already paid for the fake. It was also a fee for allowing the forger to live."

"That's why Ray sent his brother, Tony, to Feinstein's antique shop to find out who brought in the papyrus." Joe flipped to a copy of the police logbook and pointed to the nighttime complaints about the noise. "That was the night of the break-in. Feinstein didn't know Lawrence's name, just that he'd had the check made out to the Napoleon Society. Under duress, Feinstein shared that much with Tony and was scared into keeping the whole thing quiet. It didn't take Tony long to learn about the Napoleon House in Newport. He set it on fire to lure a Napoleon Society board member to him."

Joe had to admit, it was a great plan, as far as crimes went. It was a secluded area. Tony knew Lawrence would already be vulnerable because of the fire. Those injuries Lawrence had claimed were from falling on the train tracks were actually from Tony, who apparently felt that his business proposal needed a little something extra. Tony promised that full cooperation would put him in the mood to expedite the roof repair with his connections.

The deal was made.

The door hinges squeaked. Joe and Mr. Radcliffe stood while Connor entered with his lawyer, Mr. Dover. The defense attorney's thinning hair had been shellacked into place with Brilliantine, and his mouth seemed carved into a perpetual scowl. After brief introductions, they sat.

"What's this all about?" Mr. Dover tented his hands on the table.

"I need to nail a pair of slippery criminals. I have all this evidence." Joe gestured to what he'd gathered. "But I need a witness. A living witness. The two who gave me all this were shot and killed this morning in my custody." He looked to Connor, whose eyes were ringed with shadows. He'd lost weight since Thanksgiving.

Mr. Dover unbuttoned his pinstripe suit jacket, exposing the matching vest beneath. "They were shot and killed by the criminals you want to put away?"

"By one of them," Mr. Radcliffe clarified. "He left the weapon he used at the scene of the crime."

Mr. Dover nodded, apparently familiar with this tactic of using a weapon once—with care not to leave fingerprints—and discarding it on the spot.

"Big market for guns these days," Joe said, and watched Connor's gaze flick away. Both attorneys had already been given the evidence linking Connor to the weapons that had gone missing from the police's custody.

"This one caught my interest especially, though." Joe pushed an enlarged photograph of the rifle across the table. "Mr. Boyle will find that familiar."

"Don't respond to that." Mr. Dover lifted his glasses and looked under them at the photo.

"Here's the serial number." Joe shared another photo, then brought out another slip of paper. "This is a receipt from one of the raids Mr. Boyle participated in. It itemizes all the weapons confiscated and allegedly surrendered to the Property Room. That's his signature there. That's the serial number, make, and model of the rifle we recovered today. I believe the man who used it today to gun down my prisoners was Tony Moretti."

A frown deepened on Mr. Dover's face.

Connor's sallow complexion veered green. Behind his NYPD detective badge, Joe grieved again that his friend's choices had led here. But there was still time to make a right decision.

Mr. Radcliffe folded his hands on the papers before him. "Mr. Dover, we'd like you and your client to listen to a story. The ending is up to you."

And then, with the cadence of an opening statement fit for the courtroom, the prosecutor told of a young policeman, an alcoholic even before Prohibition. He had lost his way, gotten mixed up with the Morettis somehow, and ended up accepting French wine in return for four free guns a month. Then his conscience grew too heavy to ignore, and he stopped. He didn't fulfill his contract with the Morettis, which meant his life, or worse, his aunt's, might be in danger. So when Tony Moretti gave an order to kill Wade Martin, Connor did it.

From inside a manila folder, Mr. Radcliffe pulled out the photograph of Wade with Tony's writing on the back. "This was found in the city directory in Mr. Boyle's desk."

Sweat gathered at Connor's hairline and trickled down the sides of his gaunt face.

"Martin worked in one of Ray's buildings, Mr. Dover," Mr. Radcliffe went on. "He learned too much about the Moretti operations. My best guess is that the Morettis used your client to pull the trigger in what would appear to be a raid gone wrong. After all, why do your own dirty work when someone else could do it for you?"

"But today was different," Joe added. "Too much was at stake. Tony had been keeping tabs on Lawrence, so he knew ahead of time about the meeting this morning and the risks involved. The Morettis knew that if Lawrence and Fred were arrested, they'd sing during interrogation about their 'business arrangement' and the extortion, arson, and fraud that went with it. Ray couldn't risk being arrested, let alone imprisoned. So Tony silenced Fred and Lawrence—but too late." He gestured to the evidence Lawrence had gathered and shared as he died.

"As Sergeant Caravello said, Mr. Dover, I need a witness against the Morettis," said Mr. Radcliffe. "Cooperation would be rewarded."

"Rewarded in what way?" Mr. Dover asked. "The charge against my client in the case of Wade Martin is first-degree murder. Are you saying you'd reduce the charge?"

"Yes." Mr. Radcliffe leaned back. "A reduced charge and a reduced sentence. Plus, you could have a choice of prisons for the incarceration."

A frown creased Connor's brow. "What about my aunt?"

"We'll make sure she's okay, Connor," Joe said.

"How? I don't want her anywhere near the Morettis."

"I don't, either," Joe told him. "I'll make arrangements for her to move away if she wants. Someplace nice and quiet where she can begin a new life without looking over her shoulder."

The cords of Connor's neck grew taut. "Do it. I'll testify."

Mr. Dover opened his mouth but closed it again without speaking. He must have known this was the best deal his client was going to get.

361

Joe released a breath. "You're doing the right thing. She'll be safe, Connor."

"Once you've served your time," Radcliffe added, "we'll make sure you get to your aunt if that's what you want."

"By the time I'm out, she'll either be very old or will have passed into glory already," Connor said. "I don't want her to be alone in the meantime. She went to school with someone who married young and moved out of state decades ago. We heard she was widowed. Aunt Doreen would like to see her again, but they lost touch over the years."

"All the better," Mr. Radcliffe inserted. "She'll be harder for the Morettis to track that way."

"I'll find her, Connor," Joe promised. "I'll take care of everything."

"All I need is your autograph agreeing to our bargain." Mr. Radcliffe slid papers across the table. Mr. Dover read them, and Connor signed and passed them back again.

As Radcliffe secured them in his briefcase, a spark entered Connor's eyes. "I want to say something to Joe."

Mr. Dover sighed. "I suppose the risk of incriminating yourself is a moot point anyway."

Connor laughed darkly. "Now that I'm pleading guilty to murder? I'll say." He turned to Joe. "You still have no idea what any of this has to do with that oyster shell Wade Martin was holding the night I shot him."

Metal scraped the floor as Joe shifted his chair closer to the table. "I'm listening."

"You deserve to know, so here it is as I understand it. Ray got wise about Wade. Wade sensed a shift in their relationship and was anxious to get back in his good graces."

Joe held up a hand to interrupt him. "How do you know all this?"

"Ray told me." Connor continued to share the story.

Wade had known Ray was a collector. He picked up the oyster shell at Rosenberg's and gave it to Ray as a good luck token he hoped would curry favor. It didn't. Once Ray decided Wade was too big a liability, he sent the shell through Connor to be delivered along with the message "Your luck ran out" moments before Connor killed him.

Forgery had nothing to do with it.

And yet, the pursuit of forgeries had led to this chance of nailing the Morettis.

Well, that and the murders of two men in his custody.

Joe hated that Lawrence Westlake and Fred Klein had been killed today. He hated the trauma Lauren had suffered, from Fred threatening her life to her father abandoning her to Lawrence being shot and wasting his dying breath on excusing himself rather than begging for her forgiveness. He wished he could have found a path to justice without any of this.

All Joe could do now was trust the legal system to make sure the killers didn't get away with it.

Mr. Dover thumbed through the copy of the agreement Connor had signed. "Will that be all, Detective? Mr. Radcliffe?"

This wasn't all, in fact. For Connor and Doreen, the Morettis, and Lauren, this was the end of one chapter and the start of the next.

CHAPTER 37

Lauren could not get warm.

Hours had passed since she'd watched Lawrence die, and yet her pulse still pounded. Her blood rushed to her heart, as if that could help put the pieces back together. All it did was leave the rest of her cold.

"Here. Hold this." Greta bustled into the bedroom and handed her a hot water bottle wrapped in a flannel pillowcase. Curled onto her side beneath the covers, Lauren hugged it to her chest. The older woman slid another one between the sheets to warm her feet. "Better?"

"Thank you."

Voices swirled outside the bedroom. Ivy fielded telephone calls, and Elsa hosted her parents in the living room. Aunt Beryl and Uncle Julian had come with a huge vase of flowers but had little to say to Lauren. No wonder. They'd despised Lawrence even before they'd learned the depth of his deception. Their embraces and stricken expressions, however, proved their concern for their niece sincere. Sal had also arrived, and by the smell permeating the apartment, he'd brought an Italian feast to share with all gathered.

Lauren couldn't stomach a bite of it.

The mattress tilted as Greta settled onto the edge of the bed. She placed a hand on Lauren's shoulder, her quiet presence warmer than the quilt.

"Did you know," Lauren said, "that the ancient Egyptians believed that the heart was the organ for thinking, the seat of both knowledge and emotion? The brain, they thought, was mere stuffing for the head, which is why they discarded it during mummification."

"Is that right?"

"Thank goodness we know better," Lauren whispered. She did not want to rely on the convulsions of her battered heart to guide her. Her feelings were no reliable compass. She had to stand on the truth. And the truth was, Lawrence Westlake had been a liar and a thief. He'd manipulated her and forsaken her. He'd cast her parentage into question, though Mr. Clarke had assured her those doubts were unfounded. If Lawrence had escaped the authorities this morning, as he'd intended, she never would have seen him again.

But he hadn't escaped. He'd been murdered, and so had Fred. No one deserved that, either.

Greta smoothed Lauren's hair away from her face. "It's true, we cannot discard the brain, but we are not to discard our feelings, either," she murmured. "Didn't God give us both? You must allow yourself to grieve, Lauren. You can't skip over that just because of the crimes Lawrence committed."

Pressure mounted from unshed tears. "I can't mourn the loss of his deception," Lauren said, "but I hate how his life ended. I won't miss the man he revealed himself to be. But I mourn the loss of hope for a restored relationship. My mother longed for that. So did I."

"Don't you dare take on an ounce of guilt for that." Greta's soft face grew stern with conviction. "It takes two people to have a healthy relationship, and he wasn't doing his part."

Lauren squeezed her eyes shut, but her mind filled with the image of Lawrence trying to sneak away, knowing her life was in danger. He had made his choice in that instant. He had not chosen her. After he'd been shot, he could have left her with some word of affection or even regret for his behavior. Instead, he'd proven his selfishness to the end.

"I'd already begun grieving for a father I never had." Lauren's voice buckled. "I grieve that Lawrence's priorities twisted into an obsession that ultimately killed him."

"Then grieve. Don't lock that away, dear, and don't bury it. Let it out."

A knock sounded on the bedroom door, followed by a beloved voice.

With a surge of energy, Lauren threw back the covers and stood, heedless of the wrinkles plaguing her dress.

Eyes glossy, Greta embraced her, kissed her cheek, then left.

Joe came in.

No sooner had Greta closed the door than his arms were around her, holding her up, encircling her with strength she couldn't muster on her own. "I'm sorry," he whispered. "I'm so sorry."

She melted into him and wept.

SATURDAY, FEBRUARY 27, 1926

Weeks later, Lauren stood at the grave with her hand firmly ensconced in Joe's. "I wish you could have met her."

When they were children, Lauren hadn't brought Joe back to Aunt Beryl's house to meet Mother. All she'd wanted to do was escape that mansion, leaving its rules and sadness behind. Regret stabbed through her. Mother would have loved Joe, if she'd been given the chance. Even though she'd been sick, she would have loved him, as Greta had lavished her care on Lauren. "I feel like I've only just gotten to know Mother myself in the last few months." The letters had become the most precious things she owned.

A few feet away lay another grave, more recently dug and filled. But Lauren wasn't here for that man, whose name so closely resembled her own. She had not been here when he'd been buried. Her aunt and uncle had taken care of everything. Lauren wanted no part of it. She was here with Joe today to honor Mother on the anniversary of her death.

"From what you've shared with me," Joe said, "she loved you more than life. She would be so proud of you."

Smiling at the irony, Lauren nestled a pot of bright purple pansies in the slush in front of the marble headstone. "All my life, I've been trying to make my father proud. I longed for his approval. But this matters more to me now." She straightened and waited for her voice to steady. "The more I know her, the more I love her. The more I see how she loved me. Did I ever tell you that the last letter from Mother was actually written to me?"

He wrapped his arm around her shoulders. "Would you like to share what it said? Or is it better kept between the two of you?"

A smile lifted her lips. "Everything is better when shared with you," she told him. It always had been. "She wrote, 'Joy isn't just in the quest of a far-off land. It's in the coming home. It's in being here, with the people who love you, not just for the big, exciting moments but for the small ones, too.'"

"What a very wise woman she was."

Lauren slipped an arm around his waist. "She was right. It was exactly what I needed to hear."

After Lawrence's murder and the disaster that surrounded it, she knew she couldn't outrun the hollowed-out feeling within her. But she had wanted so desperately to hide. She wanted to quit her job at the Met, sure her reputation was ruined by association, but Mr. Robinson wouldn't let her, and Anita grew even more fiercely loyal. Lauren would have buried herself in the basement of the museum, under the guise of work, but Elsa, Ivy, and Joe brought her up and out of that sunless place, over and over again. Greta had even given her cooking lessons, calling good food and good work fine remedies. So while Lauren had wanted to run, she had stayed. And she had only survived the staying because of the people who stayed with her.

A mild breeze stirred the bare branches above. Warmer temperatures this week had melted snow, and the smell of wet earth hinted at the coming spring.

Lauren remained rooted with Joe near her mother, but her gaze wandered to the small stone marking her father's grave. Since his death, and even the days that preceded it, she had felt numb, angry, ashamed, and bereft by turns. She had no doubt she'd revisit all of those emotions. But when they had melted, she found a new sensation beneath.

Relief.

All her striving for his love and approval had ceased. He would never inflict new wounds on old scars again.

The Napoleon Society had died with him. Whether for Lauren's sake or her mother's, or simply to make Lawrence roll in his grave, Theodore Clarke had paid back every cent that the society had swindled from people with their forgeries. He also offered every victim an all-expenses-paid trip to Newport for a private tour of his mansion and the antiquities within. As for the Napoleon House, the mortgage reverted to the innocent board members. She didn't know what they would do with it. She didn't want to think about it anymore.

"We have company," Joe said quietly.

Nancy Foster approached with a bundle of chamomile.

"Nancy." A swell of emotion clogged Lauren's throat, and she reached out to the woman who had given so much of her life to Mother. "I was hoping I'd see you today."

Her watery brown eyes flared. "You found the letters."

"I did. I can't tell you how much they mean to me. Thank you for saving them." Lauren introduced her to Joe.

"Well, young man," Nancy said, "what is your relationship to Lauren?"

"I am the guardian of her well-being," he said without hesitation.

Lauren laughed, but he was right. "He's also my best friend, and the keeper of my heart."

A rare smile warmed Nancy's face. "Good."

They gave Nancy space to lay her flowers and pay her respects.

At length, she turned back to Lauren and Joe. "I read about your father. That's him, I suppose." She jerked her chin toward his grave.

Lauren nodded, but still she wondered. Mr. Clarke maintained there was no truth to the insinuation that he had fathered her. But would he claim her as his daughter now, even if she was his? Wouldn't he fear what that would mean for his fortune after he died?

"You have questions, sweetheart," Joe said, guessing the thoughts springing to mind. "I bet Nancy has the answers."

And Nancy would tell the truth.

"Lawrence suggested that Theodore Clarke is my biological father," Lauren said. "You were my mother's nursemaid since she was a girl. So, tell me, please. Could this possibly be true?"

Nancy's face puckered in thought. "You were born December 8, 1892, which means . . . No, that would be impossible. Your parents were living in Chicago by then, and Theodore never came to visit until after his friend became a professor at the university there."

"Dr. Breasted?" Lauren asked.

Nancy snapped her fingers. "That's the one. He didn't start working at the University of Chicago until after you were born."

"That's right," Lauren affirmed. "Dr. Breasted began there in 1894."

"Goldie's marriage wasn't what it ought to have been," Nancy went on, "but she never would have sought her own pleasure outside of it. Never. Did you doubt her?"

Cold nipped at Lauren's nose and ears. "Right before Mother died, she said, 'How I wish you knew your father.' I always thought she meant Lawrence. Then she closed her eyes and said, 'Redeem this.' And so I've been trying, Nancy. Since Lawrence came to me last October, I tried to restore our relationship. But the harder I tried, the further it unraveled, and then . . ." She motioned to his grave. "When Lawrence said he'd suspected my father was Mr. Clarke, I had to wonder if that's what she meant."

The lines in Nancy's face softened. "Oh, child, that's not what she meant."

"I know."

But Nancy shook her head. "She wasn't talking about Lawrence, either."

Lauren stared at her, replaying the words in her mind. *How I wish you knew your father. Your father.*

Your Father.

Understanding pierced, scattering all confusion.

"She was talking about the one Father who won't fail you," Nancy confirmed. "Goldie always felt bad that you didn't get to church more. She would have taken you, were she well enough. When she said, 'Redeem this,' she was praying. I must have heard her say that prayer a thousand times over the years. She wasn't giving you an order. She'd never tell you to fix what wasn't yours to solve. She only wanted you to know your true Father's love."

A guilt she didn't know she still carried took flight from Lauren's shoulders, leaving her unbalanced. Joe's arm came around her waist, holding her steady. "Thank you, Nancy," she breathed.

The old woman smiled with a kindness Lauren hadn't seen from her before. "Come see me sometime." She gave her address and telephone number. "Young man, you carry on guarding this girl's well-being. You keep her heart safe, do you hear me?"

"Yes, ma'am."

Nancy walked away.

"I need to sit down," Lauren whispered.

"Wait." Joe took off his overcoat and spread it on the ground. He held her hand, and they sat.

"I put my faith in God early on," Lauren said. "But in my teenage years, I grew angrier with Lawrence's distance. His absence. Somewhere along the way, I thought of God as remote and uninterested, too. It must have worried her that my view of God was dimmed by my view of my father."

"Your mother might not have been able to take you to church, but she showed you God's love nonetheless, didn't she?"

"Better than anyone else." Memories burst upon her with reborn clarity. When Lauren climbed the tree, pretending to be a bird while she watched for someone else, Mother had stayed, promising to be her nest when she landed. When Lauren hid beneath her father's desk, pretending to be a sleeping bear, Mother had let her, but said she would be there when Lauren woke up.

When Mother found Lauren sleeping on the hardwood floor, she forsook her own bed and came down to her.

When Lauren locked herself inside Lawrence's office with emotions too big to handle, Mother knocked on the door and even tried to climb through the window.

"I felt so alone, but I didn't have to be," she said. "Mother let me chase after something else, but she loved me unconditionally the whole time. She was there. She waited for me to reach back to her."

Joe's deep baritone rumbled as he hummed, and she recognized the tune. *"Prone to wander, Lord I feel it, prone to leave the God I love. . . ."*

"She wished you knew your heavenly Father," Joe said. "She modeled His love with her own."

"Yes, she did." The pansies blurred into purple smudges against the tombstone. "The love I chased after was false. The love she offered was pure."

"I'm sure she would be happy you know that now. She wouldn't want you to spend one drop of energy feeling guilty for not understanding that until . . ." His voice trailed away.

"Until I was sitting before her grave?" Lauren's smile wobbled.

"You were a child in an impossible situation. Your mother knew that."

He was right.

"It's never too late to feel a mother's love." She wiped the tears from her cheeks. "And it's not too late to truly grasp how wide and deep is the love of my Father."

CHAPTER

38

Lauren didn't know if she could do this. Worse, she didn't know if she should.

The curtain shielded the stage from a packed lecture hall in the Egyptian wing. Tonight was the opening of her special exhibition. Soon, the curtains would part, and she would face more patrons than she'd seen in months. Some had fallen prey to Lawrence. All of them had heard about it. None would want to see the forger's daughter.

"Mr. Lythgoe or Mr. Winlock should be here." Lauren stood offstage, nerves fraying. "We ought to have postponed the opening." But the Met's curator of Egyptian art and the expedition director had been delayed by weather and wouldn't return for another three weeks.

"We've been over this." Mr. Robinson smoothed the necktie behind his vest. "Delaying the opening would throw off the schedule for other events. More importantly, you can do this. You cataloged the art, interpreted it, designed the narrative, arranged loans from other museums, and managed a minutiae of details I'm sure I don't even know about. This is your show, Dr. Westlake. It might as well be your night."

She smiled that he'd remembered her doctorate degree. If Anita was here instead of waiting in the front row, she'd dance a jig. But Lauren remained unconvinced. "I want the art to be the spectacle. Not me. It's not too late to ask Mr. Clarke to give his standby lecture tonight instead. People would love it, and he would love their affirmation."

He lowered his chin. "What happened with your father was not your fault. If it hadn't been for you and Detective Caravello, that forgery ring would still be stealing hundreds of thousands of dollars from people. People have come tonight to see you. Now get ready, Doctor. It's time." The curtains swung wide, and before she knew it, Mr. Robinson stood at the podium, receiving a round of applause.

Lauren could barely hear his introduction over the buzzing in her head. Yet, somehow, when he extended his arm toward her, she joined him on the stage.

Then he was gone, and the spotlight fell on her alone, hot and far too bright. She felt completely exposed. The audience could not possibly hear her name and not hear her father's, too. They couldn't see her without remembering what he'd done.

She gripped the sides of the podium for support. "Thank you for that kind introduction," she began. "It would be my privilege to make a couple of my own. This exhibition would not be possible without the help and expertise of several others." She thanked the representatives present from the lending museums, and they received their own applause.

"Now I'd like you to meet two of our own here at the Met. I could not get along without my assistant, Miss Anita Young." Anita stood and turned to wave while Lauren listed her finer qualities, from clerical prowess to chocolate and coffee distribution.

When clapping subsided, Lauren spoke again. "Mr. Peter Braun." She shielded her eyes from the light until she saw him standing. "Ladies and gentlemen, Mr. Braun is our lead conservator. If you've enjoyed our galleries even before this night, you've already enjoyed the fruit of his labor. Thank you." He deserved the resounding applause that followed.

She'd talked to him several times since January, so he knew that her gratitude extended far beyond what she'd shared. He had come to her rescue, and she'd never forget it.

On Lauren's signal, the spotlight dimmed and the projector in the back turned on, showing the first lantern slide on the screen behind her. Without the blinding light, she could see the audience while she spoke. There sat Joe and his parents, Ivy, Elsa, and Aunt Beryl and Uncle Julian. She saw Miles and Victoria Vandermeer, Thomas Sanderson, and Theodore Clarke. When she recognized who sat beside him, she almost lost her place in her notes. Dr. James Breasted, her beloved professor, beamed.

"The ancient Egyptians believed the afterlife was more important than the present life on earth," she said, moving into her element. Thank God, thank God, she still enjoyed this field, even though it would always remind her of Lawrence. She'd worked in it without him for so many years, it was truly her own passion. But she knew better than to let it become an obsession.

As she advanced through the slides of exhibition highlights, she explained what the Egyptians believed about the multitude of gods they served and their efforts to appease them. She shared about the weighing of the heart, how they used the Book of the Dead, what they hoped amulets and shabti would accomplish for them in the next world. The presentation ended with the ever-popular topic of how royalty furnished their tombs.

When she finished, the house lights went up, and Lauren invited questions.

The first person stood and asked, "How do you know if a piece of art is fake?"

Lauren blinked. She hadn't spoken a word about forgeries tonight and had no intention of doing so. "Do you have any other questions related to the exhibition?"

Murmurs arose from all corners of the room. They wanted an answer to the question posed.

She glanced at Mr. Robinson, who nodded his assent.

Inhaling deeply, she scrambled to organize her thoughts. "I could tell you about case studies I've done and techniques I've used. But if we were here all night, I couldn't cover everything there is to know about what to look for. My best advice would be to study the real thing. Immerse yourself in the art, learn about it from every angle. Not just what it looks like, but the tools used to make it, where the materials come from, the historical context, the language, the people who created the art, and the purpose for it. If you become an expert on the real thing, you'll know the counterfeit when you see it."

The truth translated. If she had recognized true selfless love, she would have identified Lawrence as fake.

More questions followed, and she answered them easily. Soon, Lauren closed the lecture so patrons could visit the exhibit. Mr. Robinson joined Lauren at the podium and once again thanked everyone for coming. When he finished, the room exploded with applause. A few people stood, and then more, until no one remained in their seats.

"This is for you, Dr. Westlake," Mr. Robinson said.

"It's too much," she protested.

But the museum director backed away from the podium and clapped.

Gratitude swelled.

When at last the curtain closed again, Lauren left the stage to find Dr. Breasted. "Can it really be my favorite professor?"

"My dear Dr. Westlake." When he clasped her hand, the man's eyes sparkled, and his white mustache lifted with a smile. "You were every bit as marvelous as I knew you would be, and then some. Academics like me can be so stuffy, but you've combined the art of storytelling with the science of scholarship. A rare talent. You captivated your audience completely."

His praise humbled her. "I can't tell you what it means that you've come. Thank you." They'd corresponded several times since her father's denouement, and there had been power and healing in his letters. Still, seeing him again brought delight.

An impish grin spread. "The timing is serendipitous. I'm here to see your exhibition, of course, but I've come about something else, too. Something best discussed in person."

Joe had been the last one standing during Lauren's ovation, and he was nearly the last person in the lecture hall now, waiting while she spoke with every patron who waited in line for her. He didn't mind. He had waited years for Lauren Westlake. An extra forty minutes wouldn't hurt him.

Much.

In the meantime, he replayed music from Wagner's *Die Walküre* in his mind. Last week, Joe and Lauren went with his parents to the opera, redeeming the Christmas gift tickets at last. So much had happened since that holiday, even aside from the fall of the Napoleon Society. Doreen had moved in with her long-lost friend, where she could grow flowers in a garden of her own. She was safe while Connor served a reduced sentence in return for his testimony against Ray and Tony Moretti. The Morettis had been convicted, and though their lawyer appealed the decision, they were locked away, at least for now.

"Good evening, Sergeant."

He turned to find Beryl Reisner standing beside her husband, Julian, who offered a hearty handshake. "Good to see you, Detective."

Joe returned the greeting. "Call me Joe."

Mrs. Reisner nodded, the ostrich feather in her upswept hair quivering. "We received your invitation, and it will be our pleasure to attend."

Joe's eyebrows lifted. "I'm happy to hear that."

"You must understand something, Serg—Joe." Mrs. Reisner gripped her handbag tighter. "When I turned you away from our home when you were a teenager, I thought I acted in Lauren's best interest. The two of you were so young, and I didn't know you."

"You were also mourning your sister's recent death," her husband added, "and reeling with the responsibility of an added child in your care. Not to mention how angry you were that Lawrence had missed Goldie's passing."

"You were protective," Joe said. "I understand."

Mrs. Reisner almost smiled. "But the point is, we know you now. And we're coming."

The corner of Joe's mouth hooked up at this understated sentiment, but he felt no less grateful for it. He thanked them, and they took their leave.

At last, the lecture hall emptied of everyone but Joe and Lauren. She met him halfway up the center aisle, her shimmering eyes brighter than the peacock colors of her beaded dress. She was luminous.

"Congratulations," he said and kissed her. "You were wonderful. Everyone loved it. I'm proud of you."

A quiet laugh tripped over her lips. "For not running away or hiding?"

He looped his hands around her waist. "I know how hard that was for you, but you did it anyway. You faced it, and look what happened. Instead of being humiliated, you were celebrated."

She shook her head in apparent wonder. "That was a surprise. Thank you for coming. You didn't have to wait for me."

"I wanted to."

Lauren returned his smile. "I'm glad, because I have news. Dr. Breasted came tonight, and he told me there's a spot on his epigraphic survey team for this coming fall. He asked me to take it."

"Epigraphic Survey—that's in Egypt, right?"

"Yes, it would be for six months. We'd be recording ancient temple hieroglyphs with Dr. Breasted's system. He asked me to come and do the translation work on-site."

Six months of not seeing her face. Half a year of not hearing her voice, or holding her hand, or kissing her, when they'd lost years together already. But Joe shoved his selfishness away. Lauren wanted this, and he wanted what she wanted. Missing her already, he forced a smile. "I did get you the outfit for Christmas—it would be a shame to let it go to waste."

"I haven't said yes."

"You haven't? Isn't this one of your long-term goals?"

Her shoulder lifted and fell. "Well, yes. But it's not the only one. It's not even the most important one anymore. I once believed field experience would fill not just a spot on my résumé but a hole in my spirit. I'd hoped working in the field would please my father, and I'd finally have his approval. But that hole I felt, that something missing, isn't there anymore. I'm whole and complete as I am. I finally realize that my true Father is already pleased with me. I don't have to prove or achieve anything to earn the love He's freely given."

A hard-earned peace lit her countenance, drawing a smile from Joe. He'd seen, since Lauren was twelve years old, the way Lawrence Westlake had affected her. At last she was free of him, or at least well on her way. Deep wounds took time to heal.

"I bet you never thought you'd hear me say this," she said, "but I don't need to work in Egypt to be happy."

Joe studied her determined expression, from unblinking eyes to the set of her chin, and chose his next words carefully. As much as he'd miss her if she went, he'd feel worse if she gave up the opportunity and regretted it later.

He lifted her hands and kissed them. "I'm glad you can be happy regardless. But that doesn't mean you need to reject an unexpected blessing. Who knows but that this is God's gift to you? When does Dr. Breasted need an answer?"

"Not for a few weeks." She paused, and he could see her mind working. "It wouldn't be a career change or anything. It would be a one-time experience. As long as Mr. Robinson would allow me a leave of absence."

"He wouldn't keep you from this," Joe predicted. "And neither would I."

She laid a hand on his cheek. "If I go—and I'm not saying I will for sure yet—but if I do, I'll come back, Joe. I'm not my father. The joy is in the coming home to people who love me. To the man I love more than anything."

"Someone I know?" Joe grinned, and she stood on her toes to embrace him. He breathed in the apple blossom scent of her hair and kissed the spot behind her ear. Maybe he should put the rest of his plan for this evening on hold, since Dr. Breasted's offer had given them plenty to think about. But he couldn't wait any longer. He'd learned much from his childhood hero, Joseph Petrosino. Courage. Risk. Duty and sacrifice. And not to give up on love just because the future was unpredictable.

"I want to show you something," Joe told her. "That is, if you can spare a few more minutes?"

Curious, Lauren watched Joe's expression shift between eager and earnest. "Of course. What is it?"

"Come with me." With a subtle smile, Joe led her out of the lecture hall and in the opposite direction from the exhibition.

"Is it a secret, where you're taking me?"

All he did was smile.

In the corridor dividing the Great Hall from the Egyptian wing, Joe stopped beside a sarcophagus. "This is where we first met," he said. "The place where I first knew it was my job to take care of you."

Lauren warmed to the memory. "I'll never forget it." She paused, looking around. They'd been here together many times since then. "Is this what you wanted to show me?"

His grin deepened. "Only partially. This way."

From there, he led her into the Great Hall, through the entrance area, and to a locked door. Joe positioned himself beside it with his back to the wall, facing the doors.

"The coat-check room?" she asked.

"On the days I arrived at the museum first and didn't find you in the Egyptian rooms, this is the place I stood and waited for you during your Christmas breaks. I figured you'd come here first to check your cloak."

Her eyes misted as she thought of his steadfast patience with her. "Are you taking me on a tour of our Metropolitan affair?"

That smile again, the one that held some secret, but a secret that promised to be good. The one that quickened her pulse and made everything else fade away.

With a hand to the small of her back, Joe guided her into the Great Hall once more. Beneath soaring arches, they walked between marble statues from the ticket counter toward the grand staircase. "This—" he gestured forward and backward with his arm—"this is part of the path I sprinted the day I came back for you, October 16, 1925. I literally chased after you and found you on your way through Central Park. That was the day you agreed to help me with my forgery investigation."

"So that's why you were sweating," she teased, though she'd noticed no such thing. "I just thought you were nervous."

"You have no idea."

At the bottom of the staircase, she paused. "Going up?" She could think of several memories they'd shared on the second floor of the Met.

"We could." Joe stopped. "I could show you places all over the museum and tell you what happened there."

Nodding, she began to climb.

"But none of those matter as much as what happens here."

She turned around and saw that he hadn't followed her.

"This is the place I tell you that even though the future may be uncertain, I am more than certain about who I want to spend the rest of my life with. I don't want to wait any longer to begin our future together." Joe knelt.

Knees softening, Lauren gripped the brass railing and descended the few steps that had separated them.

He took a small box from inside his tuxedo jacket and opened it. "I love you, and have loved you, across the span of miles and years. I'm asking you to be my wife, for however long the Lord grants us. Will you have me?"

Her breath caught, then shuddered. "With all my heart."

Joe stood, and she threw her arms around him. He captured her to himself and lifted her off the stair, his lips claiming hers in a kiss that sealed the promise. A kiss that ensured they would forever remember this spot as the place where she said yes.

"Soon," he whispered, and set her down, fitting the ring on her finger.

"Yes," she agreed, and the diamond winked up at her. They'd waited long enough. She kissed him again, and he returned her warmth with the tenderness of hope fulfilled and with longing for all their tomorrows.

Joe stepped back with a smile and shining eyes. "I've kept you from the exhibition long enough," he said. "Ready?"

Her heart still thrumming, Lauren patted her hair to make sure it was in place. "Ready."

As they neared the lecture hall, Joe paused. "I left my coat in there. I should pick it up before security locks the room for the night."

Lauren joined him as they entered the hall.

Grinning, Joe took a deep breath and burst into some Italian opera.

As soon as he did, the curtains on the stage parted. Instead of a podium, the stage held a long table covered in white linen and topped with vases of red roses and platters of tiramisu.

"What . . . ? Do you know anything about this?" She set a brisk pace down the aisle for a closer look.

"Congratulations!" The sound was not one voice but many. Lauren watched in amazement as people filed onto the stage from the wings. Elsa, Ivy, Greta, and Sal, all jubilant. Even her aunt and uncle were there, expressions more subdued than the rest but still pleased.

"I hope you said yes, Lauren, or this will be really awkward!" Elsa called down.

"Don't worry," Ivy added. "We didn't follow you; we were waiting in the wings until we heard Joe's signal."

Laughing, Lauren turned to Joe. "You planned this. Pretty confident, were you?"

"If you'd said no, I'd need them all for moral support. And there would be more tiramisu for me."

They returned to the stage. The next moments blurred in a series of hugs from everyone who had come. Lauren wasn't the only one whose eyes watered.

Joe smiled. "I figured this might be an occasion you'd want to share with family. Yours, mine. Ours."

Uncle Julian stepped closer. "You have our blessing. You didn't ask for it, and frankly, you don't need it, but you have it just the same."

Aunt Beryl blinked back the moisture lining her lashes. "Your mother would be so happy for you."

"Yes," Lauren agreed. "She would."

Like the Nile flooding its banks, the place inside Lauren that for so long had been empty could not hold the joy and love that overflowed it now. The losses in Lauren's life had not been wasted. They'd been redeemed, and so had she.

AUTHOR'S NOTE

Thank you for reading *The Metropolitan Affair*! I hope you enjoyed diving into Manhattan and the world of Egyptian art in 1925. While this novel is a work of fiction, the context is historical, from Egyptomania to Prohibition to the Metropolitan Museum of Art.

Most of the characters are purely from my imagination, but Lauren Westlake was inspired by Caroline Ransom Williams, the first American woman to be professionally trained as an Egyptologist. Like my fictional heroine, Caroline earned a graduate degree from the University of Chicago under Dr. James Breasted, kept in touch with him for years afterward, served as assistant curator of Egyptian art at the Metropolitan Museum of Art, and lived in the Beresford apartment-hotel complex on Central Park West. Other museum staff mentioned in the book were real people in those positions, too: Luigi Palma di Cesnola, Edward Robinson, Albert Lythgoe, and Herbert Winlock.

The character Anita Young, Lauren's assistant, was inspired by the grandmother of my dear friend Mindelynn Young Godbout. The real Anita sparkled with wit and spunk, favored the color blue, and loved Hershey bars, especially those with almonds.

As mentioned already, Dr. James Breasted is a historical figure, and he did invent the groundbreaking epigraphic survey method in Egypt, which he invited Caroline to join. Dear reader, forgive me for taking a small liberty with Dr. Breasted for the purpose of this story. In 1925, Dr. Breasted was likely in Egypt, not Chicago, but I placed him in the Midwest in my story so he and Lauren could exchange important letters without the Atlantic Ocean slowing the correspondence, and so he could come to her exhibition opening.

The character of Theodore Clarke is inspired by the real person of Theodore M. Davis, the Newport millionaire who made significant discoveries and contributions to the field of Egyptology. Howard Carter did work for Davis before discovering King Tut's tomb on a dig funded by Lord Carnarvon. For more on this fascinating person, see *The Millionaire and the Mummies: Theodore Davis's Gilded Age in the Valley of the Kings* by John M. Adams.

My fictional hero, Joe Caravello, looked up to a historical hero in Italian-born NYPD detective Joseph Petrosino. Everything you read in the novel about Petrosino, his courtship and marriage to Adelina, and the fight against the Black Hand Society is true. Police procedures in 1925 were very different from what they are today. For instance, questioning suspects during the daily lineup was commonplace, and Miranda Rights would not be established until 1966. They also collected confiscated weapons in wooden chests and dumped them in the Narrows whenever the chests became full. The beautiful old police headquarters at 240 Centre Street now houses high-end apartments.

Unfortunately, corruption among the NYPD during Prohibition was common, especially during the early years. For an excellent book on the subject, see *Dry Manhattan: Prohibition in New York City* by Michael A. Lerner.

Many real locations were used in this story, several of which you can see today. The Vandermeer and Moretti Gold Coast mansions were inspired by Gilded Age estates on Long Island's north shore. In addition to visiting the Metropolitan Museum of Art, the New York Public Library, Central Park, and Old St. Patrick's Church, you can still have tea at The Plaza, get cannoli and espresso at Ferrara's, dine at the Oyster Bar in Grand Central Terminal, see the constellations in Vanderbilt Hall, and find the best pastrami sandwich ever at Katz's

Delicatessen. The Italian Rifle Club, Tiro A Segno, is a private club and the oldest Italian-heritage organization in the United States.

I pray that Lauren's journey touched you in some way. The most important theme in this story is that of God's true love for us, His children. Just as Goldie wished for her daughter, my wish for you is that you know your Father, too.

DISCUSSION QUESTIONS

1. Lauren craves peace and hates conflict. Do you relate to this, or are you more like Joe, who's willing to confront in order to have justice?

2. Lawrence had a pattern of running to Egypt and ignoring the hard realities in his personal life. In what ways do people commonly try to run from problems today, even if they don't leave home?

3. In chapter 6, Lauren tells Joe, "The fact that the Egyptians believed in many things to save and protect them doesn't really set them apart from our culture today." What do you think our culture believes will bring happiness and protection from discomfort? What happens when we put all our trust in those things?

4. In chapter 9, Lauren notes that seeking affirmation is exhausting. Why do you think it's so tiring to pursue affirmation?

5. In chapter 11, we read that Lauren craved her father's approval, if she could not have his love. Even as an adult, how has your relationship with your parents affected your choices?

6. A recurring theme in the story is that people see what they want to see. When have you noticed this happening in your own life or with people around you?

7. Lauren longed for a restored relationship with her father, but as Greta told her, he wasn't doing his part. Have you ever had to set aside a relationship because it was harmful to you?

8. Near the end of the book, Lauren tells her audience in the lecture hall, "If you become an expert on the real thing, you'll know the counterfeit when you see it." In what ways can we apply this to different areas of our own lives?

9. Compare the Lauren at the end of the book to the Lauren from the beginning. In what ways has she changed? What has she lost, and what has she gained?

10. In what ways has God brought new, good things out of areas of your own life that you had previously considered a wasteland?

ACKNOWLEDGMENTS

M y sincere gratitude and appreciation go to:

The many teams at Bethany House, including editorial, marketing, sales, design and art, administration, accounting, proofing, and more. I'm sure I don't know half of all the work that goes into getting every book into readers' hands.

My agent, Tim Beals, of Credo Communications, for his faithful support.

My friend Mindelynn Young Godbout, for touring Manhattan with me and lending her grandmother's muse as Anita Young. Your enthusiasm is always contagious!

Paul Friedman, general research division, New York Public Library, for all the articles you sent me and the thorough conference call to help me navigate the myriad resources available through the NYPL.

Special Agent Scott Reger, Iowa Division of Criminal Investigation, for our multiple conversations about the police and crime-related plot points and character development in this story.

Wade Martin, a reader I connected with on Facebook, who enthusiastically volunteered his name to be used for a character who "gets killed off." Thanks, Wade!

Retired attorney Jayna Breigh for helping me spitball ideas. Any legal/court case–related mistakes are my own.

My mastermind group: Kimberley Woodhouse, Tracie Peterson, Jaime Jo Wright, Becca Whitham, Jana Riediger, and Darcie Gudger.

Your brainstorming help, feedback, prayers, and general support have been invaluable.

Susie Finkbeiner, my constant cheerleader and dear friend. This book took me to the mat over and over. I'm so grateful you've been in my corner.

My amazing husband, Rob, and spectacular teens, Elsa and Ethan. You show so much grace to this writer-mama. I don't take the support for granted.

Panera Bread, for the unlimited coffee and tea subscription. I don't think you realized how much this customer would use that while writing a novel.

God, my heavenly Father and the embodiment of true and unconditional love and grace.

Jocelyn Green inspires faith and courage as the award-winning and bestselling author of numerous fiction and nonfiction books, including *The Mark of the King*, *Wedded to War*, and *The Windy City Saga*. Her books have garnered starred reviews from *Booklist* and *Publishers Weekly* and have been honored with the Christy Award, the gold medal from the Military Writers Society of America, and the Golden Scroll Award from the Advanced Writers and Speakers Association. She graduated from Taylor University in Upland, Indiana, and lives with her husband, Rob, and their two children in Cedar Falls, Iowa. She loves pie, hydrangeas, Yo-Yo Ma, the color red, *The Great British Baking Show*, and reading with a cup of tea. Visit her at jocelyngreen.com.

Sign Up for Jocelyn's Newsletter

Keep up to date with Jocelyn's news on book releases and events by signing up for her email list at jocelyngreen.com.

More from Jocelyn Green

A birthday excursion turns deadly when the SS *Eastland* capsizes with insurance agent Olive Pierce and her best friend on board. After her escape, Olive discovers her friend is among the missing victims. When she begins investigating the accident, more setbacks arise. It will take all she has to overcome those who want to sabotage her search for the truth.

Drawn by the Current • THE WINDY CITY SAGA #3

You May Also Like ...

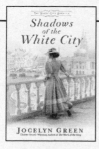

When Sylvie Townsend's Polish ward, Rose, goes missing at the World's Fair, her life unravels. Brushed off by the authorities, Sylvie turns to her boarder and Rose's violin instructor, Kristof Bartok, for help searching the immigrant communities. When the unexpected happens, will Sylvie be able to accept the change that comes her way?

Shadows of the White City by Jocelyn Green
THE WINDY CITY SAGA #2
jocelyngreen.com

As Chicago's Great Fire destroys their bookshop, Meg and Sylvie Townsend make a harrowing escape from the flames with the help of reporter Nate Pierce. But the trouble doesn't end there—their father is committed to an asylum after being accused of murder, and they must prove his innocence before the asylum truly drives him mad.

Veiled in Smoke
THE WINDY CITY SAGA #1
jocelyngreen.com

When successful businesswoman Maggie Molinaro offends a corrupt banker, she unwittingly sets off a series of calamities that threaten to destroy her life's work. She teams up with charismatic steel magnate Liam Blackstone, but what begins as a practical alliance soon evolves into a romance between two wounded people determined to beat the odds.

Hearts of Steel by Elizabeth Camden
THE BLACKSTONE LEGACY #3
elizabethcamden.com

◊BETHANYHOUSE

More from Bethany House

In 1911, Europe's strongest woman, Mabel Mac-Ginnis, loses everything she's ever known and sets off for America in hopes of finding the mother she's just discovered is still alive. When circus aerialist Isabella Moreau's daughter suddenly appears, she is forced to face the truth of where, and in what, she derives her worth.

The Weight of Air by Kimberly Duffy
kimberlyduffy.com

During WWII, when special agent Sterling Bertrand is washed ashore at Evie Farrow's inn, her life is turned upside down. As Evie and Sterling work together to track down a German agent, they unravel mysteries that go back to WWI. The ripples from the past are still rocking their lives, and it seems yesterday's tides may sweep them into danger today.

Yesterday's Tides by Roseanna M. White
roseannamwhite.com

In 1865, orphaned Daisy Francois takes a housemaid position and finds that the eccentric Gothic authoress inside hides a story more harrowing than those in her novels. Centuries later, Cleo Clemmons uncovers an age-old mystery, and the dust of the old castle's curse threatens to rise again, this time leaving no one alive to tell its sordid tale.

The Vanishing at Castle Moreau by Jaime Jo Wright
jaimewrightbooks.com

◊ BETHANY HOUSE